The Apartment
in Rome

Penny Feeny

**Tindal
Street
Press**

A complete catalogue record for this book can
be obtained from the British Library on request

The right of Penny Feeny to be identified as the author of this work
has been asserted by her in accordance with the Copyright, Designs
and Patents Act 1988

First published in 2013 by Tindal Street,
an imprint of Profile Books Ltd
3A Exmouth House
Pine Street
London EC1R 0JH
www.tindalstreet.co.uk

ISBN 978 1 90699 443 3
eISBN 978 1 90699 499 0

Designed and typeset by Tetragon, London

Printed and bound by CPI Group (UK) Ltd, Croydon, CR0 4YY

10 9 8 7 6 5 4 3 2 1

For Charles

Acknowledgements

This book has had a long gestation. It began as a short story which developed into my first (rather different) novel. I am indebted to Alan Mahar of Tindal Street Press for suggesting I resurrect and rewrite it and I am immensely grateful to him for his skilful and attentive editing. Many thanks are also due to Luke Brown and the team at Profile; to Madeline Heneghan and Mike Morris and all at Writing on the Wall; to Rebecca Goss for companionship along the road to publication; to Elinor and Elliott Elsey for help with research in Rome and to Charles, Jack, Roisin, George and Imogen Feeny for support and inspiration.

PART ONE

JULY 2010

It had seemed a small triumph at the time. Gina had been teasing Roberto, boasting about her client list until he called her bluff. Now he believed the idea was his own: a portrait of his son appealed to his vanity.

She had pushed further. 'Why don't I photograph your wife as well?'

His wedding ring winked as he flapped his hand. '*Boh*! She's far too busy. She's never at home. Besides, why would I risk leaving you alone with her?'

'What do you think I'm going to say?'

He laughed. 'I'm more concerned about what she'd say to you. She's very acute; she'd see through you in a moment.'

Gina felt confident she could handle Roberto's wife, but when she arrived at his lavish apartment complex, built around a garden as lush as a tropical rain forest and protected by tall electronic gates, she couldn't help a shiver of resentment. He'd always been cagey about his wealth. Occasionally he would overwhelm her with extravagant gifts – an expensive bottle of champagne or a box at the opera, nothing she could usefully recycle – but in general she regarded him as tight-fisted.

She'd considered getting Antonio Boletti to come to the studio, but she shared the space, which was run by an artists'

PENNY FEENY

cooperative, and she hadn't made a booking in time. Anyway, for their first meeting it would be useful to see the boy in his own habitat. She'd already guessed at his appearance: he'd have his father's nose and the sleek waves of black hair that Bertie was losing. He'd probably be wearing Prada, and a watch that would buy a year's supply of hot meals for one of the bundles of rags that curled up at night outside Rome's old city walls.

She rang the external bell and was buzzed in through the gardens. Then a maid with broad Slavic features admitted her to the entrance hall, a glistening arena of marble, and indicated a lush purple velvet sofa. Gina sank into the cushions; really it was too low. Glossy magazines were fanned out on a glass-topped coffee table; a single amaryllis bloomed in an angular pot. Evidently the touch of Signora Boletti. The effect, she thought, was of a very expensive dentist's waiting room or a private clinic; a place where you were being softened up for bad news.

As she waited she glimpsed someone flit through a doorway at the far end of the hall, a gawky teenage figure with the long loose hair often affected by the offspring of the rich. She called his name softly – she'd have preferred an unsupervised encounter – but Antonio didn't respond. She picked up one of the magazines and thumbed through it until she heard the sharp tap of footsteps. She rose.

At first she couldn't decide what it was about the woman that disturbed her. Everything was pressed into order: the straight silvery blonde hair, the wings of the collar poking in a preppy way from the neck of her cotton jumper, the turned-back cuffs, the sharp crease in her trousers running from thigh to ankle, the narrow dainty shoes. But something was not right.

'Signora Boletti?' said Gina.

'*Si.*' Her handshake was limp, unenthusiastic. Afterwards she tucked her arms behind her back. 'Roberto said he was going to call you. I'm sorry you've had a wasted journey.'

4

The phone was Gina's favourite instrument after the camera, but now and again they came into conflict. If she needed to focus she would switch off her mobile. 'Really? What's the problem?'

'Poor Antonio isn't well. That's why I've come over, to look after him.'

Come over? Didn't they live together? Was Roberto pretending to be married so she wouldn't make too many demands? She'd known men who'd done that, who'd found a wife a useful fabrication. She gazed back at Signora Boletti's smooth maquillage and all of a sudden made sense of what was bothering her. The woman was not Bertie's wife, for Christ's sake, she was his terrifyingly well-maintained mother. A far more daunting proposition.

Gina at once altered her demeanour, gave her widest smile. 'Oh, what a shame!' she said. 'But I was planning to do the studio shots some other time anyway. Part of the reason for today's visit was to get to know Antonio a little. Establish a rapport. Which is so important with portraiture, you see. The person has to really trust you and then you can discover what you want to draw out of them for the image. Is he very ill?'

'Yes, I'm afraid so,' Roberto's mother said with a finality that Gina immediately wanted to test. 'An ear infection. The doctor has insisted he keep to his bed. And both his parents are so occupied with their commitments...' She spread her hands. 'I'm sure you understand.'

Gina nodded, thinking: she knows about me and Bertie. She doesn't approve. That's why she's being so obstructive. I bet there's nothing wrong with the boy at all. 'Perhaps he's feeling better now? I thought I saw him.'

Signora Boletti moved her head a fraction. 'No, that's not possible.'

Annoyed that she was being fobbed off, Gina was determined to buy time, investigate a little more. 'It was quite a long journey here,' she said. 'Do you mind if I sit down for a few minutes before I have to go back again?'

'You don't have a car?'

'I don't drive.'

'Shall I call you a taxi?'

Gina had come to Parioli by bus. Her regular cab driver, Mario, was booked to take a client to the airport and, as usual, she'd been short of ready cash. 'Actually, a glass of water first would be lovely. If it's not inconvenient.'

'Of course. Ice?'

She was lucky. As Signora Boletti went in search of the maid, somewhere behind the panelled double doors a phone began to ring. Gina hoped the caller would be long-winded and effusive. She glided as quietly as possible across the marble to the room she thought she had identified as Antonio's. She gave a tentative knock. '*Permesso?*'

She could hear movement and the low throb of music issuing from headphones. The door was already ajar; without waiting for a response, she pushed through it. The figure she'd noticed before was sitting cross-legged on the bed, jabbing at a laptop. When it raised its head, a little sulkily, Gina felt once again confounded. This was not how she had imagined Bertie's son would look. Freckles for a start. When did Italian kids ever have freckles? And, although she was trying not to stare, the baggy T-shirt didn't hide the rise of young breasts: it was obvious the person in front of her was female.

She began to apologise. 'I'm sorry to interrupt you. I didn't realise there'd be anyone else here. I was looking for Antonio. Perhaps you could pass on a message for me?'

The girl pulled off her headphones, bemused. '*Non capisco. Sono inglese.*'

'Oh, are you?' exclaimed Gina in English. 'That explains it.'

'What?'

The freckles, she meant, but didn't say.

The girl closed the lid of her laptop and leaned forward curiously. 'Are you English too?'

'Yes – at least I have a British passport; but I haven't lived there for twenty years.'

'Wow. You've been in Rome all that time?'

'I started off in Milan, on the catwalk, but then the agency sent me down here. It suits me better anyway, more laid-back.'

'You're a model?'

'Not any more.' For a few moments they studied one another in silence. 'You're a friend of Antonio's, are you?' said Gina at length.

'I'm, like, a lodger.'

'Snap!'

The girl blinked. Her eyes and cheeks were round and childish, her lips plump, as if her face hadn't yet caught up with her adolescent body.

'You mean you live here too?'

'Not exactly. But Bertie's my landlord. My name's Gina by the way. Gina Stanhope.'

'I'm Sasha.'

'How long are you here for, Sasha?'

She hesitated as if counting the days. 'Three weeks. I'm going to this Italian summer school to see if I want to take it as an option in the sixth form. And the Bolettis are my host family. Only…'

Gina sat at the end of the bed. 'You're homesick?'

The chance to speak her own language seemed to unleash a torrent of frustration in Sasha. 'No, it's not that. Everything's a mess at home right now, anyhow. But most of the others are staying in a hostel closer to the school and they've kind of palled up. I had to be put with a family because I'm not sixteen till next month and my mate, Ruby, who was going to come with me dropped out at the last minute with glandular fever and I'm like so useless in the lessons I can't face going in. And now Antonio's got this bug and they think I might get sick too. And – '

'So he really has got an ear infection?'

Sasha tugged at a strand of hair and coiled it around her finger. 'Well, yeah, and it's going to make me even more isolated, so I might as well not *be* here...'

Gina was digesting the fact that she had *not* been lied to. She didn't like being wrong.

'...Plus we don't get on. At all. For a start he's younger than me, and totally spoilt and showing off all the time. Wears this chain around his neck like he's Johnny Depp or someone. He's really annoying, like a kid brother.'

'Do you have a kid brother?'

'No,' she wailed. 'That's why I'm not used to it. I'm an only child.'

Gina smiled. 'Me too. But you shouldn't let this put you off Rome. You should be getting out and enjoying yourself.' In truth, she'd seen too many teenagers enjoying themselves in recent years: it usually involved overdosing on cheap wine and throwing up in the gutter. Not that Gina herself was unfamiliar with wine or gutters – but the sheer quantity of late-night rabble choking the piazzas had become alarming.

'Yeah,' said Sasha, 'I know. I'll probably go to the afternoon class but, honestly, they expect us to do homework. It isn't fair. I've just taken all those GCSEs – I ought to be having a break from studying.'

'Didn't you know what you were signing up for?'

'My parents said I was too young to go raving on a Greek island. This was meant to be educational and fun. Which it would have been if Ruby had come too. Only the way it's turned out...'

From down the hall they could hear the Signora calling for the maid: 'Katya? Katya? *Dove sei?*'

'Katya asked to practise her English on me,' said Sasha, 'but I can't understand her accent. And all the TV programmes are dubbed. I feel like I'm a prisoner sometimes.' She tapped her computer. 'Sending messages to the outside world.'

'That's daft,' said Gina. She took one of her business cards from her wallet. 'Look, I'm a professional photographer. I was supposed to be meeting Antonio today, sizing him up for a portrait, but I've not been allowed to see him which has pissed me off, I can tell you. So if you want a break from the Bolettis or from your course, give me a call. If I don't answer because I'm working, leave a message and I'll try and get back to you. Okay?'

The relief that washed over Sasha and lightened her expression was surprisingly gratifying. There was something about her smile, too, that stirred a distant, buried memory. 'Anyway, I have to go now.' Gina got off the bed, slinging her camera bag over her shoulder. 'The Signora probably thinks I'm after the silverware. I'll jangle this a bit on my way out.' Sasha grinned and gave a thumbs up, as if becoming a conspirator had revived her. Gina stepped out of the room and into the path of Signora Boletti who was carrying a glass of iced water.

'I was looking for the bathroom,' said Gina. 'And – *che sorpresa* – I found *un'inglese*.'

'*Poverina*,' said the Signora indulgently. 'We must keep her away from Antonio, but it may already be too late.'

In Gina's view, the Italian attitude to malady always seemed excessive. 'Ah, but young people are made of rubber, aren't they? They bounce back.' She took the proffered glass and drained it. 'Thank you so much.'

She would have liked to explore further, sneak into other rooms to get a fuller picture of Bertie's home life – although the apartment felt less like a home than a photo shoot styled for a celebrity magazine, already airbrushed. Katya must spend all day polishing the door handles and dusting the light-fittings.

'I'm sure,' said Signora Boletti, 'that when Antonio is recovered, another appointment can be arranged. Roberto is most keen for a photograph. Children grow up so quickly these days. I will find Katya to show you out.' She extended her fingertips and withdrew them almost immediately. '*Arrivederci, signora*.'

On her way to the bus stop Gina rang Roberto. Her call went straight to voicemail so she left him a martyred message. At the very least he could take her out for a decent meal. Meanwhile, if she wanted to salvage this wasted morning, she ought to get over to the studio and do some retouching. But she wouldn't be able to concentrate for long. Her nerves were rattled, though she couldn't tell whether this was because of Signora Boletti, who, after all, had been perfectly civil, or whether there was something else, something unsettling about the girl, Sasha, that she was unable to place.

2

Gina's apartment building stood at the end of a narrow street in Trastevere. At ground level there'd once been a little hive of craftsmen's workshops; there now remained only the joiner with his random pile of chair limbs, and the upholsterer. Further along, the *lavanderia* and *alimentari* were long established but the optician with his expensive prescription sunglasses had replaced the cobbler and the bijou toyshop was changing hands for the third time. Her building was shabby: patches of plaster flaked over the lintels and paint peeled from the wooden shutters. A stone staircase twisted up to the top floor, but it was worth the climb to reach her rooftop terrace.

This was the reason she would never move. Four storeys into the sky, with the sun baking the tiles and a view that had scarcely changed in centuries, she could imagine her world was perfect – if not quite as perfect as other people's. Her neighbours across the way, media folk who considered themselves the new bohemians, had modern Perspex furniture the brilliant colours of boiled sweets, almost good enough to eat. They lounged in their jelly cubes waving matching cocktails and playing loud disco music. '*Ciao*, Gina!' they'd call and she'd wave back, not letting them see for a second any glint of envy.

Her outdoor chairs were old-fashioned, flaking wrought iron. They'd belonged to Felix, whose taste differed from hers, and she hadn't got around to replacing them.

As she reached the top landing she became aware of a disturbance, of things not as they should be. Her key spun in the lock as if it had been recently oiled, and a rich cloying scent seeped under the door. When she nudged it open, she found herself facing a showy display of lilies on the hall console. In the living room bouquets of irises, roses and carnations covered every surface: the cumbersome walnut chiffonier that was too heavy to move, the low coffee table, the two chests crammed with clothes that were waiting to become vintage (although vintage was not much sought after in Italy).

It was a long time since she'd been besieged by so many flowers. The gesture seemed suspiciously flamboyant. The apartment was gloomy after the dazzling sunshine but she knew the hazards: the trailing flex of the TV, the soft, worn rugs that had slipped their moorings. She tiptoed over them all until she reached the bedroom and gave the door a dramatic shove.

Gina's bedroom was not a sight for the faint-hearted. If you live alone there is no one to complain about the soiled laundry lying in exactly the same position for three days, the smeared make-up remover pads or the sticky Marsala glass attracting flies. Her dressing table was overcrowded and items of clothing swayed from the pediment of her wardrobe as if she lived in one large changing cubicle. She'd left the shutters closed so that light entered the room in a series of horizontal bands, slicing up its contents. She noticed immediately, however, the pale grey suit, a fine wool and mohair mix, hanging from a knob on her chest of drawers, and the pair of black shiny shoes lined up beneath it. In the middle of her double bed, his head and naked torso dark against her white pillows, the rest of his body beneath the duvet, lay Roberto. His teeth gleamed as he patted the embroidered cotton covers. 'Surprised?' he said.

Gina didn't speak.

'You like the flowers?'

'Well, they're certainly more than I expected…'

'Come here, *carina*.'

She couldn't afford to fall out with him. She moved closer until she was standing by the bed. Roberto propped himself on one elbow. His belly was a soft paunch, but he was proud of his muscular chest, the strength in his forearms. His free hand inched under her skirt, between her legs, moving up her thigh. Gina didn't look at him. She lifted her chin and raised her eyes to the ceiling. The ceilings in all the rooms, carved from pitch pine, were divided into squares; within each square the fluted edges shrank inside each other like Russian dolls, leading the eye to infinity. On a bad day she could spend a lot of time staring at infinity.

Bertie was not the sort of person to enter a florist and buy a solitary bunch of flowers. He would have stood in the centre of the humid shop, pointing at the rows of galvanised buckets with their drifts of colour: I'll have those and those and those. Once, when she'd been laid low with an excruciating migraine, a condition in which the slightest touch was painful, he had appeared with a hamper of provisions. He refused to believe she couldn't bear to swallow and had tried to tempt her by dropping quantities of grapes into his own mouth like a Bacchus. Basically, he was greedy.

'Get into bed,' he said.

'No.'

'No?' He dug a nail into her flesh where he knew it would hurt and she yelped. 'What's the matter with you?'

She pulled away from him. 'You sent me on a wild goose chase, that's what.'

'You didn't get my message?'

'No. Did you get mine?'

'That's why I'm here! To make it up to you. I have an appointment at the bank in an hour but until then…'

'Don't let me keep you.'

'Gina! I have gone to great lengths on your behalf. It was your choice, not mine, to go to my house, to meet my son. I know that really you wanted to spy.'

'I wasn't spying. I was trying to keep everything on a professional footing. Anyway, he'll have to come to the studio next time. I'm not running the gauntlet of your mother again.'

He reached for the pack of Marlboro he'd left by his phone and lit two cigarettes. Gina was supposed to have given up, but in Bertie's company this was difficult. Reluctantly she nestled beside him, took a long giddy drag on the Marlboro, then laid it on the saucer she used for spare change. She wished she could find a way to say she'd rather he didn't let himself in without warning, that all the flowers in the world wouldn't make up for the invasion of privacy.

In the beginning she'd been seduced by his aura of power (and his cashmere overcoat). Spurred on by the abrasion of their egos, they'd been hungry for each other. But lately the relationship had grown one-sided: there were few benefits to being his tenant and she was finding his demands tiresome. She was afraid she was fucking him for all the wrong reasons.

Smoke plumed from his nostrils. 'You don't love me,' he said sadly.

'And you're playing games. *You* don't love anyone but yourself.'

He was stroking her hair absently. 'He comes between us, doesn't he? You still miss him.'

'Who?'

'Your husband.'

'Of course I miss him! He was my best friend.' Five years had passed. But even if she had used Felix as an excuse too often, she didn't care to discuss him with Bertie.

'The love of your life.'

'Stop it! Are you trying to make me feel worse about everything?'

'How can I compete with him, Gina, tell me?'

'This is *not* a competition.'

'Then what's the problem? There was someone else who captured your heart, so you cannot give it to me? Or feel as I do?' He insisted on this fabrication of romance. Gina would have kicked it away if it didn't make her look so mercenary. 'Did he come after or before?' He gave an exaggerated sigh. 'Another regret?'

'My life is full of bloody regrets, Bertie.'

She hadn't thought of Mitch in years – those romantic trysts they'd kept with each other all over the world. She couldn't work out why he should have sprung to mind, but for an instant she could see his face: the quizzical slant of his expression, the twitch of a muscle in his jaw. She caught her breath at the memory.

'You need to live in the present, *cara*. *Questa bella giornata*.' He crushed the stubs of both their cigarettes into the saucer. Then, impatient with a conversation that wasn't leading anywhere, he pushed Gina's head beneath the covers, so that her mouth might seek and fasten upon his rearing cock.

It turned out to be all that was required to restore his vigour and good humour. Once satisfied, he leapt out of bed and stretched his limbs, unselfconscious in his nakedness. 'I'm sorry about this morning,' he said. 'We'll fix another date for the portrait, yes?'

Gina took a little longer to adjust her equilibrium. She shook the pillows and the duvet so the imprint of his body vanished. 'I don't want to push you into it,' she said. 'Maybe, he's too young after all.'

'Oh no, it must happen. *Sens'altro*.'

'What about your house guest?'

'Who? Oh, you mean the English girl? Strange kid. The school asked as a favour at the last minute and my wife thought the company would be amusing for Antonio. But she also thought Sasha was a boy's name. Crazy woman!' He laughed. '*Comunque*, it's not a disaster, but not a success either. If you take her picture too, maybe her parents will buy it? Make me a coffee, will you, while I wash and dress.'

Gina's kitchen was set in an alcove overlooking the building's internal courtyard of dustbins and dying geraniums. She filled the espresso pot and set it to gurgle on the stove. He had promised her a new counter-top of fine Carrara marble, yet to materialise. An electrician of her acquaintance had offered to install new halogen spotlights, but what was the point of illuminating such a dowdy space? Besides, renovation could make it harder for her to resist the inevitable rent increase.

As usual, Bertie spent ages dousing away any hint of their encounter beneath the steady hiss of water. He spent an equally long period regarding himself in the mirror, tweaking his hair, correcting the knot of his tie. Back in his tailored suit, he was the epitome of the hard-shelled businessman, driven by commerce.

By this time, the froth had disappeared on his coffee and steam no longer rose from the tiny cup. He assumed she had already sweetened it for him and drank it in a single gulp, before grimacing.

'*Mortacci tua*, Gina!'

'What?'

'No sugar.'

'Oh? Sorry.'

His eyes narrowed, examining her for evasion. Then he stepped forward and gathered her into an embrace. He nuzzled her neck, sweeping away her hair; his tongue traced the outline of her ear; his teeth nipped the tip of her ear lobe. A needle of pain shot through her. A drop of blood formed; he licked it away.

Then he let her go, fished the keys from his pocket and began spinning them around his finger. The bunch was so large she was surprised he wasn't concerned about spoiling the hang of his trousers with such a weight.

He said, as if to reassure her. 'It was lucky I got here when I did, you know. There were some rough-looking types, riff-raff, hanging around outside. But I saw them off for you.'

'Right,' she said, keeping her face a pleasant mask. She would have to tell the boys to be more discreet. They'd begged to use her address so they could receive mail and qualify for health cards, but she'd had to refuse: it would have been too risky. Like thousands of other refugees they were consigned to limbo.

Tumbling the keys from one hand to the other, he said thoughtfully, 'Perhaps it's not so safe here any more. Had you thought of moving somewhere respectable?'

'Trastevere is respectable! It's been gentrified up to its eyeballs.'

'Anywhere historic, anywhere you have tourists you have scavengers also. I didn't like the look of them. Illegals, I'm sure.'

'Bertie, I've had to fend for myself practically since I was born. I can handle what you call riff-raff.'

'I think you should consider it,' he said. 'Relocation.'

The prospect of having to leave her apartment chilled her. It was the one constant in her haphazard life. She set a tight-lipped smile as he scudded down the stairs without looking back.

3

The day before Sasha Mitchell met Gina Stanhope things had looked bleak. She'd been in Rome for less than a week and the sense of disappointment was bruising. Denied the chance to join the gang of school friends going to Zante for a fortnight (from his cockpit her father had too often seen young revellers return from holiday as bilious wrecks), the language course was meant to be the next best thing. She and Ruby had had such plans, worked themselves into a state of delirium about their trip. Ruby's diagnosis of glandular fever was devastating.

Her parents assumed she'd want to cancel, but what was the alternative? She'd be marooned in the Cheshire countryside, dependent on lifts, unable to hang out with her best friend. Besides, the atmosphere at home was decidedly strained. Her mother, Corinne, was in the final stages of a PhD, researching the care of dementia patients in hospital. The stress of co-ordinating her data and writing up her thesis, in addition to her shifts on the geriatric ward, was winding her tight as a spring. Her father seemed to be on what Corinne called 'avoidance duties'. Basically, everything had fallen apart since the dog died. The dog, Sasha concluded, had been keeping the family together. He was more important than she was and, much as she'd loved him, this rankled. He'd been the last survivor of a succession of pets and now the three of them – mother, father, daughter – were coming unstuck.

'It's not like they really care what I do,' she'd told Ruby on the phone. 'They just think I shouldn't go on my own.'

Ruby had to speak in feeble breathy gasps like an old person. 'Of course you must, Sash. It'll be brill.'

'They say I can't stay in the hostel if you're not coming. They have to find a family for me.'

'Who knows, the family might have some, like, gorgeous son, who's totally hot. Ow! Fuck, it even hurts to laugh... I feel *so* shit.'

'So you reckon I should go ahead and talk them round?'

'What else you gonna do?'

'It wouldn't bother you?'

'It'll bug me to hell. But I'd feel even worse if I thought this bloody fever was ruining your summer too.'

'When I get back, when you get better, we'll do something else, make up for all this, right?'

'But while you're there, Sash, you have to post stuff every day, so I know what's happening. Give me something to look forward to. Turn me green.'

'Oh, Rube...'

'Greener, I should have said. I look like mouldy lettuce already.'

'I'm going to miss you so much...'

'You'll have a ball!'

So Ruby had spurred her on and in the rush of last-minute arrangements she'd given no thought to failure. Now she was having to face it. While the doctor had been examining Antonio, she'd shut herself in the elegant but sterile guest room and hunched over her phone. In previous calls she'd kept up a chirpy enthusiasm for everything. Could she bear to admit she had made a mistake now? She tried her father first, without success; then she'd rung her mother. 'Do you think Dad could get me on an earlier flight home?'

'Oh, darling, what's the problem?'

'It isn't the same,' said Sasha. 'With Ruby not being here.'

'I did warn you about that, but you insisted.'

'And it looks like Antonio's getting some bug too, so it might be me next. I don't want to be sick in a foreign country.'

Corinne, as a nurse, was remarkably impervious to the threat of illness. 'You'll be fine. It's early days.'

'I suppose you like having the house to yourself. Where is Dad anyway?'

'Long-haul. Hong Kong.'

'When's he coming back?'

'I'm not sure…'

'Don't you even *speak* any more?'

'Look, Sash, I know it's tough without Ruby and it always takes a while to make new friends, but now you're there you have to stick it out. You put us under a lot of pressure to let you go – and so did the language school, come to that. But they promised me you'd be well looked after. And, my goodness, it sounded as though you'd hit the jackpot with the Bolettis. That beautiful apartment…'

Sasha gave up. How could she explain that, although the apartment was sumptuous, she didn't feel comfortable in it. Initially, Signora Boletti had been charmed by the novelty of an English guest but she soon lost interest. She gave her either too much or too little attention: pressing extra helpings of food upon her and then being distracted by something so that Sasha laboured alone at the table, pushing tortellini around her plate and hiding her leftovers under the cutlery. When he was around for long enough to notice her, Signor Boletti's gaze seemed to pierce right through her clothes and on through flesh and bone to her ungrateful, unhappy heart. And it didn't help that Antonio had turned out to be an irritating little jerk.

Having failed to convince her mother, she decided to wait before trying her father again – she was pretty certain he'd be able to slip her onto a flight home. The day after meeting Gina, however, things began to improve. She managed, for the first time, to arrive early for the lessons. She'd not missed her bus stop or taken the wrong short cut, stumbling breathless up the stairs, dropping her books on the way. Instead she joined the other language students in the corridor, making eye contact, exchanging smiles. Two German girls, Ilse and Renate, introduced themselves, but there wasn't room to sit with them so she slid into the back row, beside the shy, conscientious Japanese girl whose name she didn't know.

Sasha was not conscientious. Although she hoped to become as fluent as her father, she'd also hoped that the language would creep under her skin by some kind of osmosis and she wouldn't have to work at it. Italian was supposed to be easy, it shouldn't be giving her trouble. And, more than anything, she objected to the notion that she should hand in homework.

The tutor had arrived and was collecting the exercises set in a previous session. Some of the staff were the type who wanted to be your friend, but not this one. When she saw Sasha's pages were blank, she frowned. '*Non l'ha fatto?*'

'No.'

'*Perché non?*'

Her fellow students swivelled to stare at her. She was younger than most of them; even so, she thought it ridiculous they should be treated like schoolchildren. All her loneliness and frustration boiled up suddenly. The classroom was stuffy and humid; the windows couldn't be opened because of the noise outside. In any conversation sounds bounced off the walls and became distorted. So she lifted her shoulders to her ears, rolled her eyes, spread her arms in a gesture of incomprehension and exclaimed '*Boh!*' in exactly the same manner as Signor Boletti when he was exasperated with something.

The class erupted into giggles. The tutor's head twitched on her neck. She drawled a withering rebuke that Sasha couldn't understand, then moved away and ignored her entirely for the rest of the morning.

When the students crowded out of the room and down the stairs at the end of the class, Sasha found herself being swept along in their midst. They adjourned to a nearby bar and she was included, without awkwardness, in their number. The bar opened out into a large room at the back and there they milled: American, German, Dutch, Japanese. Sasha was the only English person – although this was the language they spoke to each other. Italian was used only to order the coffees, Cokes and beers.

Ilse and Renate took her under their wing. They had finished school and were about to go to university. She envied their effortless confidence and was grateful for the inclusion.

'Is the first time you come to lessons, yes?' said Ilse.

'Well, no, though I did miss a couple. Once because my host family took me on an outing to Tivoli.' Signor Boletti had conceived the notion and he wasn't a person to argue with. 'And then because I lost my way and didn't want to turn up late...'

'You are staying with a family? This is the reason we have not seen you before?'

'And I generally sit at the back. Maybe that's why you didn't notice me.' Her lack of significance grated, so she made a point of laughing loudly and tossing her hair lavishly.

Ilse and Renate wore cropped, functional styles that made them seem even more striking and Amazonian. Their shorts were very tight and very brief. Sasha had spent the last two years draping her limbs in jeans and sweatshirts, waiting for the bulges in her body to reassemble themselves in the right places. She knew she was a late developer – not that such knowledge was useful when her friends had long broken out of the chrysalis of puberty. 'It was the same for me,' said her mother with a smug sigh that did nothing to alleviate her sense of injustice. One day, she promised herself, one day she too would loll against the chrome counter of a bar in Rome while the ribs of a ceiling fan lazily tickled the air above and all the boys in the vicinity would gawp in lust and admiration at the tantalising creases in the crotch of her denim shorts.

One of these boys, Harry, a gangly American in a ragged T-shirt who'd been looking in their direction – at Ilse's smooth bare midriff in particular – suggested they take a picnic up to the Borghese Gardens. A delegation was tasked with choosing the drinks and a selection of ready-filled rolls to take away. The rest went outside and shuffled on the pavement.

Hovering at the fringe Sasha noticed a boy who was not as cool and self-assured as the rest. Red-faced from the heat, he was trying to keep under the protection of the bar awning. He had freckles too, but he was ginger. At least she'd been spared ginger. Once they set off again, she kept her distance from him, striding up the Spanish Steps alongside Renate and Ilse, her flip-flops flailing against the soles of her feet.

They reached the park and headed for the nearest fountain. It wasn't easy to find somewhere to set up camp. The grass, green at a distance, was coarse and sparse close up, the ground hard and dry. But there was shade beneath the trees and the muted hum of summer: children, birds, bicycle bells, even the clop of horses drawing carriages full of tourists.

They passed around the food in its cellophane packaging and unscrewed bottles of warm rosé. Renate scratched her tanned thigh, crossed one ankle over the other. She took a swig from the bottle and passed it to Sasha, saying, 'Tonight we go out, yes? To dance in a club? In Testaccio there are many, very funky.'

'D'you need ID to get in?'

The German girls shook their heads, surprised. No one had ever asked them for it. There was no age limit for drinking in Italy. 'Also, you are a girl. You need only to wear make-up.'

At home Sasha had struggled to get into clubs. No one was fooled by her fake ID. Ruby, who could talk her way in anywhere, had once said sharply that she needed to grow out of her 'My Little Pony' stage – though Sasha didn't see why a love of horses should be a handicap. She'd hoped that spending time in a city as glamorous as Rome would result in being scattered with magic dust: instant suntan, blonde streaks in her hair, a miraculously narrow waist, an elegant way of walking. Like the photographer who'd come to see Antonio yesterday, whose movements were as fluid as a dancer's.

'Sure, that'd be boss. I'd love to come.'

Drinking wine in the early afternoon made Sasha giddy; it also made her slow to grasp when the picnicking was over and the gang was breaking up. Ilse and Renate collected up the torn paper, empties and bottle tops. 'We are not like the Italians,' sniffed Renate, pinching an empty cigarette packet between her fingers and dropping it into a plastic bag. But once they'd disposed of all the debris, stepping over the low curved railings to dump it in the bin by the path, they didn't come back for Sasha. They waved and called 'See you later,' and ambled off with their arms around each other's waists. The American boys formed a phalanx that gravitated in unison towards the wide boulevard. Sasha felt a painful prick in her calf and by the time she'd finished brushing off the sharp pine needles, the only member of the group remaining was the ginger boy, Bruton.

'Whatever kind of a name is that?' she said. 'D'you get called Brute?'

He was unfazed. 'It's after my great-grandfather. I'm Scottish, you see.'

'Scottish-American?'

'Yeah. Anyway, Sasha's weird too.'

'Not to me it isn't.' At least it wasn't the kind of name you'd give an ugly dog. 'You can call me Sash if you like,' she said grudgingly. 'Most people do.'

As she rose to go, Bruton jumped up alongside her like a puppy. 'What're you doing now?'

She knew she was pickled by the heat and the alcohol, pink and slushy like a pear stewed in red wine. She planted her feet further apart so she wouldn't sway.

'Have you been to the Galleria Borghese?' he asked.

'No. I heard you have to book a ticket in advance and then you have to queue. Mental.'

'That's what you do for most places. Like, the Vatican's two hours or more.'

'Are you into art or something?' said Sasha.

He was studious-looking. Swotty. Nerdy. Not an outdoor type. 'I've travelled 4000 miles. You get this far, you don't know when you might come back to Europe, so you have to do the stuff. If I can tell my folks I've seen the Sistine Chapel, they might not ask what else we got up to, you know what I mean?'

Shit, thought Sasha who hadn't got up to anything. What was she missing out on? 'I like ruins better than art galleries anyhow.'

'You've done the Forum?'

'Yeah.' She had explored the Forum during a class she'd skipped. It had been strange wandering through the tumbled masonry by herself. Sometimes, in the street, boys on scooters had whistled and made overtures she ignored, but among the ancient temples and ruined palaces she was as inconsequential as the lizards that ran to hide in the cracks. No one was interested in her. Not that Bruton's interest was what she wanted either. People might see them together and assume they were a couple. It bothered her that the others had left the pair of them behind like the runts of a litter, easily discarded.

She didn't seem to be able to shake him off. For a nerd, he was actually quite arrogant, strolling through the park with his hands in his pockets, giving her the history of the Borghese family like he'd been descended from them himself instead of from some displaced crofter in the Scottish Highlands.

'I have to get back to the apartment to change,' she said, 'if I'm coming out again later.'

'That's hours away.'

'Yeah, but I need to get my act together too. You saw what a mess I made of stuff in class.'

The park stretched around them: drifts of lawn and parched flower beds in a web of dusty boulevards; tall chestnuts and limes shielding glimpses of palatial villas. To their right was a sign for the zoo.

'Hey, cool!' said Bruton. 'Let's go in.'

Sasha explained at some length that she didn't approve of zoos. The entire concept was horrific as far as she was concerned: animals should not be kept in captivity.

He interrupted her passionate defence of animal rights to say, 'Are you vegetarian then?'

'Duh! You can't be vegetarian if you live in the country.'

'Why not?'

'Well there'd hardly *be* any countryside if you didn't have farms. And farmers keep livestock… It isn't about what you eat anyhow. It's about how you treat living creatures. It's about *respect*.'

'Sure,' said Bruton with a patronising nod, as if she were a temperamental mare to be calmed down.

Sasha resolved to lose him at the first opportunity. His nasal whine was getting on her nerves. Emerging from the exit beyond the zoo she tried to get her bearings. In the distance a bus turned a corner and she thought she recognised the number. 'That's mine,' she said, and then, feeling she could afford to be generous, 'I've missed it, obviously. D'you want to wait for the next one with me?'

She wasn't concentrating, that was the problem. Her head was woozy from the rosé and the sudden urgent need to take a siesta. She had a blister between her toes where her flip-flop had rubbed, and needed a plaster. So when another bus pulled up, she hopped aboard. 'See you later, okay?' she said. She didn't want to fall out with someone who was offering himself as an ally, however low in the pecking order, and he was an improvement on Antonio. 'When we meet up with the others, yeah?'

Bruton frowned and began to say something, but she couldn't hear him above the engine and wasn't sure she wanted to listen. She slipped into a seat by the window and waved through the glass, miming that she would call him. With relief, she shed her flip-flop and examined her blister.

Initially she didn't pay much regard to the bus route. It trundled along the quieter fringes of the park before joining a noisy thoroughfare. Then she noticed it was approaching the Lungotevere and crossing the river. This should not be happening. The journey to the Bolettis passed through broad, tree-lined avenues, no water involved. Either this was the right bus going in the wrong direction or she'd misread the number completely. She'd have to get off.

She alighted as soon as she could, in an unfamiliar piazza hedged with orange barricades, behind which workmen were re-laying stone setts. The obvious thing to do was retrace her journey, but bus routes varied according to the one-way system and although she limped from one stop to the next she couldn't find a recognisable number or destination. This wouldn't happen to her father. He had a whole bloody crew with him when *he* travelled. She toyed with her phone and the idea of ringing him. She could leave a message on his voicemail: Come down off your cloud and rescue me! I want to go home! No, that was stupid. She did *not* want to go home. She wanted to go clubbing with Ilse and Renate and meet a handsome, brown-eyed Italian. All she really needed was someone to tell her where she was.

She was using a new Italian sim card and had very few contacts on it. Clicking down the list from 'Dad' to 'Ilse', Gina's name leapt out at her. Here was someone who'd lived in Rome for decades. She was bound to know her way around.

Gina answered at the third ring. '*Pronto*.'

'Hi, it's Sasha here. Sasha Mitchell.' A long pause. Sasha wondered if she was out of reception or battery. 'Hello? Gina?'

'Who did you say?'

'Sasha. We met yesterday. I'm the English girl, at Antonio's house, remember? And you said I should call you if I ever needed...' At this point her voice wobbled.

'Are you in some sort of trouble?' said Gina.

'I'm lost.'

'Oh, I see. Lost where?'

'I don't know! I was trying to get back to Parioli but I took
the bus in the wrong direction and it's gone across one of the
bridges to the other side of the river and I've got this awful
blister so it hurts to walk and – '

'Have you got any money?'

Sasha opened her purse. 'Not very much.'

'Why don't you ring the Bolettis and ask them to fetch you?'

'They'll be at work. I don't have to be fetched like a parcel or
anything. I just want to know how to get back and I thought
you might be able to tell me.'

'Well, only if I know where you are! What's the name of the
street?'

She craned her neck and shaded her eyes. 'Piazza Cavour,
only they're digging it up and...'

'Oh, you're not so far from me. I live this side of the river, in
Trastevere. That's what it means: across the Tiber.'

The words burst out unexpectedly: 'Can I come and see you?'

'What? Now?'

She didn't want to go back to the Boletti apartment. There
was nothing to do there except talk to the maid or check in
online with friends at home whose activities were currently
irrelevant to her; she and Antonio were no company for each
other at all. 'Are you very busy?' she asked.

After another pause Gina came to a decision. 'I'm finishing
something off but it's okay, I'll send Super Mario for you.'

'Who's he?'

'My taxi driver.'

'You mean, like a chauffeur?'

Gina laughed. 'Well he doesn't only work for me, but he's
very obliging. Not true of all cab drivers I can tell you. I'll text
you the number of his cab so you can look out for him.'

'I haven't got the money to pay for a taxi.'

'Don't worry. He'll put it on my account and I'll take some
extra photos of his grand-daughter. In this city, favours have
always been bartered. It suits the way people operate.'

Fifteen minutes later Mario drew up beside her with a flourish, a gold tooth glinting in his smile, a Madonna dangling in front of his mirror. Tucked behind his sun visor he also kept a photo of the baby grand-daughter. Once Sasha was settled, he took both hands off the wheel to release it for her to admire. As she accepted it, the Fiat jolted over a set of tram tracks and she skidded across the back seat.

'*Attento*!' he cried. '*La mia preziosa*!'

He was talking about the photo, she realised, and she passed it back with murmurs of '*Bellissima*' – a word she over-used, but it never gave offence. In any case, the picture *was* lovely. Gina had captured the child's angelic quality, and a hint of devilment too.

'You've known Gina long?' she said.

'*Ah, sì.*' He nodded vehemently. '*Però, una donna sfortunata.*'

'Oh…' She assumed he would explain and hoped she'd understand it, but there wasn't time. He shot through a red light, steered round two corners and braked inches from the pavement.

4

Sasha hadn't yet got used to the dilapidated appearance of the city: the way you'd stumble across a heap of fallen columns or a rail protecting a ditch of ancient foundations, the way cars raced around the crumbling Colosseum, and the way buildings were so often daubed with graffiti or missing chunks of plaster. However, the block Mario had driven her to was worse than most. The rendering was mottled and discoloured and layers of varnish flaked from the heavy front door. The names written beneath strips of plastic alongside each bell-push were faint with mildew, almost unreadable.

'*La più alta*,' called Mario, pointing to the top button as he reversed at speed down the narrow street.

A buzzing released the lock and admitted Sasha to a dim hallway with a cold stone floor. She took off her flip-flops with relief and sniffed a distinct odour of mould. Usually she liked warm animal scents, dense fur or a rich musky hide, but whatever she could smell here was more like something dead and quietly rotting. She was glad to reach the natural light of the landing at the top of four flights of stairs and find the door to the apartment had been left ajar.

She entered a vestibule full of flowers: so many bouquets were on the console Gina might have been preparing for a christening – or a funeral. The vases were crowded haphazardly together, as if they were a nuisance, quite unlike the elegant architectural displays regularly refreshed around the Boletti apartment. Puzzled that Gina hadn't come out to meet her, she pushed through another doorway.

The walls of this room were filled with pictures, many of them framed photographs, including some of a younger Gina, emphasising the sculptural qualities of her jaw and cheekbone, her elongated neck and legs. There were also several modern paintings: abstract compositions, daubs of colour, arrangements of line and shape – the sort you'd need a whole other language to understand – and an assortment of sculptures. A bronze egg stood on a plinth and a hemisphere of beaten zinc on a bookcase. An assembly of metal rods and cogs was positioned on a blanket box to the left of the French windows. A matching chest on the right had its lid raised like an open coffin, its contents, mostly fabrics, spilling out.

Another sculpture hovered near the chest, a life-size statue of a Roman emperor draped in a white toga and crowned with a laurel wreath sprayed silver. But it wasn't carved from marble. Although its hands and face were chalk white, its eyes were dark and disturbed. They wheeled first towards Sasha and then to the far corner of the room, and were followed by an urgent jabbering that didn't sound Italian.

Sasha turned. Set into a recess was a row of kitchen appliances: fridge, stove, sink and washing machine. Beside them stood a young man, holding a steaming cup and regarding her with horror. Unlike the friend who'd been dressing up as Julius Caesar, this figure – slim and swarthy, with a ripple of dark hair flowing past his navel to the slack swing of his genitals – was completely naked. With his free hand he scooped a tea towel from a hook and tried to wrap it around his haunches.

Sasha was too surprised and fascinated to do anything other than watch the progress of the tea towel. She'd have preferred to appear worldly and unconcerned, but in truth her knowledge of boys was far from extensive and she had to rely on Ruby for information and useful tips.

The young man sidled out of sight. The emperor called, 'Gina!' and Sasha began to speculate on Gina's role – what activity she might have disturbed and whether this was the reason she'd sounded peculiar on the phone. She was confused, too, when Gina appeared, by the fact that the woman looked so different. Yesterday her hair had been smoothly caught back, her lipstick had been bright, her dress chic and figure-skimming. Today her clothes were loose and shabby – a creased top and a pair of leggings that she'd pulled on in a hurry – and her hair was a tousled bush.

Sasha had once stumbled across a couple having sex in the stock cupboard at the back of the school art room. The boy, energetically pumping with his trousers round his ankles, hadn't noticed her. The girl from the year above had flicked a middle finger insolently in Sasha's direction. That had been mortifying; this was almost as bad.

'So Mario got you here in one piece,' Gina said, seizing a handful of hair and twisting it into a knot on top of her head.

'Yes. Thanks.'

'What did you want to see me about?'

'Well... I...' She didn't know the answer to that. She should have asked Mario to take her back to the Bolettis. She'd probably have been able to find the money to pay him and it would have been worth it to save all this embarrassment. 'You said you lived nearby... I don't know this side of the river and, um... I did *ask* if you were busy.'

'Busy? Yeah...' Gina peered at her. 'God, you look parched. D'you want a drink? Yusef's just made some green tea. Or – '

'Have you got a Coke?'

'I doubt it.' She opened the fridge and withdrew a bottle of mineral water. 'This is better for you anyhow.' She poured a glass and handed it to Sasha.

The liquid and its bubbles revived her. 'And if you had a plaster for my blister, that'd be so great.'

'You'd better wash your feet first,' said Gina, 'when Yusef's finished in the shower. Sit down while you're waiting, for goodness' sake. This isn't a cocktail party.' Then she noticed the living statue. 'Oh God, Sami, are you still here?'

Sheepishly the emperor readjusted his coronet.

'Sami does his stuff in Piazza Navona. But I help him with his make-up. Not bad is he?'

'Could you help me with mine?' said Sasha, perching on the arm of a chair.

'What? Well…' Gina came closer. She tipped up Sasha's chin, then stroked her skin as if assessing its softness. 'The whole hog?'

'We're going to a club tonight, me and some of the other students. But they're older and I've, like, got to look as though I'm one of them.'

'Hey, they're talking to you, are they? That's good news.'

'Yeah.' Sasha brightened. 'Wicked.'

'What about Antonio's mother? Can't she help you get ready?'

'I don't know. She might take me to a beauty salon and I don't like those kinds of places.'

'What makes you think you can trust me?'

'You looked amazing yesterday.'

Gina massaged the side of her swan-like neck. 'And today I look like something the cat threw up?'

'No! N-not at all.' In fact Gina's face was curiously bland, the features indeterminate apart from her eyes, which were large and intense. Even so, Sasha couldn't tell their colour: reflective as water, they might have been grey or green or hazel. 'If you do it for him,' she said, indicating Sami, 'you must have had training – as a make-up artist, I mean.'

'Actually I'm a photographer,' Gina reminded her. 'I guess there's a connection though: contouring, highlighting, retouching, sharpening. Different techniques, same results.'

The bathroom door opened and Yusef came out, fully dressed in T-shirt and jeans. He had a broad, sensitive face and a nose that was slightly crooked, as if it had been broken and misaligned. He wouldn't look at Sasha when Gina introduced them, his long lashes downcast. He joined Sami and the two of them murmured together.

'They were expecting another friend to show up,' Gina explained. 'That's why they buzzed you in and you caught them on the hop. Stupid boys! They're always looking over their shoulders, poor kids, and this is one of the places they can feel safe. But God knows, you could have been anybody! Bertie even!' She scowled in a way that was distinctly intimidating. How could a person change so, from one day to the next? 'You're not a bloody spy, are you?'

She was a schoolgirl on a language course. How could she possibly be a spy? 'Course not! What d'you mean?'

'Bertie's my landlord. He's part of a property syndicate. Didn't I already tell you that? Was he the one who suggested you come here?'

'No, like I said, I got lost.'

Gina crossed her arms, tapped a slippered foot as if unconvinced. 'I wouldn't put it past him. He seems to think he has the right to walk in whenever he feels like it. I had to shift his bloody flowers into the hall, they were cluttering the place up so much.'

'Signor Boletti bought you all those flowers?'

'I had a rat problem,' said Gina. 'He wouldn't do anything about it for ages so I had to put down poison. He brought the flowers as a sweetener, but he's up to something, I'm sure of it.'

'I noticed a smell,' said Sasha, 'soon as I got into the building.'

'The trouble is, it's not in his interests to make any improvements until my contract runs out and he can put the rent up. And if he hasn't sent you, then I'd rather you didn't tell him anything. We all have to be on our best behaviour. *Giusto, ragazzi?*'

Yusef continued to avoid eye-contact; Sami nodded. The pair of them edged towards the door and let themselves out with a soft click. Gina sighed. 'I usually work from the studio, but sometimes it's more convenient from home... Now, you go and sort yourself out in the bathroom. You'll find plasters in the cabinet.'

The bathroom had no external window. The bath and shower-head were old and ornate – practically antique. Sasha ran the tap. After a dramatic groan in the pipes, a torrent gushed over her sore foot. When she had dried and bandaged it, she stood in front of the mirror, imagining what miracles Gina might work. A shelf above the basin held a razor and shaving gel, male paraphernalia among the moisturiser and cleansing wipes. Did a man live here? Or was the razor Sami's, so he could shave before his makeover? Suddenly the impact of Gina's remarks struck her. The young men weren't making a social call; they were having their pictures taken. It didn't take much imagination to envisage what kind of pictures.

'Better?' said Gina when she came out. She'd opened the shutters to the terrace and golden afternoon light flooded the room. She also had open, on the table in front of her, a vanity case packed with tubes and bottles, brushes and cotton wool. She passed her a wide hairband. 'Put this on and sit on that low stool so I can get at you.'

'You don't have to do this, really,' said Sasha.

'I thought you asked me to? Keep still while I whisk your eyebrows into shape.'

'I mean...' The tweezers tweaked too fast to feel any pain, but her eyes watered. 'You might want to work on your photographs or something.'

'I'll look at them later.'

'Are they, like, models?'

'The boys? Yes, in a way.'

Not modelling togas, that was for sure. 'Glamour?' suggested Sasha.

Gina barked with laughter. She laid down the tweezers and soaked a ball of cotton wool in toner. 'Such a con,' she said. 'So many girls your age, they think that's the way to go, don't they? Pump up their tits and stick a feather boa between their legs. That's not modelling. Jesus!' She swabbed savagely at Sasha's temples.

'Ow! I didn't say it was what *I* wanted. What do you call it then? Porn?'

'It's not hardcore,' said Gina, as if she didn't care one way or the other. 'Believe it or not, darling, some people will pay money for a more subtle type of erotica. If it's arty enough you can get away with hanging it on your walls, you see. No need to stash it in a back room. Now, how dark shall we go for your foundation?'

'I'd like to look tanned.'

'I'll see what I can do.' She massaged moisturiser with the tips of her fingers in a circular soothing motion. 'And it's not for my benefit either. You've no idea how sordid some of these kids' lives have been. Wherever they come from – Albania, Afghanistan, Turkey, Tunisia – they've effectively been trafficked, like slaves. And things don't get much better here. Even if they manage to escape, there's nothing for them. No welfare, no jobs, just charity from the Church. Sami's a bit better off because he's good enough at what he does to earn a few euros. Illegally. No stability and not much in the way of prospects.'

'Where do they live?'

'Well, Sami and Yusef managed to find a room in a squat. Most of the others are homeless. Some sleep in the church crypt. I'm working on a project there – with the full cooperation of the priest, by the way. I'm aiming to build up enough material for an exhibition. We're hoping it will help to raise funds, or shame the city fathers into doing something – although I doubt it. Romans are too used to scavengers.'

'Is that what you'd rather be doing?'

'Rather than private commissions?' said Gina, patting on foundation with a sponge. 'Portraits for the Bolettis and their

kind? You could say so, yes. And don't forget the weddings –
guaranteed to put you off marriage, darling! They come here
in droves, the Yanks and the Brits, for the romance of nuptials
in Italy. They're glad of a bilingual photographer, especially
one who can shave kilos off them and turn them into fairytale
beauties.' She sighed. 'Though that market may have been
milked too far, there's so much red tape: residence criteria to
satisfy, documents to stamp, taxes to stump up. The important
thing is that I provide a professional service. And, in the case
of the boys, let me make it clear: I am *not* exploiting them.
If I sell they'll get paid. He has a striking figure, don't you
think?'

'Who?'

'Yusef.'

'Oh, right… I didn't really notice.'

'You didn't?' Gina sounded amused. Her phone, lying next
to the vanity case, vibrated and danced a little jig. She checked
the screen with a cluck of annoyance and switched it off. 'Don't
blink.' She began to blend shadow over Sasha's eyelids and
tease out her lashes with a mascara wand. 'A steady hand is
so important, you know. Muscle control. Ask Sami. And my
mother. It was the only thing she ever taught me actually. I
wasn't her top priority.'

Sasha reckoned she knew how she felt. 'Mine says stuff like
I've got to stand on my own two feet. She's done her bit. She
wants to focus on her career.'

'How old are you?'

'Sixteen next month.' On the plane she'd been classed as an
unaccompanied minor, but she'd known half the attendants
anyway; she'd been in good hands.

'Oh, I thought you were younger.'

Sasha bridled. 'I'm the youngest in my year, that's all.'

'Anyway, darling, your mother's probably right. And at least
you weren't abandoned aged eight so she could go off with her
fancy man.'

The remark was casual, but the notion stuck fast. For the first time, it occurred to Sasha that the PhD might be a smokescreen, that Corinne might have met someone else. It would explain why the atmosphere at home was so tense. When she'd been younger her parents had dovetailed their shifts so that someone was always around for her. This was no longer necessary, yet in the past month she could count on one hand the meals the three of them had eaten together.

'How did she abandon you?'

'Phoebe? She left me in boarding school while she went off to the States.'

'With the fancy man?'

'She was on tour – she was a dancer – but she hitched up with Mountebank Monty and got him to pay the school fees. She's on her third husband now, Carlos, and lives in Santiago. That's Chile, by the way, not Spain, so we don't often meet.'

'What about your dad?'

'Oh, he was another brilliant example of crap parenting: a serial philanderer. Absconded, then divorced. I was a mistake they both regretted. Everybody thinks of the sixties as this incredible period of freedom from constraint, but unluckily for those two I was conceived before the Abortion Act.'

The bitter brittle tone in which she delivered this was making Sasha squirm on her stool. Gina cupped her chin firmly. 'Don't move. I'm nearly finished. I always do the lips last, though I don't think a strong colour will suit you.'

'My dad…' Sasha began.

'What?'

'He's a bit over-protective, I think. He wasn't keen on my coming here. Mum had to help me talk him round.'

'Obviously some fathers take their responsibilities more seriously than others. What does he do?'

Sasha couldn't answer at first because Gina's pencil was tracing the outline of her mouth. 'He's a pilot.'

There was a momentary silence while Gina swapped the pencil for a fine brush, uncapped different lipsticks and tested them on the back of her hand. Then she said, 'Those were the days! I used to fly a lot myself. People wonder how you can get used to it, the constant hopping about, but you can adapt to anything really. Like the guys dossing in that crypt every night.'

'He's a captain,' said Sasha proudly. 'My mate Ruby does this ace impersonation of him, cracks us up every time: Morning everyone, I'm Captain Mitchell and I'd like to welcome you aboard this chicken coop with wings. Sorry about the delay you had being frisked by security and the fact that we've got to sit on the tarmac for an hour but it's raining torrents at your holiday destination so why not sit back and enjoy…' She trailed off. Gina wasn't cracking up.

'Bully for him! Should I be impressed?' Her hands fluttered slightly as if they weren't so steady after all. She laid the brush aside and passed Sasha a mirror. 'All done.'

Sasha pulled off the headband and peered into the glass. The same and not the same. Ruby had worked on her occasionally before a night out, when Sasha could be bothered to let her, but Ruby's handiwork was nothing like this. Not so much a transformation as a re-emphasis: a creaming of the texture of her skin, a definition to her features that made her eyes stand out, reduced her hamster cheeks and gave her a luscious peachy mouth. 'That's wicked!' she exclaimed. 'Absolutely ace.'

Gina was putting everything away, screwing tops onto tubes, tucking the sable brushes into their nest. 'Let's hope it gets you through the nightclub door. Here, you can keep this lipstick. You'll need to touch up before you go out anyhow.'

'Thank you so much. Will you… I mean, would you… be able to give me a make-up lesson sometime? Before I go home.'

'No, I don't think so. I've got a lot on my plate, I'm afraid. But enjoy the rest of your stay.'

She appeared to be detaching herself, keeping a distance from everything they had said and done that afternoon, almost as

if she'd changed her mind about Sasha and decided she was a
spy for the Bolettis after all.

'Can I call you again? If...'

'If?'

'If I'm at a loose end or something?'

'You should take your mother's advice,' said Gina. 'Learn to
stand on your own two feet.'

'What have I done?' She remembered the phone hastily
switched off. 'Have I been in your way? Some sort of a nuisance?'

'I assure you it's nothing personal.' She relaxed a little and
patted Sasha's arm. 'Come on and I'll take you to the right bus
stop this time. I have to get some shopping anyhow.'

As Gina checked her keys and her purse, Sasha looked at one
of the wall-hung photographs. It was a wedding group: at any
rate, they all wore flowers in their buttonholes, although the
groom was the only member of the party dressed in white. He
was clasping the hand of a sombre woman in black. Her hat
had a little veil which hung over her face but Sasha recognised
Gina. She didn't mention it. During the bus journey she got out
her dictionary and flipped through its pages. *Sfortunata* was the
word Mario had used, but it didn't, she discovered, mean lucky.

5

Gina was walking down Via Ripetta with her portfolio under her arm, containing a carefully chosen quantity of prints. She was on her way to the Galleria Farnon, which had a reputation for cutting-edge showmanship and striking visual images. She'd originally met David Farnon, its American owner, through Felix. Their first meeting hadn't gone well, but they'd overcome a mutual suspicion and over the years she'd cultivated his friendship and hoped he could see promise in her work.

The previous Sunday he had expressed an interest – which she would hold him to – at a drunken lunch party in what he mockingly called his summer residence. Like the Pope's, this was situated near Lake Albano: a converted farmhouse with a surfeit of marble bathrooms. David shared it with his partner, Sergio, who was older, indulgent and equally dapper. Sergio had cooked, with the help of a woman from the village. There were many courses, with long intervals between them and plenty of opportunity to pass the wine around the table. Discussion had centred chiefly on the forthcoming holiday season. Some guests were flying or sailing to exotic destinations; others were unwinding at their beachside villas.

'It's the busiest time of my year,' Gina explained, to excuse her lack of plans, although this was not strictly true. 'I have to snatch breaks when I can.' In practice, this meant pursuing the invitations casually dropped by the villa owners with a text or call to announce she'd found herself in the neighbourhood of Sperlonga or Santo Stefano or Pietrasanta and might drop by for a couple of days. In the past she'd had some splendid holidays, but fortunes fluctuated. Bertie had promised a trip to New York, though not until September, and Bertie's promises were rarely reliable.

While they were waiting for the cheese, Gina got up to stretch her legs. She'd ambled across the loggia, as if admiring the roll of the hills and the sparkle of the distant lake, and cornered David. 'Such a delicious meal! Sergio's a marvellous cook.'

He was opening another bottle of wine and raised his eyes to her briefly.

'Will you be closing the gallery in August?'

'I have the decorators coming in. It needs a revamp before the autumn shows.' His voice had a rasping quality, his East Coast accent thinned from years of living abroad.

'Actually I have some new work I'd like you to see.'

He sniffed the cork and laid it on a starched napkin. The linen tablecloth had been beautifully laundered too; the sun through the tracery of vine leaves had tinged its whiteness green. 'Okay,' he said. 'You should bring it round sometime.'

'When?'

'Whenever.'

Which was why she was now strolling into the gallery at an hour when she judged the place would be quiet. A smooth-shaven young man with flamboyantly trendy spectacles was sitting at the front desk. David, he said, was in the back office. She told him not to announce her and went on through.

David's office was austere and immaculate. A safe was hidden behind a large monochrome canvas; box files were ranged on the shelves in order of height and depth, likewise the reference books. His computer monitor rose on a graceful stalk.

'Gina! *Ciao!* Did we have an appointment?'

'Didn't you get my email after that lovely lunch? I said I might call by.'

'Oh, yeah. What can I do for you?'

'You remember you wanted to see my portfolio? With a view to... maybe exhibiting some of it?'

She handed over the folder, tried not to watch too avidly as he untied the ribbon and began to flick through. His actions were fastidious. He treated each photograph with care, but his face was impassive and she'd no way of determining his reaction. This was quite different from dealing with her customary clients whose purpose was to make a selection. David might yet reject everything. He waved her onto a white leather sofa and rocked gently in his own swivel chair, shuffling the photos in front of him.

'I've been working on a new project,' she said. 'Down at the crypt.'

'The crypt?'

'In Ostiense. It's an underground shelter belonging to the Church and Father Leone has agreed – '

'Father Leone?'

'Yeah.' She grinned. 'I call him the Lion King to wind him up. Didn't Felix ever introduce you? The priest who fell out with the Vatican? He can't get promoted so he's a thorn in their side instead. He runs the shelter like a little kingdom. It's a halfway house for these kids, asylum seekers mostly, while they're being assessed. Though if the authorities can drag out procedures for long enough they'll be deemed adults and then they're no one's responsibility.'

David tapped the polished surface of his desk. The door to the gallery opened; voices murmured but didn't linger. 'So tell me, what are you trying to achieve here?'

'I take a damn good picture,' said Gina, wishing he wouldn't put her on the defensive.

'Sure you do, hon, but you know what, I think you're too influenced by your day job.'

'I don't have a day job. This is what I do.'

'I mean your newlyweds. All that romantic touchy-feely stuff. I think you could be harder, know what I mean? It would make your work stronger, more acute. There's a lot of potential here.' He continued to toy with some of the nude studies. He picked up one in which the jagged scar on Yusef's thigh was echoed by the play of light and shadow across his torso. 'These are a bit sub-Mapplethorpe, but there might be a market for them.'

She had to grit her teeth. She'd always had a problem with her temper. She'd once thrown a bottle of nail varnish at the Lion King. Another man might have thrown it back, but he'd ducked and then, being a priest, he'd crossed the room to take her hands between his and calm her down. David might simply put everything away and show her the door. He was influential and it would be foolish to antagonise him.

'I hoped you'd say that.'

'There could be an issue with their age, permissions and so forth. Though no way do these look like kids to me.'

'I have the boys' consent. I've told them that anything I can get I'll pass on.'

'You want me to make enquiries?'

'That would be great, but it isn't…' She fidgeted in her seat, uncrossed and re-crossed her legs. 'I mean, those are a side line, to try and help them make a living. There's also the question of… We did talk about a show.'

'We did?' He drew his hand across his stubble and tugged an ear lobe, ruminating. His ears were remarkably small, Gina had always thought, delicate pink whorls that you might see on a young child. And weren't those scars behind them? His jawline was so tight she suspected a facelift. Gina and David were more or less the same age, both trying to preserve the illusion of youth. Unlike him, she didn't have the money for plastic surgery – but she knew how to work magic with cosmetics.

'I'm programmed up until next March,' he told her. 'I figured I could put on a group show in April. There are a few other guys who've sent me some interesting work.'

'Other photographers?'

'Well, sure.'

This was a blow. But hadn't she already learnt that life was a bloody race and there were always competitors snapping at her heels? What was the alternative? To pickle herself as her mother had done? As far as she could tell, Phoebe lay on a couch in her hacienda hooked up to a constant drip of Gordon's gin and Latin American TV soap opera. She still danced at parties but only in that brief window between inertia and inebriation, when she'd fall over.

Gina would have preferred to be the sole exhibitor, but she had to be realistic. Even a group show offered exposure; it was better than nothing. 'I'd be happy for you to consider me,' she said, not wanting to seem too eager.

'It's a question of balance,' he began, as if delivering a lecture. 'Between one's instincts for art and the need for… I guess you'd call it saleability.'

'Oh God,' said Gina. 'Not that old chestnut again. Anyhow, I don't understand what you're getting at – do you think I'm too commercial, or not enough?'

'Your work is charming,' David said, 'but you know what: charming doesn't command the same price, not with serious collectors. You could be way more hard-hitting.'

'Of course I could! If you want challenging I'll give it to you.' Images flashed through her brain of the crypt, the dark unsavoury space, barred windows, a brooding mass of vaulted stone; the scarred youths with wounds both mental and physical. 'And then you'll be telling me to tone it down.'

'No, hon. I could double your prices. So here's the deal: I'll pencil you into the programme. Show me some more stuff later in the year and if I like it and you fit in with my other choices I'll take you on. Happy?'

She nodded although she didn't see how this was an improvement. He had hedged his offer with so many qualifiers his commitment was negligible.

'These,' he added, making a neat pile of the nudes and returning the rest to the folder, 'I'll hang on to, shall I? You got anything else you'd like me to sell?'

Once, two or three years ago, when she'd had a bad run of late payments and nothing much on the horizon, she'd drawn the line at hocking her equipment or calling her mother, so had sold a couple of paintings instead. Felix wouldn't have minded, she knew, but she'd felt treacherous all the same and a failure for not keeping his collection together. David's eyes had lit up – he hadn't charged gallery commission rates, but he'd taken a cut none the less.

'No I haven't.' He'd riled her with his sub-Mapplethorpe reference and now he was expecting her to be grateful for his largesse. 'And I need to know if you're buying those off me straight? Because this is a sensitive area. I don't want Father Leone to find out or he might forbid me access. At the same time the boys need money, and I need to cover my costs.'

'Sweetheart, you know I'd no more screw you over than jump your bones...' He drew his wallet from the back pocket of his jeans and handed her a fifty euro note. 'Take them out to lunch on me. I'll give you a call if I get any offers.'

'Lunch,' echoed Gina, enjoying the crisp feel of the cash and feeling mildly insulted at the same time.

David swept back his hair and checked his handsome watch. 'Yeah, it's darn near time. I'm meeting Sergio and a couple of friends for a bite. I booked the table for four but I daresay you could squeeze in if you wanted to hang out with us some more.'

Gina marvelled at David's ability to make an invitation sound discouraging. It had been Sergio, amiable, good-natured Sergio, who'd asked her over for the Sunday meal; he loved to cook for a crowd. 'Thanks,' she said, 'but I already have a date.'

'Sure you do.' His eyes travelled to the note she was tucking into her purse.

'No, not with them.'

His thin lips cracked into a smile. 'Ah, do I detect a new man on the horizon?'

'Sadly, I'm making do with the old one. It's not what you think. I've arranged to see a girlfriend who works near here. She finishes at one, so I should get a move on. Thank you for...' For what, exactly, an offer he might not keep? 'I know it will be great working with you.'

He gave a stilted little bow from the waist. 'Take care, hon.' Then he called her back. 'Hey, Gina, you've left your portfolio behind.'

She beamed at him sweetly. 'Do you mind? I don't really want to lug it around. I'll call back for it in a day or so. Give you a chance to take another look.'

She was on the street again before he could argue, fired up for her next encounter: one where she would be calling the shots.

6

The person Gina intended to haul over the coals for the next hour was her former roommate, Vicki. They'd shared a flat when both had first come to Rome, but they no longer shared a circle of friends. Vicki had captured a dentist and lived several kilometres away on a housing development that had tried to copy the English model, with garages and unsuccessful areas of lawn. Gina visited rarely: for the christening of the couple's twins and two or three blind-date dinner parties, equally disastrous. As a rule they met in the city for occasional cocktails or lunches.

Vicki worked for an accommodation agency, whose windows displayed wide-angled shots of seemingly spacious apartments with huge monthly rents. When Gina entered, Vicki was talking into the mouthpiece of a headset and scrolling through an online magazine. She clicked off the screen and completed her conversation with a flurry of '*ciaos*' and '*grazies*'.

'Gina, darling!' Vicki seized her bag, pushed her chair beneath her desk and waved her colleagues goodbye. She used to be small and thin but was now small and plump, like a full-breasted robin. 'Where do you want to go?'

'I don't mind,' said Gina. 'You're paying.'

Vicki flushed and hunted for her dark glasses. By the time they were out in the melee of office workers lighting cigarettes and drivers mounting the pavement to negotiate inadequate parking spaces, she'd hidden her eyes. 'You're right. My treat, I said, so let's go to La Fontana.'

Gina could have put money on La Fontana a week ago. It was a traditional *trattoria* with an uninventive menu, but you could always find a seat. It was their default option. They agreed it would be cooler inside and sat towards the back, near the wall-hung air conditioning unit. A paper tablecloth was clipped over the gingham fabric one; colourful ceramic flasks of oil and vinegar and a vase of yellow daisies squatted between them.

'Heavens, it's been ages,' Vicki said with false enthusiasm. 'I feel so bad about not getting in touch. But it's been one thing after another with the twins. Everything comes in double doses… Anyway, I'm really glad you rang.'

'You are?'

'Well, of course.'

'Don't you want to know why?'

Vicki leaned forward. 'I have to take my shoes off, my feet are killing me.' There was a smack of leather hitting the tiles. A waiter was hovering so she lifted her sunglasses to study the menu but, as usual, chose a salad. Gina ordered soup, followed by veal and half a carafe of wine; she was hungry.

'I wish I could eat as much as you and not put on an inch,' sighed Vicki. 'Now, I'm going to take a guess. You're looking for a new place?'

'You always ask me that.'

'Only because I think I can find you the very thing. Somewhere the plumbing works, somewhere with a lift even – though I suppose the stairs are good exercise for you.'

'And a terrace. Can you get me a terrace?'

'I'll do my best.'

'How far out? At the end of Via Flaminia? Halfway to bloody Civitavecchia?'

'Well, the further you go the more space you get for your money. It's not rocket science.'

'And what about your commission? I bet it's generous.'

'Jesus, Gina, you know I don't do this job for the money!'

Gina did know that. It was a situation she couldn't envisage. Why would a person choose to spend their morning in a dull office dealing with dodgy landlords when they could, with a little imagination, follow much more interesting pursuits?

Vicki, formerly a holiday rep, had chased a sunny fantasy of married life which had trapped her into a rigorous observance of family traditions: anniversaries and saints' days and festivals, children's parties and concerts and school performances. She went to work for the sake of the gossip, for a bit of role-play, for the extra money to justify her designer handbags. Never in her life had Gina bought a handbag; she owned an extensive collection, all presents, which she was whittling down. Clearly Vicki was bored.

'Anyhow,' said Gina. 'I'm planning to stick where I am for as long as I can. I think you know what I'm really here for.'

Her bowl of minestrone was delivered along with a basket of coarse crusty bread; she tore off a hunk and dipped it into the soup. Vicki toyed with a breadstick, snapped it in two and crunched the smaller piece. Thanks to her husband, her teeth were in perfect condition. Gina noticed some spots at her temple that might have been sun damage and could do with concealer.

'Do I?'

'Yes.'

Vicki leant her cheek on her palm, consciously or unconsciously covering the moles with her fingertips. Eventually she said, 'I was trying to be helpful.'

Gina was in the process of adding salt. 'Helpful!'

'If you're talking about the *Scuola di lingua*, I was just doing my job.'

'Have they been clients of yours for long?'

'Who, the summer school? Yes. It's the same every year, honestly. We block-book a whole load of lodgings for their older students. The rooms in family homes are usually arranged separately but we keep a handful on our books. And, as you know, Roberto Boletti has several properties registered with us anyway so...'

'I can't believe Bertie would have the faintest interest in offering open house to some pimply adolescent. Like you, he doesn't need the money.'

'It was his wife,' said Vicki, drawing a pile of dry crumbs into a peak. A group of diners, most likely bank clerks or bureaucrats, came to sit at the adjacent table. The men loosened their ties and hung their jackets over the backs of the chairs, which squealed as they were scraped into new positions. Vicki's phone began to ring; Gina glared until she switched it off. 'His wife was genuinely interested, she liked the idea of a British companion for their son. Though when I first contacted her, I'm afraid she may have thought that Sasha Mitchell was a boy.'

'So you actually called her?'

'I wasn't being manipulative! Honestly, Gina, you have to believe me. The trouble was, it was all very last minute because the girl had been going to stay somewhere else. The school asked me as a favour to see what I could do. I tried the Bolettis on the off-chance. I was as surprised as you when they said yes.'

'You've said "honestly" twice now.'

Vicki said angrily, 'Look, we haven't seen each other in months and already you're accusing me of all sorts of shenanigans. I don't have that kind of power.'

'Why did you do it?' Gina pushed her soup away; it was too watery and she'd added too much salt. 'Was it for *divertimento*?'

'I told you, I was doing my job.'

This was too simple a get-out clause; no way was she going to let Vicki off the hook. Although if she'd been in the same position, with every day of her life mapped out, she'd probably be tempted to a little mischief herself. 'So when did you make the connection? When did you say to yourself, here's an interesting proposition: let's see what would happen if I farmed out the daughter of Gina's old boyfriend to the family of her current one. And how did you know who she was anyway?'

Their main courses arrived: Vicki's milky circles of mozzarella like slices of the moon on a plate, interleaved with tomato and basil; Gina's *scallopine* sprinkled with parsley.

'There was information about the parents on the form. Name and occupation: Paul Mitchell, pilot. I mean, it's not an uncommon surname. It could have been a different man altogether. I'd no way of knowing for certain...'

Gina doused her *patate fritte* in vinegar. 'But you thought you'd have a little fun at my expense?'

'You'd've done the same,' said Vicki defensively. 'I bet you would. And anyway, it wasn't up to me. I made a suggestion, the Bolettis didn't have to act on it. It was serendipity really.'

'What did you expect to come of it? Antonio's at least a year younger so I don't think romance is very likely. Or was it the prospect of playing God that pleased you?'

'Okay – it was a stupid thing to do. I acted on a whim, but no, I didn't have any expectations.' With fork poised midway to her mouth, she added, 'Perhaps it was a bit underhand, but there's no harm done is there?'

'Except the kid's going to wonder why I don't want anything to do with her.'

'Oh my God, you've met her! That wasn't meant to happen! I didn't think for a moment that Boletti would actually introduce you to his family. However did it come about?'

'He's commissioned a portrait of his son, as it happens. I went to visit.'

'And that's when you saw the girl?' Vicki looked crestfallen. 'You have to believe me. I wouldn't have upset you for the world.' She laid her hand tenderly over Gina's. 'So, was it really painful?'

'It was disconcerting,' she admitted. 'Once I'd realised.'

'It must have been so weird for you. Did she… look like him at all?'

'Same colouring I guess. Not much else to link them.'

This was not quite true. Already, at their second meeting, she'd been aware of something intangible in Sasha. Holding the girl's head in her hands while doing her make-up, observing the thrust of her chin, the throb at her temple, the untamed shape of her eyebrows, she had registered a sense of familiarity. The mention of Mitch's name, although shocking, had not been a total surprise. It wasn't the girl's fault. How could she know what had happened before she was born? The break-up that had been handled so badly. It wasn't an area Gina wanted to revisit; she'd spent years trying to bury her emotions. She would deny that Mitch had broken her heart, but he was the man with the worst timing in the world.

She poured the rest of the carafe into her wine glass. 'Look, this ought to be nothing to do with me. I don't want to get involved, but the kid's out on a limb and seems to need someone to keep an eye on her. I don't think either the older or the younger Signora Boletti really understands, so in the circumstances maybe you –'

'Me?'

'You dealt this hand, Vick.'

'What can I do? It would be the same whichever family she was lodging with. And I have to get back to the twin terrors every afternoon. Really, if she's in trouble it's the language school's responsibility, not mine.'

'She isn't in trouble; she just seems a bit adrift. As well as being naive for her age but, hey, what do I know about adolescence? All that angst? It was a helluva long time ago.'

'I'll check with the school,' said Vicki. 'I'll find a way of making discreet enquiries to make sure she's settling in. And I suppose I could ask her over for a meal one evening…'

'She'd never be able to find you. I already had to send Mario to the rescue when she got lost.'

'Oh well then…'

Gina pushed her plate aside. 'This situation is not of my making. I want you to be absolutely clear that if there is any fallout of any kind it's your call. Not mine.'

'Yes, of course.' Vicki's expression showed a combination of remorse and relief. She called the waiter over to ask for coffee. Gina took pleasure in adding a cognac to the order and savouring it while Vicki waited for the bill. Their parting was amicable if a little strained.

'Must rush or I'll be late for the twins. Where are you going now?'

'Oh, the studio probably. I think I'll walk.'

'We should meet up again before the holidays.'

'Sure.'

'And I'll… you know… keep my ears open. Check everything's okay…'

'Not my problem, darling.'

7

The photo shoot was to take place at the weekend, at Roma's training ground, along the Via di Trigoria. This was decided by Antonio and arranged by Roberto. He had a contact who could organise the access they needed. The pitch wouldn't be in use. But it wasn't a problem.

'I'm not a sports photographer,' Gina pointed out. 'Action shots, you know, they require a different technique. With portraiture the shutter speed is slower, the lens lingers because you're trying to probe deeper...'

'Like a lover?' suggested Roberto.

'If you want to put it like that.'

'So you cannot do what my son asks?'

'I can do anything. I thought you were after the classic studio portrait, but if he wants to be the football star that's fine by me.' She could foresee a clash of opinion. She would go out of her way to avoid the hackneyed, yet the triumphal pose was probably exactly what father and son were after; along with an excuse to parade on ground trodden by heroes.

Roberto agreed to collect her from her apartment on the way to Trigoria, a half hour drive out of town. There had been talk of the Signora joining them, to watch her son's performance for the camera. The prospect had made Gina uneasy, so she was relieved when other commitments intervened and Bertie told her his wife had changed her mind.

He hooted at the base of her building from the family saloon, a silver Alfa Romeo. He didn't get out of the car. Antonio was sitting beside him in the passenger seat, his hands loosely clasped around a new leather football. His quick smile at introduction betrayed a mixture of pride and trepidation. He didn't much resemble his father. He had limp, mousy hair and a sly, narrow face. His kit – the Roma shirt, the pristine boots – were fresh from their packaging.

Gina opened the car door and slid into the back seat, which she found occupied by another female passenger. Not, fortunately, either of the Signore Boletti.

'You have met before, I think?' said Bertie, roaring down Viale di Trastevere. 'This is the English guest we have staying with us.'

'Hi again,' said Sasha.

'Yes,' said Gina curtly. 'We met some days ago.'

'She needs to see that Roma is not all ruins and museums and *il Papa*. We have another important culture too, *davvero*?'

Sasha shifted a fraction to make room for Gina's camera bag. 'It will give my dad a laugh when he hears about this trip. But I'm going to watch from a distance; I promise I won't get in your way.'

'Don't worry. When I'm concentrating nothing gets in my way.' Making a stab at normal conversation, she added, 'How are you enjoying your visit?'

'I'm having a terrific time,' said Sasha, also with careful politeness.

Although Gina and Roberto mostly spoke Italian together, his English was good. He would understand the girl's answers.

'You're on a language course, right? How's it going?'

'We all speak English outside the lessons,' she confessed. 'We're more than halfway through now, but I'll probably just be getting the hang of it when I have to go home again.'

'Oh, when's that?'

'The end of next week.'

There was reluctance in her tone, as if she were starting to enjoy herself. Gina was pleased. Even after so many years of living in a place which combined acres of red tape with sublime indifference to rules and regulations (whoever filled in a tax form truthfully or obeyed a no-smoking sign?); even though the streets were clogged with litter and services frequently on strike (24/7 internet access – when did that ever happen?), she couldn't imagine anyone coming to her adopted city and not falling in love with it.

They were cruising through the wide boulevards of EUR. The business district's monumental marble edifices were beginning to look seedy and weather-beaten, diminished in scale now that so many glittering efforts of glass and steel were joining the party. Gina had seen these changes in England too, on rare return visits, but unlike London, Rome would always be low-rise, would never resemble a computer-generated matrix of skyscrapers. Better to be scruffy than soulless.

Suburbs thinned and fields took shape; hedges, trees, birdsong. Eventually they reached the entrance to the training ground. Roberto showed his pass at the gates and swung into the car park. Antonio got out and began jogging on the spot, bouncing the ball with each upward thrust of his knee.

'See,' said Roberto proudly, 'how well he controls it?' In a lower voice he murmured to Gina as she screwed her lens onto the front of her Nikon. 'We will have eyes watching us, *cara*.'

'I know that!' She edged away from his touch. 'Isn't this going to be a bit of a drag for you?'

'Not at all,' he protested. 'I love to watch a skilled operator. I mean yourself, naturally, as well as my son.'

Antonio was dribbling the ball towards the goal mouth. Alone on the pitch he looked small and insignificant. She raised the camera to her eye and lowered it again. She'd need to get close to create Antonio the magnificent striker. He was too tense; he should play for a bit, relax.

'Sasha,' she called. 'Let him kick the ball to you.'

Sasha, in a pair of round sunglasses and cut-off jeans that were a little too tight, was leaning against the body of the Alfa, unwrapping a piece of chewing gum. 'But I don't play football!'

'All you have to do is kick it back. Why else are you here?'

Sulkily the girl stuffed the gum back in her pocket and moved off. She walked the way Mitch did, Gina noticed, that roll on the balls of the feet, surprisingly erect for a self-conscious teenager. Perhaps she'd had ballet lessons: dancing was known to improve the deportment. Phoebe had stories of walking in a circle for hours with a dictionary on her head.

'*Brava*!' said Roberto. 'Also, I have another proposal for you.'

'An assignment, you mean?'

'No, no. Something to make your life more comfortable.'

Was it possible that at last he was going to make some improvements to the apartment? Had he been frustrated once too often by the airlock in the pipes and the erratic dribble of the shower? Did he envisage her cooking dainty meals for two in a new efficient oven? No, wildly unlikely: he knew she didn't cook. Though a fridge plumbed in with an ice dispenser, *that* would be worth having.

'You see, I know how to make you happy.'

'Bertie, you're all promises, promises. Jam tomorrow.'

'What is jam tomorrow?'

'Tell me what you're thinking of. Go on, give me a clue.'

'No, later. When we are alone.'

'*Papà, che cosa fai? Sono pronto.*' Antonio was flushed with exertion, a sheen of sweat on his upper lip and clavicle, a glow to give a portrait life and depth.

'*Adesso vengo*,' Gina called, moving forward. The sun might be a problem, bleaching the colours, but she should be able to compensate. As soon as she began to stalk the boy she lost all sense of time. Occasionally she called orders – Sasha's job was to return the ball whenever Antonio kicked it out of shot – but she didn't want to interrupt his focus. She wanted to capture the intensity of his frown, the set of his jaw, his shining pride in a well-aimed goal. When he played out his fantasies he was no longer a spoilt rich boy with too many possessions he didn't value, but as determined and defenceless as any of the migrants she'd come across, pursuing their dreams.

Initially Roberto played at being coach, shouting instructions, stamping earth that was so hard the ball sprang effortlessly into the sky. His pima cotton T-shirt was the palest pink, but it didn't feminise him; he was tanned, robust, exuding prosperity and self-satisfaction. He was a man always likely to be on the winning side. It was what had attracted Gina to him in the first place, but it was a mistake she shouldn't have made: letting herself be drawn into a relationship without negotiating an escape route. At this point in her life, she didn't imagine she could ever do away with the exit clause.

She concentrated on Antonio's performance, disporting herself in all kinds of frankly ridiculous positions to keep pace. She tried to ignore any other distraction, including the curious onlookers peering through the fence, so it took her a while to notice Bertie had given up. She saw him greeting an acquaintance, presumably the official who'd facilitated this visit, sitting on a bench at the touchline, making phone calls. Then he stood and began to semaphore. '*Basta, basta ragazzi*!'

Antonio slowed to a halt. There were large dark patches of sweat under his arms and across his shoulder blades. As footballers do, he pulled off the shirt and wiped his face. Gina's shutter clicked rapidly. This was not the picture the Boletti parents would choose, but she loved the way he looked so spent, wasted, enveloped in exhaustion. She thought of Sami holding his pose for hours on end without a crack disturbing his ivory make-up. Or Yusef, finding an illegal day's work on a demolition site, every muscle coated in a film of grey dust so that he, too, resembled a ghost. That was true stamina.

As a special privilege, Antonio was to be allowed to shower in the team's changing rooms. This was the sort of perk a useful connection could set up. His father and the official accompanied him into the clubhouse. Roberto tossed Gina the car keys so she could dismantle and pack away her equipment, and Sasha followed her. They opened the car doors to reduce the furnace-like heat and sat on the baking leather seats with their legs in the sun. Sasha's freckles climbed from ankle to thigh. She'd tried to blot them out with fake tan and spotted Gina looking.

'I hate the smell of that lotion,' she said. 'And it isn't as simple as it says on the bottle.'

'You've not done a bad job,' Gina allowed. 'You have to look twice to see the streaks. It's a question of practice, that's all. It comes easily to me because I got plenty when I was modelling.'

'Did you like it?'

'What?'

'Being a model.'

'Some of the time. It wasn't planned. I fell into it.' There were elements she had liked: the money for a start, the praise and attention, the feeling of family when the girls bonded together. She'd experienced that at boarding school too, but the sense of warm inclusion, being part of a gang, could be dangerous. It was safer not to depend on other people.

'Were you, like, scouted?'

'I answered a dodgy ad. Luckily it led to better things. I was at a bit of a loose end because I'd been thrown out of sixth form and I needed to find work before my stepfather, Monty, stopped my allowance.'

'Really? What had you done?'

'Oh, the school was one of those pricey penal institutions where anything could get you into trouble. Smoking, wearing jewellery, ignoring curfews. I mean, I did all that stuff, but the reason they gave was that I cheated in an exam. I didn't, as it happens. The girl sitting next to me copied my maths paper, but they assumed it was the other way around because they wanted rid of me anyway.'

'Wow, how totally unfair. Didn't you complain?'

At the time she'd been glad to leave, but it had given her a jaundiced view of justice. 'Actually I learnt two useful lessons: trust no one; cut your losses.'

'Oh,' said Sasha with a sharp intake of breath. 'That's so bleak.'

'Lesson number three,' said Gina. 'Enjoy the good times. Shit, you're making me sound like a walking book of clichés. Drop the subject, shall we?' She couldn't risk letting something out of the bag about Mitch.

Sasha scuffed the toe of her trainer against the tarmac. After an interval, she said, 'I don't get why we had to come all the way out here so Antonio could run around with a football. I mean, all pitches look the same and no one's going to be able to tell, are they?'

Privately Gina agreed with this, but she said, 'Well, this is his team, so it must be like treading on hallowed ground or whatever. He probably thinks it will bring him good luck.'

'But you've been taking portraits, right? You can't even see the background.'

'In some of the distance shots I can make it look like he's scoring a goal.'

'It could be any goalpost,' Sasha persisted. 'Who's to know?'

'*He* knows, so that will make it valuable to him. It's not always what you actually see that's important. A particular location can create a mood. Maybe I'll find it reflected somehow in his face.'

'Can't you tell?'

'Not until I get to the studio and run everything through the computer.'

'Is that where you're going after this?'

'I don't know. I haven't decided.'

Roberto and Antonio emerged from the clubhouse and approached the Alfa in ebullient good humour. Driving back they chatted with much laughter and gesticulation, as if they were alone in the car. Gina resented this, although she was perfectly aware she was only the hired photographer. Antonio wouldn't expect his father to treat her any differently from the way he treated Katya, the maid. She kept her gaze fixed out of the window so she wouldn't have to make any more small talk with Mitch's daughter. She considered mentioning Vicki's name as a possible contact, but decided against it; Bertie seemed to be looking after the girl.

They re-entered the city walls at the Pyramid, the landmark tomb of Caius Cestius. Addressing her for the first time since they left Trigoria, Roberto said, 'Do you want me to take you home, Gina?' She answered without thinking, her decision taken on the spur of the moment, 'No, drop me here.'

'*Managgia la miseria!*' He was trapped in the central lane of traffic. 'Why didn't you say so earlier?' The inconvenience didn't deter him however. He crossed three lanes at speed and swerved to a stop behind a bus. His eyes met hers in the mirror and she saw that they were sorrowful. 'Forgive me,' he said. 'I should have understood. You want to visit him.'

'I... I...' She stopped. She did visit Felix's grave regularly; often she brought flowers. As she squatted to arrange them in their little brass pot she would talk to him, conjure his responses: wise, sardonic, sometimes impossibly pompous, and feel comforted. But in July, although the Protestant Cemetery was awash with roses, cut blooms shrivelled in the heat. They would have no life at all. She hated to see the petals browning, limp stalks failing to bear their weight.

'*Anche tu*, Sasha?' said Roberto.

'I'm sorry?'

He switched to English. 'You have visited this cemetery before?'

'No, why?'

'Why? Because it's important to your culture, no?'

'You see,' said Gina, amused by Bertie's solemnity, 'the Romans, they like films and music and football and racing rallies. And technology – anything that's up to the minute. Whereas we Brits are into art and archaeology and dead poets.'

He pounded the dashboard in mock annoyance. '*Che cazzo dici*?'

'I'm explaining the historical reference. Keats and Shelley,' she told Sasha helpfully, 'are buried by the Pyramid. Signor Boletti thought you'd be interested in a visit.'

'What, now?'

'*Certo*,' said Roberto.

'Oh, sure, great.'

Gina was lumbered: the girl was already getting out of the car.

'Afterwards,' said Roberto, 'be sure to send her safely back to us. And I'll call you about those photos.'

'I'll email you the proofs as soon as I've sorted through them,' said Gina, striving to sound as formal as possible in front of the two teenagers.

The lights changed; the Alfa sped off. As they waited at the busy intersection, Gina said, 'I'll point you in the right direction but it's not actually convenient for me to be a tour guide. Bertie got the wrong end of the stick. I'm sorry he threw you out like that before I had a chance to explain.' She started to cross and Sasha hurried after her. 'Still, you should see it – it's such a wonderful peaceful spot, given it's in the midst of all this clamour.' She windmilled her arms in the centre of the road and trucks and scooters darted around her. Sasha looked scared.

'Don't dither,' said Gina. 'You'll get yourself killed.'

When they were both safely on the opposite pavement, she veered down the quiet side street that led to the cemetery. She pointed through the aperture set into the wall. 'If you look through that you can see Keats' grave. The main entrance is a little further on.'

'What are you going to do?'

'Oh, it's a business matter. I'm going to see the Lion King.'

'Do you mean the film?'

'God no! He's a priest called Leone, who has a church not far from here. But you'll be fine.' She wasn't a babysitter; the girl was none of her business. Anyway, what could go wrong?

8

The Protestant Cemetery was closed. Sasha pushed fruitlessly against the lock before thinking to study the timetable screwed to the heavy gates and cursing. Just her luck! She took out her phone and sent a text to Renate. She and Ilse had gone with some boys they'd met on a trip to the beach. Sasha wished she'd muscled in, instead of letting Signor Boletti persuade her she shouldn't miss a rare and privileged opportunity: every football fan's dream. She should have made it clear she wasn't a football fan. It was at times like this she could have done with Ruby, whose resistance to being pushed around was super-human.

Sullenly she retraced her route to the main road. In the distance she spotted a flash of red that might be Gina's T-shirt, drawing closer. An arm waved, a voice called out; Sasha ran towards her.

Gina was taking long impatient strides, her bag thumping against her hip. 'Damn, I'm sorry!' she shouted. 'I should have remembered they're shut on Sunday afternoons.'

Sasha supposed it was nice of her to have turned back, though it was her fault Signor Boletti had dumped her out of his car in the first place. 'What am I going to do?'

'Well, I don't want you to get lost again so I can give you directions to Parioli if you like. Or you could call Bertie and get him to pick you up. He won't be far off yet.'

Sasha considered. She certainly didn't want to struggle home on public transport – though at least when she got there she'd be able to log on and disappear into the virtual world of Facebook. Annoying as it was, she would have to ring for a lift. She flipped open her phone again and Renate's response pinged into her inbox. They would be leaving the beach soon and taking the train to Ostiense. The prospect boosted her spirits.

'That's near here, isn't it?' she said to Gina.

'What is?'

'The station for Ostia. I'm going to meet my mates there so it's not worth going back to the Bolettis. If I could kill a little time, hang out with you for a bit longer…'

'Come with me to the crypt, you mean?'

'Yes please.'

Gina gave a quiver of irritation. 'If you must. It's a bit of a walk so we need to hurry.'

She marched off, crossing onto the broad busy boulevard; Sasha kept pace. She could have said, No, she thought to herself. She didn't have to do all this sighing, this martyr act, like her mother tried sometimes. In fact, both Sasha's parents made a big deal about the lives they were responsible for – when they were only doing the job they were paid to do, after all.

They passed under the railway bridge and on a piece of wasteland alongside the line she noticed an encampment of cheap nylon tents. From a distance the bright colours and bil- lowing shapes could have been a flock of butterflies. As they got closer she could see that some of the tents were ripped and stained; there was a coil of sluggish smoke and a stench of burning plastic. Two men were shouting in an argument that seemed to be escalating; their fellow campers watched, cross- legged on the ground, in an aura of apathy. Afraid they would beg for money she didn't have, Sasha stuck close to Gina. 'It's a bit scary round here.' The wall opposite was sprayed with graffiti; discarded bottles and cans rolled in the gutter. Rubbish overflowed from a row of skips. A train gathered momentum along the tracks.

'You're getting a glimpse of the underbelly,' said Gina. 'It's a different kind of grim. When I first came to live here all the shanty towns, tin shacks, cardboard shelters, whatever, were on the outskirts. The bits the developers hadn't got to yet. They were mostly Roma, Kosovan Albanians and a few Africans in those days. Now there are so many of them, the migrants have moved into the centre. They spend all day looking for work or queuing for handouts, but they can't find anywhere to live. Half the time they can't move on either.'

'Why not?'

'It's all down to something called the Dublin Regulation. You're supposed to claim asylum in the first port of arrival, which for most of them is Italy. They wind up in detention centres where they're fingerprinted and given temporary papers. The country can't actually cope with the influx, but because they've been registered they get sent back if they try to move elsewhere. Guys have even set fire to their fingertips to destroy their prints.'

'Does it work?'

'No.'

'And do they really have to sleep on the street?'

'Scandalous, isn't it? Worse than refugee camps in the third world. Would you believe the company who wants to develop the site has cut off their water supply? At least this might force the city's hand. If they don't find them accommodation, God knows what trouble will break out.'

A few minutes later she added, 'Right, we're here. Be careful. These steps are steep.'

They'd arrived at it almost without warning: an unassuming church with a Madonna lurching above the main entrance like a figurehead on a ship's prow. Sasha followed Gina down a cast-iron spiral staircase into the gully of a basement area; then through a wooden door. There was no natural light in the crypt; fluorescent tubes swayed overhead, illuminating half-empty crates and cardboard boxes, bin bags of old clothes. Beneath the vaulted arches were spools of bedding rolled up like sausages. In a corner, a heap of clothing stirred: someone was sleeping. A group of young men seated around a large square table seemed to be learning English. Their teacher, a plump, fair-skinned woman, raised her eyes to Gina and continued the lesson without acknowledging her.

'Here he comes,' muttered Gina as a slight stooped figure detached himself from another small knot of people and approached.

Sasha was unprepared for the fact that the Lion King was bald. She'd expected an impressive creature with a flowing mane, who could double up as a medieval king. Or Jesus. She almost said, 'Are you sure this is the right guy?' even though the long black folds of his soutane swished as he walked.

In spite of his nondescript appearance he had an air of authority. He was speaking to Gina in Italian and Sasha couldn't follow, but she got the impression he was angry in a quiet steely way. And she could tell that Gina was arguing, denying something. She shook her head, even stamped her foot. Words tumbled out of her in indignation and Sasha was surprised she would shout at a priest. Feeling awkward, like when she stumbled on her parents having a row, she wandered off. The underground air smelled musty and stale but it was deliciously cool. It made her think of diving into river water and swirling up the mud from its bed. A youth with a bandaged arm, the yellowing crepe matching the roll of his eyes, shouted at her as she passed. She'd no idea whether it was in greeting or anger.

Then Gina caught up with her. 'Come back, Sasha. Don't intrude.'

She's been told off for something, thought Sasha, so she's taking it out on me. 'I'm not intruding!'

'These boys don't have any homes or any privacy. You must understand that, show some respect.'

'I wasn't doing any harm. What is it anyhow, this place?'

'It's Limbo,' said Gina. 'Better really if it were Purgatory. If your loved ones say enough Masses for you, you have a chance of getting out of Purgatory.'

Sasha wasn't stupid. She could see that it was a homeless shelter, that the occupants, like the men camping behind the station, were as hopelessly stranded as if they'd been washed up on some desert island. She knew how desperate people could be to reach what they believed was a land of opportunity. Once her father had had a stowaway on his plane: a man curled inside a suitcase who suffocated in the luggage hold. Corrupt baggage handling was suspected. There'd been an investigation but there was no conclusive evidence. Her father had been angry and shaken; tangential responsibility, said her mother – whatever that meant.

'If the authorities believe these kids,' said Gina, 'they'll treat them as minors and find them a place in a hostel, whatever. But it's a lot less bother and expense, actually, to disbelieve them. Father Leone is trying to bridge the gap by providing this space. I need to have a word with him in private. There are issues we have to resolve over this project I'm working on. How far I take it, that sort of thing. It's complicated… But it's not like with Antonio. These guys aren't pretending to be hotshot sportsmen flashing their studs. It's a whole different ball game. I call them the Lost Boys.'

'I don't know why you didn't say this when we were still in the car,' protested Sasha. 'Why you let me think…'

'Because I didn't want Bertie to know where I was going. So you mustn't tell him. Is that absolutely clear? He claims he doesn't like riff-raff. He'd rather send them back out to sea in a leaky boat and maybe take a few potshots while he's at it.'

'Why do you hang out with him?'

'For one thing, I didn't choose him as my landlord. He's in a property consortium who bought out the previous owner. And two, I can't afford to turn down work.'

Sasha wasn't convinced. Why would she give the guy a pet name if he wasn't a friend, if their relationship were purely professional? Not that she could ask such a question. She tried another: 'Couldn't I stick around anyway? Maybe I could do something to help?'

A pair of volunteers were sorting through the donated clothes. Sasha didn't like the look of the job, but no one who's mucked out stables could describe themselves as squeamish.

'You're a good kid,' said Gina, which infuriated her. 'But the Lion King's got to take another Mass soon and this isn't really the place for you. You'd be better going to find your friends.'

Sasha responded stiffly, 'Okay, I didn't mean to hassle you. I'll go.' Perhaps, by the time she'd retraced her route, she'd have heard from Renate which train they were on.

Gina nodded absently, but then looked concerned. 'Are you sure you'll find the way? This isn't the most salubrious neighbourhood and you do stick out like a sore thumb.' She fiddled with her phone. 'Reception's poor down here. Hang on a minute.' She disappeared through the door and up the staircase, a streak of red.

Sasha thought, why do I need an escort? Why do people always assume dreadful things are going to happen because you're a girl? All the same, she was wary of taking a wrong turn, making a fool of herself again.

When Gina returned she had a young man in tow. He seemed familiar but Sasha couldn't place him until Gina said: 'You remember Yusef? I started calling him Joe and he rather likes it so I expect you can do the same. He's agreed to take you back to the Pyramid so you can meet your friends. Spend a few months living rough and you know your way around better than most of the locals – and that includes me.'

'*Ciao*, Joe,' said Sasha.

The youth held out his hand. He was not much taller than her, which was good because she hated to be towered over. He moved with a delicate grace and would have been remarkably handsome were it not for the crook in his nose which gave him a piratical air. She wondered whether he found the memory of their first meeting as disconcerting as she did.

'His Italian's not bad,' said Gina, 'and he knows a bit of English, so you should be able to understand each other.'

Joe was an odd mixture of the deferential and the streetwise. He treated Sasha with immense old-fashioned courtesy; helping her across the road as if she were blind or lame; he'd also curse and gesticulate at careless drivers, as excitable as any local.

Sasha said, 'Actually, Joe, I don't want to get to the station yet.'

'No?' When he frowned his eyebrows met. It made him look as though he were thinking hard, as if the slightest deviation from his orders could have serious consequences.

'No,' she repeated. 'It's too early. I'm waiting for a text.' A few metres ahead, a bar shimmered in the heat rising from the pavement. The two small tin tables under the striped awning were unoccupied; a gumball machine stood sentinel. 'Why don't we get a drink? *Qualcosa da bere*?' When he hesitated, she added. 'I have money. I'll buy you one.'

They sat with two Cokes poured over ice. 'God, I get so thirsty here!'

His skin was a deep glowing coffee colour. Next to his forearm, hers looked pasty and anaemic. When their hands touched by accident his flesh felt so hot she expected a scorch mark.

'*Da dove sei*?' she said, since it was what people asked her all the time, part of the currency of vocabulary in a place where so many people were in transit. She wasn't being nosy.

She asked her questions by degrees and by degrees he answered. He was from Afghanistan. He was eighteen. He'd left his country two years earlier, spent months travelling across mountains on foot, hiding in containers, clinging to the chassis of trucks, gambling with his life. He was applying for his official papers. He had no family.

'What, none at all?'

His eyes were extraordinarily large and luminous; she was afraid he might be about to cry. He'd been her age when he set out – she couldn't imagine it. After fending for himself and depending on charity for so long, wouldn't he have wept himself dry?

With a circular sweep of his arms, he mimed an explosion, blew out his cheeks. 'Not living,' he said.

And the horror and simplicity of those two words chilled her. She could only ask, feebly: 'A bomb? But you survived?'

'I was not there.'

'God, that must have been so awful, to come back home and find...' She sucked noisily through her straw as if the action could blot out such an atrocity. He didn't say anything. The only way to break the silence was to change the subject. 'Gina,' she began. '*E una buona amica?*'

It worked. '*Come madrina,*' he answered, with a smile that sparkled.

Relieved, Sasha pretended to click a shutter. 'She takes your photograph for magazines?'

The charming smile broadened. '*Si.*' He squared his shoulders so she could see his pectoral muscles ripple under his shirt. 'I make exercise,' he said. 'Is important. Also...' He tapped his thigh and she remembered the scar she had seen there like a fork of lightning. 'I walk. Always walking.'

'Where do you live? Is it far?'

He jerked his head, gesturing behind him. 'I have room with Sami. *Cognosce?*'

'Sami who was Caesar?'

'*Si.*'

Sasha drew up her legs, resting her heels on the lip of her tin chair and her chin on her knees. Was it peculiar to Rome, all this dressing up? Antonio and his football kit, Sami and the living statues in Piazza Navona, tour guides disguised as senators, Roman centurions presenting photo-opportunities, monks in cowled habits, priests in dog collars. Like the whole place

71

was a stage or a filmset. And added to the mix were all these
thousands of refugees desperate for new identities.

The warmth of the afternoon folded itself around their bodies.
The ice melted in their drinks. Joe said, 'You are student, yes?'

'Yes.'

'England is very fine country.'

'It's okay.'

'I want come to England. *E migliore.*'

'Better for what?'

'*Per tutto, non?* Everything. Every person have place to live,
to work...'

'No, not everyone has work. And, like, for me it's really difficult. No one wants to employ you till you're eighteen. And
we live in the middle of nowhere, so all the kids who are nearer
to town than me get any Saturday jobs going in the shops and
stuff...' She broke off; he'd probably only have caught half of
what she'd said. 'Plus you'd have to speak the language.'

'When I have papers,' he said, 'I go to England, find job...'

'One day,' agreed Sasha, finishing the dregs of her Coke.
'Yeah, you'll get over to us. Course you will.'

'Where is you?'

'You mean where do I live? I'm in the country, outside
Manchester.'

'I can visit?'

'Well, gosh, um...'

'You live with family? Mother and father, *tutte le due?*'

It was a harmless enough question but the context rendered
it somehow momentous. Instead of saying 'yes', she let out a
sob, which was all the more absurd because of course she lived
with both her parents in the traditional nuclear unit and she'd
never had anything awful happen to her, apart from a broken
leg – even that hadn't been so bad because the plaster cast
and the crutches had got her loads of attention. However, she
was miserably aware of the fragility of her family unit at this
particular time – like a bubble too easily pricked.

It was pathetic to come over so emotional in front of Joe after what he'd been through. He must think her a wimp of the first order. She could never have wobbled like this in front of Renate and Ilse or any of the other language students; they were all so determined to get out there and *have fun*. It would have been different with Ruby, tough bossy Ruby, because she knew her so well.

Joe took the initiative. First he patted her on the back. Then, tentatively, he put his arm around her and drew her closer. She was aware of a strong masculine smell and a scrape of stubble against her hair. She pushed him away. He pulled a paper napkin from the dispenser on the table and passed it to her. She dabbed her eyes and sniffed.

'Sorry,' she said. 'It hits me sometimes, I guess. Feeling homesick.'

'Homesick?'

'It means...' Sasha wondered how she might explain. A person who had no home couldn't sicken for one, could they? It would be an insult. 'My dog died,' she said instead, which provoked a nostalgic yearning for the touch of a wet nose and the thump of a tail against her leg. She dug in her bag for a fresh tissue and found some loose coins which cheered her up. 'Hey, but that's enough whingeing. Why don't we have a real drink?'

'*Cosa?*'

'Like a cocktail?' She leaned from her chair and peered into the dim interior of the bar. The door was curtained with strips of plastic to keep away the flies. On the counter a dish of panini oozed yellow mayonnaise, on a shelf above stood bottles of obscure aperitifs and liqueurs. But what was she thinking? This was hardly the spot for cocktails. 'No, bad idea. Forget it.'

Her phone was ringing with the call she'd been waiting for. She moved away from the table to answer it. They were on the train, Renate told her – 'the beach was so busy and the water *so* dirty, you would not believe it!' – and would be getting in shortly.

'I'm only five minutes away,' said Sasha, pleased that for once she was in the right place at the right time. 'I'll come and meet you, yeah?' As long as Joe pointed her in the right direction she wouldn't need him any more. She could put their second mildly embarrassing encounter behind her. 'That was my friend, Renate,' she said. 'We're meeting outside the station.'

'I carry you,' he said.

She giggled. 'No, Joe. Take, not carry, but I can handle it, no worries. Left and left again, right?'

He blinked. '*Scusi?*'

Her shorts were sticking to her thighs; trickles of sweat were running down the backs of her knees. She longed for the evening. 'That way?' she said, pointing.

'I show you.'

He was determined to follow Gina's instructions to escort her, so she had to let him take the lead – though she was able to orientate herself within moments of turning the corner. And even when they arrived at the station he hovered in the background like a bodyguard, unwilling to leave her by herself.

Renate and Ilse strolled off the Ostia train and down the platform arm in arm, swinging their beach bags. They were followed by four Italian youths talking with animation among themselves, but failing to keep up. '*Ciao*!' said Renate, embracing Sasha. A dusting of sand freckled her left cheek. 'How was the football?'

'Not great. I mean not great for me. Antonio was, "Wow, this is so cool, I'm a real hero." Imagine!'

Ilse peered beyond her, at Joe, who was keeping his distance. 'That's not him?'

'No.'

'He is your date?'

Sasha turned, trying to see Joe through the German girls' eyes. He was holding himself very erect, but there was something louche and untamed about him too, barely reined in. Actually, she thought, if you didn't know anything about him, you'd think this guy was well fit.

'He's someone I met through a friend,' she said casually.

'He is student also?'

'No, he's, um, a male model.'

The girls both looked approving. 'He will join us?'

But this, Sasha was not ready for. 'He's got stuff to do,' she said. 'Maybe later.' It was too big a step to include him but, if he asked, she might be prepared to exchange phone numbers.

9

Gina preferred to have notice of Roberto's visits. She didn't like him to catch her unawares. She needed time to clear away disordered magazines and dirty crockery – especially the latter, in case he'd assume it was recent and react as if she had someone hidden in her wardrobe. If she said, 'Actually it's my cup from yesterday', he'd be appalled by her slovenliness, and if she said, 'A friend was here', he'd want to know who and when, male or female? She'd find herself seething at his questions and not at all mollified by his insistence that he found her so fascinating he wanted to know everything about her. And the worst of it was when her rage translated into arousal, making her growl like a cat on heat, biting and scratching as he tried to pin her down. The sex that followed would be tremendous and the man with whom she had this entirely unsuitable love-hate affair would strut off preening, like the bloody cock of the walk.

It had disturbed her to discover he'd used his key to let himself in and although it had only been the once – allegedly for her benefit – she didn't want it to happen again. So she arranged for him to collect the photographs late one afternoon. She'd compiled a presentation pack of half a dozen 8x10s for him to take home. Her favourite showed Antonio with his head tipped back, the ball suspended like a saucer of leather, almost out of the frame. The line that flowed down his throat and sternum bisected the shot in an unbroken arc; the expression on his face was rapturous. She hoped her selection would satisfy the family, that she wouldn't have to edit another bunch of images.

Roberto had a site visit; he wanted her to join him there but she refused. He was so used to people marching to his orders it didn't occur to him they might have other priorities. Gina was adamant. 'Bertie, I don't want to tramp around some dusty tip where I'd have to wear a hard hat.' And then she got him to admit he'd also scheduled another appointment at the bank, who were being difficult but not so impossible that a little pressure wouldn't work its charms. No doubt representatives of the bank would be invited away for the weekend – or perhaps the house party had already taken place and they required reminding of any indiscretions.

'Text me when you've finished with them. I'll be home waiting. And the least you can do, if you're going off on your family holiday, is come over and say goodbye properly.'

The Boletti household would soon be relocating, along with other family members – grandmother, aunts, cousins – to the villa they owned in Fregene. Built in the sixties when the resort was in its heyday and much envied for its generous size and prime position, it was near enough to Rome to enable Roberto to trot regularly back and forth, attending to his affairs. His wife, ensconced in an undemanding career as a civil servant, would be taking her full holiday entitlement. Sasha Mitchell, whose course was almost over, wasn't going with them; she'd be flying home at the end of the week. Gina didn't expect to see her again.

When her doorbell rang and she picked up the intercom she assumed Bertie was early.

'*Ciao*, Gina!'

'Oh... Sami, it's you.'

Sami was a frequent visitor. Like some of the other lost boys, he'd turn up at the slightest excuse. Some people, who didn't approve, warned that she was courting disaster; she would be robbed and deceived. But her expensive equipment was at the studio, and her treasure chest – repository of her few items of sentimental value – was kept locked, the key buried in a kitchen canister. Besides, Sami was no stranger. She'd taken him under her wing three years before, seen him gain in confidence and prowess. He'd finally been granted leave to remain but there was little chance of legal work or getting a permit to perform. Every time he took his stand in Piazza Navona he was taking a risk. He'd decided this risk was small compared to some of the others he'd run. One of the worst, he'd told her, was the dogs used to sniff out human cargo as well as narcotics; he'd escaped them by hiding in a container of fish, partially rotting. He could no longer eat fish.

'I can come in?' Sami asked.

'No, I'm sorry, not today. My landlord's due.'

'Five minutes only? Please! For my make-up.'

She sighed, reconsidering. 'Okay, if you must, but we have to be quick.'

She sat him on the swivel chair under the anglepoise lamp. The shutters were wide open but the day was dull; an overcast sky threatened thunder. She smoothed a thick white base over Sami's face and neck and with one of her fine sable brushes traced a web of light grey to create a marbled effect. He could do the backs of his hands himself.

'How's Joe?' she asked casually. 'I've heard nothing lately.'

'He's seeing the English girl.'

'What English girl?' Even as she spoke, she realised he meant Sasha. 'What do you mean? They've been meeting each other? More than once?'

Sami nodded.

'What on earth are they doing together? Not *dating*?'

'They walk.'

'Walk? I see.' But she didn't. 'Where?'

She tried to picture them wandering in the area around the Pantheon, blending into the mass of sightseers, maybe drinking at night in the bars around Campo de' Fiori where the foreign students clustered like iron filings. Was that likely? What did girls of Sasha's age drink? Syrupy slugs of sambuca or limoncello? Pina colada? As for Joe, he wasn't used to alcohol. Although he'd been excited to discover its effects, most of the time he couldn't afford to go to bars. She wouldn't have thought the pair had much in common, but she couldn't stop the images forming. There they were: a couple of misfits – one who had seen too little of life, the other who had seen too much – holding hands in front of the Trevi Fountain, or leaning over the parapet of the bridge to Isola Tiberina, watching the river gush around the forlorn fragment of the Ponte Rotto, sharing the experience of being in tune with somebody else, if only for a fleeting moment.

Sami said, 'I don't know where, but he meet her again tomorrow.'

Gina couldn't help feeling twitchy. 'Look, I know it's nothing to do with me – apart from the fact that I introduced them – but warn him he shouldn't get involved, will you.'

Sami's eyes were uncannily round and dark in their ivory mask. 'I tell him?'

'Yes, I think it's better coming from you. She's a kid, he's an adult. Do you understand what I mean?'

He gave a non-committal grunt. She stood aside to let him out of the chair. 'Shit, what am I doing, leaping ahead, jumping to conclusions? Mountains out of molehills. Forget it.'

'I'm sorry, what you want me to do?'

'*Niente*. Forget I said anything.' In a way, she wished he hadn't said anything either. Imagination overdrive, that was her trouble. Packing away her tubes of greasepaint, she added, 'Right, you've had your five minutes so you better get going. I need to buy some more sugar for Signor Boletti's coffee so I'll come out with you.'

She was anxious to escort him from the building herself, she didn't like to think of him lurking, inviting Bertie's suspicion. He was looking especially incongruous because he hadn't yet changed into his full costume. He was carrying his cloak and toga in the crate he used to stand on. He would cut a bizarre figure on the bus: a sculpted laurel-wreathed head rising from the collar of an everyday polo-shirt, but Rome was a place where people regularly stared at extraordinary sights. Gawping was something you got used to.

She accompanied him down the road and then dived into her local *alimentari* for the sugar. Once inside, inhaling its ripe and salty air, it was not hard to be persuaded to add a carton of olives, maybe some artichoke hearts and ham to her purchases. While slicing the transparent crimson wafers of *prosciutto crudo*, Signora Bedini updated, for Gina's benefit, her lengthy and convoluted feud with her daughter-in-law. The bones they quarrelled over were son and grandson and resolution seemed unlikely. The Signora had won the most recent round. She'd refused to babysit on the occasion of a formal dinner. 'At very short notice, when it becomes impossible for them to find an alternative. *Magari*! Next time maybe she won't be so quick to criticise the way I treat my son's child.' Her lips smacked in satisfaction and Gina nodded in approval. She'd been a customer here for several years, listening to the Signora's laments for the way things used to be, and had joined the ranks of her confidantes. She looked forward to her tales of one-upmanship.

'They had to pay for the dinner in advance, I suppose?' she said as she was handed her waxed paper package of ham.

'*Naturalmente*!' They smiled in harmony at each other.

She had been longer in the shop than she intended. As she stepped outside she felt a fat drop like a tear on her cheek. She looked up. The sky was livid, a puddle of spilt petrol, dark and iridescent all at once. It wasn't surprising; humidity had been escalating throughout the day. More drops splashed around her. She cradled the shopping bag close to her chest for protection, put her head down and ran into Sami who was trying to shelter under the awning of the nearby bar.

'Sami, what are you still doing here?'

He regarded her mournfully. 'I cannot work in the rain.'

'Bollocks, it's only a shower. It will be over in minutes, you know that. By the time you get off the bus the sun will be out. *Sbrigati*! Hurry up.'

He didn't move. 'There will be no sun today.'

'It's a summer thunderstorm,' Gina insisted. 'It'll clear the air. And if everyone else is rained off, you'll have the piazza to yourself. The tourists will be grateful. They need extra diversion in the rain.'

'I can come inside again?' he said.

'No, Sami, you can't. And you know why. Do you have enough money to get yourself a coffee? You can sit in Gae's place till it stops. Quit acting like you need a bloody mother to hold your hand.' She broke off. 'Hey, I'm sorry… I shouldn't…' The rain was pelting them both. Her hair and clothes were plastered to her skin. His make-up was running. 'Go,' she said, giving him a gentle push through the doorway of Gaetano's bar. Then she took a deep breath and sprinted home.

It was amazing how wet you could get in such a short time, she thought, as she squelched up the stairs and fumbled with her keys. If Sami hadn't appeared she could have popped out twenty minutes earlier and escaped the downpour. And it turned out to be a wasted errand: as she let herself into the apartment she loosened her grip on her shopping. The olives careened across the floor in all directions and the sugar, its packaging already damp, burst open on impact, scattering grains like white sand, coarse and sticky underfoot. Maybe she could rescue some of it, scoop a few spoonfuls into a bowl. Who would know? Then she'd sweep up the rest, collect and rinse the olives, take a shower and, if there was time, effect all the other little touches that would show Bertie she was a good tenant: taps sparkling, rubbish emptied, CDs in cases, pillows plumped in readiness…

She was part of the way there when she recognised his peremptory ring on the doorbell and had to admit him in her bathrobe.

'Ah Gina,' he said, tugging her towards him by its cord. 'I'm sorry if I'm late. You're impatient for me?'

'No,' she said, towelling her hair. 'I was caught in the rain. I got soaked.'

He let her go and rested his umbrella by the door. He took off his jacket, gave it a little shake and hung it on her coat stand. He removed his tan leather loafers and lined them up under the jacket. He padded towards her again, not the type to waste time. '*Allora*,' he said. '*Al letto*.'

'Don't you want to see the photographs first?'

'The ones you emailed? I've already seen them on the computer.'

'But those were raw unedited shots, like old-fashioned contact sheets. I've printed up the ones you said you liked so you can frame them. Or you can choose one or two to enlarge even more. It's up to you and Antonio, whichever you prefer.'

'I'm sure they're magnificent,' he said, slipping his arms around her waist, inside the bathrobe, squeezing a handful of flesh.

'Bertie! This is unprofessional.'

He was perplexed. 'How?'

Gina couldn't bear to admit to herself that he'd no interest in her skills as an artist. Why should he? They'd kept up this fiction for nearly two years: that she was a lonely widow and he was saddled with a wife who was '*un po' stronza*'; that they could comfort each other without making unreasonable demands. In practice this spelt escape for Roberto from his witchy wife, security of tenure for Gina and athletic love-making for them both. But there were limits.

'Right now,' she said. 'I've got my photographer's hat on, so you need to treat me properly, as you would your architect or your accountant.'

He laughed. 'You think I sleep with my accountant?'

'No! That's my whole point.'

'My wife does,' he said, trying to push the robe off her shoulders. 'So I let her think it. That way she doesn't suspect anything about us.'

'Just look at the damn photos, will you.' She grabbed the folder and thrust it into his straying hands, determined to keep up appearances.

He loosened the ribbon and opened the cover, picking up the prints one by one and holding them gingerly at their edges. She watched closely, hoping she'd see him register delight and admiration, but in truth it was hard to tell. 'Very good,' he said.

'Very good, you mean that?'

'*Certo.*'

'You're happy with them?'

'Yes! You've done an excellent job. What more can I say? What else do I have to do?'

'You could pay me.'

He laughed again. 'Of course I'll pay you.'

'I've included my invoice, as you'll see. Cash would be good. Now, if possible.'

This time he scowled and his tone was contemptuous. 'This is the behaviour of a *puttana*.'

'Why?'

'To ask for money in advance.'

Gina could feel the heat rising in her face. 'In advance of what?' she said furiously. 'I've done the work. I've given you and your son my time and skill. It's true that my usual terms are thirty days, but since you're about to go on holiday I thought you'd prefer not to have an outstanding debt to me.'

'*Calma, calma, carina mia,*' said Roberto, unembarrassed, but backing away from her towards the coat stand. He plucked his wallet from the inside pocket of his jacket and pulled out a handful of notes. She'd known he would have the cash. Credit cards did not grease palms in the same way; they didn't offer the casual flourish of a colourful euro note.

She accepted his payment, signed a receipt and retied the folder, all the while trying to control her breathing.

'I love it when you're angry,' he said and she knew, as he propelled her towards the bedroom, that she'd blown it again, worked herself into a state of over-excitement. He shed his trousers and chased her across the sheets, tugged her legs up by the ankles and wrapped them around his neck; she drummed her heels against his back.

Afterwards, he didn't leap straight for the shower. He drew her head onto his breast and said, 'I have a proposition for you.'

Gina, lulled into his warm embrace, murmured to him to continue.

'I mentioned this, at the football ground.'

'Oh yes, I remember. Jam tomorrow.'

'It's a pity you couldn't come on the site visit this afternoon.'

'I was working. When you're self-employed, you know, there's no let-up. I can't drop my clients for something that isn't even built yet. I mean, if you wanted to commission before and after shots that would be different, but you've been very secretive and I don't have the time or inclination for a magical mystery tour.'

He twisted a lock of her damp hair around his finger. A blade of sunlight crept through the window, striking the costume jewellery heaped in a bowl on her dressing table, her glass perfume bottles; the rain storm was over. 'Actually one of the apartment blocks has been completed,' he said. 'The builders are in liquidation. That's why the rest of the development is only at foundation stage. I don't know if we can raise the money, but we're negotiating. We're hopeful. You see, the block that's finished is very fine, the fittings are lavish: travertine marble on the floors, granite worktops in the kitchen, the best appliances. The shower is so powerful it can give you a massage. There's a lift, very fast. Each apartment has a balcony with a superlative view: one way the sea, the other way, the city – '

'Why are you telling me this?'

'I think you would enjoy living there.'

'What!' Even Vicki had shown more sensitivity. 'Bertie, you're crazy. I'd be miles from everyone and everything I know.'

She couldn't take his suggestion seriously. The bed had served the function of a wrestling ring and she had collapsed against the ropes. All she wanted was to lie in the half-light with familiar noises a stone's throw away. She knew the voices of her neighbours, the rhythm of their footsteps; she could tell when the market stalls were setting up and winding down, when an accident had been averted, when the children were let out of school. She had always valued being in the heart of things.

'There is a sweetener.'

'Oh?'

'The apartment is rent-free.'

'Why? Is it for a caretaker?'

'It's because I have bought it.'

'You bought this place,' Gina reminded him. 'So what's the difference?'

He shifted onto his side, his body touching the length of hers, his penis nudging her lightly as if it hadn't yet decided whether to rear into another bout of action. 'This is owned by the consortium,' he said. 'The apartment I'm telling you about I've bought personally. A present for you.'

She sat up, shocked, tipping him away. 'A present? You mean it's in my name?'

'Well, no,' he allowed. 'I am the owner naturally. But I'm happy for you to live there for nothing.'

She might have known the offer was too good to be true. 'You think I'm going to let you treat me like a kept whore? What fucking century are you living in?' She leapt out of bed, falling over herself to pull on a pair of knickers and a jersey maxi-dress. She grabbed the pack of cigarettes he'd left on the bedside table and lit one. She felt smoke pluming from her ears.

'Gina,' he said placidly. 'I'm offering you a deal. You know me. I don't grant favours. You don't have to be insulted. This is a solution that would suit us both.'

'No it isn't. A solution to what, anyway? You're asking me to go and camp out in the middle of some arid building site where I probably won't have any neighbours for years. I'll bet there isn't even an *alimentari*.'

'There's a supermarket, a huge Conad.'

'And no buses or trams. I'd be completely isolated.'

'You could learn to drive. It would be useful for your assignments.'

'I don't know if I can afford to run a car, plus it would take me for ever to get to the studio. But the main problem – and I don't believe you can't see this – is that I'd have no bloody rights at all.' She would not be bought off. Bertie might think he could put her in a box, visit her when he felt horny, and meanwhile make a killing on her lovely home, but he'd find she didn't give in so easily.

He climbed out of bed, stocky, bullish, unrepentant. 'I can't talk to you while you're like this.'

'Like what?'

He ignored her, headed for the bathroom and slammed the door. She heard the pipes groan. In agitation, she released some ice cubes into a glass, poured a shot of grappa and took it out onto the terrace. The rain-washed tiles steamed, the potted plants – aromatic bushes of rosemary, bay, sage and citrus – looked perky and refreshed. Her gaze skimmed the rooftops of Trastevere in all their shades of terracotta, russet, ochre, rose and apricot, their irregular muddle of peaks and slopes and gables, their balconies crammed with greenery and aflutter with laundry. How could she leave this?

Bertie wouldn't understand. Apart from being a rogue and an adventurer, he was also a family man. He couldn't fathom her lifestyle and she'd no desire for his. They had reached an impasse. She'd have to call it a day before things got any worse, before he backed her into a corner from which she had no retreat. Bye bye, Bertie.

Taking the decision pleased her, gave her a sense of liberation. Now that he'd paid her for the photos, she need have nothing more to do with him. She'd jettison her chances of home improvement, but what the hell, she'd managed long enough with the way things were. He could sod off and sweet-talk his sexy accountant into bed. It was obviously a possibility at the back of his mind.

She broke off a leaf of lemon-scented geranium and dropped it into her glass. She returned inside to top up the grappa. The bolt on the bathroom door shot back and he emerged, hair slick against his head, tucking his shirt into his trousers. She didn't offer him a drink. Watching him put on his socks and shoes, she reflected on the vulnerability of the naked foot. How it lacked the power of the clenched fist, how it could so easily be cut or damaged, how it could only inflict pain when shod in leather, how a kick was so much crueller than a punch.

When he stood again, she said, 'It's stopped raining, but don't forget your umbrella. I don't want you to leave anything here.'

His head jerked on his neck. 'I'm only going to the beach for a couple of weeks. I'm not deserting you.'

'As far as I'm concerned you can stay there as long as you like.'

'Gina! Are you trying to break my balls?'

'No, Bertie, I'm trying to break off our relationship. We want different things and it isn't working. You need to go.'

His expression was hard to read. She estimated two parts astonishment, two of wrath and one of admiration. Then he guffawed. 'We shall see.'

'You don't believe me?'

'You're going to need me, *cara*, and then what? I can make things very difficult.'

'I think I'll manage.'

She held the door open to make her point clear. He paused on the threshold where they usually kissed goodbye, then gripped the banister as if he wished it were her wrist. Or neck. She knew she was taking a gamble. He was treating her like an intransigent child; later he might just feel insulted. She closed the door.

Her hairbrush was lying on the sideboard. She knocked it off with an impatient movement and started flicking through the local edition of the *Pagine Gialli*. She ruffled the directory's thin pages several times until she traced the number she was looking for. Then she picked up her phone and dialled a locksmith who owed her a favour.

IO

The language course was over. The days that had dragged at the beginning had speeded up alarmingly as the third week ended. In Parioli, Katya was the only person who seemed upset by Sasha's imminent departure. Antonio was far more interested in his beach holiday, as if he fancied himself a bit-part player in The O.C. Katya had helped to pack her suitcase, standing zipped and ready in a corner of the guest room. She'd even ironed clothes it would never have occurred to Sasha or her mother to press and thus made room for extra purchases and the presents for her parents and Ruby.

Sasha had bought a box of handmade chocolates for her hosts, but decided to give them to the maid instead. Katya accepted them with a lip-smacking conspiratorial grin. She crushed her in an energetic embrace and blessed her in the names of a dozen obscure Catholic saints. Sasha promised to send her a postcard from England. The chocolates probably wouldn't have suited Signora Boletti anyhow. She wore wide shiny belts that cinched the waists of her pencil skirts and tight trousers: there was no room for expansion.

Sasha was spending her final evening in celebration. The students were gathering in Renate and Ilse's room in the hostel to prepare for a night on the tiles, getting wasted. Until now, she'd always returned to the Bolettis before midnight. An exception was being made for the farewell party. The Signora had told her they wouldn't worry, even into the small hours, so long as she kept enough money in her purse for a taxi and didn't get separated from her friends. Signora Boletti herself would be leaving early for Fregene, but Roberto would put Sasha on her plane.

The German girls had shifted the furniture in their room so their beds were against the wall and there was space in the centre of the floor to slice up the takeaway pizza and dole out the vodka and Red Bull. The aim was to get tanked up to save money on drinks later and to have enough cheap carbs in their stomachs to avoid being hungry. After all, as Harry, one of the American boys, had pointed out, they'd have the entire duration of a flight the next day in which to sober up.

Harry had been hitting on Ilse for some time, but she was waiting to hear from the Italian she'd been seeing since last Sunday's trip to the beach. She crouched over her phone, swatting him away like a fly when he pretended to jog her elbow or ruffle her cropped hair. He joined some rowdy comrades in the corner, in a downing the shots competition. The atmosphere in the room was steamy with alcohol and anticipation. The mousy Japanese girl, generally regarded as a teacher's pet, had already drunk far more than she was used to and was weeping at the prospect of losing her new friends. Renate was refilling her plastic beaker and consoling her.

Sasha was sitting on a pillow on the floor, munching through a slice of pizza Napoletana, forcing herself to eat the anchovies because, like olives, they indicated you had grown-up tastes. Bruton, who'd arrived late, came to sit beside her.

'We didn't see each other so much,' he said.

She shrugged. She hadn't been avoiding him, but she was hardly going to seek him out. 'Yeah, well... Did you have a good time?'

'Sure. You should have come on the outing to the Catacombs. It was awesome.'

It was also expensive, she remembered thinking when people were signing up for the tour. 'I knew it would give me the creeps.'

'Too right. There were all these underground passages you could so easily get lost in. And the walls were hollowed out in rows like a locker room but instead of storing your possessions in the spaces, they were full of dead bodies.'

'Really?'

'Not any more! Though we did see some bones casually lying about. Hey, but the best place for a real fright, if you're interested in skeletons, is the Capuchin cemetery. It's at the bottom of the Via Veneto – do you know it? The chapels are totally decorated in bones and body parts and you have these dead monks standing around in their habits like evil ghosts. It's mind-blowing.'

'I didn't get there either.'

'St Peter's cell? The Garibaldi family tomb?'

'No, afraid not.'

'What have you seen then?'

'I went to the Protestant Cemetery,' she offered.

'Yeah, that was cool. Did you find Shelley's grave? D'you know the story about his heart being snatched out of the fire on the beach because it wouldn't burn? And how his grieving widow, the one who wrote *Frankenstein*, kept it in her desk for years, wrapped in one of his poems, till she died too?'

Sasha grimaced. 'Actually it was shut the afternoon I went, but you can see where Keats is buried through a window in the wall.'

Bruton looked pitying. 'Seems to me you missed out on one helluva lot.'

'Oh no,' she insisted. 'I did all the regular sights. I even got taken to Roma's training ground.' When he failed to look impressed, she added, 'No, it didn't do anything for me either. But I went up the Gianicolo for the view and got to explore the gardens of Villa Doria Pamphili. That was lovely, it's a huge park, almost like being in the country. I really liked it.'

Joe had taken her there. She might not have discovered it otherwise. Although they'd exchanged numbers and a couple of texts – '*Come stai? Bene*', was about the sum of them – they hadn't made any plans to meet. But earlier in the week he'd been loitering by the railings of the school when she came out of class and she wasn't certain, when she saw him at the bottom of the steps, whether this was simple coincidence. Renate, close behind, had no such doubts. She nudged her in the small of her back. 'You did not tell us, Sash, you had this date.'

'I didn't know he was coming.'

'Why don't you bring him with us for a coffee?'

They greeted each other shyly and tagged along at the back of the group that was winding through the streets off the Corso. There was talk of lunch and they ended up in Campo de' Fiori, bunched into a gaggle again at the spectacle of the market. In fact, the stallholders were beginning to pack up, restoring cheese and salamis to their cool boxes, stacking their unsold fruit in plywood crates, loading buckets full of flowers into the backs of their vans. Passing one of the fruit and vegetable stalls, Harry had plucked a small Galia melon from its pyramid and started to fool around with it, pretending it was an American football.

The stallholder had his back turned and didn't notice. Joe frowned and lagged behind, as if to detach himself. Harry tossed the melon to a friend and they began running a little way with their heads down, passing it back and forth between them. Others joined in, laughing at the wild surreal freedom of playing ball in a Roman market so many miles from home. A handful of shoppers and the many curious tourists watched in bemusement.

'Hey,' shouted Harry, hurling the melon in Joe's direction. 'Your turn, man!'

Joe took a step back; the melon fell to the cobbles and exploded, scattering seeds like shot.

'What d'you do that for, you jerk? It was an easy catch.'

Joe, wrapping his arms around his torso, was frozen to the spot. Sasha was torn. She'd have preferred to keep a neutral stance, but moved surreptitiously to his side.

'It's okay,' she said. 'He was just arsing around, being a dickhead.'

'He steal the fruit,' said Joe, shocked by the blatancy of Harry's performance.

'Oh he'll *pay* for it,' said Sasha. 'I mean, he might not have done if it hadn't smashed. He'd probably have handed it back again, no worries. But now…' She could see Harry unbuckling his money belt (they'd all been warned about pick-pockets) and counting out coins for the stallholder, adding more to the pile until the man was prepared to grunt in satisfaction. Then he gave a thumbs up. 'See? He doesn't give a toss.'

The crowd dispersed. The melon seeds were rinsed with a jet of water into the gutter; the remaining rind rocked gently on the cobblestones. The atmosphere of revelry dissipated.

Joe said to Sasha, 'Is not good here. I know better place for games.'

'You do?'

Which was how they slipped away from the others, took a bus across the river and up the Gianicolo to the entrance of the Doria Pamphili estate. The classical villa with its formal parterre was grand and imposing but Sasha preferred the untamed parkland. She and Joe reverted to child's play, darting around trees, following trails, chasing wildlife. They lay on their backs on the grass, staring at the patterns thin clouds made in the sky, rolled onto their stomachs beside the lake, trailing their hands in the water.

She hadn't giggled like this since she last saw Ruby and she wondered how strange it must feel to Joe – he wasn't much older than her when his family was blown to bits and he embarked on his exodus – but he didn't have the words to tell her what his life was like before and she was wary of asking. Instead, he listened to her explaining the way things worked in England, the way they were different to Italy (and Afghanistan) while his supple fingers plaited a wreath of wild flowers and arranged it on her head.

They repeated their excursion a couple of days later. Sasha brought sandwiches made from the leftovers in the Boletti fridge and Joe carried the heavy bottles he'd filled from a water fountain. That second time, as they walked along he took her hand. It seemed a natural gesture, friendly but innocent, as did the brush of his lips at her cheek as they said goodbye. Nothing more.

She hadn't been back to Campo de' Fiori since, but Renate, self-appointed team leader, had decided it was where they were going when they'd finished the vodka. At night the square, already crammed full of bars, turned itself into an outside disco frequented by students and other young foreigners. They couldn't afford the club they'd previously tried in Testaccio; two cocktails had cleaned them out. Far better to get lashed at a bar and dance in the piazza if they felt like it.

It was fun, Renate insisted, dancing in the street. She added, cocking her eyebrow, 'He is coming also, Sash? Your friend?'

'Who?'

'*Come si chiama*? Joe?'

'He's not, like, my boyfriend or anything.'

'So? He comes or not?'

'I don't know. I said I might text him.'

Athletic leggy Renate was as light-fingered as she was quick on her feet. She had Sasha's phone in her hand and her thumbs were clicking over the keys. 'I'm writing in Italian,' she said. 'This is better for him than English, yes?'

'Writing what? What are you saying?'

'Only the name of the bar, that's all. He will find you,' reassured Renate, pressing send.

'I don't know if I want him to find me.' It was one thing to amble around a beautiful park together on a mellow afternoon, but he wouldn't slot easily into the rabble of a Saturday night send-off. Everyone would already have drunk themselves silly and she didn't think he was used to that kind of carousing.

Suddenly, however, things were moving very fast. Bruton and the Japanese girl were trying to crush the pizza boxes into an overflowing waste bin. Ilse was circling the room with the second vodka bottle, topping up all the plastic cups until the bottle was empty. She clapped her hands and shouted '1-2-3-Go' and at the same moment they all raised and drained their drinks. Then they bundled themselves out of the building and onto the bus. Sasha was squeezed up against Bruton but he didn't make any advances.

She was relieved when they arrived at the bar Renate had nominated and Joe was nowhere to be seen. Inside the place was small and funky, bathed in an orange glow. A tape-deck at the side of the counter was playing The Killers' live album. This was a big improvement on the Italian music she'd had to listen to, which veered between woeful laments and chirpy teeny-bop pop. The group had already pooled their remaining euros for a drinks kitty. The girls ordered rosé, the boys lager. Outside, most of the chairs and tables were occupied and many of the drinkers were standing. Customers of one bar merged into another, the ambience was friendly and festive; even the sky, which had been overcast for much of the week, was clear and studded with stars.

'Oh my God,' said Sasha, cradling her pretty pink glass. 'I can't believe it's my last night. I actually don't want to go home.'

Renate and Ilse were lucky they could go back to Munich whenever they fancied, by hopping on a train. They were talking of travelling up Italy's Mediterranean coast, stopping off at seaside resorts for a spell of snorkelling. Ilse's Italian admirer – strongly scented with aftershave, a powder blue jumper draped across his shoulders – had joined their table and invited them to visit his family place at Porto Ercole en route. Sasha was envious.

'You could go to Fregene with Antonio, no?' said Ilse.

PENNY FEENY

'I don't think there'd be room in the villa. They're meeting up with their cousins. He wouldn't want to be bothered with me. Anyway, I'd rather be with you guys.'

'Sure,' said Renate in her low drawl. 'You may come also.'

'Really? Do you mean that? I could bunk in with you?'

'Why not?'

For a while she basked in this fantasy. She wouldn't have to return to a lifeless house with no dog in it. She could put off worrying about what she was going to do for the rest of the holidays if she couldn't find a job, as well as the gnawing prospect of her GCSE results. God, when you looked at it that way, what on earth was she going home for? She hadn't even spent all her money yet. How could her parents possibly begrudge her a couple of days on a beach? The gang from her year who *had* been allowed to go out to Zante would be well-tanned and well-toned from all their swimming and sunbathing. Sounds fun, she imagined saying to them on the first day of the new term, but my experience was more... sophisticated.

The noise was escalating: the hoots of laughter and clink of glasses, even the scrape of matches and flare of lighters. The taped music, running in a steady loop, battled the output from other bars. She could hear shouts of 'Bet you can't!' 'Bet I can!' 'Bet you five!' 'Raise you ten!' Harry had gathered an audience of onlookers at the promise of his party trick. The aim was to balance a Peroni bottle on his forehead, flick it upwards so that it somersaulted, and catch its neck between his teeth, whereupon he'd glug the contents. A bottle shot skywards and he missed it, to a general howl of disappointment. Fortunately it was rescued mid-tumble before its contents were lost. This didn't deter Harry from trying again, but Sasha was distracted by a shape looming at her elbow.

'Oh my God, Joe!'

If he'd arrived an hour earlier, she might have been self-conscious, unsure whether to include him in the party – whether he'd be accepted like Ilse's dapper boyfriend or considered an interloper. But now the night was buzzing – actually her ears were buzzing – his presence would be easily absorbed. She might even give him a proper kiss, right at the end when they all said goodbye, when they parted maybe for ever. Chances were she'd kiss everyone anyway.

'You send me message?' said Joe.

'Yeah, it's my last night and for a lot of other people as well, so...'

'*Ti voglio bene*,' he said.

'What?' Italian was supposed to be the language of romance, so it didn't make sense to her that the phrase they claimed meant 'I love you' was, if you translated it literally, an unabashed come-on: '*Ti voglio bene* – I well want you.' She hadn't expected to hear Joe use it.

In reply he handed her his phone so she could read the text on the screen. She flushed deeply in embarrassment. 'I didn't send this.'

'No?'

'No.' She pointed at Renate. 'She was messing around. She sent it.'

Renate was no longer coherent. She wore a sleepy grin and her head swayed from side to side.

'It was a mistake,' Sasha apologised, trying to salvage dignity. 'Don't take any notice. It's good that you came though.'

He put his phone back into his pocket, as if undecided what to believe. There were no free chairs so Sasha rose to stand beside him. Another Peroni bottle rocketed through the air. Joe ducked. Sasha reached up and miraculously it sailed into her hand. There was a stuttering round of applause.

Harry, who had so far notched up one success, three failures, came barrelling over and stumbled en route into Joe. 'You again,' he muttered and made a grab for the bottle.

'Hey,' said Sasha, needled. 'Finders keepers.' She passed it to Joe who probably had some catching up to do.

'That's my beer,' said Harry.

'Not any more.' He scowled and tottered a little, looking more intimidating than perhaps he had intended.

'Go away,' said Joe. 'Leave her.'

'Then give it to me.'

'No.' Defiantly, Joe drank it down.

Harry lunged towards him. 'Bully!' shouted Sasha.

Joe side-stepped with a swift neat grace, but something in Harry's behaviour had agitated him. 'You kill my family,' he said, his eyes glittering. 'But you cannot hurt me.'

'What the fuck are you talking about? I haven't killed anyone!' In his indignation Harry was shouting and at the word 'killed' heads turned. The audience who'd been laughing at his tricks were massing around the three of them, curious, over-stimulated and, in some cases, spoiling for a fight. Sasha just had time to appreciate the irony of the playlist – 'I Predict A Riot' was starting up – as Harry raged, 'You fucking apologise, man. Who the hell d'you think you are?'

Renate, from her seat at the table, growled, 'He's from Afghanistan.'

'He's not Italian? Is that right?' Harry lit up. 'Well, you know what, my family had losses too, because of that bloody pile of shit you call a country! Why d'you have to mess up our lives? Why can't you smoke your own dope, mind your own fucking business? What you doing over here anyhow? You belong back in the caves, man, or in the gutter at the very fucking least.'

Somebody was trying to pull at Harry's sleeve, to calm him down, but the interruption goaded him further and his fist shot out and cracked against Joe's collarbone. Joe, sober, was quick to retaliate, but this wasn't a wise decision. The news that he was an asylum seeker had circulated rapidly. He had no protection, he was alone.

A number of youths began to exchange blows. It was a hot night, they'd all had too much to drink. The scene took on the appearance of an athletic but undisciplined ballet. Some of the bystanders were applauding and enjoying the spectacle;

others drifted away. Ilse and her boyfriend hauled Renate from her chair and scooted with her to safety on the far side of the piazza.

It took Sasha a few moments to register that Joe, the target for this sudden release of aggression, was on the ground and the blows were not playful. She was outraged that tempers were so out of control; she had to put a stop to them. She launched herself to the ground, covering Joe's body with her own. She didn't believe that any of these boys, who normally acted like civilised human beings, would hit a girl. But that was before the boot collided with her face.

The stars were still visible when she closed her eyes, imprinted on her eyelids. She was still conscious, her thought processes hyperactive. She was aware of voices cursing, receding, the focus of the fight realigning. It continued though; in fact it spread, rippling outwards to the surrounding bars, involving more eager participants. She thought she heard a police siren. The students had been warned against tangling with the police. They were advised to carry their papers at all times and keep them safe. Any theft should be reported and a *denuncia* at the police station famously took hours to complete.

Sasha's documents were in her suitcase. She did not want to be arrested on her final night; that would be *so* gruesome. Her school friend, Jordana, had been done for shoplifting once and although she'd been brittle and defiant, like 'Yeah, so what?' she'd basically come across as a frightened kid. You blew everything if you got caught, you might as well wet yourself in public. The frightening thing was that, actually, Sasha was wet: wet on her hair and down her front and on her legs and she didn't even know if it was blood or tears or wine or wee. Every bit of her hurt. Her head felt as if it had been crushed by a giant nutcracker. She was terrified her limbs were paralysed. And the police sirens were coming closer.

Somebody had an arm around her and was trying to raise her. Someone else said she shouldn't be moved, but the person with the arm ignored them and got her to sit. She hoped it was Joe, but it was Bruton. 'Can you walk?' he said. ''Cos you'd better get out of here fast.'

'What about Joe? Is he okay?'

'I reckon that's him.' He pointed to a dark huddle a few feet away.

'Oh God, he needs help.'

'My sweet lord,' said Bruton. 'Aren't you just asking for it.'

'What?'

'Trouble.'

'That's not fair.' There were definitely tears running down her cheeks. She got into scrapes, as everybody did, but not like this. This was for Jordana and Co., mouthy types who liked a challenge. Sasha's parents had drummed into her the importance of respect and sensitivity towards other people, standing up for those who couldn't stand up for themselves. Yet wasn't that why she'd been laid out flat on the cobbles and thumped, because she'd gone to the aid of a friend?

'Can't you walk any faster?' said Bruton.

'We have to take Joe with us.' He'd be fingered as the scapegoat and if he was arrested, he might be deported too: to the place where there was nothing left for him. She imagined a crater in the earth where his house and family and childhood had once been.

Joe must have been used to making quick getaways, stumbling to his feet and limping to keep up as Bruton chivvied them down one of the alleys leading from the piazza. 'You were lucky,' he said. 'Some other guys got involved so the fight moved away from our crew. Plus the police were slow on the uptake. I figure the bar owner must have called them straight off.'

'Thanks for helping,' said Sasha.

'Heck, I didn't want to hang around any longer. Leaves a nasty sour taste, that kind of hassle. It's not the way you want a party to end. Harry was nuts to freak out like that. The guy can't hold his liquor.'

Appearances were so deceiving. There was Harry, tall and rugged and upstanding; put him next to nerdy little ginger Bruton, and who did she think would have more maturity? Well, events had proved her wrong.

Sasha needed to get her breath back so she stopped in the shadow of a doorway. The others halted too. They hadn't yet had a chance to examine their respective wounds. 'How do I look?' she asked.

'Frigging awful,' said Bruton. 'You should get yourself cleaned up.'

'How am I going to do that?'

'Okay, here's my idea. We head for Corso Vittorio and you can use the toilet in one of the bars there, then pick up a cab home.'

Strolling through a brightly lit café while covered in blood and snot didn't appeal to Sasha. Fortunately they passed a drinking fountain and she was able to dab at her face. She wouldn't let Bruton help her; he was bound to be heavy-handed and she was already trying her best not to scream from the pain. 'If you could hail us a cab,' she said, 'that would be brill.'

'You can't hail them,' he said. 'They never stop. You have to go to a rank. I think the nearest's at Largo Argentina.'

But when they got there, the rank was empty. Sasha and Joe leant against the railings that surrounded the sunken ruins while Bruton made sure he was at the head of the queue. When a white taxi pulled up, he waved them forward. 'Where are you both going?' he said. 'Same direction or what?'

'What about you?'

'Hey, I got no injury. I can walk.'

'Well, okay. Ostiense first and then up to Parioli.'

Bruton opened the back door of the cab and she started to climb in. The driver turned, saw the state of her and waved an angry arm. When she didn't respond to his diatribe, far too fast for her to follow, he stamped on his accelerator. The taxi jerked forward, Sasha lost her footing and the door swung closed; the car raced away.

This happened twice more, though with less drama. Bruton asked politely if the cab driver would take his friends who had been involved in a minor *incidente*. On hearing his American accent and then seeing Sasha and Joe, the driver would regretfully refuse the fare.

'Maybe we should call an ambulance,' said Bruton.

'No!' She couldn't spend her last night in Casualty, that would be too awful, and Joe was determined to stay away from any form of authority. 'Let's give it one more go. Perhaps if they see me before I get in, there won't be any explaining to do. They'll either stop or not. And if not, I guess we'll have to find a night bus.'

'There's one coming now.'

Sasha moved boldly into the taxi's path, her condition illuminated by his headlights. When he braked she fully expected to be rejected, the automatic door locks to descend and the driver to speed off with a weary shake of the head. But for once this didn't happen.

'*Porca miseria*!' exclaimed Super Mario. '*Che successo qui?*'

11

Gina had not been home long. She'd eaten out with friends at a new restaurant they'd all decided was disappointing. They'd moved on to a late-night bar with low-level seating, low-level lighting and a comprehensive array of whiskies. In the corner a long-haired man played lazy jazz piano, accompanied by a saxophonist in a trilby. She'd left earlier than her friends because she had two weddings to cover the next day and didn't want to be tempted into drinking too much. When Mario rang, so soon after dropping her off, she assumed she must have left something behind in his cab.

But no. 'She is in distress again,' he said.

'Who?'

'*L'inglese.*'

'What d'you mean?'

'I'm on my way to you,' he said. 'You'll need to come down, I think.'

'What's going on? Whereabouts are you?'

'Crossing the river. I'll be with you in moments.'

She hadn't begun to get ready for bed so she went out on the terrace to watch for him. It was a warm night, too warm for sleep to come easily. Lighted apartment windows formed an irregular pattern of dots and dashes like a message in Morse code. Revellers were wandering through the streets, scooters careened around corners, Gaetano had not yet closed up his bar. She saw the taxi draw up and hurried down the stairs in a mixture of curiosity and irritation.

Mario rarely left his driver's seat. When necessary he would help her with heavy bags and equipment, but most of the time it was as if he were glued into position, so she was surprised when he was the first out of the car. She couldn't recognise the occupants of the back seat.

'What's going on? Who've you got with you and why the hell did you bring them here?'

'Because you're nearby,' he said. 'And the girl needs help.' He opened the car door and offered his arm as support as Sasha inched her way out.

'Jesus!' said Gina, half joking. 'Have you been in a fight?'

'Yes, actually.'

'Oh, right... Well, if somebody attacked you, darling, you ought to go to the police.' Another figure crawled out behind her. 'Joe? Is that you?'

'I'll help her up the stairs,' said Mario, clearly less willing to assist Joe and ambivalent about his presence. His was one of the voices regularly warning Gina that she was exposing herself to exploitation.

'I can walk,' Sasha said. 'So can he. We just need to get cleaned up.'

From the speakers on Mario's dashboard came the call of a fare waiting. 'You should take that,' Gina told him. 'We can manage.'

'You're sure?'

'Yes, I'll be fine to deal with them for now and if they need a ride later, I'll ring you. How long are you out for?'

'Another couple of hours? It depends on the fares.'

He was peering into the back seat as if checking for blood stains. Sasha scrabbled in her bag. 'I have money. I must pay you.'

He waved her away. '*Non c'e bisogno*. There's no need, it's no distance.'

The note flapped in her grubby hand. 'Well, if you're sure...'

He hopped into his seat, gave Gina a thumbs up and revved back onto the main road.

Once inside the apartment Gina avoided turning the lights up too brightly. She wasn't keen to see the damage these two foolish young people had done to themselves.

'Joe will need the first bath,' she said, turning on the taps and flinging open her medicine cabinet in search of witch hazel, iodine, TCP, bandages and paracetamol; cursing because her stocks were low. 'While you're waiting, Sasha, I'll get you an ice pack.' Really, she could do without a drama at this stage of the evening. She hustled Joe into the bathroom and then wrapped the contents of an ice tray in a plastic bag, which she covered with a tea towel and handed to the girl. 'I'm popping out for some more painkillers,' she said. 'You're both going to need them.'

'Will any chemists be open?'

'Oh, I'll get them from Gaetano, he usually keeps some behind the bar.'

Sasha covered her face with the ice pack and muttered, 'I'm so sorry.'

Sorry! raged Gina, as she clattered downstairs again. I'll give you sorry! She couldn't articulate why she felt so angry with the girl. After all, Joe had been beaten up before – and worse. But she clung to her conviction that Sasha would have been the catalyst. She'd seen it before: a typically careless teenager, sodden with alcohol, flirting her socks off until things got out of hand. The girl was naive, unaccustomed to drinking, unaware, like so many of them, of the messages she was transmitting. Joe presumably intervened to protect her from some other drunk's advances.

Gaetano's bar was empty; he was clearing up. He'd been serving coffees since seven that morning and was polishing to an immaculate shine the chrome of his trusty machine. He shook his head as she came in. '*Mi dispiace*, Gina. I'm closing.'

'Ouf, I don't want a drink. It's aspirins I'm after. Or paracetamol. Have you any to spare?'

He tutted in sympathy and she decided it was best to pretend the need was hers. 'I can't afford to get a migraine. I've a big day tomorrow.' She was glad his father, who in theory had retired years ago, wasn't on duty. He missed the interaction with customers and would have insisted on a ream of information: where precisely was the pain that she was trying to treat? How long had she endured it, had it travelled at all? There could well be a more accurate remedy, to which he could offer the key. Had she not heard that a paste of lemon rind on the forehead could work wonders? Or a poultice of cabbage leaves?

Gaetano fumbled below the counter and produced a full packet of paracetamol.

'Gae, you're brilliant! I'll replace them tomorrow, I promise, as soon as the *farmacia* opens.'

He wrang out a soapy dishcloth. 'No hurry.'

'I don't suppose you've a big bottle of *acqua minerale*? I've a feeling I'm going to need plenty of liquid too.'

He produced a bottle from his chiller, cloudy with condensation. 'Thanks a million. My saviour!'

Re-entering the apartment she found Sasha in the hallway, scrutinising her reflection in the long mirror. There were grazes on her knees and scratches on her arms but, when she lifted the ice pack, Gina could see her face was the real casualty: a closed eye, a puffy cheek, an egg-like swelling on her forehead. The eye that was open was stricken and appalled.

'Not pretty,' Gina said.

'Oh my God, I can't believe it! I can't let anyone see me like this.'

'The swelling should go down quite quickly. But you're going to be colourful for about a week, I'd say.'

'That long? Oh no!' Her legs crumpled and Gina supported her into a chair in the living room. Sasha clamped the ice pack back onto the left-hand side of her face.

'Do you want to tell me how it happened?'

'Everything was going really well. We were having a wicked time. Truly.' Her mouth quivered and she sank her teeth into her bottom lip.

Gina held out two paracetamol, poured water into a glass. 'Where were you?'

Sasha gulped them down and continued. 'Oh, it was a bar in Campo de' Fiori. Nice chilled atmosphere and stuff, great music, no aggro. But Harry was showing off, playing silly buggers a bit and that's how it started.'

'Who's Harry?'

'One of the Yanks. Normally he's, like, sound, but I don't know whether he was pissed off because Ilse has this new bloke or whether he was just rat-arsed. Anyway, he was doing these stupid tricks with a beer bottle and he ended up arguing with Joe.'

Why, pondered Gina, would Joe get into an argument with an American? He knew how vital it was to stay out of trouble. Could he have been trying to impress Sasha?

'So then,' the girl said, 'these other guys joined in, like they'd been waiting for a chance to have a go. And it wasn't even fair. Joe was way outnumbered, so I tried to stop them.'

'*You* did?'

'Yes.'

'Why?'

'I don't know why. Well, because I wanted them to stop and I thought they'd back off. Which they did... afterwards.'

'You mean, after you got involved?'

'Yes. And I suppose I felt a bit guilty because I was the reason Joe was in the piazza in the first place. I mean, Renate was the one who sent the text message, but...'

Gina was revising her opinion of Sasha: foolhardy, but the girl had spirit. This was Mitch's daughter, all right. She recalled

him trying to break up a fight in Sydney. Mitch claimed he'd
acted instinctively. He hadn't anticipated the knife blade that
only just failed to puncture his lung. 'Nine lives, see,' he'd said,
trying to make light of the incident, though it had cast a shadow.

'When Joe comes out of the bathroom,' she said, 'I'll check
him over in case he needs any stitches. You can get yourself
cleaned up and I'll put you in a cab back to the Bolettis.'

'Oh no, please! Don't make me go back there.'

'Why, what have they done do you?'

'They haven't done anything,' wailed Sasha. 'But look at me!'

'They'll be worried about you.'

'No, they won't. They knew this was my last night and I was
likely to come in late. As long as I contact them in the morning,
it will be fine. Can't I stay here? Please?'

'I only have one spare bed. I think Joe needs it more than
you do.'

'Couldn't I crash on the sofa? Maybe I'll look better in the
morning. You could make me up a bit. What are they going to
think if they see me like this?'

'You could tell them the truth,' said Gina. On second thoughts,
that was not such a good idea. She didn't want Bertie to make
any connections between Joe and herself. Now she had finished
with him, it was more important than ever to stay beneath his
radar. She contemplated her bedraggled visitor and sighed.
'Okay then, I'll make an exception. I understand the need to
lie low and lick your wounds, but you'll have to get on to the
Bolettis first thing or they'll report you missing or something
and there'll be hell to pay. We don't want that.'

'I'm so grateful, really…'

'And I've got a lot on tomorrow, work-wise, so I can't hang
around being your nursemaid. Is that understood?'

'Sure.'

Gina did not sleep well. How could she when her home had been
turned into a field hospital? Joe's face had escaped injury – he'd

become practised in protecting it – but the rest of his body was covered in bruises, and a flap of skin hung loose on his calf. Gina had given him ointment and bandages to apply and made up the bed. She'd found Sasha a pillow and a duvet and then barricaded herself in her own bedroom, alert for any cries in the night.

At seven she got up again and woke Sasha, who was curled dormouse-like on the sofa. The girl wriggled and jerked upright, alarmed and disorientated.

'You should ring the Bolettis.'

'Isn't it a bit early? I don't want to disturb them.'

Gina had long nourished a fantasy of disturbing Bertie's wife, whom she imagined to be complacent and insensitive. 'It will be the lesser of two evils,' she said, handing her the phone. 'Your luggage is in their house, right? So you'll have to collect it before your flight.'

'Couldn't I ask them to send it over here?'

'Bertie and I aren't seeing eye to eye at the moment, so I'd rather you didn't involve me. Anyway, aren't they going to take you to the airport? Or put you on the shuttle or something?'

Sasha swallowed with some difficulty. Was she trying not to cry? It was hard to tell. 'I can't go home,' she whispered.

'Of course you can. Home is exactly where you should be, with your mother looking after you.'

'But they'll never let me go anywhere by myself again! They won't understand the way you do. And it will be so rank, travelling all bashed-up like this.'

'Look, I do sympathise. Maybe you could buy a baseball cap, pull the brim way down over your eyes.'

'I wouldn't have to bother you much longer. Renate and Ilse have invited me to go to the sea with them.'

'So you don't want to make a spectacle of yourself on the plane, but on the beach you don't mind?'

'I can't go home like this,' she repeated.

'Oh, for God's sake! I'm going to put the coffee on. You'd better make that call.'

As she prepared the coffee and boiled the milk, she could hear Sasha mumbling in broken Italian. She didn't ask what arrangements she made; she didn't want to know the detail. The girl began telling her she'd spoken to Katya, the maid, but Gina brushed this information aside. She gave her a steaming latte. 'That should revive you. I have to go out on some errands this morning – to the *farmacia* and the post office – so if I don't see you before you leave for the airport, good luck and have a good trip.'

If she had thought that by refusing to debate, she would win the argument, she was wrong. When she got back to the flat, to prepare herself for the first of the weddings, Sasha Mitchell was still there.

12

In the gym changing room, towelling himself after a shower, Paul Mitchell could hear a phone ringing. He thought it might be his own, but he couldn't find it. He dragged his clothes from the locker but each pocket he tried proved empty. Where could the damn thing have gone?

The oddest things had been happening lately; like the disturbing incident in the cockpit when a glitch on his ADIRU had caused him to lose data. He'd watched in disbelief as figures peeled away from the computer screen, the autopilot and autothrottle disconnected and most of his navigation display disappeared. He'd transferred to the back-up unit and crisis had been averted, but it continued to haunt him: the notion that such essential information could evaporate like clouds on a hot day.

An even greater fear was that of losing his family. Sasha was growing so rapidly and Corinne becoming so distant, he was almost superfluous in their lives. He could kid himself, when flying towards the midnight sun, or trying out a new sushi joint in Tokyo or simply enjoying the camaraderie of the mess room, that all was well. But on ground leave the day was a void. Hence the jogging, the gym, and what Corinne called his utterly pointless decision to uproot the privet hedge at the bottom of the garden and build a dry stone wall. He had got satisfaction from selecting and arranging his stones, conquering the challenges of weight and volume, stress and balance. He didn't allow himself to consider the possibility that, if family life disintegrated, the house, garden and new stone wall would have to be put up for sale.

He was tying his shoelaces when the phone trilled again. This time he could tell it was coming from inside the locker, which meant he had to fumble for a coin to open it. The phone was at the back, where it must have fallen from the pocket of his jacket. Both missed calls were from Corinne. He rang her straight away.

She sounded flustered. 'Paul? Why didn't you answer before?'

'I was in the shower. I told you I was going to the gym.'

'You said you were going to pick up Sash.'

'She won't be landing yet.' He glanced at his watch. 'She'll scarcely have taken off.'

Corinne said on a note of high pique, 'She *hasn't* taken off.'

'You mean the flight's delayed?'

'I mean she hasn't got on the plane.'

'What?'

'She rang to say she's been invited to stay on for a few days. She wants you to get her onto another flight.'

'Jesus, Corinne! And you said yes?'

'She hadn't even left the city centre, she'd no chance of making the check-in. I'm as angry as you are, but there's not much I can do about it. She thinks planes are like buses – better actually – you just pick up another one. You and your perks.'

'You can't blame me for this. Anyway, I thought she wasn't happy there. She wanted to come home early.'

'That was two weeks ago, Paul. Things obviously improved. This was the first call I've had in days, which ought to have been a good sign.'

How on earth could you tell when a teenager's behaviour was typical or erratic? Sasha was like a yo-yo. 'Is she staying on with the Italian family then?'

'Well, no.' A little sigh of frustration. 'I asked to speak to the mother and Sash admitted she wasn't actually there. She was in the flat of some Englishwoman she's made friends with, lives in an area called Trastevere.'

'What Englishwoman?'

'Her name's Mrs Raven. A widow, apparently, but a long-term resident.'

Mitchell pictured an eccentric bag lady, feeding leftover spaghetti to stray cats; not an uncommon sight in Rome. Ministering to dumb animals would appeal to his soft-hearted daughter. 'Do we know anything about her? Did you talk to her?'

'Yes.'

'What did she sound like?'

'She sounded English. A bit posh. Otherwise normal.'

He swapped his phone to his other hand and hefted his backpack over his shoulder. 'I don't like it,' he said, banging out of the changing room and into the lobby.

'No,' agreed Corinne. 'I don't like it either.'

'Are you suggesting I should go out there and drag her back?'

'I think you need to get hold of her, find out what she's up to.'

A fellow gym member, waiting by the drinks machine for his can to descend, hailed Mitchell as he passed. Usually he'd have stopped for a chat, maybe got a drink for himself, but in this instance he charged through the swing doors and into the car park. 'I'm on my way home. I'll ring her as soon as I get in.'

'I won't be here,' said Corinne. 'I'm meeting Nadia. We have to go over some stats.'

'It's Saturday.'

'It's the best time for both of us.'

Nadia's PhD was on a subject similar to his wife's. Even so, he felt their meetings were far more frequent than strictly necessary. Suspicion burrowed beneath his skin like a maggot. He'd barely met Nadia but he knew she wasn't one of Corinne's closest friends. How could he not conclude that she was a front for someone else?

113

Five years ago, entering his house, particularly after a spell away, had been a joyful experience: Sasha, peachy, pre-pubescent, hair in a high ponytail, rolling on the carpet with the dog; Corinne, calm, capable, singing in her glorious husky voice as she turned the meat or drained the vegetables, responsive to his embrace. Today there was only the disembodied beeping of the burglar alarm, which he switched off.

He poured himself a beer and went up to Sasha's room, where the ghost of his little girl lingered. A medley of stuffed toys was lined up on her bed, some stained with spilt squash from childhood tea parties. The walls were patterned with horses' heads. The wallpaper had been a trial to match up and, though proud of his handiwork at the time, it looked especially incongruous now it was plastered with posters of Daniel Radcliffe and the Arctic Monkeys. The contents of the wardrobe, where a galaxy of high street labels spilled off their hangers, was the only other sign that this was the bedroom of a young woman.

He set his beer can on her desk, sat down on her bed, pulled out his phone and dialled her Italian number.

She answered straight away but her voice was wary. 'Hi, Dad!'

'Your mother's given me some guff about you missing the flight this morning. What the hell do you think you're up to?'

'I'm sorry. Truly. It just seemed too good an opportunity to pass up.'

'What did?'

She was instantly defensive. 'My German friends, you know, I already told you about them loads? They've invited me to go with them to the beach and it's not like I've had a proper holiday this summer. I took all those GCSEs and then what? I go off and do even more studying! It would be kind of nice to have a break.'

He hated coming over authoritarian and high-handed. He longed to indulge her, sweet sassy Sasha – and protect her too. 'As I remember, it was your choice to go to Rome.'

'Well, you always used to go on about how great it was!'

It was true he counted it as one of his favourite cities, although he hadn't flown that route for years.

'Plus you wouldn't allow me to do anything else. Anyhow, I've had an ace time. My Italian's really come on. I fancied a couple of days swimming in the sea. No big deal.'

His antennae were wired for duplicity, but she sounded plausible. And perhaps she had missed out compared to other classmates, with Ruby's glandular fever throwing a spanner into the works. 'So why on earth did you wait till the last minute to tell us? It would have been easier to rearrange your flight than sort out a fresh one.'

'Because we only decided at the last minute. We fixed it up yesterday. They're travelling by train, you see, so it's easy for them.'

A detail was nagging him. 'Hang on a second. We don't know anything about these German girls.'

'Yes, you do. Renate and Ilse?'

'But Corinne said you were staying with an Englishwoman.'

'That's for tonight, before we set off. So I thought maybe Thursday, if that's okay, for the flight? No sooner, really, and Gina said – '

'Who's Gina?'

'She's the woman who's putting me up. Honest, you'd like her.'

It was a coincidence, it had to be. How likely was it, after all, that she was still in Rome? 'This is the Mrs Raven your mother mentioned? Is she there? I'd like to speak to her.'

'Sorry, no,' said Sasha. Did he sense relief rather than regret? 'She's got a wedding.'

'She's getting married?'

'Duh! She's a photographer. It's her job. I can give you her number, but I don't think you should call her for a bit because she'll be, like, really busy. She's got two, one after the other. But Mum's already spoken to her, so it's cool.'

'Give me the number anyway,' said Mitchell, reaching into the jar on her desk for a pen. Not wanting to mark her school folders, neatly arranged by Corinne, he wrote it on the palm of his hand. 'I'll call you back when I've sorted something, but you ought to know that neither of us is too pleased about this. In fact we are seriously pissed off.'

'No worries, Dad,' said Sasha, too damn perkily, he thought. 'It'll be fine.'

When she'd hung up, he clenched and unclenched his fist half a dozen times. And each time it reappeared, Gina's number. The digits, unlike those on his ADIRU screen, wouldn't vanish until he washed his hands.

Anyone could be traced these days, through a search engine, Facebook or LinkedIn, though it wasn't the sort of thing he'd ever bothered to do. It would be easy enough to enter Gina's name to settle the issue, but he resisted the temptation. What would be the point? Their parting, all those years ago, had not gone well. He'd tried to be so delicate, so tactful, but perhaps he'd been kidding himself. Perhaps a tactful split was an oxymoron, and she wasn't the type to smooth anybody's path. Fortunately, the break-up had been made easier by the fact that they were living in different countries and the fact that Corinne, with her ready laugh and warm freckled arms, had been waiting for him.

But if it turned out this Gina Raven really was his former girlfriend another conundrum presented itself: was Sasha's meeting with her a totally random encounter? A trick of fate or engineering? For a while he sat on his daughter's bed, debating. Then he thought, what the hell, opened his palm to read the number again and punched it into his phone.

13

Sasha clicked her mobile shut. She decided to contact Ilse and Renate later, when she knew what she wanted to say to them. She felt lousy, not just because of lying to her parents, or because she'd had to throw herself on Gina's mercy, or because her head was throbbing so much – but because she was screwed, basically. She couldn't handle being gawped at, so she couldn't go out. And now she'd burnt her boats, she couldn't even go home.

While Gina had been out on her errands, she had lain on the sofa listening to the clock at Santa Maria marking every quarter hour. At each chime she had thought, there's time yet, I can make it. She'd had to go downstairs when the taxi arrived from Parioli. She was glad Signor Boletti wasn't accompanying her suitcase; he'd presumably found it convenient to believe the excuses she'd made to Katya. It would have been easy enough to climb into the cab and ask to be taken to the airport. And then the midday cannon boomed from the Gianicolo and she knew she was too late.

Gina had not been pleased to find her still ensconced. Sasha prepared herself for a scene but Gina, though tight-lipped, had rallied. She'd even vouched for her when she rang home, which was by far the most difficult step of the enterprise. Once she'd cleared everything with her mother, who was hard to deceive, laying it on for her father was a relative cinch.

Gina had breezed out again with her equipment, looking almost as if she might be one of the wedding guests, elegant in linen trousers and silk shirt, her hair tied back, her nails perfect. 'Attention to detail,' she'd snapped, when Sasha paid her an innocent compliment. 'And this time, while I'm gone, you'd really better think about what you're going to do.' Sasha couldn't respond with either a woeful or a meaningful look because half of her face was frozen and her good eye was red and raw from rubbing.

She mooched around the living room, lifting objects, photographs, the funny sculptures, and replacing them carefully. She switched the television on to a bright and squealing game show, then flicked through the channels in search of MTV, which was mainly what she'd watched at the Bolettis. She couldn't use her laptop because she didn't know Gina's wireless code. She pushed open the shutters to the terrace but the light dazzled her, so she retreated. Two matching wooden chests stood either side of the French windows. One was locked; the other opened onto a selection of clothes, mostly men's shirts, trousers and jumpers in expensive materials – cashmere, mohair, sea island cotton. She wondered why Gina was hanging on to them, whether for dressing up her portrait sitters, or because they had sentimental or financial value.

She was curious to see what Joe was doing. He had scarcely come out of the second bedroom. He'd used the bathroom once and Gina had gone in to talk to him and take him more painkillers. Sasha assumed, like herself, he'd been dozing on and off, but he couldn't stay in bed for ever. Besides, the spare room was also a study. It had a desk and a computer in it – a regular PC, nothing fancy – so as long as it wasn't protected with a password she'd be able to log on to Facebook.

She put her head cautiously around the door. Joe was propped, bare-chested, in a half-sitting, half-lying position against the pillows. He stirred awake as soon as she entered. The computer was in an alcove beyond the bed. '*Ciao*,' she said. '*Come stai?*'

'*Bene*,' he said, '*anche tu?*' You too? Their private joke.

She moved further into the room. 'Gina's gone out to work. Can I get you anything?'

'*Acqua, per favore.*'

Behind the theatrical swoop of curtain that obscured the kitchen area, she filled a jug with ice and water and set it on a tray with two glasses. She carried the tray to a small chest beside the bed and passed him one of the glasses.

'You haven't washed that cut properly,' she said, pointing at a scrape on the span of his shoulder.

He twisted his neck to try to spot it. 'Where is? I cannot see.'

'And there's you with two functioning eyes! Here, let me.' She broke off a piece of cotton wool from a pad Gina had left nearby and dipped it in the water jug. Very gently she dabbed at the raw flesh. The impact of his fall must have driven the cobbles through his T-shirt, ripping fabric and skin. She'd noticed a blue holey rag on the bathroom floor.

'You have kind hands,' he said.

'My mother's a nurse. I suppose I must have learnt something from her.'

'I want to be doctor.'

'You do?' Was that possible? How would he do the training, take the exams? 'Aren't you too old for school?'

'Yes,' he sighed. 'When I arrive, I want to go to school, to study. Father Leone, he try to find me place but I must take tests.'

'To see what you've learnt already, you mean?'

'No. Bones. Teeth. For my age.'

'What the fuck!'

'Leone, he write many letters, for me and the others, but we wait long time and now is too late.'

'There must be another way,' Sasha said. 'These days, it's easy to be a mature student – like my mum. She's going to become Dr Mitchell, though that's philosophy not medicine.

Me, I wanted to be a vet, but it's really competitive and you have to do all science A levels to have the best chance and my Chemistry's crap. So I'm planning to do Biology, Geography and French, plus Italian maybe, that's why I came here…' Why was she nattering like this when he wouldn't be able to follow her, when most of the time they exchanged simple sentences in a mixture of halting English and Italian? Probably she was nervous because he was staring so steadily at her awful hideous, swollen face.

'Don't,' she said.

'*Cosa?*'

'Don't look at me.'

'*Perché?*'

'Because I look a fright. Much worse than you.'

'*Non è vero,*' he said, but he dropped his glance to his chest and began counting the bruises.

'You missed one,' said Sasha. 'There.' Her fingers brushed the side of his ribs. He seized her hand. 'Sorry,' she said. 'Did I hurt you?' But he was spinning the silver bangle on her wrist so it caught the light. She was afraid it might have dented in her fall, but although the silver was scuffed the marks could be polished away. 'Pretty, isn't it; it was a post-exam present.' She really must stop talking about bloody exams, when Joe'd had no chance of taking any. His own wrist, she saw, was almost as slender as hers; she would have offered to let him try it on, but his hand was already moving up her arm, pointing now at a graze below her collarbone.

'*Anche tu,*' he said.

The graze ran under the strap of her vest and it seemed perfectly natural that he should slide it away for closer examination. And perfectly natural that the other strap should slide off too and the vest wind up around her waist so she was sitting in front of him in only her bra. And what was perfectly amazing was that she didn't feel the least self-conscious. What was the point of being ashamed of her figure when her face already looked like the back end of a bus? Joe was the only person in the world she could countenance right now; the only person she could allow to get this close. So she helped him unfasten her bra and her skirt, and crawled into the bed alongside him.

They started to caress each other, trying to avoid any wounds or abrasions. It was like the game Operation, which she'd played as a child, in which you had to remove a body's organs without setting off the alarm. At each accidental wince or tremor they would draw back, gasping, then giggle and begin again. Sasha's injuries were mostly to her face, but the touch of Joe's lips on her breast, her stomach, the inside of her thigh, seared. Her fingers skimmed his sternum, travelled lightly to his waist and buttocks, ventured towards his groin, the parts of him that were not damaged. She recalled, two weeks ago, her first sight of his lithe nakedness. She could never have imagined becoming so dangerously intimate.

'Hang on a sec,' she said eventually, hopping out of bed to fetch her bag from the next room. A packet of condoms was zipped into the inside pocket. They'd been secreted there ever since she and Ruby had first formulated their plans for Italy, when they'd anticipated cruising the clubs and bars and pulling as a pair. When they'd had high hopes.

She released a condom from its foil wrapper and passed it to Joe to put on while she wriggled out of her knickers. They lay on their sides facing each other because it was the only way to be comfortable. Although he was trying to be tender, she could sense his impatience and did her best to guide his urgent thrusts. She braced herself for the shock of fresh pain, but so many other parts of her were aching and sore she wasn't aware of any; only of excitement and the rich warm substance of this boy inside her.

His movements began to increase in speed and rhythm. She sneaked a look at his face; his eyes were closed, his lips were parted, his breathing fast. She drew up her leg and hooked it over his hip, tensing her thigh muscles, feeling the satisfaction of the deep connection between them. Then he bucked and groaned, she assumed with pleasure, and for a few moments they both lay completely still. He withdrew from her with caution and she could feel the heat that had built between their bodies slowly fade. He rested his hand low on her abdomen. '*Non ti fatto male?*'

'No, it didn't hurt at all.'

His eyes were open now, looking at her searchingly. '*Ti voglio bene*, Sasha,' he said.

She wanted to squeeze the breath out of him, but such an embrace would be far too painful so she contented herself with stroking his face. 'Me too.'

He raised himself a little and brushed his lips against her ear. '*Grazie.*'

She couldn't smile properly but one side of her mouth curved with happiness. 'Thank you too, Joe.'

Gina had had a long day. After her back-to-back assignments, she'd gone to the studio to upload the photographs and check she was satisfied – not a cliché among them. The in-box of her phone was jammed with messages she'd ignored: details of times and meeting places if she wanted to go out that evening. She didn't. She wanted to go home and lie in the bath with a drink and empty her head of clutter. She couldn't. The children, as she thought of them, would be occupying her precious space. She could get Sami to come and take Joe off her hands. What she was to do with the girl, she'd no idea.

She didn't know whether they'd be hungry, but she called into the *alimentari* because she needed something to eat herself. She seized a pack of linguine and a tin of *vongole* – there would have been juicy fresh clams in the market, but she was far too late for that. 'Meagre rations again,' she explained to Signora Bedini. Really it was sheer laziness and a reaction, possibly, to the dainty jewel-like canapés at the wedding reception. She'd never pretended to be much of a cook.

The apartment was oddly quiet when she got in. She looked out onto the terrace, thinking her invalids might be enjoying the fine evening – healing in the fresh air – but it was empty, as was the living room. She noticed Sasha's bag was gone from the floor by the sofa and, having missed her suitcase under the hall console, supposed the girl had already left. She was glad to be relieved of the responsibility but puzzled too; it didn't seem in character.

Then she opened the door to the spare room and found them both spreadeagled, partially covered with a rumpled white sheet, sleeping. The picture they created trumped her indignation; she couldn't resist. Quietly, soft-footed, she took out her camera and began to click the shutter. The north light was perfect. The images were stunning: these battered, spent bodies, the angles of their youthful limbs, the fall of light on the folds of the bedlinen, the setting that veered between tawdry and romantic. Sensational.

Sasha stirred, opened her eye. 'Did you just take my photograph?'

Gina sat back on her haunches. 'Did you just sleep with Joe?'

'Is it any of your business?'

'I think if it happened in my house, yes, it probably is.'

Sasha flushed and tried to cover herself. Joe was quickly awake. 'What the hell did I tell you?' Gina raged at him. 'She's too young.'

'It wasn't his fault,' said Sasha. 'Anyway, we didn't do anything. Honest. We were a bit lonely and looking after each other.'

'Like I'm going to believe that!'

'Please don't shout. Please don't be angry.'

The child was so woeful with her distorted, discoloured face, her plaintive voice. Gina decided to dismiss the possible repercussions, decided it was preferable not to know the truth. If she'd made more noise coming home, they might have been alert to discovery, found time to disentangle. She couldn't forget what she'd seen: after all, she'd captured the evidence and was looking forward to examining it. But it showed the aftermath, not the act, and part of its power would reside in the anonymity of the figures.

'I think you both better get dressed.'

Realising that no one was going to move, exposing themselves, while she was in the room, she added, 'Now, I'm starving so I'm going to make a quick meal of *linguine alle vongole*. Only tinned, I'm afraid. The *vongole*, I mean, but they're not bad. D'you want some?'

Sasha nodded doubtfully. Joe reached for his jeans, some fresh rips in the knee. His top, Gina remembered, was ruined, unwearable. She would have to find him something of Felix's, from her standby selection. He'd had some beautiful possessions but she wasn't a hoarder; she only hung onto objects of value because she never knew when she might need to cash them in.

She left them to it and set a pan of water to boil, poured a glass of white wine, chopped cloves of garlic. She opened the tin and up-ended the clams; the small jellied blobs hit the smoking olive oil with a hiss. She threw her pasta into the pot and the wine into the clams, stirring with unnecessary vigour.

Sasha and Joe shambled out of the bedroom, more or less dressed. 'Can I do anything?' said Sasha. 'I'd really like to help.'

'Help! What you need is a big placard round your neck that reads "Hindrance". Just sit yourself down somewhere out of my way.' She noticed their hands creeping together for reassurance and jerking apart when she banged three dishes down on the table. She drained the pasta, mixed it with the clam sauce and set the large bowl in front of them.

'What are those things?' asked Sasha.

'*Vongole*. I hope you're not one of those teenagers who lives off McDonalds and won't eat anything else?'

'No... not at all.'

'And you're not allergic to shellfish?'

'No.'

'Well, you'll be fine then. Tuck in.'

Perhaps Sasha sensed that if she didn't eat her hostess's indifferent cuisine, Gina's tolerance would wane further. She said, 'It would be brill if I could stay here tonight. I'm just waiting to hear from my dad about my return flight and then I'll clear out and hook up with Renate and Ilse. They know what happened so I won't have to do any explaining to them.'

The girl's skin was stretched purple and shiny across her cheekbone. Not the best advertisement, Gina had to admit, for a Roman holiday. 'I suppose what you want,' she said, 'is for me to boot Joe out so you can take over Felix's room?'

Sasha looked nonplussed. 'Felix?' She was twisting linguine around the prongs of her fork, but the strands kept sliding off.

Joe was shovelling food into his mouth as if it had been a long time since his last meal. '*Devo andare*,' he said. 'I go.'

'Yes,' agreed Gina. 'You must.' She might have to make an exception for Sasha Mitchell but there was no way Joe could stay another night. Such a precedent would be risky and Father Leone was already suspicious of her relationship with the lost boys. She knew he distrusted her motives. 'It's actually the nicer room,' she went on, 'but I'd been in mine for so long, from when I was his lodger, that I never got around to moving out.'

'His lodger? You mean he was your landlord, like Signor Boletti?'

'No, not at all like Boletti. Felix had a tenancy. He believed in spending his money on art, not property.'

Sasha had hidden some of the clams under a wodge of stuck-together pasta. She put her fork down carefully. 'I'm sorry. I thought it was, like, a spare room or a study...'

'Yes, that's why there's a desk: he taught at the university. Now it's my study too.'

'But weren't you married to him? I mean...' She was all the colours of the rainbow, blushing through her freckles. 'Obviously I don't know anything about him, but...'

125

'No reason why you should. Only, as it happens, it wasn't that kind of a marriage.'

'Oh, I didn't realise…' She didn't give up, this girl, she had the curiosity of youth. '…I thought there was only one kind of marriage. Apart from civil partnerships of course. But they're same sex, aren't they, and –'

'Darling,' said Gina, 'You're going to find there's a lot you don't know about yet.'

PART TWO

THE YEARS BEFORE

14

Five Years Earlier: 2005

The plastic telephone cord was twisted twice around Gina's arm. Her head was tipped sideways at an awkward angle, trapping the old-fashioned receiver between shoulder and ear. In her left hand she held a pot of nail varnish; with her right she was painting her toenails a deep dramatic blackcurrant. She thought, if she had an activity to focus on, she could remain detached; she wouldn't experience the sense of hurtling headlong into pointless confrontation. In Rome it was seven thirty in the morning, already warm as a caress. In Santiago, she knew it would be late, but Phoebe had always been a night owl.

'A wedding?' Her voice floated astonishingly clear and girlish across the thousands of miles that separated them. 'You mean, yours?'

Gina was almost certain she could hear the ice cubes cracking in her mother's glass: testimony either to the quality of satellite communication or of Phoebe's determination never to be further than six inches from a drink.

'Yes.'

'Oh darling, how marvellous!' Phoebe was of the generation who believed spinsterhood to be a curse rather than a pleasure – which was why she had collected three husbands.

'I'm afraid this isn't an invitation.'

'Oh, but why shouldn't I come? I haven't been to Europe for years.'

'It's for information only.'

'Go on then, tell me about him.'

'You won't like what you hear.'

'I see…' The wheedling tone pulled itself together, became waspish. 'You're not getting mixed up in anything foolish, are you? It's not that old boyfriend of yours who nearly went to prison, is it? Gun-running or drugs or something.'

'Black market cigarettes, actually.' As if Phoebe cared; as if, dancing from one sugar daddy to another she'd given a rat's arse what Gina got up to. Gina had never come first in her mother's life. 'Of course it isn't him.'

The ice cubes clinked together. 'So who is he?'

'His name's Felix Raven.'

'Felix and Eugenie! What a splendid combination. I've not met him, have I?'

Gina spoke to her mother about twice a year, rarely saw her more than twice a decade. 'It's possible. We've been friends a long time.'

'Oh, you know that's quite common,' said Phoebe. 'I've seen it a lot. People who've known each other for ages, or childhood sweethearts who've diverged and met up again. They realise in middle-age how much they've got in common, how nice it would be to spend the rest of their lives together. A second chance doesn't have to mean second best.'

Gina's hand was shaking, smudging the varnish. She reached for a wad of cotton wool to wipe it off and start again. Knowing already that her marriage would be short, this happy-ever-after talk was excruciating. She couldn't help snapping, 'We are not sweethearts. It's not a romance, okay? It's convenience.'

'Convenience?'

'You've already reminded me how old I am, and he's a good deal older. Perhaps when you get to thirty-nine you stop looking for love.'

In fact Gina relished the thrill of a new relationship, never knowing when it might arrive and soar into flight. She sometimes wondered if she was addicted to the first flush: the glorious beginning that could go to your head and make up for all the misery that came later. None of this, however, was anything to do with Felix.

'I'm not sure I understand. Do you mean it's to do with money? Because...'

Because you'd know about that, thought Gina grimly. Hunting down the money, shoring yourself up against troublesome inconveniences. Like a daughter. Aloud, she said, 'I don't expect you to understand. It's complicated. But I'm getting married this afternoon to my very old friend and I thought you should know.'

'Today! You didn't say it was today!'

'Didn't I? What difference does it make?'

'Well, I can't possibly come, can I?'

'It's a very low-key do. I can guarantee you won't be missing out on anything.'

Gina knew she never managed these infrequent conversations well and it was with relief that she restored the receiver to its cradle, cutting off her mother's protests and the faint chirruping of crickets in the South American night.

The shutters to the terrace were half open, beckoning, promising another glorious day. Gina wasn't usually up so early unless she had an assignment which required her to capture this particular fragile light. She had planned to spend the morning making preparations, but there wasn't much left to do. Later their friends would come to help Felix down the stairs and into Mario's cab. Then, slowly, very slowly, they'd mount the steps of the Campidoglio to the Sala Rossa to take their oath. They were going to have the wedding breakfast in Pierluigi's so she only needed to chill some champagne and perhaps buy some fruit. Although, as it happened, visitors kept bringing fruit. Torrents of grapes, figs, nectarines flowed over the shelves of the fridge.

She replaced the cap on the nail varnish and threw away the smeared pieces of cotton wool. Felix was sleeping. Barefoot, wearing a long baggy T-shirt, she edged around his bedroom door. He was covered up to his neck with a sheet woven from fine cotton lawn, its touch the most he could bear. A pair of embroidered Moroccan slippers lay on the floor at the end of the bed, neatly positioned for his feet – those long thin feet with the prominent ridge of bone rising to the ankle. On the pillow, his large, apparently disembodied, head with its high brow and imperious nose, resembled a bas-relief of a Roman emperor – Augustus perhaps. His eye sockets and cheeks were sunken shadows; she could make out the bones of his skull beneath the taut skin.

The empty slippers, his inert body, the thick sweet air of a sickroom, induced a crashing wave of grief. It disturbed Gina that the pain of loss was so acute, that she could be knocked breathless this way. He must have heard her enter the room – or perhaps he noticed the strong almond smell of nail polish overlaying those other smells of medication, disinfectant and decay. He opened his eyes but didn't move.

'Are you okay?' whispered Gina. 'Can I get you anything?' He smiled but didn't speak. 'Hey, I'm sorry. I shouldn't have woken you.'

He found his voice, lurking somewhere at the back of his throat. 'What time is it?'

'Eight o'clock.'

'What have you been up to?'

'Pretty disagreeable stuff actually. Phoning my mother. I'd left it to absolutely the last minute to tell her, but I don't know why the hell I bothered.'

'Ah, the dreaded Phoebe.'

'Do you want me to help you up?' She delved beneath the sheet, supporting his armpits, and gently raised him into a sitting position. She thumped the feather pillows one by one and bent him forward so she could mound them against the brass bedhead. Through his thin vest she could identify each vertebra: a row of knobs descending his spine like organ stops. He leant back against the pillows with a sigh.

'Breakfast?'

'Tempt me.'

'Peach and banana *frullata*?'

'I'm not really hungry yet.'

She patted his leg beneath the sheet and his lips compressed in a small grimace. 'I thought whoever gets here first could help you change into your suit, make sure the fit's okay.'

The white suit, collected yesterday from the cleaners', was hanging on the wardrobe door, glinting under its layer of polythene.

'The fit will be lousy.'

'I think you'll get away with it. Especially if you wear the fedora.'

'It's not a fedora. It's a panama.'

'That's what I meant. Anyway, you'll look classy.'

He smiled. 'And you, dear heart, how will you look?'

She twirled, thrust forward her pelvis, let her hands rest on her hips. 'Devastating, darling.' Gina was not planning to wear white. She had a short, tight, black silk dress which flattered her minimal curves. She liked the idea of breaking with tradition. Weddings were so over the top these days, she craved austerity. She blew invisible dust from the panama hat and returned it to its hook. She rummaged in the chest of drawers until she found a red silk handkerchief to adorn the pocket of the white suit; the crimson rosebud for the buttonhole was still wrapped in its damp cocoon. A heavy watch and a couple of rings lay nearby: Felix hadn't decided yet whether he would wear them, whether the watch might chafe and rattle like a manacle instead of a functional timepiece.

'Tell you what,' she said. 'I'll make the *frullata* anyway. You don't have to drink it but it's going to be so creamy and delicious you won't be able to resist.'

'I need to shave.'

'We've plenty of time.'

A sudden surge of activity from outside: the clatter of iron shutters rising, of awnings unfurled, the screech of a television advert, the buzz of a bell.

'Was that the door?'

Gina went out onto the terrace and hung over the railings. She had a foreshortened view of a man's hat and a bicycle. Should she pretend it was the postman? Or no one at all.

'Well?' called Felix faintly.

She came back inside. 'I think it's the Lion King. He seems to have his bike with him.'

'He can leave it downstairs.'

'I don't know what he's doing here. We agreed not to invite him.'

'Did we?'

'It's a civil ceremony. Secular guests only, we said. People who are on our side.'

'Leone's not our enemy.'

'Well, I know he's not yours.'

'Anyway, I didn't invite him. If you let him in I don't suppose he'll stay long.'

The priest wasn't a frequent visitor, although he had been calling more often in recent weeks, as Felix became confined to the apartment. In the beginning he'd been a shadowy person Gina only heard talk of. Two years before, when Felix first took on English classes for the asylum seekers, he always went to the crypt; he never brought anyone home. By degrees she'd noticed his wardrobe emptying, the clack of the empty hangers as his clothes disappeared. She pictured his linen jackets and cashmere jumpers on the younger fitter bodies of other men, who wouldn't take care of them – shrinking them in the wash or snagging them on nails – but she never said anything.

It was when Leone's name began to pepper Felix's anecdotes and observations, when there was evidence of his visits – a book on philosophy or a cake made by nuns – that she found her jealousy inexplicably mounting. Once, her return home had interrupted the two of them in passionate discourse that floundered at the sight of her into awkward silence. Leone had been wearing an open neck shirt – she could see the throb of his throat; his hand had been resting on Felix's knee. He'd left soon afterwards – sheepishly, in Gina's over-active imagination. Glancing into Felix's room she was sure she could see the sheets disarranged. She hadn't been able to keep her suspicions to herself.

'You're fucking him, aren't you?'

'For God's sake, Eugenie, he's a priest.'

Felix only used her full name when he was annoyed with her, but she didn't care. 'When did that ever stop them?'

'There are other kinds of relationship, you know. Besides, where am I going to find the energy?'

And that was the irony. Gina wouldn't have minded if Leone had been his sexual partner, but she was supposed to be Felix's soulmate, his closest companion. No one else. 'You're not even a Catholic.'

'Is that what's bothering you? Don't worry, he's not trying to convert me. We do talk about spiritual things, it's true, in a way you couldn't with a lay person. But mostly we discuss what's going to happen to those boys; there's a constant stream and he can't see the end of it.'

'That doesn't explain why he's around so much, like he's got a hold over you, persuading you to give all your stuff away.'

'You've got completely the wrong end of the stick. Have you ever thought about why he's stuck in that parish? Why he runs all those activities the Vatican doesn't really approve of, however Christian they might be? Because they're never going to advance him anyway. He blotted his copybook years ago. Like me, he wants to make his peace with God.'

She hated it when he became sanctimonious. Her Felix, long-time mentor and confidante, was refreshingly sharp and sceptical. 'Well, I can tell he doesn't think much of me.'

'You are so paranoid.'

'He thinks I'm bad for you,' Gina complained.

'Does anyone really give a monkey's, at this point in time, about what's good for me?'

She had left it at that. She didn't want to row with him; she didn't want him to see the shallow resentful side of her (although he knew it well enough) and Leone had continued to visit. They'd both agreed he wouldn't fit in with the other wedding guests (or be interested in attending), yet now here he was, ringing the bell for the second time, knowing they had to be at home.

Gina crossed into the hallway and pressed the intercom. She left the front door to the apartment ajar and went over to the kitchen counter. She packed coffee grounds into the basket of an espresso pot and set it stuttering on the hob. Then she chopped peaches and bananas into the goblet of a liquidiser and added a stream of milk to the churning fruit. As the *frullata* foamed and settled, the visitor pushed the door shut behind him.

The Lion King was wearing a grey suit; he took off his hat, ran his hand over his balding scalp, polished his glasses. Apart from his clerical collar, his appearance was unobtrusive, discreet: a low-grade functionary, someone who had no wish to stand out. His skirts, as Felix called them, turned him into a different person altogether, a man of power and charisma, but they were inconvenient on a bicycle.

He held out a small parcel. 'Forgive me for disturbing you so early,' he said. 'I've brought some more CDs for Felix. There's a recent recording of *Aida* from La Scala and...' When Gina

THE APARTMENT IN ROME

didn't take it from him, he put the packet down on top of the bookcase. 'How is he today?'

'Hard to tell, he's only just woken up. Not too bad, I think.'

'And how are you?'

'Me?'

'Yes.'

'Well, I'm on top of the world, aren't I? It's my wedding day. Or had you forgotten?'

'I hadn't forgotten.' He smiled, acknowledging their edgy relationship.

She couldn't resist baiting him. 'But you thought you'd make a last ditch appeal to my noble nature? Call a halt.'

'The Church regards marriage as a sacrament,' he said mildly.

Gina, suddenly aware the shirt she'd been sleeping in was ripped and stained, felt sluttish and dirty. 'Here,' she said, pouring a coffee and handing it to him. 'Take this.'

He poised the cup on his palm. 'I don't condemn…' he began.

She was already backing into her bedroom. 'I need to get my dressing-gown. I won't be a minute.'

When she returned in a pink silk wrap, brushing her hair loose from the band that had held it, he was roaming the walls – walls which had once displayed three pictures deep and a dozen across. The white spaces left behind were framed in a darker, dingier shade of emulsion.

'See how many he's sold off already! It's not like I'm his only beneficiary.' She filled a second cup and clasped it with both hands, looking down into the black swirl of the coffee. She thought about spiking it with a dose of grappa to make *caffè corretto*, but it was a little too early, even for her. 'And that closet in the hallway that used to be full, you know, of Armani, Versace, whatever, is practically empty.'

Father Leone observed, 'He's a very generous person.'

'Exactly! You've done well out of him too.' Gina's reflection bounced back at her from the priest's lenses. She couldn't make out his expression. There was no sound or movement from Felix's room. 'I'm not holding a gun to his head, you know. As if I cared about any of this *stuff*!'

'You will acquire it, however,' he reminded her. 'Also the lease of the apartment.'

'Are you blackmailing me, Father?'

He spread his hands – a common enough gesture, but unusually flamboyant for him.

Gina pressed the heel of her palm against her temple as if it were the only way to stop her head exploding. Then she said, 'He booked his plot last week, you know.'

He looked puzzled at the change of subject. 'I'm sorry?'

'The same day we went to choose my ring, which I paid for myself, by the way, with my own money. It's in the Protestant Cemetery, his plot I mean, along with Keats.' She sat on the worn velvet of the chaise longue, pulling up her legs so her chin was resting on her knees. 'Do you know what happened after his funeral?'

'Keats'?'

'Felix told me. Apparently he had to be buried before daybreak – that was the law for non-Catholics. Outside the city walls too. And then by the time his friend, Severn, got back to the lodgings they'd shared, the police were there. The police and his landlady. D'you know what they were doing? They were destroying everything Keats had ever touched. Bed linen, cushions, every bit of furniture. They were even scraping down the walls and taking out the windows. Because they thought consumption was contagious. They thought you could catch it by sitting on the same chair, playing the same instrument, drinking from the same glass. Severn was so angry he took his stick and smashed all the crockery to smithereens to save them the trouble.'

She sprang to her feet again, driven by her own restlessness. Her wrap billowed open in the movement; she pulled the tails of its belt together and knotted them tighter. Her fingers curled around the small pot of nail varnish that she'd dropped into one of its patch pockets. In a fit of frustration she raised her arm and flung it across the room. She was aiming at a blank patch of wall rather than Leone, but she nearly hit him all the same; her aim was lousy. There was a small tinkling sound.

The brief moment of satisfaction left her. 'Damn!' She foresaw the ineradicable trail of deep magenta splashed onto wall and rug. Nail varnish – what an idiotic choice. But the bottle hadn't broken. It had caught the edge of one of the remaining pictures, splintering the glass. As Gina watched, the rest of the glass shivered and fell out of the frame which slowly dropped off its hook and onto the trunk beneath.

In two strides, Father Leone was beside her, taking her hand between his. She held his gaze. 'It's possible, wouldn't you say, Father, for a bad person to do good things?'

'Who is this bad person?'

'Me. I'm talking about myself. I'm trying to explain that even if I'm the self-absorbed gold-digging all-round bad influence that you think I am, I can do the odd good deed without needing to be bullied or cajoled or made to feel guilty.'

'Gina…'

'I'm the opposite of you, that's all. As a good person, I mean, who did a bad thing.' She regretted the words as soon as she'd spoken them. It was an intrusion. She wasn't supposed to know about the priest's past; Felix shouldn't have told her.

A movement from the bedroom made them both turn. A shuffling in the doorway, a voice croaking: 'I was promised a *frullata*.'

His breakfast was still sitting in the liquidiser, a brown crust forming on its surface.

'We thought you'd gone back to sleep.'

He was leaning on a cane. His other arm was outstretched, the white suit flapping across it like a ghost. 'Something must have woken me. Morning, Father.'

'Good morning, Felix.'

'God, I'm sorry about this.' Gina waved at the shards of glass scattered on the floor. 'I'll sweep them up.'

'Oh,' he said, without much interest. 'The Twombly. You really should control your temper, darling. That could be your nest egg.'

'Yes, I know.' Carefully she rescued the precious drawing and stored it inside the trunk for safety.

Father Leone said, 'I came to bring you some music, Felix, and to give you my blessing. I have to leave now, but I wish you both well for today.' Turning to Gina, he said with a faint smile, 'It's not a question of good deeds or bad deeds. It's about forgiveness. Absolution. This is the problem for you non-Catholics. You have to learn to forgive yourselves.'

15

Two Years Earlier: 2003

Large black ants were scurrying through the cracks in the paving. Lanterns swinging between the potted shrubs caught their movements as they transported tiny morsels of food with a rhythm and dedication that was awe-inspiring. Felix had been watching them for some time, surprised to see them so active at night. They put him in mind of the myeloma cells twitching and dividing inside his bone marrow. Treatable, but incurable, he'd been told. Like the ants. They could be kept at bay with powder or insecticide, but they'd always come back.

He was waiting for Gina. They'd planned to arrive together, but she was working late at the studio and had urged him to go on ahead. She had been wearing him down – at first in regard to the flat, pointing out repeatedly that his second bedroom was unoccupied, that he was in need of TLC, that they could be good for each other. And then she'd insisted he set up this meeting with David Farnon. It was David who suggested they got together for a drink in the Club Salamander, which had sprung up in a converted warehouse in Ostiense.

Felix sat in the courtyard looking out for her; the ants at his feet, a canopy of starlight above his head, the ice melting in his drink. Below, in the belly of the club, the cellar vaults churned with music and sleek, barely dressed bodies. The upper levels – the lounge, the cocktail bar, the silvery circular tables in the courtyard – accommodated those who couldn't keep up with the frenetic pace of the dance floor.

A few years ago he would have sweltered with the rest of them. Now he felt distaste for the salty slick of sweat collecting between shoulder blades, the reek of crotch and underarm. His energy, his appetites, were reduced. His love of collecting had been a driving force but there was no magic in it any more. He could no longer go to a new exhibition and pick out the most likely success story. He could no longer find those rare and precious items that multiplied in value simply by sitting on his chiffonier. He'd lost his touch.

When he'd first come out to Rome as a young man he'd been full of enthusiasm, undeterred by having to start from scratch. An interest in metaphysical poetry and beautiful boys, a doctorate in the work of John Donne were his credentials. He'd begun by teaching English privately, then in institutions, until he finally acquired tenure at the university. Expatriate life agreed with him, enhanced his standing and gave allure to what could have seemed mere drudgery in England. And when both his parents had died, leaving him a small legacy, he'd been able to indulge his passions, now evaporated.

A man dressed in a collarless shirt and combat trousers brushed against his table. Pausing to steady himself, he smiled and raised his brows in query. Felix shook his head and turned away. He moved his chair further back into the shadows. Behind him came the rustle of glossy green leaves, the scent of blossom lightly disturbed. He took his phone out of his pocket and cradled it in his palm warily as if it might erupt. Gadget-loving Italians had more mobiles per head than any other nation, but he struggled to master the functions; he found texting particularly difficult. He scrolled through his contacts and rang Gina. 'Are you still coming?'

'Of course I am! There was just this *tiny* delay...'

'So why didn't you call me?' He couldn't help sounding petulant.

'Because I thought you'd be downstairs where there's no signal and you probably wouldn't hear anything anyway.'

'Look, I'm not in a club mood. I'm thinking of leaving.'

'But I'm on my way. Isn't David with you?'

People were flowing in and out of the various doorways. Music accompanied them fitfully. 'He's prowling around somewhere.'

'Then do hang on for me. Please.'

She gave him no chance to argue. Felix stared at his silent phone. Really, he was a dinosaur. One might think that part of the charm of Rome was being surrounded by ruins and relics far more ancient than oneself, but the locals – the real, living inhabitants – embraced modernity. In the English department, they were addicted to their computers. They admired Felix's fine calligraphy but they laughed at his adherence to books and print.

He tried not to think about the department, about the office, the desk and chair that were no longer his. The chair had started it all – suffering from lower back pain, he'd hoped to persuade Administration to provide one that was more ergonomic. Such a simple request, leading to blood tests and then diagnosis. His ability to teach wasn't impaired, but his need to take time off was deemed unfair on the students. Plenty of other aspects of university tuition were unfair on the students, who were fodder for an institution obliged to maintain its intake at all costs: insufficient resources and reading materials; over-crowded lecture theatres; ingrained nepotism, but these were troublesome to address. Easing out a foreign employee in poor health, whose original mentor had retired, was altogether simpler. When September came he found his name omitted from the timetable and staff lists, his classes taken over. The shape of his days – once he might have enjoyed the freedom to do nothing – imploded.

In private he clung to the idea that one day he might go back. In public he didn't mention it.

Some twenty minutes later Gina materialised. 'Why, darling, you're all alone! What happened to David?'

'Pickling himself at the bar.'

'What? Is that a good idea?'

'Somewhat inevitable, as you're over an hour late. I would have thought, if you ask me for a favour, the least you could do is turn up on time.'

'Don't be so priggish. I've arrived, haven't I? And I could really do with a drink.'

'Right then. Let's move.' He rose slowly, coughing a little, feeling the ache in his bones. Gina reached out to pat his back, her hand suspended. He straightened up and she slipped her arm through his in a fluid movement as if that was what she had planned all along.

On a stool at the far corner of the bar sat a man with startling white-blond hair and piercing blue eyes. From a distance he appeared youthful and languid; on closer view he was not as young as he looked. He was accompanied by a tall glass of bourbon on the rocks and a boy with a fuzz of hair as dark and velvety as moleskin. 'A recent acquisition,' murmured Felix. 'I'm not sure, to be honest, whether these are the best conditions for you to meet him.'

'Let's just see how it goes.'

David raised his glass as soon as he saw Felix approaching. 'I thought we'd laaaast you,' he proclaimed, the drink drawing out his vowels.

'I was waiting for my guest. And here she is.'

'Sooo, *this* is your new roommate?'

Felix winced a little. 'We've come to an arrangement,' he said. 'Of mutual convenience.'

'Absolutely,' agreed Gina.

David lifted her hand and affected to kiss it. 'Good evening, Empress.'

Felix noticed that she looked irritated. 'I think he means it as a compliment,' he said. 'Because the Empress Eugenie was famous for her dress sense; she was a fashion icon really.'

She withdrew her hand. 'Actually I hate the name Eugenie. Beaten only by Phoebe in the sick-making stakes. I think my mother was out for revenge. Please call me Gina.'

'Well then, *Gina*, what would you like to drink?'

'White wine, please.'

'Felix?'

'I'll have another whisky sour.'

David relayed the order to the bartender and squeezed his companion's slender thigh. He'd introduced him so perfunctorily neither Felix nor Gina caught his name. When the drinks were poured he didn't suggest moving to another table, so Gina perched on a stool and Felix leaned against the marble counter. He preferred to stand. Brass fans like propellers stirred the air above their heads; the walls were painted in the deep moody colours of Rothko abstracts: aubergine, mulberry and plum. Their reflections were distorted in the mirror behind the banks of bottles. The light was dim.

After an awkward pause, Gina said with a wide red-lipped smile, 'I've heard that you're opening a gallery.'

David swallowed his bourbon; he moved his hand further up his companion's leg. 'Well, if you're gonna have a dream...' he said, and hummed a few bars from *South Pacific*.

Gina looked disappointed. 'Is it only a dream? I thought...'

'What?'

'Well, um... that if you'd got to the stage of considering work to exhibit, you might be interested in seeing some of mine.'

'You're an artist?' mused David in a tone that might have been ironic.

'An artist-photographer, yes.' When he made no response she began another tack. 'Felix has such an amazing collection, don't you think?'

'Collection's too grand a word for it,' Felix protested, though he was proud of his eye. There was kudos in being a talent-spotter. 'You make me sound like a Guggenheim.'

'Of course you've had some lucky breaks.'

'Skill, darling. The trick is to get in at the beginning, before anyone else cottons on. I can't afford not to buy early. Then, if a work becomes so popular it destroys your pleasure in it, you can sell at a profit and move on to something new. Also, I happen to believe in being a patron to the living. Money's no good to the deceased.'

'Hey man,' said David. 'You ever want to sell your Cy Twombly you let me know.'

Gina put her head on one side as if conjuring up the drawing. 'I don't really get it. I can't see beyond the squiggles.'

'Because you've yet to look at it thoroughly,' Felix said. 'That's why Twombly's work is so interesting, there's so much depth to it. He doesn't deal in superficial images. If you think about it, letters, hieroglyphs, marks on paper – they all require interpretation. You can't just give them a quick once-over – although the general effect is superbly melancholic.' He added, 'I know it's only a small sketch on paper but one doesn't look a gift horse in the mouth.'

David became more alert. 'A gift? Not from the artist?'

'No, from a generous old friend. No longer with us. He knew I was an admirer.'

'However you came by it,' said David, 'it's your hedge against the world. Isn't art sublime! Nothing compares. Still, I'm aiming to be more than a collector. I plan to be a king-maker.'

Gina broke in. 'So maybe you *would* like to see some of my stuff? Can I give you my card?'

He snatched it from her, borrowed Felix's pen, and scrawled 'Empress' across the back.

'The way I see it,' said Felix, wondering how long it would take him to catch up with David and stop feeling so damn sober, 'I'm just a curator anyway. A temporary

THE APARTMENT IN ROME

guardian. Good art should have – will have – a life of its own, beyond me.'

A gaggle of young men had collected at the bar. They were all wearing low-slung trousers, vests clinging to their pectorals and belts like charm bracelets festooned with keys, lighters, phones and fobs. They snapped their fingers, calling for drinks, a sheen of moisture on their upper lips, their cheekbones, the bulging curves of their muscles. David's companion gazed at them through his feathery lashes. He drew a cigarette from the pack of Marlboro Lights lying between their glasses on the bar, rolling it, tapping it and sniffing it, as if he were a connoisseur of the finest Cuban cigars. David adjusted the position of his stool to form a protective barrier against the crush. 'If you're feeling kinda low, Felix,' he said, 'my suggestion to you is to try one of these.'

'One of what?'

He ruffled the soft pelt on the youth's scalp. 'My Iranian.' He bared his white, evenly capped teeth, a tribute to advanced American dentistry. The Iranian didn't seem to want to expose his own in comparison. He inserted the Marlboro, unlit, into his mouth and tugged at the row of small hoops that ringed the outer rim of his ear

'Does he understand anything you're saying?'

'Not if it's in English. He's got a bit of Italian though. *E un culo magnifico.*' The boy smiled, leaning forward to reach for his cigarette lighter in a movement which lifted his magnificent arse from his seat. 'You know,' David carried on, 'that could be a neat number for you if you're at a loose end. Teaching a little English could get you a long way. Know what I'm saying?'

'English Lit,' said Felix. 'Not, what-is-way-to-station-please.'

'So sooorry, *professore.*'

Gina cut in unexpectedly. 'Don't be such a snob, Felix. You've done it before and you're very good at it.'

'Gratitude,' said David, 'will be your reward.' He leant forward and planted a lascivious kiss on the Iranian's lips.

Gina bent to Felix's ear. 'He's completely trashed. This isn't going to get us anywhere.'

He shrugged. 'I said you'd be better off visiting him at the gallery.'

'But you also told me he hasn't found the right premises.'

'Well, yes.'

'So what was I supposed to do?'

'Well, you could have tried a little patience,' Felix pointed out. 'A few months further down the line, I could have asked him over to dinner. By then he might have got around to signing a lease and you could have shown him your portfolio. Or you could have got here on time tonight.'

'I knew this was coming! I knew it would somehow end up being all because of me that your Yankee Doodle Dandy with more money than wit was out of his head.'

'Darling, he's not out of his head and there's nothing wrong with his hearing. Try and keep your voice down.'

David's face set like a sulky child's, with the lower lip pushed out. Then he glimpsed Felix's reflection in the mirror, and winked. 'I don't generally like women who come over strong,' he said. 'You want me to make an exception?'

Gina put down her glass. She shook her head at the suggestion of a refill. 'I guess there's no point in staying,' she said. 'I've blown it, haven't I?'

'So what's new?'

'You don't want to come home with me?'

Felix felt entitled to be annoyed. 'Probably not.'

David swayed a little, dropped his foot onto the floor to steady himself. 'You run along there, Empress,' he said dismissively. 'We'll look after your friend. Come on back downstairs, Felix, and we'll see what we can find for you.'

This was not a good idea. After a handful of abortive encounters and several more drinks he recognised that his evening was disintegrating. David and his protégé were still dancing, but Felix felt a sudden urge for solitude. Without saying good-bye, he left the Salamander, staggering a little as he turned the corner away from the club. Behind him were vibrant lights and throbbing music; ahead lay shadows. He'd intended to call up a taxi – Gina had programmed the number for him – but he felt the need, initially, for a walk in fresh air.

It only takes one wrong turning for a less-than-sober person to become disorientated. Felix appeared to be walking through a channel with high oppressive walls on either side and no clues as to where he might end up. A car swished past him, its headlights flashed and dipped from view. The stars blurred alarmingly when he looked up at them; the moon sagged, yellow and heavy, as if exhausted. He decided to concentrate on his feet, on putting one shoe in front of the other, keeping parallel to the wall. Eventually, this corridor would open into a piazza or turn into a junction of some sort. He'd be able to see a sign or a landmark, chart his way back to civilisation.

This was not the first time Felix had wandered through the city at night. One never knew who one might meet when the clubs disgorged. A brisk unbuttoning, a meaty cock, a brief but satisfying fumble in the arch of a doorway – eye contact avoided – offered a particular pleasure of its own. He enjoyed the attention of the crowd when he was holding forth, but he was a solitary hunter. As a rule, being alone didn't frighten him. He'd recovered from the occasional mugging and worn his scars with pride. But being ill brings with it a new kind of vulnerability.

Finally the long street segued into another. Shabby shops had their iron shutters pulled down; the apartments above showed no light at their windows, played no music, everyone was sleeping. A barren swathe of scrubland occupied the corner. Perhaps by day it was a park or a playground; he could only make out a few ungainly shapes. Another high wall – maybe a school or a cemetery – was sprayed with an unreadable scrawl; he felt there was something menacing in the arrangement of loops and jagged shapes.

He pulled his phone out of his pocket but his fingers were

sweaty and it slipped from his grasp, clattering onto the narrow pavement. As he stooped for it, he heard footsteps. He hoped, naturally, that they belonged to somebody pleasant and helpful, someone who could direct him to the nearest cab rank. He glanced behind him. All he could see was a dark form – or maybe two – probably male, probably younger and taller and stronger than he was. Should he stop, let them accost him? They'd be after his wallet, money and credit cards. No, dammit, they could make do with the mobile – he hated the bloody thing anyway.

Leaving it for them, he began to run. The footsteps wavered and halted, but they must have been after greater booty. Within seconds they were pursuing him again, gaining on him. He didn't feel a blow, but was aware of the ground rising to meet him, of crashing all at once into black oblivion.

Gina was in bed when the call woke her. She groped for her phone and answered it in an automatic reflex. '*Pronto*.'

'Leone,' said the stranger.

Befuddled, she began to envisage the arid desert of spaghetti westerns. With the shutters closed, the room around her – which she had not yet got used to – was a dark mysterious space filled with murky shapes. 'What time is it?'

'I'm sorry to disturb you,' he said. 'I have called because yours was the last number dialled.'

'The last number dialled,' she repeated. 'Oh my God, Felix! Has something happened to him?' It was rare for her to be the first to leave a social occasion. Usually Felix would be dragging her off the dance floor or away from the bar, telling her she'd had enough. And she would be disagreeing.

'He has had a fall.'

'A fall? That could be really bad for him! Dangerous, I mean. How is he? Has he broken anything?'

'We think not. We think, if so, he would be in more pain. Presently he is sleeping.'

'Where? Where are you?'

'You are his wife?' said Leone.

If she had been less worried, she might have laughed. 'We're just good friends. He isn't married,' she added, remembering the demonstrations Felix had attended out of a sense of duty to the cause – though it was hard to foresee a prospect for civil partnerships in Italy. 'Who are you?'

'I am Father Leone from the Madonna of All Mercy. Your friend lost his way and stumbled upon us.'

A priest. God almighty. 'What do you want me to do?'

'You could take him to the hospital.'

Felix hated hospitals, especially since he had become so dependent on the treatment they offered. Her job, as she saw it, was not to let him wallow. 'You'd better give me your address and then I'll come and fetch him.'

Dawn was breaking when she arrived at the crypt and hammered on the door to be let in. Felix was wrapped in a blanket on a spindle-backed chair, looking shamefaced. And grey.

'I don't know how you managed to get yourself into such a state,' she greeted him.

'Isn't that what I always say about you?'

She rested her hand on his arm. 'I'll have to get you checked out.'

'Just as well I've been taking the steroids,' he muttered. 'Could have been worse.'

'How did it happen anyway?'

'What, that I drank too much? Or got lost? You shouldn't have abandoned me, you know.'

'It was a disaster, wasn't it? Is he always like that, the Farnon guy?'

'Not really. He had a row with his partner last month and they're temporarily estranged. So he's a bit derailed, showing off his wild side.'

'No kidding?' She peered at bodies unfurling from thin foam mattresses. The priest was moving among them, his rosary clanking at his thigh. 'What is this place?'

'Some sort of haven for lost souls,' he said. 'Extraordinary, really, that I should stumble upon it. But I did, literally.'

'How do you mean?'

'I fell down the steps. I tripped over because I was running away from these fellows I thought were muggers. In point of fact they were trying to return my phone – I'd dropped it, you see. They raised me up like bloody Lazarus and brought me in here – though at the time I was convinced I'd arrived at the gates of hell. This creature in long black robes came gliding forward. The Grim Reaper, I was sure of it. In fact it was my saviour, Father Leone, who has patched me up.' He waved towards the priest and flinched. 'I'll have to find some way of thanking him.'

Gina pushed back the blanket and rolled up his sleeve. 'You're damn lucky your bones haven't snapped, you're covered in bruises. We need to get them seen to.'

His voice dropped. 'All I really want to do is sleep. You know how important it is for me to be in my own bed these days.'

She laced her fingers in his. 'Come on then. Never mind the priest; we can come back later. Didn't I always promise I'd take good care of you? Repay you for what you did for me?'

'When in particular?'

There were countless times, it was true, in the past decade, when Felix had come to her aid. 'Right at the beginning, remember? The clinic...'

'Darling, it was the indefatigable Vicki who rescued you in your darkest hour; she hardly let me near you.'

'I meant before, that day on the beach.'

16

Ten Years Earlier: June 1993

G ina and Felix had struck a chord almost from their first meeting, although to other people the relationship appeared perverse. Her flatmate, Vicki, who was inclined to be bossy, too ready with her advice and opinions, declared, 'I can't understand why you're hanging around so much with that Felix Raven. He's far too old for you.'

'Perhaps I like older men.'

'And you yourself call him the Raven Queen!'

'He's promised to advance my education,' said Gina. 'He says my own fell short. And I don't want to be thought an airhead because of the work I do. Plus he's good fun, and that's what I need right now.'

Their friendship was cemented by the common strand of abandonment. Gina's lover, Mitch, had called an end to three years of globe-trotting, of wild weekends in far-off cities which they never saw because they scarcely left their hotel bedroom. The previous year he had helped her move down from Milan to Rome and hinted that they should be looking for a place together. The sudden break-up had sent her reeling, she was so unprepared for it – although she'd pretended quite the opposite.

In Felix's case, his companion Maurizio, a charming boyish Sicilian, had returned to his roots. He'd gone home for his father's funeral and announced he would not be coming back. 'Under Mamma's thumb,' sighed Felix. 'I should have guessed.'

One sunny June morning he called on Gina, hooting outside in his small red Lancia that would not, after all, be driving to Siracusa for the summer. She'd gone out the night before with a group of people she didn't know very well. They had hopped through a string of noisy bars, finding none satisfactory; she had developed a splitting headache. She leaned out of her window; he leaned out of his.

'Let's go for an adventure,' he said.

'What, now?'

'*Carpe diem!*'

'You'd better come up.'

Suitcases gaped open on her floor, some half-filled with clothes. Felix skirted round them. She'd closed her shutters again so the room was dim.

'It's a glorious day, you know.'

'Is it?'

'Absolutely. I'd planned to go bargain hunting in Porta Portese as distraction therapy. But then I thought, no, bugger the market. What's the point of haggling over more bric-a-brac that I don't need? Why not head for the beach?'

'The beach?'

'Sure. It will do you good – the tang of sea air.'

He hadn't mentioned the suitcases. He hadn't asked her how she was or why she had started a flurry of packing at two o'clock in the morning. She'd been tramping about in a torment of indecision with armfuls of clothes until collapsing in a heap at 4 a.m. She was never good-humoured after a rough night, but Felix knew that she rarely refused an invitation, even when her head was pounding. He'd argue she could catch up on her missed sleep, lying in the sun.

'How long will it take you to get ready?' he said. 'I'll go for a coffee, shall I? Wait for you outside.'

He hadn't given her any option. Still, maybe he was right: a change of air could be a real tonic. Cities were always claustrophobic in summer, whereas even a small sea like the Mediterranean appeared to promise infinity. Gina kicked the cases out of her way, prowling the room with far less delicacy than Felix as she sought towels, bikini, sandals, sun cream. She filled a large straw basket with everything she thought she might need, including paracetamol and indigestion tablets, and pulled an equally large straw hat onto her head. She suspected she looked like a holiday advertisement and was quite prepared to snap at Felix, should he mock, but all he said was, 'Not sure you're going to fit into my car, darling.'

The car was not air-conditioned. As they crawled towards Ostia with thousands of other Sunday sun-seekers, Felix's idea seemed less attractive, less spontaneous. His complexion darkened with annoyance when the engine over-heated in the traffic jam for the second time and he had to top up the radiator with expensive rations of mineral water. As he climbed back into the driver's seat, Gina exhaled a long sibilant whistle through her teeth.

'Christ, what's the matter now?'

His agitation might have amused her if she'd been feeling better. 'I was wondering,' she said, 'what is the point of being here?'

'Well then,' he said, 'perhaps you should have told me an hour back: Listen, Felix, you know you'd far prefer to go shopping for antique crystal than get your rocks off with a rentboy picked up at the seaside. Or you could have insisted we took the train. And don't give me that hangover nonsense – you always have a hangover. You know why you get so sick all the time?' Recently she had thrown up, spectacularly, over one of his Moroccan rugs. The dry cleaners had done their best, but the rug's colours had shifted into a different spectrum and it had to spend much of the day over the railings, soaking up the fresh air. 'You have a drink problem, that's why.'

'Fuck off. Who said anything about a hangover? Anyway, if we'd taken the train we'd have had miles to walk and it's too hot for walking. But what I was trying to say was, well, I'm thinking of leaving.'

'What, Rome?'

'Italy.'

'Why?'

She was feeding the brim of the hat through her hands, revolving it on her lap; the straw felt dry and brittle. 'I have to think of the future. I don't know what's going to happen to my career... I need to decide whether I should do something different altogether.'

'Don't I recollect an excited phone call? Weren't you, a few weeks ago, limbering up for the contract of a lifetime?'

'And was I completely trashed when I told you that?'

He changed into third gear, easing his foot off the clutch as the queue gathered speed. 'Jewellery, you said. Because you had the longest brass neck in the business.'

Gina put her hands around her throat and squeezed. 'Yeah, well, it'll probably never happen. And I was so looking forward to it. Flaunting my baubles in the Trevi Fountain like Anita Ekberg.'

He began to hum the Sinatra tune. Gritty gusts of hot air blew in through the windows along with blasts of music from competing car radios. A pair of drumsticks tapped vigorously on the membrane of her skull. She resisted the urge to scratch at a mosquito bite on her wrist – and to scream at Felix for dragging her out of bed. She said, 'I might go back to England. Or America.'

'America?'

'My mother's over there, remember.'

'I thought you couldn't stand your mother.'

'In particular I can't stand the man she's married to, Mountebank Monty. But I think they're splitting up.'

'Talking of splits… this is about Mitch, isn't it?'

'Bastard. He never checked, you know, to see how I was. Out of sight, out of mind. We used to have these long conversations at crazy hours because we were in different time zones. Now I'm dead meat.'

'You're nothing of the sort.' He took his right hand off the steering wheel and stroked her arm. 'Please don't go. I'd miss you if you left.' Then he swung onto the coast road, bordered with low-lying sand dunes, and pointed through the windscreen and the heat-haze. 'At last! Now to find somewhere to park.'

Along the beach, oiled bodies were laid out in rows like seals basking. A parade of muscular beauty wandered up and down the shoreline. Few swimmers were tempted into the water, opaque and murky beneath a glittering surface. Gina settled their belongings around the chairs and umbrella they had hired and lay back, topless. Felix set off to the bar for a couple of beers. He was wearing a loose cotton shirt with the collar turned up to protect his northern skin from the sun, and a very small pair of swimming trunks. Most of the other men wore even scantier versions; the sheer mass of tanned and toned buttocks cresting the sun-loungers was eye-watering.

Gina sat up again when he returned and took one of the proffered beers. They'd been opened by the bartender and Felix had carried them with such circumspection he hadn't spilled a drop.

'Thanks.' She swallowed a mouthful, then tucked the bottle in the shade of her basket.

Neither of them could see the other's eyes behind their sunglasses. In fact nearly everyone on the beach was masked by dark lenses – a covert tool of inspection and examination.

'Such a feast of flesh,' he said. 'Surely you can enjoy just looking?'

'Not as much as you, evidently.'

'I met Maurizio here, you know.'

'Oh God, did you?'

Two lean young men sauntered by, close enough to touch, their arms entwined, their profiles sharp against the light. One wore a gold crucifix, the other a silver. Maurizio had been a homespun unassuming type. It was hard to imagine him flirting in the manner of those on the beach.

'Perhaps some of us are destined for the single life,' Felix said, a trifle mournfully. 'Or perhaps we get exhausted by our mistakes. So much easier, don't you think, to divorce the two?'

'What two?'

'Sex and companionship.' He tipped some more beer down his throat.

'You've left out love,' said Gina, picking up her detective novel. The words danced on the white page, undermining her concentration.

He turned his head and looked along the rows of sun loungers as if searching for a familiar face. He moved his watch to admire the white strap mark it had left. He drank some more beer, wiping the neck of the bottle each time. He picked up the copy of *Vogue* Gina had brought and put it down again. He returned one or two bold stares with a faint lift of his chin. His long upper lip folded over his bottom one in a sly smile, giving him the look of a refined goat. 'It doesn't seem to me that you're in the mood for a chat,' he observed after a while.

'I guess not.'

'Are you feeling all right?'

'Touch and go, to be honest. But I've brought my medicine chest so I'll be fine.'

'I think I might take a walk along the shore. If you don't mind?'

'Of course not. You go along, bag yourself a hunky new set of cock and balls.'

'Will I look pathetic if I keep my shirt on?'

'Like you're afraid of exposing yourself, you mean? Yes, you will.'

Reluctantly he took it off and she slathered high protection suncream across his neck and back. She gave him a little push to send him on his way and then closed her book again. She was no more in the mood for reading than she was for gazing at nearly naked men. So many people were passing up and down the shore that the sea itself could only be glimpsed in patches. A couple of North Africans in vivid kaftans were walking at the edge of the water. They were strung with ropes of carved wooden beads, leather belts and sprays of exotic plumage. They stood out among the sunbathers and were, for the most part, completely ignored as they tried to access one private *stabilimento* after another. A handful of young men were playing a ball game choreographed to display their physique rather than service the ball. There were no children squabbling, wheedling or wailing, in sight. Gina closed her eyes.

'*Ciao, carina*.' A young pretty woman was perching on Felix's abandoned cushions.

Gina peered through her sunglasses. 'I'm with someone,' she said.

The woman, a girl really, with a bountiful mass of black hair, said, 'Yes, I saw him.' And it was all she needed to say, to point out that she knew perfectly well what kind of man Felix was, what kind of relationship he had with Gina.

The woman was small and evenly bronzed. She wore white sandals, four triangles of tight white bikini and white-rimmed sunglasses. These, she took off. She had tigerish eyes flecked with gold, matching the bangles that clinked on her arms and the chain fastened around her ankle. 'Stefania,' she said, holding out her hand so that Gina could not ignore it.

'I'm Gina.'

'I know.'

'You do?'

'We met before, a brief introduction only. You don't remember?'

'No, I'm sorry.'

'You're a model, I think?'

Gina couldn't rid herself of the suspicion that the woman was lying, that she'd simply seen her photograph somewhere. Somehow that was more palatable than total blacked-out memory loss. 'And you?' she said politely.

'I'm a swimming instructor.' She flexed her biceps so they rippled in her upper arms. 'There are too many people in this country who can't swim. So I have plenty of work.'

'That's great, Stefania, but actually – '

She interrupted. 'My friends call me Fani.'

'Really?'

The tiger eyes glinted. A pink tongue flickered across her lips. 'Really.'

Gina tried to wriggle into a better position and turned towards the sun.

'I think you will burn,' said Fani.

'Oh, I tan easily enough.' When she'd been at school in England, her classmates had envied the natural way she shaded to brown; she was never pasty. Here, though, among Romans who took the cultivation of colour so religiously, she lagged behind.

Fani picked up the bottle of suncream. 'Let me help you,' she said.

Gina didn't move. Her indigestion was getting worse, not better, and she wanted the woman to go away. She gave a sigh, which Fani misinterpreted. A stream of Ambre Solaire landed on her chest. She shot upright. 'Hey! What was that for?'

'You will burn,' Fani said again. A packet of menthol cigarettes was trapped against her hip by the cord of her bikini bottom. She offered one to Gina, who shook her head, and lit her own with the composure of someone who has no intention of moving.

'I had a late night,' said Gina. 'I was hoping to nap.'

Fani exhaled with unruffled assurance. 'It's dangerous to sleep in the sun, you know.'

'Look, I don't want to seem rude, but I honestly don't remember ever having met you...' Her voice rose irritably. 'Am I not speaking your language? What part of Go Away and Leave Me Alone do you not understand?'

Crinkles of worry clustered on Fani's forehead. 'Are you quite well?'

Gina clutched her book, thinking what a pity it was only a paperback and how much she would like to aim it at her tormentor's head, when a fist slammed into her stomach, cutting off her breath. The book fell to the ground; her mouth opened silently. Once more the fist crashed into her gut, winding her. She stared at the other woman as if she were holding her down under water, gripping the tops of her arms and kicking her mercilessly below the waist.

Fani gouged a small hole in the sand and buried her cigarette stub. Then she laid her hand lightly on the gentle swell of Gina's abdomen and said: 'It hurts here?' And Gina finally found sufficient air to scream. A few heads turned, but not many, because half the sounds on the beach were shrieks and bellows and catcalls and the sheer expanse of air and water absorbed them.

Felix, returning unrewarded from his stroll, had not recognised Gina's cry among so many others, but as he approached their pair of hired chairs and their blue-and-white beach umbrella, he noticed something odd in the way she was sitting: no longer a languorous siren, but splayed as if she'd been dropped from a height. Bending over her was a woman with a bush of black curly hair and strong sinewy legs like a gymnast.

Felix walked awkwardly in flip-flops. He needed to protect his feet from the searing heat of the sand, but he couldn't run in them. He could only lengthen his stride and focus on his target. Although it was after two and the sun had passed its climax, he'd been going to suggest they escaped it for lunch. A seafood risotto, a mixed salad and plenty of mineral water would be his choice; it was important not to dehydrate. He was not as fit as he should be, so when he reached the parasol he had to hold onto its pole for a few seconds to catch his breath. Then he said: 'What's going on?'

The bracelets on the woman's arms rattled, her sunglasses glared at the sky. 'You are her friend, I think?'

'Yes. What happened? Gina, are you all right?'

Gina lay back, her head resting at an angle, her body damp and crumpled as a used towel. 'Tell her to piss off,' she said in English.

'What?'

Before she could answer her limbs jackknifed again. Felix looked at the woman. 'Do we know you?'

Her manner was brusque, impatient. 'I am Stefania,' she said. 'Gina has become very ill.'

He knelt down beside her. Her face was alarmingly white, her eye sockets a dark purple. She winced when he touched her. 'I'll go to the bar and call a doctor.'

'It is Sunday,' said Stefania. 'Finding a doctor could take time.'

'Gina, do you think you could walk to the car?' He started to pick up the debris of their outing: books, magazines, fruit, bottles, towels, a large sun hat, packets of pills. He counted the empty foil cartridges. 'You always eat too late.'

'Not so,' said Stefania.

'Excuse me?'

'This cannot be indigestion, it's too severe.' Again she tried to probe and again Gina yelled. 'I think it's probably the appendix.'

Gina bit so hard on her bottom lip her teeth left their imprint.

'Are you a nurse?' Felix asked Stefania. 'Or medically qualified in any way?'

'No.' She folded her arms, pulled at her twisting curls. 'But we Italians are very experienced in *mal di stomaco*. Also, my cousin was sick like this, a few months ago. It was lucky he got to the clinic in time. If the appendix bursts the results are serious. You can get, what's it called, peritonitis.'

'I hate being ill,' muttered Gina.

'They gave him only a very small scar,' Fani said. 'Very discreet. He can still wear his preferred bathing suit.'

'She might need help getting to the car,' said Felix. 'Are you free for ten minutes?'

'*Certo.*'

'She'll have to get dressed first.'

Gina insisted on putting on her own T-shirt, wincing as she had to stretch her arms. She refused the shorts: saying she couldn't bear the restriction at her waist. Strong and sturdy, Fani supported her right-hand side; Felix, her left. 'It's all right, I can walk,' she said crossly. But she didn't disengage herself.

Felix had been obliged to park the car some distance away. He left Stefania and Gina sitting at the parched roadside verge while he went to fetch it. In the stifling heat the air shimmered, refracted like water. A slow stream of cars trawled past, searching for parking spaces or companionship. More than once a crop of male heads poked through open windows and called invitations to the two women. Fani responded with a choice array of insults; Gina dropped her head between her knees and retched.

Felix knew he was not much good in a crisis. When, in recent years, friends, ex-lovers and acquaintances had succumbed to the stealthy onslaught of Aids he had, he freely admitted, avoided dealing with 'the manky bits'. He'd written cheering missives, he'd sent thoughtful gifts, he'd telephoned. But he couldn't cope with the physical reality of sickness: the distortion of features, the wasted limbs, the distressing loss of bodily functions, the smell. He gagged in hospital corridors and recoiled from the sight of blood. He had been brought up to be fastidious by his elderly parents; he pulled on gloves to dispose of household rubbish; he was the most regular customer at the local laundry. He was relieved that, at this stage, Gina was merely a pale doubled-up version of her usual self – quieter if anything – she hadn't even vomited yet.

He got out of the car and came towards her. She was using Stefania as a mounting block, pushing down on her shoulders so she could stagger to her feet. Stefania, trim and unfazed in her immaculate white bikini, pulled open the passenger door and helped Gina into the seat. 'You must let me know how she is,' she said to Felix. 'I shall worry all the time she's lying on the table in the operating theatre. I shall worry that the surgeon holds his hand steady, that the cut will not be one millimetre longer than it needs... that she recovers well.'

Gina gave Felix an agonised look, as if to say: is this woman for real?

Felix said, 'Well, um, that's very thoughtful of you. Give me your number and I'll call you.' He leant past Gina and hunted in the glove box for pen and paper, among the neatly labelled cassette recordings of Monteverdi, William Byrd and Thomas Tallis. Gina sighed and squirmed away so that Fani's goodbye kiss met the clench of her jaw.

'Jesus!' said Felix, starting the engine. 'I know you're feeling rotten, but do you have to be so ungrateful?'

'*What*?' Another spasm sucked the air from her lungs. Some moments later she said: 'She kept hassling me. On and on and on. I am *not* queer, for God's sake.'

'Well, if you're sunbathing half naked on a gay beach,' said Felix mildly, 'it's an easy mistake to make. Actually, I thought you already knew her, that you two had met before.'

'That was some bullshit she invented. Men do it all the time. I mean, why can't they come up with a sassier pick-up line? Do you know what Mitch first said to me...?' She yelped with pain again, adding, after an interval, 'So I don't want her calling on me. Anywhere.'

'Okay, okay. It's just, you know, I think I told you, I'm not too good in hospitals. I have this recurring nightmare – I wake up in a complete sweat – about coming round after an operation and finding they've taken the wrong bit of me away.'

'And what bit would that be?'

He laughed. 'My tongue – so I can't even complain about it.'

'Actually.' She slid further down in her seat, as if her neck were too brittle to support her head. 'This sort of talk isn't very comforting.'

'Sorry, I'll shut up.'

He fiddled with the controls of the radio cassette and two opposing voices soared through one of Monteverdi's madrigals. The body of the small stuffy car, smelling of over-heated plastic, was filled with the torment of lovers parting in a heart-rending lament.

'Please, Felix,' Gina whispered as they approached the out-skirts of Rome.

At once he switched off the tape. 'Heaven forbid that you should have to listen to any music composed before you were born. My apologies.'

Somewhat feebly, she batted his hand as he changed gear. 'It's not that. You aren't going to take me to a public hospital, are you? Only... I'm scared...'

'Darling, I'll take you to this lovely clinic I know run by nuns. I haven't used it myself, as it happens, but I've heard very good reports. They're perfectly sweet, the food is excellent and all you have to do is pay them.'

'Well, let's hope I don't have to stay in for too long.'

'If it's only an appendix, it shouldn't be more than a week. Lucky you'd already started your packing too.'

She shot him a quick furtive look. 'Ironic, don't you mean?'

'I'll drop you off and go and pick up your suitcase.'

'Listen, Felix. I know you hate these places, but you will stay with me a little while, won't you?'

'Well, of course I will.'

'Also, there's something else I should have told you. I'm not sure it is my appendix actually. I know you'll be cross with me for not saying anything sooner, but...'

He could see her struggling for breath and patted her hand. 'Save your energy,' he said. 'It can wait.'

165

17

Six Weeks Earlier: April 1993

G ina replaced the small flat stick in its tube; she returned the tube to its carton, the carton to the paper bag imprinted with the name of the pharmacy. She tied the paper bag inside an anonymous pink striped plastic carrier, let herself out and dumped her bundle in the nearest skip. Now that it was lost, swallowed up amongst so much other refuse, so many other bin bags of rotting waste, she would not be tempted to look at it again, re-examine the little stick as if it could tell her a different story.

On her way back up the stairs she thought of Phoebe. Most of the time she tried to forget she had a mother, just as her mother probably tried to forget her. Since she'd grown up and moved abroad they'd found more common ground and learned to tolerate each other, but tolerance was as far as it went. Empathy, understanding, were not part of the deal. Yet now, unbidden, rose the image of Phoebe as a frightened young woman, her hair teased into a roll of candyfloss, her eyes winged with black pencil, secretly letting out the pleats of her skirt, stitching elastic into the waistband with neat little running threads. Contemplating what to do next.

Gina was alone in the apartment: two lofty rooms with a kitchenette and half a bath, in the San Lorenzo district. Vicki was away for the weekend, which was just as well because she wasn't yet ready to confide in her. Vicki would draw up lists of options and outcomes and Gina balked at that level of detail. Anyway, Mitch ought to be the first person to know, although she'd no idea how he would react to the news.

It must have happened over a month ago, on their ski break in the Dolomites. Snow was melting on the lower slopes so the skiing wasn't particularly good, but the resort had a reckless end-of-season air which was catching. When she proved herself swifter than Mitch on some of their downhill races she was determined to out-do him in other aspects too: drinking, partying, card-playing, acrobatic sex. She was on a newly prescribed progestin-only pill because of her migraines. Could she have been lax in timing her dose? The whole five days had passed in a magnificent blur: a contest of speed and stamina, a rush of blood to the head. She'd never be able to pinpoint the moment.

It couldn't have happened at their last meeting, that was for sure: a single night's stopover which had gone badly. Mitch had been argumentative – for no good reason she could see. Then, as each restaurant they'd tried had been full, he'd got hungrier and grouchier. They'd snapped at each other relentlessly and ended up with a greasy takeaway. They'd turned their backs in bed and both had slept poorly. Their fall-out had escalated in the morning when he discovered she'd switched off the alarm and he'd nearly missed reporting for duty. (Though they'd made up, after a fashion, on the doorstep.)

She'd delayed the pregnancy test till the very last minute, but she couldn't put it off any longer, because Mitch was on his way over again. She returned to her bedroom and opened the double doors of her wardrobe to find something to change into. All these beautiful clothes – how much longer would she be able to wear them? How much longer would she be able to work? Head and shoulder shots for jewellery might be a possibility – though wasn't the shape of the face and the texture of the hair supposed to change too? Defiantly she dragged a tight pair of trousers off a hanger. This was ridiculous: there was no way she could have a baby. She pulled the trousers over her thighs, drew up the zip and fastened the metal stud without difficulty. See, she told herself, there's time yet to make up your mind. Important decisions shouldn't be taken in a hurry.

Did she want it to stop, she wondered, all the flying about? It was three years since she and Mitch had first met, during a photo-shoot in Egypt. He'd been billeted in the same Cairo hotel and somehow they'd switched drinks at the bar during a brief power cut. She could still recall the shock of the unpalatable single malt on her tongue – and the taste of Mitch himself later. Then came the calls: 'Where are you next Thursday? Striking distance of Basel by any chance?'; 'A few days exploring the Great Barrier Reef – tempted at all?'

Gina always said yes.

One of the delights of their relationship was the fact that so much of it took place on neutral ground. They didn't have the chance to get bored or bogged down in dreary mundane tasks; everything was an adventure. They came together like dancers, their passion fresh and sparkling and newly energised. But lately she'd detected a shift. When he'd hired the van to drive her stuff to Rome, he'd said, 'I hope you're not planning to do this again in a hurry. I want to know where to find you.' And, by degrees, the border hopping, the intercity rendezvous had become less frequent. Usually they met in Rome, occasionally in Manchester. He'd even talked about buying a property, which to Gina had been a step too far. Until now. Until this.

At the bottom of the wardrobe, where it had fallen, she found her favourite crimson shirt. There was no time to iron it but as she fed buttons into buttonholes the fabric strained a little. Could her breasts be bigger already? All to the good: she wanted to look desirable. She wanted Mitch on her side; she wanted them both to be in agreement.

She would have to proceed carefully. First, they would go out to eat. She'd booked a table at a place which was reputed to have an Arabic influence because one of the partners was Syrian. Along with bread and olives, a dish of chillies was routinely served as an accompaniment to the meal. Mitch thought Italian food was too predictable, so she was pleased at the find. Afterwards, when he was mellow with food and wine, she would lay her cards on the table.

She went to sit in front of her make-up mirror. Her routine was automatic; she knew exactly how long it should take – but he arrived early. She was clamping curlers to her lashes when the doorbell rang. 'Just a minute!' she called blithely through the entry phone. She needed to paint a juicy kissable mouth.

But when she let him in, he ignored her lips and pecked her cheek like someone who could scarcely be bothered. He had a stooped, weary air.

'I bet you're ready for a drink. I've got a nice Pinot Grigio for you in the fridge.'

'No, I'm fine, thanks.'

He must be tired again, she thought, though she should have spotted the clues: he had no bag with him for a start, and he was unshaven – usually his fair, square jaw was razored smooth so as not to give her a rash. She shouldn't have been so busy telling him about the restaurant and making a half-hearted apology for the dishevelment of her room. The contents of two handbags were scattered on the bed, an obstacle course of key rings, pens, combs, notebooks and scissors. 'Another ten minutes,' she said, 'and I could have cleared it all away. You'd be able to find somewhere to sit down.'

There was too much jauntiness in her voice, contrasting with his flat delivery. 'Is that a problem? Do you want me to go?'

'Of course not. Vicki's away and we have the place to our-selves.' She returned to the stool by her dressing table, half expecting him to follow, to take her hair in his hands and pull the brush through it in slow sensuous strokes.

Instead, he went to stand on the other side of the room, by the window. He thrust his hands in the pockets of his jeans. 'We need to talk.'

She nodded agreement. 'My thoughts exactly.'

It was that moment of gloom before sudden nightfall, when the swifts spun in black arcs against a copper sky; she hadn't yet switched on the lights. Mitch cleared his throat and said in the same neutral tone: 'Well, that's a relief, I suppose, if we've both come to the same conclusion. And not surprising really, after last time. We always said we'd be absolutely straight with each other, didn't we? So yes, I agree with you, we should call it a day.'

She stared at him. His face was partly in shadow. 'What did you say?' She half rose. 'Oh for goodness sake, Mitch! Stop winding me up.'

'But I'm not... I thought that's what you meant.'

She thudded back down onto her dressing stool, alarmed. Once, in Milan, she'd arrived home to find the television miss-ing. Nothing else was disturbed so she thought her eyes must be deceiving her. She had taken a few moments to register it had been stolen, and then she'd felt like the most naive idiot in the world. Which was exactly how she felt now. She didn't understand how it could have happened. How, one minute they couldn't get enough of each other and the next he was this unrecognisable stranger.

'Is this because of last time? Because if it is –'

'Let's just say it didn't help.'

'Meaning?'

Clamour from the street filled the room: a flamboyant exchange of greetings, the buzz of a Lambretta drowned by a wailing siren. Mitch took his hands from his pockets, closed the window and said: 'Christ, Gina! I'm trying to do the right thing here.'

'All the while we've been seeing each other,' she said, 'I thought we had something special, that other people didn't have, that...'

'We did! You know the way I felt. You were the one who refused to commit, who didn't want to be tied down.'

Neither of them had professed love – from a combination of pride and a mutual competitive streak – but the emotion had been there, even if the words were lacking. This was all wrong, it shouldn't be happening. It was like tasting a disgusting obscure malt instead of a lovely mellow Armagnac all over again. 'But that was what you liked about me,' she protested. 'Admit it.'

'Gina, we live in different countries. Be practical. It couldn't go on for ever.'

'It wasn't a problem before.'

'Well, logistically, it was a bit easier when you were in Milan...'

'So it's my fault, is it? I'm too inconvenient for you?'

'It's not a question of convenience. Look, you're never going to give up your kind of life...'

'How do you know?'

'Would you move back to England, to the north-west?'

'Would you move here?'

'No, not any more.'

'What d'you mean, "not any more"? Were you thinking about it? Has something made you change your mind?'

Did he flinch or did she imagine it?

'Be honest,' he said. 'We've not really been getting along. But because we have this artificial sort of set-up, when we're not seeing each other, in the gaps in between, we tend to forget...'

'But last month in Cortina...'

'You were completely over the top. It was embarrassing.'

'You're just jealous because you couldn't out-ski me. Because I won nearly every race.'

He ignored this. 'And the other night was a total disaster.'

'Is this all over a stupid alarm clock? I've said sorry a hundred times, haven't I? And I wasn't messing, I was just trying to get some sleep. Talk about overreaction!'

'Gina, it's nothing to do with the alarm clock – though it's typical of you not to think of the consequences. They might have been bloody serious for me. I could have been disciplined for being late – but it kind of brought things into focus.'

She crossed one leg over the other and her shoe swung loosely from the end of her foot like a person clinging to a window ledge several floors above the ground. When her knee juddered and the shoe fell off, she imagined she heard an almighty crash and wondered who would pick up the pieces. 'Oh my God, you're seeing someone, aren't you?'

He had the grace to look sheepish. 'It's actually not that simple…'

She plucked a cigarette from one of her cartons of duty-free Marlboros and gripped the filter between her teeth. 'Who is it?'

'You don't know her.'

The lighter flame soared to her eyebrows. 'Of course I don't know her! In our "artificial set-up" we don't meet each other's friends, do we? We're self-sufficient.' She took several jerky puffs and with her left hand restored her shoe to her foot.

'This isn't getting us anywhere.'

'No,' she snapped. 'So where do you want to go?'

He jumped at the chance to take her literally. 'Probably back to the hotel.'

Who was this stranger? She itched to throw something at him. If she could smash his shell she might rediscover his core, lay her head on his chest to listen to the thud of his heart. 'Well, don't let me keep you.' She could hear the snarl in her own voice but she couldn't control it. 'It's perfectly clear where your priorities are.'

'Look, it seems we've been at cross purposes. I didn't expect it to come as such a shock but I should have timed it better…' She didn't say anything. He went on, 'Do you want to meet tomorrow for a coffee? It might be easier to have a discussion when you've calmed down. I can't talk to you when you're like this.'

'What would be the point?'

'I didn't want to end on a sour note. I didn't want to hurt you.'

'Hurt! Like I pricked my finger or something.'

'Gina, you have to believe me...'

'Why should I?' Why listen to him defend himself over a cappuccino? What did it achieve or change, if he'd already fallen for someone else? She was appalled that they could have misled and misread each other so. And then she thought: the bastard, what right has he got to know anything now? I can solve my own problem. It's none of his business.

He sighed and looked as though he might approach her for a farewell embrace. She held out her palms to ward him off, so instead he moved in his solid unhurried way to the door. Grasping the handle he said, 'Look after yourself, won't you?'

Gina watched him go and counted to twenty. Then she let her feelings fly. She flung whatever was in convenient reach at the door's blank expanse: books, shoes, heavy brass table lamp and, ultimately, the stool she'd been sitting on. The door withstood the assault, but for weeks afterwards she continued to discover new chips and nicks in its paintwork.

Mitchell, retreating down the stairs, heard the thumps. Part of him wanted to go back but he had to confront the truth that he and Gina were going nowhere. Her fecklessness could be charming but she had less sense of responsibility than a kitten. Once, her ability to recompose herself had been part of her attraction: her hair constantly changing colour from creamy blonde to foxy red; her eyes green or gold or bronze depending on the light. Often his colleagues didn't even realise he was meeting the same person. But now he found this chameleon aspect exasperating; it was like grappling with water. You never knew what you were dealing with. Tonight, for example, she'd behaved like a petulant, needy kid.

Meeting Corinne, who was attentive and serene and all that Gina was not, had alerted him. He hadn't set out to find a new partner. Corinne had entered his life at a particular moment – just as he was beginning to look for stability, to appreciate the appeal of coming back to a well-kept house, a warm bed, a loving woman. Maybe even a child. He had considered the contrast between the two women, as he considered everything, and come to his decision. He didn't doubt it was the right one, that it would bring him the future he wanted.

PART THREE

APRIL 2011

18

It was afternoon by the time Mitchell left the airport. He drove through country lanes where tight whorls of green were beading the hawthorn hedges and daffodils clustered on the banks as if to welcome him home. He turned through the open gate and crunched to a standstill on the gravel behind Corinne's Toyota. She was in, then.

He pulled his case from the car boot and stood leaning for a moment against the warm metal. He often experienced a slight sense of dislocation after being away, especially on a long-haul trip. Sometimes he insulated himself by keeping within the confines of his bland international hotel with its fitness centre, restaurant and casino: places where the air was continually recycled. At others he was more than ready for the full-on assault course of colour, sound and smell that was Hong Kong or Mumbai or Nairobi. Immersing himself in exotic culture was as good a distraction as any.

Coming home had generally provided an interlude of calm – apart from the dog, who'd been prone to over-excitement. They hadn't replaced him, so there was no barking at the sound of his car, no frantic scraping at the door. Nor had he yet got used to the gap in the garden left by the pear tree, which had fallen in a winter storm. Although it rarely fruited, the blossom had been joyous. The new, open aspect gave him clear sight of his wall, finally finished. He'd laid the last stone shortly before the snow came. It was too low to keep anyone out, but when the snow melted he lost interest in making adjustments. There was a limit to tinkering.

It had been a hard winter in more ways than one; the atmosphere in the house as chilly as the temperature outside. Only Sasha, bless her, to provide a leavening. She was the cog that kept their family life ticking over, but not, he knew, for much longer. Within eighteen months she'd be off to university and he and Corinne would be left with, possibly, nothing to say to each other. The bright sun on the daffodils was misleading, he thought, as he wheeled his case to the door. There was no warmth in it.

Had they heard him come in? Music drifted from the radio in the kitchen, along with the fragrance of vanilla and melted chocolate and the interplay of their voices – Sasha's sentences had the choppy rhythm affected by her generation; Corinne's were low-pitched and melodious. He observed them from the doorway, their chairs drawn close together at the table, their heads almost touching as they focused on the screen of Corinne's laptop. Sasha noticed him first. Sensing his presence, she peered over her shoulder and jumped up. 'Dad, you're home!'

'You were expecting me?' This addressed wryly to Corinne.

Corinne shut the laptop with a snap. She was wearing a blue-grey angora sweater that matched the colour of her irises. She looked as soft and strokable as a rabbit, but they'd hardly touched each other in months. She rose, allowed him to kiss her cheek and went to fill the kettle. A mixing bowl and baking tin lay soaking in suds in the sink.

'Are you jet-lagged?' said Sasha. 'Only if you are…'

'No, I'm fine.' Why could they never remember his itinerary, even though each month's was pinned up on the corkboard along with postcards, invitations, appointments and other messages? 'Cape Town's in the same time zone.'

'Oh good, then you'll want to try my brownies with your tea. They're really squidgy.' She handed him one on a plate.

'Mmm, excellent.' As he took a second bite of the warm moist brownie, he became aware of a tension in the two of them. Sasha, in particular, was prowling around him like a hungry cat. Lately she had sprung from the cocoon of adolescence into fully formed womanhood. She used to shroud herself in baggy sweatshirts, but now there were at least two inches of bare flesh between the hem of her clinging top and the belt of her skin-tight jeans. No wonder he was always being asked to turn the heating up. Her feet, however, were well encased in thick sheepskin boots.

'Is there something you're trying to tell me?' he said, half curious, half amused.

'Go on, Mum. Ask him.'

'Ask me what?'

Corinne poured three mugs of tea. 'Sash is planning an Easter break.'

'Oh?'

'Me and Ruby,' she said, and stopped.

'You and Ruby, what?'

She danced up to him as well as she could manage in her furry boots and put her arms around his waist. Her face was close to his and pleading. 'We want to go to Rome.'

'What?' he bellowed.

'Dad, don't shout.' She put her hands over her ears. 'I'm not at the other end of the house.'

'No,' he said.

'What d'you mean, no?'

'What do you think I mean?'

'How about if you came as well? You could take us to places. That'd be cool.'

He glanced over at Corinne. As if she were no longer involved, she started to deal with the washing-up. He had to move away from the draining board to give her space. Five minutes I've been home, he thought. And now this.

'It will be good for us,' Sasha insisted. 'Because Ruby couldn't make it before and we both need to get conversation practice. This will be our only chance before the exams.'

'I think you burned your boats after last time,' said Mitchell.

'That is so unfair! I only got back a few days late.'

'With a black eye.'

'So? It could happen to anyone! I told you at the time, those Italian beaches get so crowded and there was this volley ball game going on as well. It wasn't anybody's fault. It was an accident. And anyway, we won't be going to the beach at Easter. I'll be showing Ruby around the ruins and churches and such. It's supposed to be really amazing when everyone gathers in front of St Peter's to see the Pope. It was tough on her missing out last summer, so this will, like, be a good chance for us both.'

'It wasn't just the business of your black eye,' he said, 'though God knows why that family you were staying with didn't take better care of you.' He wasn't likely to forget the shock of seeing his daughter stumbling through customs with her listing suitcase, battered and dishevelled beneath an absurd baseball cap. He'd thought at first she'd been in a fight. 'It was the casual way you treated us to information. You took advantage and it's made us feel we can't trust you. I wouldn't be happy about you going again.'

'Look, I could go anyway. Without you. I've got my passport and the money I've been earning from the waitressing. I mean, this is a study-related trip, you know.'

Corinne was drying knives and spoons and filing them in the cutlery drawer. She didn't look up, but she coughed reprovingly and Mitchell latched on to this hint of reservation.

'Don't push your luck, Sash.'

He had to clarify it in his own mind. Were his misgivings connected to the suspicion that she'd lied last summer? Or the fact that while she was in Rome, she'd apparently met Gina Stanhope? He'd no idea whether she'd kept in touch or whether they would meet again, but the prospect made him uneasy.

'We really want you to take us, Dad,' said Sasha, holding his gaze with her round innocent eyes. 'We'll be, like, eternally grateful.'

'No,' he said again.

Her bottom lip pushed forward and trembled, exactly the way it used to when she was small. It didn't belong on the nubile body with its exposed navel. See, he thought inwardly, she's not grown-up at all. She was a child still, bewailing the death of a pet or a horse gone lame. She needed taking care of, she wasn't yet ready to make her own decisions.

'You are so mean!' she said in a fierce whisper, presenting him with an eloquent back and stomping out of the room.

'Christ,' he said to Corinne. 'Why'd she have to be so impatient? I'd hardly got through the door...'

'It's her age, isn't it? Teenagers don't understand deferred gratification. She was trying to make an effort. She was really anxious to get you on side.' She waved at the forlorn plate of brownies and he began to feel churlish. Then she added, 'Mind you, I don't know why you bother.'

'Bother with what?'

'Pretending to make a stand, when you know she'll win you round eventually.'

'It might be more effective if you backed me up,' he said mildly.

'Yes, but I'm not going to.'

'Why not?'

'Because I don't see the harm.'

'Corinne! After last time?'

'I don't see why there should be any problems if you go along with them.'

'Okay, she needs a chaperone, but why does it all hinge on me? Why are you staying out of this? Won't you come too?' They hadn't holidayed together for over a year, she'd been so swamped with case studies and data collection, but now the research was concluded; she had her doctorate. He allowed himself a mild dig at her Quality of Life questionnaires: 'Where, on a scale of 1-10 do you see yourself on the Ladder of Life? Are you very satisfied? Quite satisfied? A bit satisfied? Not satisfied at all?' She didn't even smile. 'Don't you feel the need for a break?'

'Yes, actually. I have been thinking about it.'

'We could all go together then. Rent an apartment. You've never been to Rome, have you? I could show you around.'

She didn't pause to consider the offer. 'As it happens, I have other plans.'

'Other plans? What the fuck does that mean?'

She cocked her head as if listening to the vibrations on the floor above. Sasha would be playing music, talking on the phone, messaging on the computer, or possibly all three at once. Until recently she'd been going out with a boy called Liam and was now absorbed in deconstructing every stage of the relationship with her girlfriends. Although Mitchell had welcomed its end, for some reason he couldn't help feeling sorry for the boy.

Corinne said, 'I'd rather not have a showdown while Sasha's in the house.'

'Why does there have to be a showdown?'

'Because you won't like what I'm going to say.'

'Try me.'

'All right. Don't pace up and down though. Come and sit at the table.'

He pulled out the chair opposite her. The afternoon light fell in shafts between them. In her natural element, Corinne could spread calm like butter. It was one of the reasons she was so good with disturbed patients. Mitchell, too, considered himself tolerant. The two of them didn't argue, they didn't even have rows, but they'd been going their separate ways for longer than he cared to calculate.

She rested her arms on the cover of her silver laptop. 'I have to think about my next step,' she said. 'I've spent too long putting other people first.'

'Other people?' he said, trying to suppress annoyance. 'You mean your father?'

It seemed to him that his father-in-law's Alzheimer's had dominated the first ten years of their marriage. Corinne had claimed his needs meant she had no energy for any more children. Mitchell stifled the notion that he had been cheated of a son, but from time to time her sacrifice rankled. After her father had died, she devoted herself to the cause, nobly determined to improve the lot of dementia patients.

'And you. And Sash.'

'Me? I don't think so.'

'I'm not going to bicker about it,' she said, as if this were an act of great generosity. 'You asked me a question and I'm trying to answer it. I feel that I've moved onto a different stage and – '

' – Now that you're *Dr* Mitchell.'

'Don't mock, Paul.'

'I'm proud of you,' he said. 'You've worked incredibly hard and done incredibly well. I'm not trying to put you down. I'm trying to understand why your success should have negative implications for our marriage.' He was pleased with the way he sounded fair and reasonable, even though his fist was clenching and unclenching under the table.

Corinne matched his equable tone, but she was twisting a lock of hair and avoiding eye contact. 'I'm finally at the point where I can advance my career. It's different for you, you made it a long time ago, but I can have ambitions too.'

'So you think Sash and I are holding you back?'

'No, of course not. She's grown up, for goodness' sake and you've always been self-contained.'

'Self-contained? What's that supposed to mean?' He dug his nails into his palm. 'That I don't easily lose my temper?'

'You absent yourself,' she said. 'You're never here.'

'It's my job,' he said, bewildered. 'I fly.' He used to marvel that it only took four letters of the alphabet to spell out the exhilaration, the power, the unbelievable thrill of finding your-self airborne. Twenty years on, the process had become familiar, not quite so dizzying, but the lift was still there, it hadn't dulled.

She shrugged. 'Even when you're on leave you're off doing something else, at the gym or some endless cricket match.'

'But your father enjoyed the cricket! You used to encourage me to take him.'

'Or building that damn wall.'

'You wanted me out of the house, Corinne. Out of your way.'

'The point is,' she said coolly, 'that I've a lot to think about. Future-wise. I might be applying for jobs in other parts of the country. And you might not want to come with me.'

This was the scenario he'd feared, the three of them scatter-ing in different directions. It had been a constant he'd never underestimated: the pleasure of touching base, coming home to his family.

'I'm thinking of booking a walking holiday, which is why I don't want to go to Rome with you and Sash. I wouldn't be able to get to grips with any decisions on a sightseeing trip.'

'We've talked about this before,' he said. 'You could take a walking holiday with me.'

'But it wouldn't work. I need to get away.'

'From me?'

'From the general home environment.'

It had happened so gradually, this slow erosion of common ground. At what point could he have called a halt, engineered a different direction? 'So you're going alone, are you?'

'With Nadia probably.'

Mitchell remembered that Nadia had recently celebrated her divorce, which was not encouraging, but with any luck Corinne would get sick of her after spending a whole week in her company. Assuming 'Nadia' wasn't a codename for someone else entirely. Another man? Would Corinne be so devious? He noticed she'd taken her wedding ring off to wash the baking pans. It glinted from the window sill. He wondered how often this happened and she 'forgot' to put it back on. He rotated his own around his finger, the gold band a snug fit. 'So when did you plan all this? While I was the other side of the world, so I couldn't interfere? And when were you going to mention it? The night before you left?'

'Don't be silly. Nothing's set in stone yet. But I thought if you took Sash and Ruby to Italy, I might as well go away at the same time. When you got back just now, we were looking into options, that's all.'

'Where does that leave me?'

'It wouldn't do any harm,' said Corinne with some asperity, 'for you to do some thinking too. You've been taking me for granted for an awfully long while.'

'So that's what this is all about? It can work both ways, you know.'

'Paul, be honest. We're in a rut. We need to stop avoiding the issue and take a good look at ourselves.'

He wished he could puncture this sanctimonious air of hers, but she was entrenched on the moral high ground with her dignity of care for the demented, whereas all he did was ferry the able-bodied to and from their frivolous holidays. The fact that they placed their lives in his hands was not one she'd consider pertinent.

'You ought to go to Rome with the girls,' she said again. 'I think it's a good idea. You can keep an eye on them, take them out for meals, spoil them a bit.'

'While you get your hiking boots and thinking cap on?'

She pushed her hair off her face and he could see the fine lines drawn on her forehead, the slight woeful droop to her mouth as she said, 'Yes. And I reckon you'll be grateful in the end. I can't have been much fun to live with lately.'

'True enough.' He smiled to bridge the gap between them, but was flummoxed by her next remark.

'Don't you have some friends in Rome anyway? That woman.'

'What woman?'

'Don't you remember? She kept ringing up, soon after I moved in with you, and leaving messages. But you'd never ring back. It was ages ago. What was her name... Vicki?'

'Vicki Harris? God no, I hardly knew her. She was some ex-pat, probably moved on.' He waved his hand as if to bat away the distant Vicki. He'd forgotten all about her, but the precision of Corinne's recall alarmed him.

Even more alarming, on reflection, was the licence she was giving him to return.

19

Gina opened her internal mailbox on the ground floor and withdrew a white envelope. Her hands shook; there was a tremble in the back of her calves as she climbed the stairs. Should she open it once she got in or throw it straight into the bin? This must be the fourth or fifth she'd received – she hadn't kept count – and she knew it would contain another notice to quit the apartment. In theory she was protected for a further eighteen months, until her lease came up for renewal, but Bertie wouldn't let a bit of legislation get in the way of his ambitions.

He hadn't forgiven her for dumping him, that was the truth of it. After his holiday last summer he'd rung her several times, remonstrating, trying to coax her back. When this failed he'd turned irate and vindictive. There had come the occasion when the police battered at her door with a search warrant. She had been denounced for indecency.

Later, with friends, she could laugh at such absurdity, but at the time she'd had to hide both her shock and her desire to giggle. 'What sort of indecency?' she'd demanded, admitting two officers into the hallway. She was confident that she was dressed demurely and all her sensitive prints were safe in the studio.

The complaints, she was told, concerned the fact that she was running an unlicensed business, a casino or bordello. People had been seen trooping up the stairs either to supply or to pay for sex.

Gina had kept her nerve. 'This is a private residence,' she'd said with dignity. 'Look around if you like, but most of what you'll find here belonged to my late husband. I can't imagine where this lurid suggestion has come from.'

Sheepishly, the police agreed their informant must have been mistaken. Their glance into the rooms was cursory; they didn't open a drawer or a cupboard. They issued an apology, which was also part warning, and left on good terms. Gina resolved to take extra care in future – and then the writs started to arrive.

The legal advice she'd sought had not been reassuring: fighting Bertie would drain time and money she didn't have. On the other hand, his tactics were scaremongering rather than enforceable. The easiest response was simply to ignore them.

Which was why she did not now open the fourth (or fifth?) letter. She crumpled it into a ball and plunged it into a mess of coffee grounds, orange peel and yoghurt pots in the bin under the sink. She sought something mouldy from her fridge to pile on top. Frankly, she didn't have time to be cowed by Bertie's bullying. Clearly she would have to devise a strategy of her own, but not yet. She had other, far more exciting, priorities to occupy her: tonight was the opening of her exhibition.

David had honoured his commitment and in between commercial assignments, she had been selecting, editing, retouching and recomposing her images for his satisfaction. He had a good eye, she had to admit, and he'd agreed to her chosen title, *I Vulnerati*, which she hoped suggested the wounds and scars of her vulnerable subjects. They'd had a few arguments over what to say in the publicity and whether any of the boys in her photographs should come to the opening (answer, no).

And of course it wasn't a solo show. But, minor niggles apart, she owed a debt of gratitude to David Farnon.

She was turning away from the sink, switching on the iron, blotting out the very existence of unwanted post, when he rang her. 'Hope you're putting your best party frock on.'

'I'm about to iron it now. Red as sin, it is. Knock out.'

'I have a nice piece of news for you.'

'You do?'

'You remember,' David said, 'I have a client, an art-house publisher, on the guest list and I reckoned you'd be right up his street? Well, I've been speaking to him and he's kinda keen to meet you.' There was a pause; she could hear him giving directions to a minion.

'Sounds almost too good to be true,' said Gina.

'Have faith, hon. He has a crowded schedule, so he can't stay long. But he's going to swing by early so if you want to make the right impression roll up in good time, that's all I'm saying.'

'You think I'd be late for my own show?' She'd allowed plenty of time to prepare herself and already made a booking with Mario.

Three hours later he dropped her off in front of the Galleria Farnon. She mounted the shallow stone steps and pushed through the swing doors. A vast reception table was beached on the limestone floor, spotlights dazzled from the ceiling. Waiters in slinky black outfits posed with trays of fizzing prosecco. David was deep in conversation with one of the other exhibitors. He waved but didn't come over. Gina could have joined them, but she wanted to savour the pleasure of seeing her images so well ordered on the walls. She lifted a glass of prosecco to her lips and enjoyed the first surge of alcohol.

There was another person already studying her portraits, a lanky man in a brown suit. Ideally David should make the introductions, but why wait if the publisher was in a hurry? As she hesitated, the man turned and approached her, holding out his hand. He had a formal old-fashioned air. 'Signora Stanhope? I have been hoping to meet you.'

'Gina, please.'

'I am Franco Casale. I admire your work very much.'

'You do? Thank you.'

Casale had a beard that emphasised the jut of his jaw – more Venetian than Roman, she thought – and he stroked it as he appraised her, rather as if she too were for purchase; her composure didn't falter.

'So, Gina…' He tapped the catalogue pinned under his arm. 'I have been reading about you. You have been following these people who live… on the margins, shall we say?'

'I find them interesting. Of course, I realise the images could be seen as a statement on society…' They were standing in front of a shot of refugees lined up along a graffitied wall. She'd used a long exposure so the men appeared like wraiths, the belligerent slogans harshly visible through their bodies. 'But I'm not making a judgement. I want my work to be seen as art, not propaganda.' This was not exactly what she had told Father Leone.

'This is a new development for you?'

'In that it's not a private commission, yes. I do enjoy working for my clients, but there are restrictions… I mean you can't always be truthful. And that's what I aim to do as an artist, convey the truth.'

A waiter approached with a platter of canapés. Casale helped himself to two crostini and an anchovy stuffed tomato. He must be one of those men, Gina decided, who was permanently hungry. She couldn't eat a thing. He dabbed oil from his mouth with a small paper napkin. No crumbs in his beard fortunately. 'But you have not always been a photographer?' he said.

'True. I began as a model.'

'So what made you switch to the other side of the camera?'

She was feeling exhilarated and a little reckless. This man liked her pictures. And if he wanted to learn more about

Gina Stanhope the person, she would do her best to entertain him.

'Let me tell you a funny story.' She allowed her glass to be topped up and continued. 'You know the famous scene in *La Dolce Vita* where Anita Ekberg wades into the Trevi Fountain? Well, I'd been booked for a high-class jewellery campaign and we were going to reproduce it.'

Casale tipped his head to one side, he seemed to be listening with interest.

'We had to shoot in the early hours of the morning with the area cordoned off. So there I was in the middle of the fountain in a peroxide wig, a black silk taffeta dress and this string of topaz stones on a gold chain. We'd been hanging around for so long I'd folded my arm, *cosi*.' She demonstrated, cupping her elbow in her left hand, caressing her collarbone with her right. 'Then, just as the photographer raised the camera, some kids on a scooter came charging through the cordon. You know what the *carabinieri* are like, all posturing and pistols. They whipped out their guns, though the kids had gone before they could do anything. But because I was startled my fingers caught in the chain and it snapped.

'The guy took the shot anyway, at the very moment the topaz went spinning off like great balls of fire. It was fantastic actually, but it couldn't be used for the campaign, so he entered it for a competition instead and won a major prize. Meanwhile, what had I got? Wet feet!'

This was a tale she had told before and it usually made her listeners laugh but Casale, if anything, looked disapproving. Puzzled, he said, 'You mean you were obliged to stop modelling because of a broken necklace?'

'No, not at all!' He had completely missed the point. Gina was annoyed with herself. She had wanted to show him, what, that she was someone with a colourful past? Marketable. But a photographer didn't need a personality; she had to remember this. She was only a filter.

'I think the story is not true,' he said.

'Excuse me?' Had he actually called her a liar? She gulped at the rest of her drink.

After an uncomfortable silence he added, 'I'm sorry if I offend you.'

This was not going well. She needed to change the subject. 'It's my fault,' she said lightly, 'for talking too much about myself. What about your projects? I've seen some of your books, I think. Those beautiful editions following the routes of the pilgrims…'

'My books?'

'You are – ' Hell, she couldn't remember what the company was called. And why hadn't David given her his name? 'I mean, you do publish…'

'But no, *mi dispiace*, this is not my profession.' He repeated, 'I am Franco Casale,' and handed over a business card.

She accepted it with forefinger and thumb and slipped it between her palm and the base of her wine glass, too mortified to read the details. It was enough that he wasn't who she thought he was.

'I believe we have an acquaintance in common.' He had an unswerving gaze and was watching closely for her reaction. 'Roberto Boletti?'

Gina blanched. If the man was a friend of Bertie's, there was no knowing what he might be devising. She raked the room for rescue. Friends had begun to arrive; she thought she spotted Vicki with her husband. 'I'm afraid there are other people here I need to see.'

'If this is not a suitable occasion, I apologise, but with regard to Boletti – '

'I'm sorry. I really don't think we have anything else to say to each other.' She edged away, not wanting him to see how he had unsettled her. She ripped the small white card in half and discarded it. She took a fresh glass from the waiter's tray and allowed herself to be drawn into a warm clutch of well-wishers. As long as she could keep herself cushioned by drink and company, the rest of the evening should swim along perfectly.

The following day David sent her a series of urgent texts. When she rang him back he said accusingly, 'You didn't answer your phone.'

'I went to bed late. I had it on silent. What's up?'

He wasn't calling to gossip or dissect the occasion, that was for sure. He sounded agitated. 'You'd better get your ass over here, pronto. And bring your laptop.'

David was no longer her favourite person. The promised publisher had failed to materialise altogether, and despite, or because of, oceans of prosecco, she had a nasty taste in the back of her throat and a sharp pain at her temple. She bridled. 'What's the problem?'

'I'll tell you when I see you.'

Gina refused to be rushed. She took a long shower, tossed down a scalding espresso, and chose to walk. She needed the fresh air.

When she arrived at the gallery, David was halfway up a small stepladder unhooking a pair of photographs from the wall. She held the door open, not wanting to call out while he was on the ladder. As soon as his pristine moccasins found their footing she let it click shut. 'What are you doing?'

He beckoned her to follow him into the back office. 'We're in trouble,' he said.

Gina balanced herself against the edge of his desk and drew her toe along the outline of a floor tile. 'Why? What have you been up to?'

'Not me. You.'

'Me!'

'Afraid so.'

'What am I supposed to have done?'

He laid down the photographs and indicated the long-haired football player in mid-leap. 'This is the Boletti boy, Antonio, isn't it?'

'How on earth do you know that?'

He pulled a white-tipped menthol cigarette from the packet he kept in his shirt pocket and toyed with it. 'A representative of the family called in earlier.'

'Who?'

'It was a lawyer actually. Apparently the Bolettis were not too happy to learn from the grapevine that their young son was being displayed in public.'

'Oh for God's sake! That's ridiculous. They'd given me full permission to use them. They were impressed with my client list.'

David was flicking his cigarette between his fingers like a conjuring trick, obviously desperate to go outside for a smoke. Instead he sat in his swivel chair and drummed on its arm. 'Not on this occasion, it seems. They don't care for the company you've put him in.'

'Who could have told them anyway?' Then she remembered Franco Casale.

She unbuttoned her jacket, tried to relax her shoulders. 'You loved that sequence,' she said. 'Because it was so retro.' In a series of prints reminiscent of post-war Italian cinema, half a dozen youths played football in a run-down piazza, laundry flapping overhead, a pair of scooters for their goalposts. Energy radiated from their scrawny limbs, the whole group configured into a striking ballet. 'And these shots of Antonio in his Roma gear – just look at his wonderful, intense expression – were a perfect foil for the others.'

'Sure, but that was before I knew who he was.'

'I don't see why it should make a difference.'

'It's a risk I can't take,' he said.

'What do you mean? Why is it a risk?'

'I'm not fighting your lawsuits for you, hon. The deal is, we take them down or he'll get the whole show closed.'

'But that's outrageous! He can't do that!' Her mouth was so dry she couldn't swallow. She had to lean more firmly against the desk to stop her knees wobbling.

David smacked his forehead. 'Hey, I'm being dumb here. Boletti's the landlord who's after your apartment, isn't he? The one you thought you'd seen off?'

She'd already told him about the visit from the police. 'I got another letter from his *avvocato* yesterday. Probably the same guy who's hassling you. If only I'd realised, I'd've knocked his teeth out. Franco Fucking Whatever.'

David was not much given to gestures of affection, but he squeezed her arm in sympathy. 'I know it's tough, Gina, but I'm a foreigner here. So are you. We have to be on our best behaviour.'

'This might not seem such a bloody disaster if only your publisher had turned up.'

'I told you he was on a tight schedule. I guess he lost his window, but I'll chase him, I promise.'

'If there's anything left for him to see...' Then she rallied. 'You're not really going to let Bertie dictate to you, are you?'

'Well, we have a problem to address here. If we take these two down I'll have a wall with a crazy gap in it.' He smoothed back his white-blond hair. 'So that's basically why I called you over. Is there anything you haven't shown me?'

'How d'you mean?'

'Let me see what you've got on your laptop.'

'Oh right...'

She took it out of its sleeve and laid it on his desk. She had lost her equilibrium and everything took longer than it should have done. The keys slipped beneath her fingers, the cursor skated across the screen. Eventually she set up a slide show of the work she'd previously submitted to him.

He sat down and scanned through the material, shaking his head. 'I thought so. We already picked the best.' As he closed the programme he spotted the folder she'd labelled 'Aftermath'. He leaned forward and opened it. 'Hey, what's this?'

Gina said, 'They're not ready.'

'No?' He clicked from image to image. 'They look kinda interesting. Holy shit!'

'Honestly, I haven't done anything with them yet, they're just raw takes.'

'Raw,' he agreed, wincing. 'And new, huh?'

'No, actually I took them last summer.'

'Why didn't you show me before? I can't believe that, with a theme like yours, you didn't think of including them.'

'I wasn't certain they fit with the rest of the selection. And I'm still kind of ambivalent...'

'Did you set them up in the studio?'

'No, in the apartment.'

'You've sure done a convincing job.' His tone was half-admiring, half-appalled. 'The guy looks familiar.'

'Yes, he's one of the Afghanis. He's in the football sequence too. I call him Joe.'

'Hey, didn't he pose for those studies I sold privately?'

She nodded.

'They were quite a hit,' he mused. 'So I vote we go with these. I'll need two edited prints – you know the dimensions – and I'll need them fast.' Then, as if he sensed some reluctance in Gina: 'Is there a problem?'

What choice did she have? And the Aftermath shots were indisputably spectacular. David had sensed their erotic charge. 'No, no problem.'

20

Sasha closed the shutters and then opened them again. No, she wasn't dreaming. There it lay before her: the cobbled pedestrianised street, the crimson awning over the bar on the corner, the cast-iron balconies opposite with their ugly air-conditioning units. Except to her they weren't ugly. Everything in view was beautiful because she was back in Rome.

The apartment was tiny. Ruby was currently washing in what was described as a wet room because when you stood under the showerhead the basin and loo were drenched as well. The two of them were sharing the double bed and off the kitchen was another small room where her father would sleep. He hadn't seen it yet because he'd been delayed. A security threat had disrupted his schedule and he'd overrun his flying hours. When he joined them the following day he would be annoyed, she suspected, because this apartment wasn't the one they'd booked but a last minute substitute. The agent had been apologetic – something about unfinished building works – but so charming. He'd driven them to the new place which was, he promised, in an even better, more central location, and he'd given them a bottle of white wine from Frascati. The girls had been too excited to complain.

Sasha loved the way that the sounds and aromas filtered up from the street, that she could simply step outside for her breakfast. The area had been noisy overnight but she'd decided that she loved noise too. She'd spent so much of her life begging her parents for lifts, struggling to get to the heart of things. This was a taste – glorious, heady – of her future.

Ruby came out of the shower, only half-wrapped in a small towel, and joined her at the window. They used to be the same height, but Sasha had acquired another inch; her slimmer frame had also affected her carriage: she appeared taller, and able to look down on her best friend.

'*Cosa facciamo oggi*?' said Ruby in an exaggerated comedy accent.

'What do you want to do?'

'What do *I* want to do?' A wicked dimple quivered in Ruby's cheek. 'Aren't we, like, going to play detective?'

Two young men emerged from an open doorway for a smoke. One bent to light his cigarette and then threw back his head to take his first drag. He spotted Ruby in her towel and whistled. Sasha pushed her out of sight. 'I'm not sure,' she said.

'Hey, why so chicken all of a sudden?' Ruby was on the floor rummaging in her suitcase. Neither of them had unpacked anything and yesterday's clothes, the ones they had travelled in, lay in a dirty heap. She seized a pair of red lace knickers and shimmied into them.

'That's so unfair. I'm not chicken.'

Ruby foraged for a T-shirt, changed her mind and discarded it. Sasha had a strong suspicion that her father's arrival would make it impossible for them all to share this cramped space. He was, she thought, unnecessarily conscious of health and safety, always pointing out hazards that she could happily ignore. Ruby's cotton top in the middle of the shiny floor would be an example. This could be turned to their advantage, however, if he felt obliged to stay somewhere else.

'You don't want me to meet him,' said Ruby.

'And that's totally untrue too. It's not my fault I haven't been able to get through to his phone. I think he must have had it nicked.'

She had kept in touch with Joe intermittently, by text. When she'd started going out with Liam on a regular basis, her messages had become less frequent. But things had never really gelled with Liam. He couldn't help being an average bum-fluff sixth former, his hands clumsy and his kisses too wet. She knew she'd probably romanticised Joe out of all proportion, but the fact remained that he was mysterious and thrilling and tragic. And her first. And maybe, if she met him again, they could take up where they had left off. Or not. If, on their second encounter, he turned out to be nothing like the heroic figure her imagination had conjured, she'd be rid of the fantasy and that would be a good thing too.

The only problem, as Ruby had reminded her, was that he wasn't returning her calls. She'd had no response since he'd wished her a happy new year in January. She wasn't going to let this scupper her trip – she and Ruby knew how to enjoy themselves – but it was undoubtedly a setback.

'He'd've got another handset by now,' Ruby pointed out. 'Even if it was just a cheap thing. Or he could've lent a mate's to tell you what was going on.'

'If he's lost his phone, he'll have lost all his contacts too.'

'What about that photographer? Didn't she have your number?'

'Gina was dead against us,' said Sasha. 'Beats me why it was anything to do with her. I told you, didn't I, how I sent her a friend request on Facebook and she blew me off. Cow.'

'I thought she was cool? She let you stay over.'

'Yeah...' In truth, Sasha felt ambivalent towards Gina. She envied her lifestyle and her undeniable sophistication and she supposed she owed her – she'd helped her out of more than one scrape. But she was aware of an undercurrent of disapproval which she thought unjustified. She longed to challenge it and put her right.

'Why don't you send her a text? Ask if she knows what's happened to him.'

'I told you, Rube, she didn't like us being together. She won't tell me.'

'How d'you know?'

'There's other places I'd rather look first, that's all. Like Piazza Navona. You need to see it, it's truly awesome. This guy Sami, who's a mate of Joe's – they room together – does this living statue thing there. Julius Caesar, I think. And if he's not around we can go to the church, see if the priest knows where he is.'

'He might not even be here any more,' said Ruby, pulling on a tight pair of shorts. 'Hey, d'you think I'll be let into the church in these?'

'It's only a crypt, the bit I went to,' said Sasha. 'What d'you mean, he might not be here?'

'He might have gone to another country.' She stuck out her tongue and waggled it at the mirror. 'Reckon I'm dehydrated. Have we got anything to drink?'

'We'll have to go out and buy some.' When they'd arrived, late at night, there'd been nothing in the fridge but the Frascati and a bottle of mineral water, both of which they'd drunk. 'Anyway, he *can't* go to another country. You only get one chance to claim asylum and if you try to move on somewhere else for a better deal, you get sent back again. It's plain crazy because even if you have friends or family who could help you out, you can't go and join them.'

'You could try though,' said Ruby. 'I bet that's what your Joe's done. How come you know so much about this anyway?'

'I said I'd try and help him come to the UK so I had to, like, find out stuff.'

'You sly bitch, you never told me!'

''Cos I failed,' said Sasha sadly. 'The whole thing was hopeless. I reckon that's why he gave up on me.'

'He was using you, then? One-way ticket.'

'Shut up!' She closed the shutters again and strapped on the leather messenger bag that contained everything she considered important. 'I'm ready to go,' she said. 'I'm starving.'

It was an odd experience for her to be leading the way. The previous summer she'd been endlessly tagging along – whether with Antonio, Bruton, Joe, Gina, Ilse or Renate. Half the time she hadn't liked to voice an opinion, afraid of being thought naive. That didn't matter any more. She was in charge and Ruby couldn't boss her about; she could only follow.

The apartment was, as promised, central. Within a couple of twists and turns – Ruby pausing to peep into courtyards or shop windows – they arrived at a flock of white canopies protecting market produce from the day's glare. Sasha drew Ruby into the gangway between the stalls. 'And this,' she proclaimed, 'is Campo de' Fiori.'

'Oh my God! Where you were in the riot!'

'Yep.'

It was strange to be back there again, in a different season, at a different time of day. She pointed to a dark stain on the cobbles a few feet from the statue of Giordano Bruno and joked, 'That's my blood. Won't wash off.'

Ruby hooted with laughter. 'We can come back tonight, can't we? I'd like to see it when everyone lets rip.'

'It'll probably be really staid. People sitting around yammering. Italians yammer *a lot*.'

She avoided the bar where they'd been drinking last summer and led Ruby to a small café offering breakfast. They sat outside on wicker chairs, pretending they were actors on the set of a movie. It was one of their routines, each trying to keep a straight face while being the first to make the other laugh. Usually the incongruity of their location would be funny in itself, but this place, with its picturesque stalls and swathes of flowers and chic passers-by, could have been a filmset in any case. Not quite real.

They moved on to Piazza Navona, which was thronged like an open-air circus with buskers and jugglers and artists and hawkers. Ruby stopped to examine a pair of feathery earrings pinned on a black display board. Sasha pulled her away, cupping her hands around her eyes to scan the piazza. She hadn't underestimated the crowds, but she hadn't considered the difficulty of steering a way through them.

'How do you know that Joe's mate's going to be here?' asked Ruby.

'I don't. But Easter's a really busy time, innit? So if you want to make money off tourists you're going to put yourself out there.'

'Is that him?'

'No, you dork, that's Christopher Columbus.'

'How can you tell?'

She couldn't, in fact, but she could take a guess, and since she was the old hand, Ruby wouldn't know any better. 'Because he's *gold*. That's what Columbus did, wasn't it? Discover gold. And he's wearing a hat. Julius Caesar is white and has a laurel wreath.'

'I don't believe you.' Ruby went up to the statue and said, hands on hips, 'You're not Christopher Columbus, are you?' The statue didn't even blink.

'You'll have to give him some money,' said Sasha.

'Why? It's not like he answered me. Who's that over there?'

A tall white-robed figure stood motionless in front of the church of Sant'Agnese. As they approached they realised it was a woman: an ice queen or a ghost.

'I don't think he's here,' said Sasha. 'We could come back later, have another look. It will be really busy in the evening too and, like, he probably can't stick around all day long.'

Nevertheless, she slumped against the rail of the fountain in disappointment. The waters representing the four great rivers of the world splashed and mingled behind her back. Ruby perched beside her, flicking through a free magazine she'd picked up, promoting exhibitions, concerts and nightlife.

'There are some clubs here that have free entry before eleven. Maybe we should check them out. Google them on the ipad when we get back to the apartment, see if they do decent music.' Ruby shuffled her feet in a two-step and clicked her fingers; she fancied her dancing skills.

Sasha leaned across, riffled through the assorted adverts and yelped. 'Oh my God!'

'What?'

'Have you got the map?'

'No, you have. I saw you put it in your bag. What is it?'

She jabbed excitedly at the page. 'That's her.'

'What is?'

'See this advert for an exhibition? That's her name: Gina Stanhope. I want to look up the gallery. It might be near here.'

There were two further names beside Gina's and, in smaller print, details of an address and opening times. The central image was eye-catching: an other-worldly landscape that had a hypnotic quality if you stared at it for long enough.

'This isn't one of hers,' said Sasha. 'She takes portraits. She was having a session with Joe when I first met him. Maybe I can show you what he looks like and you'll believe me. He's well fit, honest.'

Ruby was enthused. 'Come on then, get the map out.'

As Sasha unfolded it, a middle-aged man stopped to ask if they needed help; she quickly refused.

'Why did you do that?'

'Because he'll offer to take us there. And then he'll want to buy us a coffee and we'll never be rid of him.' This wasn't necessarily true, but Ruby had a way of inviting attention that made Sasha uneasy. It was true that Renate and Ilse had worn scanty revealing clothes last summer but, like the local girls, they had given off an air of superior confidence. Ruby had swagger a-plenty, but she was also like a puppy who wanted to play with everyone. Indiscriminate. 'Anyway,' Sasha carried on, 'I've worked it out. It's between here and Piazza del Popolo. It shouldn't take us long to find.'

She handed Ruby the map on the pretext that she was a better navigator and they set off for the gallery. Was it possible Gina would be there too, curating her own show? Did artists do that? She wasn't sure. She wasn't sure, either, whether Gina had exhibited before. She'd thought she took portraits, families, weddings, all that commissioned stuff – and a bit of erotica. Maybe there'd even be a full frontal of Joe? She could feel herself going hot all over at the thought. She'd no idea how Ruby would take it; Ruby wasn't predictable. She might be well impressed. Or jealous. Or she might think it was hysterically funny, which would be hard to handle.

It was bizarre enough being back here, nine months on, searching for that elusive sensation she remembered as a warm glow: a lovely fusing of novelty and fantasy. Sometimes she wondered if it had happened at all, if the twenty-four hours with Joe in Gina's apartment was a dream invented by her subconscious. There'd been something so unexpected and tender about their coming together that she couldn't bear the prospect of ridicule – even if it was only directed at a two-dimensional black-and-white image. She began to drag her feet.

'Wassup?' said Ruby, noticing that Sasha had fallen behind. 'Have you got a blister or something?'

'Not yet,' said Sasha, grateful for the excuse. 'But I should have worn my old trainers. I don't want to do too much walking in these.'

'No worries, we're nearly there. It's up here on the right.'

The street widened into a lozenge-shaped piazza, its walls pasted with torn and flapping posters, its gutter clogged with litter. A sleek and magnificent Porsche was parked alongside a glossy glass entrance. Above this the words GALLERIA FARNON were etched into steel. Sasha grabbed one of the door handles ahead of Ruby and hesitated.

'Now what's the matter?' Ruby demanded.

'We might have to pay to go in.'

'Dumbo! It's a commercial gallery. They want to get people inside to buy. Come on!'

She pushed past Sasha with her usual bustling impatience but, once they'd entered, the lofty white space intimidated. A young man with long hair and a perfectly ironed cotton shirt was seated at a desk in the corner. He was conferring with a bearded man in a well-cut suit; the latter spread his hands flat on the surface of the desk as he leaned forward, a briefcase tucked between his ankles. The gallery assistant's gaze flickered towards the girls as if they were intruders and then returned to his customer.

'What is it about these places?' whispered Ruby. 'Why do they always make you feel like you're in church?'

'Ssh,' Sasha whispered back. 'He probably understands English.'

They both moved over to the far wall and a sequence of what Sasha had assumed were wild landscapes, like the one on the poster. In fact, on closer inspection, they were industrial wastelands: abandoned silos, cooling towers and decommissioned factories, raw and monstrous.

'This isn't hers,' said Ruby skimming the labels and moving around the walls at speed. The assistant at the desk was on the phone, speaking in a mannered intonation and rolling his eyes now and again at his client. Another couple came into the gallery; they had the look of serious seekers of culture and Sasha was glad of the cover. She couldn't explain why she felt so apprehensive and, if this was the way she was going to react to seeing a photograph of Joe, how the hell was she going to cope with actually meeting him again in the flesh? If she ever did.

'Is he one of these?' said Ruby.

She had moved on to the wall which showed Gina's photographs. Three bare-chested youths were clambering over each other in a fountain like porpoises, mirroring the sculpted marble from which the water gushed. They gave off an air of wild exuberance and abandon until you looked closer and saw their painful scars.

'No,' said Sasha.

They were nothing like Gina's wedding photos or the retouched portraits of her wealthy sitters. These damaged subjects were in sharp focus, though they seemed ready to sink back into the shadows. A body was trapped in a broken section of piping, asleep; a face was raised in supplication, tears magnifying the eyes in a way that was almost grotesque. There was a disturbing close-up of the blistered hands of a man who'd tried to burn the layers of skin from his fingertips.

'A bit grim,' was Ruby's verdict.

'Not this one.' Sasha pointed to a surreal shot of Sami-as-Caesar sailing past the Circus Maximus on roller blades with his arms stretched wide. The quirky image made her smile.

'Is that him?'

'No, that's his mate we were looking for, Sami. Cool, no?'

Then, abruptly, she reached the end of the row. Here were two framed pictures of a naked couple, lying face down on a wide white bed.

'*I Vulnerati*,' said Ruby who had picked up the catalogue from a side table and was leafing through the English translation. 'It means wounded. And vulnerable too, according to this. Well, it fits, doesn't it, if they're all asylum seekers. Hey, Sash, what's the matter?'

'I think I'm going to be sick,' said Sasha.

'Was it the custard cornetto? You'd better not throw up in here.'

Sasha gave a strangled moan. Ruby felt her forehead. Then she turned to see what she was staring at. 'Fuck, is that you, Sash?'

Sasha swallowed, she couldn't speak.

Ruby said reassuringly, 'It's only your hair and a bit of your cheek showing and that's much too swollen for anyone to recognise. Your bum looks great though. Sorry! Only kidding. Is it really you? And him?'

She had to hide behind her hands. 'I don't believe it.'

'It's no big deal. What about those pics we posted for a laugh after the results party?'

'That was different. I mean, for one thing we were drunk, and anyway they were, like, between friends – not for the whole world to see.'

Ruby indicated the empty space around them. 'Do you see the whole world here? I bet hardly anybody ever comes in or buys anything.'

'Oh my God, they're for sale?'

'Didn't you know she was taking them?'

'I was asleep! She came in on us. I knew she had the camera, but I didn't think... Christ, Rube, what am I going to do?'

Ruby jerked her head towards the gallery assistant with his client in the corner. 'Ask him to take them down. If she didn't have your permission, it's gotta be illegal, right?'

'I can't!' wailed Sasha. 'I don't want him to know it's me. I don't want anyone to know.'

'Then keep quiet, because nobody could possibly tell. Or get her to do it.'

'How?'

'Call her,' said Ruby. 'Fucking tell her right now.'

Sasha stumbled to the exit, pulling her phone from her bag. She'd been back in Rome for half a day and already the time she'd spent with Joe had been reduced to a sordid sideshow for strangers to gawp at. She didn't know if she could bear it.

21

The spring sunshine was dazzling and Sasha's vision was blurred by tears. She could just make out an apparition in white scooting across the small piazza. She began to chase after it, calling 'Sami! Sami!' but the robed figure was elusive. Rounding the corner in pursuit she found herself in an empty street. She rubbed her eyes; she must have been imagining things, her brain confused by what she'd seen in the gallery. No one could disappear from view that quickly. Behind her, Ruby, who'd been struggling to keep up, tripped and cursed.

'Look at that! I've trodden in fucking dog shit. Slow down, Sash. Where the hell are you going?'

'I thought I saw him.'

'Who, Joe?'

'Sami.'

Ruby hopped on one foot and tried to scrape her shoe against the kerb. 'Have you got through to her yet?'

'No.' Sasha pushed her silver bracelet up her arm and stabbed again at the redial button on her phone. Gina wasn't answering, every call went straight to voicemail. Briefly, she considered going back to the rented apartment, curling up on the bed, pulling the covers over her head and blotting out the world. It was what she did in the throes of acute period pain, what she'd wanted to do after the Campo de' Fiori incident, until Joe had turned horror to joy. But now there was no Joe and their coming together, their most private moment of intimacy, was on public display. Gina Stanhope was totally shameless.

'You should go on trying,' urged Ruby. 'She's probably talking to someone.'

Sasha sniffed and strode away from the sickly shitty smell.

Ruby panted after her. 'Hey, wait for me! Where are we off to anyhow?'

'I'm going to have to go to her bloody flat, aren't I?'

'What if she's not there?'

'Then I'll wait.' Her feet, she realised in some surprise, were familiar with the route, and already pounding across Piazza Farnese. 'It's not far from here – we only have to cross the river. You will back me up, Rube, won't you?'

'Of course I'll back you up. She should never have done it! You're meant to pay people to use their pictures or get them to sign for permission. I reckon you could sue her, Sash. It's a flippin' nerve she's got. She must've thought she could get away with it because you'd never see it. She's going to get one massive shock.' Ruby relished a challenge, a storming confrontation. She grimaced happily at the prospect.

They were emerging from Via Giulia onto the Lungotevere and Sasha's steps began to falter. 'You're right,' she said. 'No one who matters is going to see it. Perhaps I should leave it.'

'What about your dad though? S'pose he, like, wandered in there?'

'Why would he do that? It's not the kind of thing he's into: arty farty photographs.'

'Then you could use it to guilt her into telling you how to find him. Your Joe, I mean.'

They crossed at the pedestrian lights onto the Ponte Sisto. Sasha leant over the parapet. The colour of the Tiber, flowing far below, echoed the vivid green of the fresh new leaves on the plane trees. Last summer they had been limp and dusty.

It was weird, when you came back to a place, the way things were subtly different. It could be like that with Joe, too, if she ever saw him again.

Ruby tugged at her sleeve. 'Come on. You've made it this far, you gotta see it through.'

During their canter towards Trastevere, Sasha had made regular attempts to call Gina's number. When they finally entered her street, she punched the redial button yet again. This time there was ringing and her stomach lurched. The ringing stopped and Gina's husky voice came on the line: '*Pronto.*'

At the same moment they reached the apartment block and Ruby, scanning the labels, pressed the top bell.

'*Pronto?*' repeated Gina. '*Chi è?*' Then: '*Momento. Suona la porta.*'

The front door swung open and Sasha clicked to end the call. Why give her any warning now that they were here and she had let them in? Why not wait until they were face to face? In fact, she wouldn't even need to speak. Gina would only have to see her, standing in front of her, to feel as guilty as hell.

The light was dim, the only sound was their footsteps echoing on the stairs. Ruby's mouth was set in a rictus of determination, as if she were the one about to chivvy this stranger she'd never met into abject apology. Sasha couldn't possibly have expressed the confusion of emotions consuming her with every tread.

When they reached the top floor they had to knock again; the door was not already ajar, inviting them in, as it had been on Sasha's first visit. However, Gina drew back the catch and flung it open with a flourish. This must be one of her good days. She was looking particularly glamorous and she had the merry demeanour of someone who's just heard exciting news. Her wide smile became a puzzled frown at the sight of the two girls. She started to speak in Italian – they identified the word '*bagno*' – until Sasha stepped forward. She couldn't believe she hadn't been recognised.

'Gina, it's me, Sasha Mitchell.'

'Oh my God!' She clapped her hands together, then laid them on Sasha's shoulders, appraising her. 'I would never have known. What happened to you?'

'What d'you mean, "What happened"?'

It wasn't fair, the way Gina did this, putting her immediately on the defensive, when it should have been the other way around, like she'd been in another fight or whatever.

'Darling, you're so… grown-up. Not the girl from last summer at all.'

'Oh.' She felt flattered, but wrong-footed too. How could she launch into her diatribe when Gina was beaming in such a positive and admiring fashion?

'You've really blossomed.'

'I have?' Ruby nudged the small of her back. Sasha didn't know how to continue. 'Um… thanks.'

Gina seemed abstracted – half pleased to see her, half eager to get on with something else. Ruby shoved Sasha harder this time. 'Er… this is my mate, Ruby.'

'Oh,' Gina's eyes glowed. 'The famous Ruby.'

The famous Ruby scowled with a touch of petulance. 'What've you been saying about me, Sash?'

'I never said anything.'

'She missed you,' said Gina smoothly. 'In fact, I'd go so far as to say that at first she was completely lost without you.'

''Cos Antonio was such a tosser,' said Sasha. 'I told you that, remember.'

'Well, it's fantastic that you're here again,' said Gina in her cat-that-got-the-cream voice. 'And with your friend this time. But I'm sorry I can't stay and chat. I'm due to meet a client.'

'We don't want to chat,' muttered Ruby, but Gina didn't appear to notice.

'And although it's so lovely to see you, actually I had hoped you were the plumber.' She gave another dazzling smile. 'Pity.'

'The plumber?' echoed Sasha, edging further into the hallway. She could see a slice of the living room, untidy, unchanged.

'My boiler's been on the blink for two days. Nightmare. The only upside is that cold water makes your hair shine.' She flicked it, gleaming, and it fell neatly back into position.

'You've got no hot water?' Ruby shuddered. 'That must be gross.'

'I do wash,' said Gina sharply. 'He was supposed to come yesterday, but reliability isn't one of the strengths of functioning Roman society. Plus plumbers operate under different laws to the rest of us, don't they, so when he promised he'd turn up before midday it was crazy of me to believe him.'

Ruby said, 'If you gotta go out, we could stay here and wait for him.'

'What?' Gina's first instinct was to dismiss this bold suggestion. 'Why ever would you do that?'

'If you're cool with it, we don't mind. Sash says you can get English channels on your TV; you can't in our apartment.'

'You didn't come to Rome to watch TV?'

'Course not! Just while we're, like, waiting for you to get back.' Ruby massaged her shin vigorously, pretending she had cramp. 'We've been walking around all morning.'

Gina began to waver. 'Well...' She stood back, assessing them both, as if weighing up the benefits of hot water against the occupation of her flat by strangers. Except they weren't strangers exactly – wouldn't that make a difference? 'He did text to say he's on his way,' she admitted. 'He must have sent it while I was on the phone. I don't necessarily believe him, but I really do have to get to my appointment. This could be a good commission.'

Sasha cast a quick glance at Ruby, who winked back.

'I'll only be an hour or so,' Gina went on. 'An hour and a half, tops. So if he turns up before I get back, do feel free to leave. I've used him a lot, he's perfectly honest. On the other hand...'

'We can stay till you're done, can't we, Sash?'

'I wouldn't want to disrupt your plans.'

'We haven't made any yet.'

Gina's mobile trilled in her bag. 'That will be Mario,' she said, without bothering to check, clearly too distracted by her important meeting to consider why Sasha had suddenly materialised on her front step. 'I have to go. These are my spare keys. Make sure you double lock the mortise and then drop them into my mailbox on your way out. Oh, and shut the *portone*. I appreciate the favour. Thanks, girls.'

'"Thanks girls!"' mimicked Ruby, watching from the landing as Gina descended the staircase. When the *portone* slammed, she punched the air. 'Success!'

'What I don't see,' said Sasha, 'is how hanging around for the plumber is going to do us any good.'

'I don't believe you!' said Ruby. 'The way you wimped out. You are a total wimpette, babe. You were shouting all the way here like you were mental and then when you get close up and personal it's all yes miss, no miss, three bags full miss.'

'I was going to get around to it,' insisted Sasha. 'But I didn't have a chance.'

'You could have *so* scuppered it for her. Imagine what state she'd've been in if you'd had a go, laid into her? You could've lost her that precious commission if you'd gone at things right.'

'Maybe it's more important to me that she tells me about Joe.'

'Whatever.' Ruby's dimples twitched. 'Anyhow, I stopped her from sending us away, didn't I? And she really owes us, so she'll have to do what you say. D'you need a bit of practice? We could have a rehearsal if you want. I'll be Gina.' She lifted her chin and gurgled in a throaty drawl: 'Darling! What's with this growing-up business? Is it hard? How do you do it exactly?'

'Lay off,' said Sasha. 'Let me look around a bit first.'

'Feeling sentimental?'

'Something like that.'

She stood in the centre of the living room, inhaling traces of Gina's perfume, a tang of citrus from recently juiced oranges, sunlight baking wood. The same pictures were on the walls, the furniture was in the same position – though a new throw was draped on the couch where she had slept, a deep emerald green mohair. There were fashion magazines on the coffee table, along with some scribbled post-it notes, reminders, phone numbers, what might have been a shopping list. In Gina's bedroom, she saw the bed was unmade, shoes had been kicked into a pile, the side lamp had been left on. She closed the door; there was a limit to snooping and anyway it was the other, larger bedroom that held attraction for her: Felix's room.

The sight of it was, in the end, confusing. It didn't resemble anything she recollected. The bed, which had dominated the space, had been folded back into a sofa, and a large North African style rug was squared in front of it. The computer was a blank screen in the corner; Gina's overflow clothes were presumably still stored in the wardrobe, but there were rows of photographs framed around the walls, which she didn't remember. Surely she'd have been aware of all these faces watching her?

'So this is it,' said Ruby. 'Your crime scene. Wicked.'

'It's not a crime scene.'

'You were underage, so technically that means...'

'So were you!'

'No I wasn't. Anyway, my first time was like, totally shit. I've wiped it out actually. I'm not even thinking about it. Or the grotty broom cupboard we did it in. But for you, wow, teen queen of romance, this could be a massive moment.'

'Fuck off.' Nearby noises, a thump and a shuffle, unnerved her and she spun around. 'Hey, what was that?' She was jumpy, horribly jumpy. The place taunted her somehow – perhaps because the spare room looked so completely different from its incarnation on the gallery wall. She could almost hear Gina saying, What bed? There's no bed here. What girl? Can you see anyone who remotely resembles her?

214

For a moment she wondered – and the thought was pleasurable – whether the sounds she'd heard indicated a visitor and whether that visitor might be Joe – although Gina didn't encourage him to call, she knew. He'd only been there on that first meeting for a photo shoot and it was Super Mario who had delivered them on the second occasion. 'I can hear somebody coming up the stairs.'

'It'll be the plumber, you idiot,' said Ruby as the bell rang.

They opened the door to a harassed man in overalls who seemed surprised to see them.

'*Siamo amice di Gina,*' explained Sasha. '*Lei aveva bisogno d'uscire per un'ora.*'

'Hey, well done,' applauded Ruby.

'*Inglese?*' said the plumber with a smile.

They nodded. Ruby added her contribution. '*Non c'è acqua calda.*'

'*Lo so.*' He heaved his bag into the bathroom where the wall-mounted boiler awaited his attention.

'I guess we could go,' said Sasha.

'Go! What are you on about? We said we'd wait for her to come back.'

'I don't think I can face it. Anyway, I'm hungry. I'm ready for my lunch.'

'You've dragged us both all the way over here and now you're bottling it!'

'I'll text her or something. After all, she knows I'm back and, like you said, she owes us. She'll have to do what I want. Only, I'd rather, like, not have a full-on showdown.' Gina's reaction had been unexpected. She'd been hoping for a prickle of annoyance or antagonism: so much easier to have a satisfying argument if the other person was angry too.

Ruby was inspecting cupboards in the kitchen area. She opened the fridge and scrutinised its contents thoughtfully. 'There's food in here. Looks a bit rank though. D'you think the plumber wants a cup of tea? Should we ask him?'

'Italians don't drink tea!'

'Don't they?'

'Well,' allowed Sasha, 'some of them go in for the fancy herbal sort, but generally they have coffee.'

Ruby had moved on to a row of canisters, picking them up and shaking them. 'Oh, this one rattles.'

There came a clanking in the pipes; the plumber called out something they didn't understand. Sasha turned on the cold tap but no water escaped. 'We can't even make coffee.'

'Look at this.' Ruby held up a small key. 'What d'you think it's for? It's not big enough for a door. A jewellery box perhaps?'

'How should I know? Anyway I'm not after her jewellery.'

'It must open something important if she keeps it hidden away.'

'People get robbed all the time in Rome,' said Sasha. 'It's famous for it, like Barcelona. That's why you have to be careful of pickpockets. It's probably for some money box she keeps under the bed. She told me how people like to pay in cash or in kind 'cos then the taxman doesn't find out.'

'A money box under the bed?' said Ruby. 'I don't think so. I think it's dirty pictures she's hiding. There might even be some more of you. D'you reckon she could be a blackmailer?'

Sasha glanced towards the bathroom. She could hear the heavy breathing of a man exerting himself, a few curses, the chink of tools being jostled. 'Then it'll be for the chest.'

'What chest?'

'Over there, that pair either side of the window. The one on the left, which I've seen open, has clothes in it, men's clothes mostly. The other one's locked.'

Ruby grinned and tiptoed towards it with an exaggerated sense of drama. She fitted the key in the lock and lifted the lid. Sasha who had been holding her breath, as if a whole host of demons were going to leap out, came closer. She was disappointed to see more clothes, though these were female: sequinned vests and silky tops, pashminas and palazzo pants, interleaved with black tissue paper, all bearing the labels of French and Italian designers. They lay delicate and fragile like sleeping beauties, unworn for some time.

'I reckon these must be valuable,' she said. 'If they're haute couture or whatever.' Nevertheless the discovery was an anticlimax.

'Just a minute!' said Ruby, slipping her hands between the layers and down the side of the chest. 'I can feel something stiff.' She tugged at a corner and pulled out a heavyweight folder. 'There must be, like, some major secret in here, else why would she have hidden it?'

In the bathroom the plumber was whistling, his confidence restored. Sasha was increasingly agitated. If the folder held more compromising photographs, close-ups of body parts or indecent acts, she didn't want to see them. 'Whatever it is, hurry up. Let's get it over. I think he's nearly finished.'

'Cool it, what's it got to do with him?' Ruby closed the lid of the chest and then sat on top of it to open the folder. 'Who's Eugenie Raven?'

'Who?'

'Eugenie Raven.'

Sasha was flummoxed. 'Haven't a clue. Why?'

Ruby waved a printed document. 'That's what's written here.'

'Where. On what?'

'Dunno. Tenancy agreement maybe? *Affitasi*. That's the sign you see hanging on buildings, innit? To let.'

'Eugenie… oh my God! It must be her, Gina.'

Ruby snorted. 'For real? Sounds like a character from a Disney film, doesn't she?'

'Is the agreement with a man called Boletti? They're the family I was staying with, they're how I met her.'

Ruby turned the pages. 'It's got the name of some company but yeah, Boletti signed it.'

'She was worried he was going to try and evict her. Maybe that's why she's keeping it safe.'

'It's not the only thing in here,' said Ruby, her eyes widening. 'There's like a marriage certificate to the Raven guy and then another when she's still Eugenie Stanhope, *madre*… Stone me – doesn't this look like a birth certificate?' They regarded it together. 'You never said she had a kid.'

'She never told me. Anyway, he'd be what, eighteen now? Old enough to leave home.'

'There's nothing in this flat,' said Ruby, 'that would belong to a teenage lad. No sports stuff, no music, no computer games, no clothes…'

'And no dad named,' said Sasha. 'So she must have been a single parent. Bet she had him adopted and that's why he never lived here. What's his name?'

'Thomas. English, huh?'

'Put it all back, it's nothing to do with us.'

Ruby drummed her heels against the side of the trunk. 'Hey, babe, I'm not done yet. Look, there's this too.'

It was a child's drawing, protected in a transparent envelope. Some squiggles in one corner, some objects that might have been mushrooms or, more likely, flying saucers and some oddly pretty patches of coloured crayoning.

'How old d'you reckon he was when he did this? Three at least? Four? So she can't have had him adopted right away. Maybe this was the last thing he drew for her and that's why she's kept it. Look, he's even put a little signature on the back. Doesn't that say Tommy?'

'Dunno. Can three-year-olds write?'

'Come on, Sash. Get in the frame. There's more to your mate Gina than meets the eye.'

There was a powerful hiss and the gushing of water. Quickly Ruby sat on the folder, and Sasha stashed the picture out of sight in her messenger bag. The plumber emerged beaming, rubbing his hands together. '*Tutt'aposto*,' he said. '*Scaldacqua funziona*.' The girls nodded and smiled.

'Close one,' breathed Ruby, after he'd seen himself out.

'I need the loo,' said Sasha. 'I've been bursting all the time he was in there.'

'Then what?'

'Then we...' Her phone started to ring and she fished for it anxiously. She was relieved to see it was her father calling. 'Oh, Dad, hi. Have you landed?'

'I'm on the fast train to Termini,' he said. 'Where are you?'

'Um...' Too much information wouldn't be a good idea. 'We're in Trastevere.'

'Have you had lunch?'

'Not yet.'

'Everything okay with the apartment?'

'Yes. Fine and dandy.'

'Okay, I'll pick up a cab when I get to the station and buy you something to eat. Dump my bag later. Can you see anywhere you like the look of?'

'Let me talk to Ruby,' said Sasha. 'When we've found somewhere nice I'll text you.'

'See you later, sweetheart.'

'Well, that's it,' she said, snapping her phone shut, only partially regretful. 'If Dad needs us to meet him in, like, half an hour or so, we can't wait around any longer for Gina.'

'We're not letting her off, though.'

'No way.'

Ruby restored the folder to the trunk and the key to its hiding place. Sasha used the bathroom. She wasn't planning to keep hold of the drawing for long – she wasn't a thief – but since Gina had stolen something of hers and violated a precious memory, she could do with a bargaining tool.

22

Gina slid into the seat behind Mario and he smiled at her in the mirror. '*Buona giornata, oggi?*' he said.

'*Benissima!*' she agreed joyfully.

Less than two weeks ago she had been fraught and frazzled, preparing the replacement photographs for the exhibition and trying not to panic over Bertie's threats. But she'd heard no more from Bertie or from Franco Casale and now it seemed things were looking up. Maybe not in the bag yet, but she was optimistic.

Mario was driving her to the offices of a company who published illustrated travel books and guides to social and cultural history. She was meeting a commissioning editor there, Luca Morani. She would overlook the fact that he hadn't managed to make the opening of her show – and all the confusion caused as a result – because David had kept his word and persuaded him to visit since. It had been a pleasant surprise to get a call saying he wanted to discuss a project he was working on.

Mario dropped her in Viale Mazzini, not far from the RAI studios where her neighbour with the colourful outdoor furniture worked as a producer. The company was an offshoot of a larger publishing house and she'd imagined books tottering in dusty piles, but the reception, with its fresh flowers, quiet air con, and elegantly framed samples of cover art, was slick and modern. She didn't have to wait long for the editor to appear. Luca Morani wore a snowy white shirt; his silver hair was swept back like an aesthete's, but he had the dark twinkling eyes of a true Roman. Not easy to manipulate, but hopefully susceptible to charm. As they shook hands she gave him her warmest, sincerest smile. 'It's an honour to be here,' she said. 'You produce such lovely books.'

'We have high standards,' he acknowledged. 'Would you like a coffee?'

'No thank you, I'm fine.'

The walls of his office were papered with a collage of striking images but she didn't have time to examine them because he began to speak and Luca Morani could talk for his country. She'd barely sat opposite his desk in a pose of interested enquiry before the flow began. And it was like listening to music. Flattery, maybe, but that didn't detract from the charming enthralling cadences of his speech. He was saying things she had longed to hear ever since she'd first picked up the camera and she didn't dare interrupt the momentum. At any point, she feared, he might break off, re-examine his diary and burst out: '*Madonna mia*! This is a terrible mistake. You're Gina Stanhope, no? But I was expecting Gina Stanowski.'

She kept waiting for the 'But'. There was always a 'But'. You couldn't get through life without one. That was why Felix had been good for her. He explained it was her natural tendency to be contrary, which meant she had to be positive when she was around him. He was a born pessimist so he brought out her sunny side.

'*Però*,' said Luca.

Okay, not a But, a However. Gina crossed her legs in their slim trousers and locked her hands over her knee. She offered him another slow smile of utmost sincerity and leaned forward slightly to show she was willing to compromise.

The phone rang. '*Scusi*,' he apologised, raising the receiver on his desk.

She caught the vibrations of a high-pitched female voice, though not the words. A harangue, she guessed, probably his wife. She tried not to appear to be listening, not to appear impatient, though she couldn't stop her foot tapping. When luck see-saws so violently from one extreme to another, the desire to pin down a moment of triumph is overwhelming.

Morani ended the call and rotated his expensive pen. He straightened a small pile of papers in front of him and it struck her this might be the contract he wanted her to sign.

'I'm so sorry,' he said. 'Where was I?'

'*Però*,' she said reluctantly. 'You were going to tell me about the catch.'

'The catch?' And then he laughed, a rich booming laugh. They both relaxed.

'The brief is tight,' he said. 'The deadline too.'

'Well, it's true that I'm very busy. Spring and early summer are prime time for weddings. They're my bread and butter and I have to eat. But they're generally at weekends so I have some weekdays free.'

'There would be some travel involved. But you are independent? This wouldn't be a problem for you?'

'I love to travel.' This wasn't true, not any more. In the past, when she'd flown business class it had been different, sometimes a positive delight. Like those far-off days when she'd met Mitch in a string of exotic locations. But budget airlines had destroyed the excitement of flying, turned the process into a chore and a scrum.

'That's good. Excellent. *Allora…*'

She waited.

'Regrettably, the photographer who was working on this assignment for us is unable to continue,' said Luca.

Gina stared at him. 'This book, the project… it's already been started?'

'But yes. It's due for publication at the end of the year, to tie in with the market for Christmas. We could take it out of our schedule completely, or defer it if necessary, but we prefer first of all to investigate other options.' He spread his hands, palms upwards, and then clasped them together, smiling at her. 'So, by happy coincidence, I hear of your exhibition. I visit. I tell my colleagues this woman could be perfect and so we have our interview.'

'You want me to finish off someone else's work?'

He went back to fiddling with his pen, a little defensively. 'Did I not explain the book itself is the work of a journalist? The photographs are illustrations only. However, you may have heard of him, Nico Stakis? He is Greek, but based in Bologna.'

'Possibly,' said Gina, almost certain she hadn't, but she didn't want to sound too grudging. 'What happened to him?'

'He has been in a road accident, broken his arm and his collarbone. Such bad timing! The car is totally destroyed. He is presently in plaster, but he has made us some *raccomandazione*.'

Could news of her style have reached Bologna? That would be a fillip. 'This Nico, you mean he recommended me?'

'Not exactly,' he admitted and Gina envisaged a long list of names scrubbed out because they all had more important things to do. She reviewed those reams of flattery she'd enjoyed so much. There might be a principle at stake here. Would a person who was trying to be taken seriously as an artist agree to subsume their vision to another's? How would it work out if she stepped into the injured man's shoes? Who would get the credit? Who, apart from herself, would care?

'We are hoping for a seamless transition,' Luca continued. 'It's not precisely reportage that we're after. We want to aim for something more enduring. But you call yourself a street photographer, is this not correct?'

She'd insisted on it, in the piece she'd prepared for the exhibition catalogue. Of late she'd been using the studio less frequently for photo shoots, though she preferred the editing equipment there. She liked to think that out of doors she could create an air of untrammelled spontaneity, even if every item in the frame was tightly controlled.

'Yes I do – since I've been following *i vulnerati*, and they live and sleep where they can. Being on the streets becomes their natural habitat, turns them into foragers.'

'The changing face of Italy,' he said, 'is our theme. In particular, we don't wish simply to produce vacant beauties. We are looking for portraits of character to illustrate this position of flux. I will give you the full brief with the manuscript.'

'I promise you, my portraits won't be lacking in character.'

'*Bene*. I think, from what I've seen, that your work and Nico's has much in common.'

Gina didn't care for this. Nobody likes to hear they aren't unique. 'Really?' she said, as non-committal as she could manage, given that she was being compared to an accident-prone Greek she'd never met.

'Well, you are both, if you like, immigrants yourselves. Perhaps you are attracted to rootlessness.'

'Actually I've been based in Rome for the best part of twenty years.' She paused. There was every chance the actions of Bertie and his henchman Casale might render her not only rootless but roofless too. As vulnerable as her subjects. She should not argue with this man. He had influence and contacts, the parent company was prestigious. 'Sorry to be so prickly,' she said, all honey again. 'I'm sure you know the insecurities we freelancers suffer from. The project sounds fascinating and I would love to take it on. With the appropriate credits, of course.'

'Of course.'

'We would need to discuss a fee. Plus expenses.'

'You have an agent? Does David Farnon represent you?'

'Only as a dealer.' There was no need for David to have a larger slice than he was entitled to. He was already in an enviable position: a dabbler, as she thought of him.

As it turned out, the fee Morani quoted was not especially generous. However, he reminded her of other openings the project might lead to and she agreed to take away a detailed brief and the contract, which she would go over with her *avvocato* – not that she had one. She'd sacked her previous lawyer when he'd been incapable of dealing with Bertie's ridiculous writs; David had offered to find her another. The actual manuscript, with accompanying images, would be emailed. Most of Nico's work had covered the northern industrial cities. Gina's focus was to be Rome and the south: Brindisi, Taranto, Naples, Catania. Bandit country, as she thought of it. Places where finding beauty could be a challenge, although there would be no shortage of character.

He then rose and shook her hand warmly across his well-ordered desk. More like a bank manager than a publisher, she thought to herself when he failed to ask her out to lunch. Not that she would have accepted; she'd no time for a leisurely meal. She had to get home to check the plumber had turned up. That would be the icing on her perfect cake: hot water.

Or so she thought, until she checked her phone on her way to the bus stop and saw that David had sent her a text. *Possible buyer alert. Call me.*

The bus was approaching. She caught her breath, didn't breathe out until she had swung aboard. Then she dialled, the mobile sweaty in her palm. 'Hi, David, it's me. Mission accomplished.'

'How did it go?'

'Good, I think. Morani's offered me first refusal on the commission.'

'You aren't going to refuse it, are you?'

'I need to check over the terms before I sign but, you know me, I'll do anything that raises the profile.'

Progress as they wound towards Castel Sant'Angelo was slow. The area around the Vatican was always a bottleneck and in addition they were halted by a temporary traffic light. She had a good view of a piece of stone wall. She added, 'So if you're looking for gratitude, darling, you have it. In spades. He wouldn't have noticed my work if you hadn't given me the show and nudged him to come along… so do you want me to lick your shoes now or later?'

'You sound high, hon.'

'I feel high. Get on with it, tell me the big news.'

'Are you sitting down?'

'Well, I'm on a bus, but yes, I've managed to get a seat. It's not that crowded, but they're digging up some gas pipe in the road so we're stuck a while. You have my full attention.'

'You got my text?' said David. 'I think we may have a buyer.'

'That is *so* delicious! I hardly dared hope money would change hands. I thought the subject matter would be too challenging. Anyway, no matter. Tell me which one?'

'Two, as it happens. Numbers 42 and 43.'

'I can't remember your damned numbering, David! What are their titles?'

'You numbered them yourself. Aftermath 1 and Aftermath 2.'

'Aftermath?' said Gina as the bus finally lurched forward and gathered speed along the riverside. Through the streaky window she could see a party of schoolchildren strapped into backpacks, a daredevil scooter nipping along the narrow space between their crocodile and the side of the bus.

'The pair you produced,' he said, 'when we had to take down your young football player. You are one hell of a chancer, Gina, I'll give you that. But it turns out to be the best thing you could have done. No?' She didn't respond. 'Are you still there? We have to figure out a price. Do you know which shots I'm talking about?'

'Aftermath,' she said slowly. 'Yes, I know exactly which prints you mean. And they're not for sale.'

That steely voice of David's sharpened a fraction. 'Not for sale? What's your *problema*?'

'They were a last minute substitute, weren't they, because Bertie was putting pressure on and because you'd planned everything so rigorously we couldn't possibly allow any blank spaces. According to you, the whole world would cave in if the proportion of gallery wall to frame was not absolutely precise. So I had to come up with the Aftermath pictures. But I don't want to sell them.'

'Why the hell not?'

'Because...'

Because Sasha Mitchell was back in Rome, and might actually still be in her apartment. This was extraordinarily bad luck and something she could never have foreseen. She hadn't expected the girl to return, let alone seek her out. But it seemed she'd only just arrived. If Gina acted fast enough there need be no repercussions, but she couldn't explain all this to David. He'd berate her for being unprofessional. 'I have my reasons,' she said.

'They'd better be good ones.'

'Just take them both down, will you?'

'What, in the middle of the show? Gina, you can't do this to me.'

'I'll find you something else.'

'We already went through your portfolio. Those were the most stunning. And the buyer thinks so too. What am I going to tell the guy? He's coming in to the gallery this afternoon and my instructions were to find out your price. *Capisce*?'

'Let me think about it then.'

'Half an hour,' said David. 'Don't keep me waiting.'

'Okay. Okay. I got the message.'

She switched off her phone, too agitated to make or receive any more calls. At Piazza Trilussa she stumbled homewards through the narrow streets. Moments ago she had been on cloud nine; why should anything change because Sasha Mitchell had reappeared? The girl need never know. In fact, the sale of the pictures presented a solution. If the buyer took them away at once and she replaced them, David might not be happy, but hey, she'd have the money and he'd get his cut. She should ask for the highest price she dared. She toyed with numbers in her head and her step lightened.

Signora Bedini was out on the pavement in her slippers, pulling down the shop's shutters for lunch. She hardly ever left the premises or the flat above where she lived with her younger son. He sat at the till by the door collecting payment or raced around in a delivery van, dealing with orders. '*Ciao, come stai*?' the signora hailed her, as if hoping for a chat: another chapter in the battle with her daughter-in-law. In the last instalment the grandchild had developed a shocking McDonalds habit.

'*Bene grazie*,' Gina called, not wanting to be delayed, speeding up as she neared her front door.

She was, she had to admit, apprehensive about dealing with Sasha and her friend. Arguably, since the girl's face was scarcely visible, permission should not be necessary. She'd prefer to get it, naturally, but doubted it would be granted. Gina had learnt, in her years of being photographed, to detach herself from the end product. The extraordinary looking person on the magazine page wasn't her; it was a two-dimensional creature, preened and primped and painted. In real life no one would recognise her. But try telling that to Sasha Mitchell. She would be far too self-conscious to appreciate the power of the image Gina had created.

She needed to find a way of getting rid of the girls without arousing suspicion. If she could sweet-talk them, send them on some wild goose chase to another part of the city, out to the Catacombs for instance, it would give her time to get over to the gallery. Whereupon she'd have to sweet-talk David, who was a much tougher proposition, but she'd think of something.

She reached the top landing. No voices in her apartment: perhaps the girls had left, which would be a temporary relief. The tension constricting her neck and shoulders eased. She pushed her key into the lock. At least, she tried to push it but met resistance. Perplexed, she tried again and then thumped on the door.

'Sasha, are you in there? Stop playing silly buggers.'

Silence. Why on earth would the girl block up her keyhole? She banged and listened once more; it was hard to tell whether there was anyone inside. She knelt and peered into the lock: nothing was visible. She poked at it uselessly with the key. Glue, that's what it must be. She'd heard of it as a student prank, like an apple-pie bed. Then it struck her that Sasha might have been after revenge, that she might already have visited the exhibition and seen the shots of herself in abandonment.

Gina grew cold. The day that had begun with such promise was splintering into fragments. She would not let the bad luck win out. She still had the girl's number on her phone, though she'd need to do more arm-twisting than sweet-talking at this stage. Standing in the small square of sunshine pooling from the rooflight, she thumbed through her contacts' list. She didn't preamble. 'This is Gina Stanhope,' she said when Sasha answered. 'What are you doing right now?'

'Right now?' Evidently the girl was too flustered to think of lying. 'I'm having lunch.'

'Where?'

'Oh, um, in a pizzeria called Ivo's. I'm sorry we didn't wait for you but the plumber came and fixed whatever it was, and then – '

'Ivo's? San Francesco a Ripa?'

'Yes.'

'Don't leave,' said Gina. 'Wait for me there. I need to speak to you.'

She hung up without giving the girl time to reply. If she hurried she could get to the pizzeria in five minutes. She wouldn't allow Sasha Mitchell the chance to run out on her. Meanwhile she had another call to make – and she was well within her allotted half hour.

'David?'

'Yes, hon?'

'I'm willing to sell. The sooner the better.'

'I knew you'd see sense. So, what – '

'Get as much as you can for them. I hope he's loaded, this buyer.'

'Could be. I've not come across him before.'

'What's his name?'

'Let me check.' She heard the rustle of papers, diary pages perhaps or filing cards. He spoke in a low tone to the pretty boy who worked for him. Then he came back to her.

'Franco Casale,' he said.

23

The girls were waiting outside the pizzeria at a table covered with a green checked cloth. Sunlight dappled the paper place mats, sparkled on the glasses and the cutlery. Sasha and Ruby with their tousled hair and little pastel cardigans looked fresh, young and expectant – though not as relaxed as Mitchell had anticipated. Sasha was chewing her bottom lip, a habit of hers when she was troubled. He hadn't wanted them to arrive in Rome ahead of him but it had been unavoidable, and they'd insisted they could cope for such a short length of time.

He dumped his soft holdall – no need for a trolley case on a casual trip – and hugged his daughter as she rose to greet him. 'Hello, sweetheart, everything all right?'

'Yeah, fine.'

'No problems on arrival?'

She flashed a quick eye-roll at Ruby. 'No, not really.'

'Not really? Did the airport transfer meet you okay?'

'Sure.'

'The apartment,' Ruby began.

'What's the matter with it?'

'Nothing, Dad. It's great. Only...'

'Only what?'

'Wicked location,' said Ruby. 'Done up recently too.'

'It isn't the one we thought we'd booked, that's all. It's similar though.'

'Oh well.' He was annoyed by the substitution, but glad it was nothing more serious. 'These things happen. Not worth stressing over.' The girls exchanged a look of surprise tempered by relief. 'Have you ordered yet?'

'We were waiting for you.'

'And now I'm here,' he said jovially, determined he was going to enjoy this week and the company of the two young women. He was not going to dwell on what kind of holiday his wife might be having. No point even in wishing a downpour on her: she'd probably revel in it. 'Choose whatever you like. Let's push the boat out.'

Their order was modest: Coke and pizza Margherita. He went for Peroni and a Capricciosa. The drinks and a basket of bread were soon set in front of them.

'So tell me,' said Mitchell, 'what have you been up to this morning?'

Ruby jumped in. 'We went to Piazza Navona but it was murder.'

'So what brought you over here?'

It was a simple enough question but they seemed uncertain of the answer. At length Ruby said, 'I wanted to see the river and Sash said there were all these dinky shops over this side. So we've been, like, browsing.'

'Did you buy anything?'

'Not yet. We don't know how far our money will go. But Sash saw these earrings she really liked, turquoise and pearl and silver. They were in this proper quirky shop full of random accessories, peacock feathers and stuff and…'

Ruby was keeping up her end of the conversation but Sasha wasn't joining in. He'd expected her to persuade him of the necessity of viewing these earrings, of coming up with a hundred reasons as to why she couldn't go home without them – although she must know he'd say yes. Sasha had never been a greedy or demanding child, easily contented with small things. And if some of her wishes had been unfeasible – like a horse – it was all the more reason to indulge the harmless requests.

Ruby's account was interrupted by the waiter arriving with their three crisply baked pizzas. Sasha was bringing her first forkful up to her mouth when her phone rang. Mitchell identified its distinctive ring tone, a clip from the Arctic Monkeys' *505*, but she appeared not to notice until Ruby nudged her. And when she answered, she paled as if she'd heard bad news.

'Right now?' she said. And then something about a plumber. She was mumbling, half turning aside.

His eyes met Ruby's across the table. 'Something up with the apartment?' he said. 'I thought you might be trying to let me down lightly. God, they're villains, aren't they, these short-let landlords. Take the money and run. At least you know where you are in a hotel.'

'The apartment's sound,' said Ruby. 'Not massive, but it's okay.' To Sasha, she said, 'What was all that about?'

'I don't know. She says she can't get into her flat. She can't unlock the door.'

'That's nothing to do with us.'

'I know! I told her we didn't do anything. It wasn't like we were supposed to hang around and wait for her to get back. She said we could go.'

'D'you think something's fallen down behind the door and blocked it?'

'Even if it has, it's not like we planned for it to happen.'

Mitchell had been sawing through his crust. He noticed that Sasha hadn't picked up her fork again; her mozzarella was congealing. 'What's going on? If it's not the place we're renting, what apartment are you talking about?'

'Oh...' Sasha's explanation came in a garbled rush. 'You remember the Englishwoman who put me up last year? Mrs Raven? She lives nearby and because we were in the area anyway we called on her. We weren't going to hang out for long, only she had this plumber due and he was late and she was busy and... oh heck... it doesn't matter, it's way too complicated. She'll be here in a minute anyhow.'

'She'll be here in a minute,' repeated Mitchell, a piece of anchovy fillet catching in his throat. He knew, from accessing her website, that Gina Stanhope was a photographer working in Rome; he'd worked out from what Sasha had told him that she and Mrs Raven were the same person. So how did he feel about this information? Curious probably. Twenty years, no, eighteen, was a long time. 'What does she want you for?'

'I don't know,' said Sasha miserably. 'Except that she's locked out.'

She had hardly dented the cartwheel of her pizza. Most of the time she spent peering at the view behind him. He would not turn. You came across old girlfriends from time to time; it wasn't a big deal. Generally the meeting would be uneventful, inauspicious: a brief embrace, an exchange of news and you moved on.

Gina, he suspected, would be different. She'd always been volatile and their relationship tempestuous – though with such long intermissions that every encounter had been like rain after a drought. Mobiles were scarce back then. If they were lucky they could both access a landline on the same continent; if not, they'd developed a convoluted method of passing on messages and arranging escapes. Theirs had been the mad passion experienced in youth – they'd met in their twenties and were completely taken up with each other – until real life and common sense had intervened.

Ruby spotted her first and elbowed Sasha. Mitchell laid down his cutlery, prepared to rise in greeting, to show irreproachable courtesy to this woman whose history his daughter had no inkling of.

At his back a whirlwind approached, slammed an enormous handbag on the table top, from which came the jingle of keys, and roared, 'What I want to know is what the fuck were you two playing at?'

It was difficult for Mitchell, hemmed in by container-grown shrubbery, to push back his chair, but he managed to get to a standing position, to touch her upper arm with a tentative gesture. 'Hello, Gina.'

'This is my dad,' said Sasha.

Gina was looking straight at him with what he thought of as her cat's face: wide green eyes, narrow pointed chin. You couldn't say to a woman like Gina that she hadn't changed a bit because she reinvented herself all the time. She was still lithe, still carried herself with assurance, but would he have known her if they'd passed in the street? Her skin wore the soft honeyed sheen of a life lived in the sun; her hair was short and streaked; her brows were finer than he remembered, arching expressively above deep shadowy sockets. But the eyes – the eyes don't change and once you gaze into them all the minor amendments of time become irrelevant.

'I know,' said Gina. '*Ciao*, Mitch.'

'How are you?' he asked, because he couldn't think of anything else to say.

'Do you, like, actually know her already?' said Sasha, chewing her lip furiously.

'It was a long time ago,' he began.

'Since you ask,' said Gina, 'I'm bloody fuming. Someone's been messing with the lock to my front door.'

'Well, I don't see why you think it was us.'

'You were the last people there, darling, that's why.'

'Sit down,' said Mitchell, out of his depth. 'Please join us. Let me buy you a drink.'

'Join you? Do you really think I can afford the time to… Oh, what the hell.' She semaphored at one of the waiters. 'Renzo! *Mi porta una birra? Grazie.*'

Then with the effortless elegance of her training, she slid into the seat. Compared to her, the girls opposite, so appealing on his arrival, looked clumsy and raw, like unfinished sketches.

Mitchell was sitting beside Gina because there was no other option. Their bodies were a few inches apart. It might have been a pleasant enough scenario: the two of them reminiscing about some of their more outrageous adventures – his intervention with the knife wielding thief in Sydney was the one he was least likely to forget; a small white scar still hovered between his ribs. Digging into the past, stirring up old emotions could be dangerous territory, but there was no doubt she'd remained a very striking woman. And in other circumstances...

Sasha had given up her lunch, pushed her plate aside. 'I don't believe this.' She was staring at Gina in bewilderment. 'That all along you knew my dad.'

'Like he told you, it was years ago, before you were born.'

'Well, obviously. Did you work together or what?'

'I guess you could say we were both frequent flyers.'

Mitchell didn't feel he could add to this.

'Why didn't you say something last summer?'

'How could I have known you were related? It's not exactly the rarest surname in the book.'

'I told you he was a captain.'

'Did you? Four stripes? Oh well done, Mitch.' But her tone was perfunctory, underlaid with sarcasm. 'And, of course, I'm pleased to see you again. Only I'm struggling with this happy reunion concept because I have a more pressing problem.'

She put her hand on his sleeve in a softly familiar way that sometimes used to irritate the hell out of him and at others made him want to devour her on the spot. The moment of confusion it aroused passed when the waiter set down her foaming glass of beer; he ordered another for himself. 'What problem?'

Gina drew a line in the condensation on the glass. 'Your daughter came to see me this morning with her friend. This was, I assumed, a social visit.'

Sasha squirmed and nodded, but didn't speak.

'Unfortunately I couldn't show them much hospitality. I was

due to discuss a publishing contract. Maybe she told you I've become a photographer?'

'Er, yes. A logical career choice, I thought.'

'An *artist*-photographer,' she stressed. 'Spare me those macho guys who are for ever insisting their lens is bigger than yours. So anyway, I had to go out and these two offered to wait in for the plumber who was, *naturalmente*, overdue.'

'He came,' said Ruby. 'Sorted.'

'You can see how desperate I must have been for hot water or I wouldn't have been so ready to trust them. And clearly this was stupid, because they decided it would be fun to play a trick on me and put glue in my lock. I can't imagine why?'

She was focusing on Sasha, whose complexion alternately reddened and blanched. He sensed threats and counter-threats, but neither his daughter nor his ex-girlfriend gave anything away and the accusations remained unspoken.

Ruby said with some belligerence, 'That is so unfair. We didn't play any trick. We did what you said. We shut the door behind us after the plumber had gone, posted your keys, and then we left the building.'

'When? What time?'

'I dunno. We moseyed around a bit. About an hour ago.'

'Did you shut the *portone* too?'

'What's that?'

'The main door into the street.'

'Did we, Sash?'

Sasha considered. Mitchell was disturbed by the unhappiness in her eyes, but he didn't believe for a moment that she'd have any motive for a stupid pointless prank. 'I'm not sure,' she said. 'I think maybe one of your neighbours was coming in as we went out.'

'Have you met any of my neighbours?'

'Um... no.'

'What did this person look like?'

'I think it was a man coming home for lunch or something.'

'Old or young? What was he wearing?'

'I... I don't remember.'

He reckoned it was time to interrupt the inquisition. 'What exactly is the problem, Gina? What are you accusing these girls of? As far as I can see, they did you a favour, waiting in so you didn't have to miss your meeting. What grounds have you got for blaming them?'

'Then who the hell else – ?' she began. And stopped.

Renzo reappeared with the second beer and took away Mitchell's empty glass. A cloud scudded across the sun, a Lambretta passed perilously close to their table and a small dog leapt up into the safety of its owner's arms. Sasha's eyes were downcast, examining a blob of tomato paste that had spattered onto the paper place mat.

Mitchell said, 'You're suggesting someone tampered with your lock by squirting glue inside it? It's a Yale, is it?'

'No, a mortise. I asked the girls to double-lock it, because you can't be too careful. They should have shut the *portone* though.'

'If it's not some joker, could it be a person with a grudge? Have you talked to your neighbours?'

'Not yet.'

'You could try to dissolve it with acetone. That might work. Nail polish remover.'

'I know what acetone is.'

'Well, have you got any?'

'Not on me, no! Plenty in the apartment which I can't bloody access.'

'Do you want me to help you?' he said.

Now she swivelled and looked at him full-on: those eyes he'd never expected to see again, unleashing so many memories. '*You* help me, Mitch?'

'That's what I said.'

'You with your PhD in letting a girl down? What use could you be?'

'Gina,' he said carefully, aware that Sasha was alert and quite possibly about to interrupt. 'I don't know what you're getting at. I was simply suggesting we went to the chemist, bought some nail polish remover and tried it in your keyhole. Or else you could call a locksmith.'

'It's a brand-new lock. I had to change it last year.'

'Well, do you want me to have a go or don't you?'

'Have-a-go Mitch is back in town,' she said, but he could see, beneath the bravado, she was close to tears.

Sasha opened her mouth to speak but closed it again when he frowned at her. He gobbled the rest of his meal and downed his second beer. Gina recovered herself, broke off a section of Sasha's abandoned pizza and nibbled at it without disturbing her lipstick.

At the pharmacy, Gina knew the girl behind the counter and soon the other assistants were drawn into debating solvents and remedies. Mitchell's Italian was rusty but he concentrated on trying to follow the discourse – otherwise God knew which direction his thoughts would take.

They came away with both the acetone and an empty nasal inhaler which they could pump full and use as a spray. Ruby and Sasha were hanging back, conferring in whispers – although Ruby's voice had a strident tendency and he distinctly heard: 'No, Sash, stick it out. Everything will be fine.'

The streets were quieter now that many shops had closed for the afternoon lull and Gina led the way through them unhesitatingly. It reminded Mitchell of being twenty-nine again, helping Gina move down from Milan. That first apartment had been in a different district, but the ochre buildings, the washing clipped to wires strung between windows, the fragrance of roasting garlic and rosemary – these were the same.

They arrived in the narrow street; the buildings were tall and cast deep shadows. Gina let herself in through the main door ahead of him because he'd waited for Ruby and Sasha who were dawdling. He caught up with her talking to a retired couple who lived on the ground floor.

'They've had no problem,' she said, as they began to mount the stairs. 'Which shows it can't have been kids fooling about, doesn't it? In their position they'd have been the first target.'

'And it wasn't us,' protested Ruby. 'Where were we going to get the glue from? It's not like we carry it around in our pockets.'

'You could have found it in my flat. For all I know you turned the place upside down.'

'We did not!'

'Look.' Mitchell wasn't as used to the stairs as she was; he had to catch his breath. 'You don't really think Sasha would do something so stupid, do you? I mean, for Chrissakes, why?'

'There's no knowing what teenagers will do when they get together and egg each other on,' said Gina darkly.

They reached the top landing and she demonstrated her predicament. 'There! See!'

Sasha leant against the wall, staring at her shoes. Ruby joined her, fastening her arm through Sasha's in a protective way. Mitchell knelt and squirted acetone into the aperture. The fumes made his eyes water. 'It'll probably need a few attempts,' he said. 'We'll have to wait a bit in between each one.'

A little over an hour ago he'd been looking forward to a leisurely lunch, followed by an inspection of the rented flat, a change of shirt and a sally forth into the vibrancy of the city. Instead he'd been brought face to face with his past – and not in the way he would have chosen. 'You think the person who did this was being vindictive?' he asked.

Gina was watching him with her arms folded. 'Oh, I'm sure they are.'

'You've got an idea who it might be?' he persisted, as he sprayed the lock a second time. 'Excluding present company.'

'I have thought of someone else, yes. It could be the landlord who wants to evict me.'

Sasha jerked to attention. 'Signor Boletti?'

'The family you stayed with?' said Mitchell, beginning to make the connection. 'God, that was a disaster. We were taken in by all that luxury. They were completely unfit for the job.'

'I'm not making this up,' said Gina. 'You might remember, Sasha, he was giving me grief last summer? I got bored with trying to keep him sweet so he's trying other methods of harassment. Legal and not so legal. Would you believe he tried to denounce me for keeping a bordello?'

'What's that?'

'A brothel, darling. Because, you know, it was sometimes less trouble to take portraits at home than in the studio, so there was a certain amount of... traffic. I had to stop having anyone come here and I took to the streets. He's one devious bastard. This is nothing for him. This is a little taster. He was furious with me for changing the lock last year. He's probably got some cat burglar to trash everything inside and the glue's a delaying tactic.'

'Aren't you being a touch paranoid?' said Mitchell.

'No, I'm not. He's trying to force me out so he can do up the place and sell it. It's falling to pieces at the minute but what does he care? A bit of refitting and refurbishment and whambam he's on for a handsome profit. Have you any idea how much property costs in Trastevere nowadays? I should have bought ages ago when I had the money. Holy Year: that was when it started – the stampede of people falling over themselves to exploit their assets. Cheap borrowing sent the market wild and bringing in the bloody euro hiked the prices even more. People are having to move further and further out of town, which is what Bertie wants me to do. Then he muscles in for a makeover.'

'You've been living here since the nineties?'

'I've moved a few times since we last met, believe me. I've been in this place for seven years. First I was Felix's lodger and then we married to get me onto the lease.'

'Felix?' The name stirred distant inconclusive memories.

'The Raven Queen? I don't think you ever met.'

'When did you marry him?'

'Three months before he died,' said Gina.

Mitchell didn't know what to say to that. Her morality was in a different league from his; how could they ever have been compatible? He whistled as he sprayed the keyhole a third and fourth time, trying to relieve the tension of their curiously assorted unit, marooned on this stuffy landing. Eventually his efforts were rewarded and the key slotted into the lock. It didn't operate smoothly though, and he warned her there might be damage.

She brushed this off, more concerned about the damage inside – and was taken aback to find no obvious signs of disturbance. She opened doors and turned on taps, checked the TV, CD player and computer. Her eyes flickered to two trunks standing either side of French windows, covered in embroidered throws.

It was a strange sensation to find himself in her apartment, observing the trappings of her single life and experiencing a combination of envy and panic. Envy of all these indicators of freedom and spontaneity; panic that he would never escape the dreary straitjacket of middle age.

He coughed; it was as if she'd forgotten about the three of them. 'Everything all right?'

'Yes, I don't think anyone broke in after all. I guess it was a pathetic attempt at a warning.'

'So he *is* threatening you, this guy?'

'Ouf, I don't take fright easily.'

'Well, if there's nothing more we can do…' She wasn't giving any indication that she might ask them to stay. 'We'd better get moving, girls. Leave Gina in peace.'

Sasha, he noticed, was telegraphing anguished messages to Ruby.

'Though perhaps…' he began tentatively. He knew his manner was stiff but he didn't see how it could be otherwise; there was no handbook for this multilayered situation. 'We could meet up for a drink or a meal at some point? We're only here for a week.' It was so long since they'd been in the same city and so unlikely to happen again. 'Would you want that, Gina?'

'Would I want that?' she repeated.

'You must know the best places to go.'

'I suppose it would be rude of me to turn down the offer.'

'Look, it's quite possible you'd rather not...'

'Quite possible,' she agreed.

Was she brushing him off? 'Think about it. And if you get any more hassle from your landlord, you should call me. Or I'll contact you. Sash has your number?'

'Indeed she does.'

An oddly meaningful look passed between Gina and Sasha.

Ruby had been hopping from foot to foot, unable to keep still. 'Before we go, Sash has something to ask you.' When Sasha remained mute, she added in a rush: 'She wants to know what happened to Joe.'

'I'm sorry,' said Gina. 'I can't answer that. He's gone, Sasha, do you understand? And nobody will be able to tell you where.'

'Nobody? Do you mean that?'

'Yes.'

'Not even Sami?'

Gina shrugged.

'Did he change his phone number?'

'I've no idea.'

'Who's Joe?' said Mitchell.

'A friend of mine,' said Gina, in a manner that suggested it was none of his business. 'And though I'm grateful to you for helping me get back in, I actually have another appointment to go to shortly.'

He had the impression she wanted to be rid of them. Sasha was plainly discontented with this lack of information, but they'd been stuck in a stalemate for long enough. He hustled the girls ahead of him through the door and wondered for a second what it might feel like to kiss Gina goodbye. Then the opportunity passed and they were out on the street, searching for a taxi.

The girls had some difficulty recalling the address of the rented studio. You couldn't describe it as anything else, thought Mitchell, when they finally found it. Their double bed was on a raised platform above the eating area and his cell was probably a converted pantry.

'You don't like it, Dad, do you?'

'It's poky as hell,' he said, feeling the need to slow down and take stock. 'But it will do for now. I'll get onto the agency tomorrow and make them move us somewhere bigger.'

The girls sat out on the balcony while he showered and changed. The cacophony from the street masked Sasha's words, guarded and low, but then Ruby's strong emphatic voice rose to dominance.

'Three months before he died,' he heard, as he zipped up his chinos. 'Just about made me flip when she said that. I went, like, shivery all over.'

Some mumbling from Sasha.

'Why couldn't it be his baby?' demanded Ruby loudly in the gap between the sustained bleating of a horn and the revving of a scooter. 'But then, you're right, she'd've married him earlier, wouldn't she, and kept it.'

In the act of buttoning his clean shirt, Mitchell's fingers seized up. He eased open the door that separated his cubbyhole from the living space and listened more closely. They were talking about Gina, of that there was no doubt, talking with some incredulity about the fact she'd had a baby she'd never mentioned.

'Maybe your dad would know,' said Ruby. 'Maybe we should ask him?'

'Ask me what?' said Mitchell, emerging.

'Nothing,' said Sasha. 'It doesn't matter.'

'If you had your kid adopted,' said Ruby, 'like we think Gina did, you'd want to hang on to something, wouldn't you?

A memento. That's what people do, right? Baby's first shoe, or a lock of hair or a photograph – *especially* a photograph. A drawing seems kind of odd, that's all…'

'Sorry,' said Mitchell. 'You're confusing me. You're suggesting Gina Stanhope has recently given up a child for adoption, which is why she's in a bit of a fragile state?'

'Not recently,' said Ruby. 'Yonks ago.'

'When?'

'Leave it, Dad,' said Sasha. 'Please.'

24

It quickly became apparent that the apartment wasn't going to work out for a middle-aged man and two teenage girls. Space was limited and privacy absent unless Mitchell kept to his cramped windowless cubbyhole. 'I may be used to small spaces,' he told Sasha the following morning, 'but this takes the biscuit, sweetheart.'

'We like it here,' said Sasha. 'We like being in the middle of everything.' She was squatting in the midst of her unpacking; she and her dad were both waiting for Ruby to finish in the wet room.

'Well, I'm going straight round to the agency. They need to find us somewhere else.'

Alarmed, she said, 'We don't have to come with you, do we?'

'Not if you don't want to. But why are you getting all your stuff out of the bag? You'd be better off packing it up again so we can move promptly.'

'It won't take a minute to sort it,' said Sasha, scrabbling for a pair of socks. She was hoping he'd be the only one to move.

'So what are your plans for this morning then?'

'We thought we'd go to the Vatican. Ruby wants to see the Sistine Chapel.'

'I suppose she ought to see it,' he said, 'but you should have organised yourselves sooner than this. By the time you get over there the queue will be a mile long and you'll have to wait for hours to get in.'

'We don't mind. We like queuing. It's social.'

'It's a museum, not a nightclub.'

'We know that!' Sasha and Ruby had already agreed that pretending to be stuck in a queue and spending an eternity traipsing the Vatican corridors would give them an alibi. Sasha's objective was not sightseeing at St Peter's but a visit to the crypt of the Madonna of all Mercy. 'You'll be all right on your own, won't you, Dad?' After all, she was the expert now. It must have been years since he'd done anything other than touch down at Fiumicino airport. 'You won't be bored?'

'Not at all. I have some old haunts I might revisit.'

'Are they places you used to go to with her?'

'With who? Gina, d'you mean? I couldn't say. That far back, it's a bit of a blur. We'll meet up for lunch again, shall we?'

'Okay, I'll text you when we're through.'

It crossed her mind that his manner, his attitude to Gina, was deliberately vague, but she wasn't going to let it bother her because she'd got what she wanted: another morning to track down Joe.

It was strange to be getting off the bus beyond the railway bridge in Via Ostiense and walking towards the waste ground. In fact she had to do another double take, for that's all it was: an empty piece of land. Yet her recollection of the nylon tents and cardboard shelters, the atmosphere of desperation, was vivid and indelible. If she shut her eyes she could still see the stained mattresses set out to air, the clothing, rinsed but not very clean, draped out to dry, a limp Afghan flag, a tumult of litter.

'It was here,' she said.

'What was?' Ruby looked around, not understanding.

'Where all the refugees lived, in a sort of camp.'

'Right by the street, you mean?'

'Yeah, it really freaked me the first time I saw it. But it was 'cos they didn't have anywhere else to go. There isn't enough housing.'

'They were, like, gypsies?'

'Afghani mostly. I told you before.'

'But… you don't mean to say…' Ruby was wrinkling her nose in disgust. 'This Joe of yours, you made out with, was actually a rough sleeper? Rank and smelly.'

'It's not a person's fault,' said Sasha furiously, 'if they haven't got sanitation.'

'But, Sash, really, that is gross.'

'You saw him in the photo. The only gross thing about that was Gina's nerve in taking it: Joe was totally buff. And anyway, he wasn't living on the street. He roomed with Sami *and* they had a shower and everything. He was earning a bit of dosh and applying for his documents.'

It wouldn't have occurred to Sasha to keep any secrets from Ruby. They shared their most intimate experiences – that was what best friends did. But those three weeks last summer, Ruby hadn't been able to share. She'd missed out and it was going to be difficult to bring her up to speed. 'I thought the same as you,' she said loftily, 'when I first came across those guys. I thought I was going to be mugged or something. But I wasn't. And nobody should have to live like that.'

She lengthened her stride and veered down the road that led to the church. Ruby stumbled after her, apologising. 'I wasn't disrespecting him,' she said. 'Or them.'

Sasha stopped so abruptly in the middle of the pavement Ruby almost crashed into her. Across the street was the dowdy bar where she and Joe had had their first halting conversation.

'You know what, Rube, if you'd've come with me it would all have been so different. Everything. We'd have hung out more with the other students. We'd have gone clubbing together over in Testaccio and found ourselves some cool Italian boys who wore Dolce & Gabbana and were ace on the dance floor. We'd have gone on day trips to the beach with them, or the lakes. Or maybe we'd even have hooked up with that knob-head, Harry, and one of his mates, because they were so pissing rich. We'd have got them to buy us loads of cocktails so we could get absolutely blasted before we went back to their room and let them take our pants off. But the fact is, you *weren't* here and it didn't happen like that, none of it. Don't ask me why.' She rubbed her eyes with the back of her hand.

'Hey... Sash. I'm sorry.' Ruby put one arm around her and fumbled in her pocket for a scrap of tissue. 'Here, you can't turn up all snotty. The way you're talking, it sounds like you're glad I didn't come with you.'

Sasha sniffed and blotted her tears. 'That's not what I meant. It's just that if you're two mates you're more likely to hang around with your own crowd. It's because I was on my own things ended up the way they did. There it is, ahead of us. Do you want to have a look in the church first?' The closer they drew, the more she wanted to delay. Gina had warned her off, hadn't she? Don't ask, she'd said and that was precisely what Sasha was planning to do.

'Why?'

''Cos when my dad says what else have you seen, we can say the Madonna of all Mercy and we won't be lying and he won't know it's nothing special.'

'Bollocks,' said Ruby, giving Sasha a little shove so that she almost tripped at the top of the spiral staircase. At the bottom, the doors of the crypt stood open.

Sasha paused on the threshold, scouring the vaulted space for the Lion King, unsure whether she would recognise him. Balding? Glasses? A dog collar would help. Instead, a plump woman with soft white hands and soft white hair bustled up to them. In her sprigged linen dress she resembled a well-padded armchair. '*Buon giorno ragazze*,' she said in a strong American accent. 'You've turned up good and early.'

'We have?'

'You are my volunteers?'

Sasha was trying to place the woman. She thought she remembered her from her first visit. Wasn't she the one who'd been running the language session?

Ruby said without hesitating, 'Sure. What do you want us to do?'

'Oh my Lord, you're British.'

'Is that a problem?'

'Of course it ain't. A good Catholic is a good Catholic. We have a whole heap of donations and we need to sort the bedding from the clothing and adult clothes from the kids', and then anything saleable that might raise us some funds can go into another pile. You've done this before, back home?'

'Oh yes, often,' said Ruby as the woman led them to an anteroom where a mass of black bin bags oozed their stuffing. 'Do you get a lot of English-speaking volunteers?'

'It depends. Mainly for teaching in the language classes.' For the first time she seemed to assess them thoroughly. 'Though that requires some experience and you're a little younger than usual, I'd say. Now, I'm Annie and you are...?'

'Ruby. She's Sasha.'

'Oh.' She frowned a moment. 'My memory for names is like a sieve but I didn't think... Hey, but that's how it goes in this city. You never get what you expect!'

'Is Father Leone here?' said Sasha, finally finding her voice.

'He never lets up, that priest. He's in a meeting but he'll be back here soon enough, sorting out the problems of all these guys. And the paperwork! Well you should see his office – it overflows. His dedication is terrific.' She beamed. 'And don't worry, he won't let you leave without a thank you for all your hard work. He's a very gracious person.'

'I have met him before actually. But it was when I visited last summer and I don't know if he'll remember.'

'Were you over with your church group?'

'No, I was on a course.'

'And you've come back to us! My, that is impressive.'

'I had a friend... an Afghan boy who was helping out in the crypt too. He was called Yusef. Maybe you knew him?'

'My lord, there are hundreds of Yusefs! These Afghanis often only have the one name until they're obliged to fill in a form and then they pick another right out of a hat. It doesn't make identification too easy.'

'He liked to call himself Joe.' Annie didn't seem any more enlightened, but Sasha persisted. 'Do you think he still comes here?'

'I wouldn't know, sugar. There are boys passing through daily, moving on. If they get absorbed and settle down, well, that's a good sign, but this country ain't too hot at absorbing folk, you may have noticed. I stick out as much as you young things and I've been here too many years already. Don't let me hold you up any longer – I talk far more than is good for me – you go right ahead.' Cheerfully she trundled away.

'Now we're stuck with all this,' said Sasha, surveying the black plastic mountain. 'And it'll be worse when the actual volunteers show up, it's going to make us look proper suspicious, like impostors or something.'

Ruby slit open a bin liner with her fingernail and a hotchpotch of colours flooded out. 'Do you really think they're going to care that they've got two extra pairs of hands to do their dirty work? Well, maybe not exactly dirty work but it is effing boring. My mum does this kind of thing when she's on one of her fundraising jags. Tries to guilt me into helping her and now I know why I don't.' She tugged out a shirt with a large rip in the elbow and held it at arm's length. 'I'm already feeling like an old bag lady. Honestly, Sash, the scenes you get us into!'

This wasn't how Sasha had planned it. She didn't mind doing the work; in fact it made her feel better about pursuing the information she was after. But being stuck in a little underground chamber, unable to see who was coming or going – which had been the whole point of the enterprise – was completely useless. And they weren't making much of a dent in the mountain. Their progress was slow, pulling out items of clothing one by one, trying to decide whether they would fit an adult or a child, whether they were good enough to sell. Perhaps they shook the fabric too vigorously: fluff and dust particles flew about making them wheeze. The artificial light and lack of air was enough to give anyone a headache.

They began to think they had been forgotten – and no other mysterious volunteers arrived to challenge them – but some time later Annie returned with two mugs of weak coffee. Sasha was folding a yellow knitted blanket into quarters so you couldn't see the moth-holes.

'No, don't try to hide them,' said Annie. 'These people have little enough cover – just a few pieces of cardboard sometimes. They're entitled to know what they're getting. Here, I brought you some drinks.'

'Thanks.' Sasha took the coffee which was so hot it burned her tongue.

'It's warm in here,' said Annie. 'Step outside if you need a break. The main body of the crypt is pleasanter. And you don't want to spill coffee on the clothes.'

'Is Father Leone free yet?'

'I believe so. If you…'

Sasha charged ahead without waiting – she didn't care to be shadowed by Annie – but she had to pull herself up, undecided. There was a man who *could* be Leone, but he looked as shabby and seedy as some of his homeless charges. Only his way of standing set him apart.

She approached warily. 'Father Leone?' she said. '*Buon giorno*.'

He turned and grasped her hand between his. 'My young helpers!' he said in heavily inflected English. 'Thank you. We appreciate very much your efforts. How do you find us?'

Sasha wasn't sure what he meant by the question, but she answered. 'Actually I've been here before. I came to visit and met you last summer.'

'*Davvero?*'

'With Gina Stanhope, the photographer?' He nodded, but he wore an expression she couldn't altogether decipher. 'I was also a friend of Yusef. He used to hang out here a lot because you'd helped him. You'd tried to get him into school, he said, but nobody believed his age so he wasn't given a place. He told me he wanted to be a doctor.'

The priest was standing motionless, with his arms folded. His immobility made the girls look as though they couldn't stop fidgeting, shuffling, scratching, twitching.

'Ah,' he said. 'Yusef.'

'I used to hear from him,' Sasha went on, 'until a couple of months ago. Since then he's never texted me back.'

'It is unfortunate,' said Leone.

'What is?'

Even with the electric lights blazing the crypt was an underworld, a no-man's land cut off from the streets above. Holy Week was approaching with all its palm-waving and pageantry, and across the river in Piazza Risorgimento, which was where they were supposed to be, the queue of tourists would be snaking past gaudy stalls selling purses and T-shirts and snow domes and sacred hearts, and the steps of St Peter's would be overflowing with the faithful hoping for a sighting of their Holy Father. And what possible connection could there be between all that religious pomp and these destitutes, who were mostly Muslim anyway?

'We are trying to help him,' he said.

'Help him? Yusef? Why, what's happened?'

'It is not so uncommon. He is imprisoned.'

'Holy shit,' muttered Ruby.

Sasha couldn't articulate her thoughts, though she had a million questions.

Ruby had greater presence of mind. 'What's he been arrested for?'

The priest indicated that they should follow him into his office, the shrine to paperwork Annie had described, so they could speak more privately. He started to explain. 'He wanted to leave Italy. Many do. Germany, Sweden, UK, these are all better destinations. Here, you see, there is no assistance, no requirement on the state to provide housing. No access to health care without permanent address. No chance of work without *raccomandazione*.'

'He was trying to get to England?' said Sasha. 'He never told me he'd started out!'

'To travel without documents is always a risk,' said Leone. 'There was some altercation, we have heard, at the border. Yusef was crossing into France when he was mugged. He was carrying money, maybe too much, because when the police intercepted they didn't believe it was his own. Also he had no permit. They hadn't far to transport him back to Italy, but we don't know where precisely he is being detained.'

'They thought he'd stolen the cash?'

'He claimed he earned it through working for our friend, Gina. *Comunque*, this is difficult to prove.'

Those nude pics, thought Sasha instantly. She'd said she'd give him a cut if she sold them, but probably the buyer didn't want to get involved. Especially not with a legal case.

'It is,' he sighed, 'a great shame.'

A great shame? Sasha wanted to yell. Joe locked up for something he didn't do? That was a howling injustice!

But Leone was talking about something else. 'We were trying to raise funds for a lawyer to assist him,' he said. 'We know a few who work, pro bono, but there are always expenses. Gina had something she was planning to sell – perhaps she felt responsible a little, I couldn't say – but I have been talking to her in these moments and there has been a calamity in this regard.'

'A calamity?' Wasn't it enough that Joe had lost his earnings and been incarcerated? No wonder Gina hadn't wanted to tell her anything. 'How do you mean?'

'Without the money for representation, his chances are not good.'

'What will happen to him?'

Leone was patting the piles of paper on his desk into neat rectangles, but it didn't reduce their volume. 'It is hard to conceive what Yusef has endured. His family in Ghazni is killed in a mortar attack. He has to travel across mountains, in terrible conditions, and then across the sea to reach us. He has the winter in Rome with nowhere to sleep, only here. He waits for a year, more, for schooling and it is denied. He begins to earn a little. He's young and impatient, frustrated also. He thinks he will take his chances, but he lacks the preparation. I see this all the time. However, it is expensive to keep a person in detention. He may be deported.'

'To Afghanistan?'

'It's possible.'

'After everything he went through to get here?'

'First we must locate the detention centre. Then, with the aid of a lawyer, we can get him brought back to Rome and, with God's grace, he can fight for his right to remain.'

God-talk always made Sasha feel uncomfortable.

He added, 'But we have this setback in the finances and Gina, she troubles me.'

She's been screaming at him, Sasha interpreted, as she screamed at us over the stupid glue business.

'I only met her yesterday,' said Ruby. 'But she was, like, full-on. She said everything was going great.'

'That was yesterday. Unfortunately today she has bad news. She too has been robbed.'

Sasha and Ruby exchanged glances. Sasha felt her heart battering her ribs as if it wanted to break out. Her mind raced ahead, imagining the priest saying, 'The one precious memento she kept of her little boy is lost.' She should have confessed before this, sorted out the swap: the photos for the drawing. She'd been building up to it; she hadn't quite got there.

'A very valuable picture,' said Leone.

'Oh…?' The pictures were hanging on the walls for all to see. Probably the intruder who had tampered with the lock had nicked it and Gina had taken a while to notice it was missing. She was relieved not to be responsible, but put off trying to negotiate an exchange. They'd have to work out how to get the drawing back discreetly. Or maybe it would be simpler to destroy it? If Gina had already flipped out so badly, how would she react when she discovered what they'd done? Sasha didn't even want to think about it.

25

Old haunts. What in the end did they amount to? A room above a bar where he'd spent too many hours playing poker; a German style *birreria* where beer spouted from the brass taps of huge wooden barrels; a restaurant where they were always treated like royalty; a certain bench under a certain tree in the Giardini Borghese, which had once been a favourite rendezvous. You'd have to be excessively sentimental to want to revisit any of them – and he wasn't, not really.

Not sentimental, no, but at this particular moment, stomping down the Via del Tritone, Mitchell felt he could do with a boost of some kind. He hadn't even been able to beat the hell out of some slimy Roman lettings agent who'd regarded him sorrow-fully through his Armani-framed spectacles and apologised that there was nothing he could do.

'There must be something!' The open-plan office had been divided by screens flaunting wide-angled photos of modernised flats and studios. 'Are you telling me every single apartment on your books is fully occupied?'

'You are in a most desirable area,' the agent had pointed out, twiddling his pencil. 'Close to Campo de' Fiori. The *signorine* were very happy.'

'Suppose they hadn't been? What would you have done? What else would you have offered them?'

'Well...' A resigned shake of the head. 'That was already two days ago. It's true we had a fine apartment available then, a better size for three people, but it was a little further distant from the *centro storico*. The *signorine* chose to stay where they are and, regrettably, the other has been taken. Easter is a busy time.'

Mitchell asked to see a schedule of the agency's listings, available or otherwise. He asked for further details of the original property he'd booked and why it had suddenly been withdrawn.

'Unfortunately, we don't have control over the owners' decisions. Or over the problems which can beset old buildings. In this case, there was a leak, the redecoration is not yet finished. What can we do?'

'More likely they got a better offer,' said Mitchell sourly. 'So if you can't deal with my problem, perhaps you have a manager who can?'

It was at this point that the young man started muttering about a possible *sconto*, taking out a pocket calculator and tapping its keys with the tip of his pencil. Mitchell sat back, folded his arms across his chest and gave what was intended to be an intimidating glower as the agent nudged his figures upwards, ten euros at a time.

When he unlocked his petty cash box and counted out 200 euros in twenties, Mitchell pocketed the notes and considered himself the victor. But not for long. As soon as he was out on the street he felt cheapened. He might be able to buy a couple of nights in a hotel but it wouldn't be at the standard he was used to and it would mean abandoning the girls, which he was most definitely not about to do. They could be left to their own devices during the day, but he was determined they would sleep safely at night. He'd been made a fool of and it rankled that he'd allowed himself to be disadvantaged so easily, that he'd been paid off with petty cash, for chrissakes!

His equilibrium had been further unsettled by Ruby's gossip about Gina. He hadn't wanted to press for information, but he'd been left with the disturbing impression that she'd had a baby a couple of years before Sasha was born. Which meant that it might be his. He could understand she'd have found it difficult to cope as a single parent, but surely she would have contacted him before contemplating adoption? Surely not even someone as capricious as Gina would deny a man knowledge of his own child? The very thought stifled the air in his lungs. He had to get a grip on himself, push such speculation aside.

He wished he could feel positive about the money burning the lining of his pocket, but that, too, was lowering his mood. Perhaps a drink would help. It was almost midday and he was thirsty. He veered left towards Via San Marcello and before long found himself in front of one of his old haunts, the Antica Birreria, which was opening up. He was greeted with warmth as the first customer, ahead of a rush for *wurstel* and *sauerkraut*, and he was pleased to see no change. The art deco mirrors, the wooden panelling, the casks behind the bar were exactly as they had been on his last visit, God knows how long ago.

He sat at one of the old scarred tables. Maybe he could confront Gina – no, confront was too strong a word – probe tactfully into the past. Meeting again like this, it would be churlish to ignore her, not to recover some lost ground. From his jacket he pulled out the flyer he'd taken the day before from the pile on her sideboard. When he unfolded it he expected to see a brochure for wedding clients, but the flyer turned out to be advertising an exhibition. He noted the address: it wasn't far, so perhaps he would stroll there after he had eaten. He sent Sasha a text and she replied that they were still queuing, but they'd bought some panini from a stall. He was free to order himself a snack and another *stein*.

While he waited he toyed with his phone, with the idea of calling Corinne again. He'd rung yesterday, on arrival, to let her know that everything was fine. She had cross-examined him on Sasha and Ruby and seemed satisfied with the answers. She'd been halfway up a Scottish mountain at the time and had described the view – damp but breath-taking – and the inn – yellow and smoky like kippers – where she and Nadia were staying. That was all. He hadn't mentioned Gina. He put down the phone without dialling; there was nothing else to report.

Afterwards he regretted the *wurstel*. The greasy sausage lay heavily on his stomach and slowed him up as he made his way to the gallery. From time to time he was diverted by the passage of gorgeous Italian women with spiky heels on their feet and phones and sunglasses clamped to their heads. Yet even their appeal would be trumped by the glimpse of a powerful Ducati. In his late teens and early twenties he'd owned a bike, an old Yamaha. It was nothing special but it was as near as you could get on the ground to flying. He'd had to sell it to finance further training and he didn't replace it because flying in the air was the real deal, but the sight of a fine specimen could rouse a momentary thrill.

He found the gallery with relative ease; its appearance more discouraging than inviting. He liked things plain and simple – the *birreria* hadn't disappointed in that regard – but there was a difference between simple and acute trying-too-hard minimalism. Gina had always hung around with posers – she'd been part of the fashion industry, however much she might have mocked it – so it wasn't surprising she should feel at home in a pretentious place like this.

As he gazed around the walls, the pictures that first caught his attention were not hers. They were shots of abandoned factories and warehouses in desolate settings, taken at night. They were almost bereft of colour, though there were token splashes: a gloomy green door, a rusty roof, a bluish chimney. Their surreal quality, the brooding atmosphere, chimed with his mood.

He ignored the work of the next exhibitor, whose vivid hyper-active photographs of dancers, acrobats and jugglers conveyed

THE APARTMENT IN ROME

the superficial glitz of performance but left him cold, and moved on to Gina's black and white images. He was genuinely curious about what she might have produced, as if her work could illuminate her character and give him clues as to how she had spent her life. Some shots had surprising energy: half a dozen boys lining up to play leapfrog or scaling the wall around the Pyramid – but for the most part they were sombre portraits, stark and shocking in their intensity. The subjects were victims of one sort or another; battle-scarred.

He remembered there'd always been mutilated beggars on Rome's street corners or blind men flogging lottery tickets. A tradition of charity from penitent pilgrims hoping to ease their way into heaven. But now the pilgrims were outnumbered by avid shopaholics and the scale of the needy swamping the streets was beyond the redistribution of a bit of small change. He was surprised, frankly, that Gina had chosen to work with the socially excluded. It was a long way from designer frocks and handbags, though that may have been the point for a woman of such extremes.

He wondered how much she was charging and gave an involuntary pat to the cash in his trouser pocket, which he ought to stow safely in his wallet. He reached her final portraits: two lovers on a bed, labelled Aftermath. They'd been in a fight, that much was clear, presumably with each other. He was surprised, first of all, that any woman would so readily sleep with a man who'd beaten her, and secondly, that Gina had been allowed to take the photograph.

Then he realised the whole thing was an elaborate set-up, the participants actors and the fierce bruising created with theatrical make-up. Did that mean the rest of her images were faked too? They did, on second inspection, look almost too controlled. Powerful, yes; beautiful, even, if you liked that kind of thing. But genuine? He doubted it.

The girl on the bed reminded him in a way of Corinne. She used to sprawl in similar fashion when sleeping, with her knee bent and her buttock curved like a peach. Now she always wore pyjamas. He saw her naked sometimes in the bath or in the shower, but at night she turned away from him, presenting her back. He would not think of Corinne, it would only set his doubts rumbling.

He sauntered over to the desk where a blond man, dressed from head to toe in white, was seated. He raised his eyes to Mitchell and must have decided at once that he was English. 'Can I help you?'

'I'm interested in the work of Gina Stanhope.'

'Fascinating, isn't she? A true artist's perspective. You think you know what you're looking at and then she subverts it and you find yourself having to look again. Strong stuff, no?' The man's accent was camp American; he exuded a self-confident languor. He was older than he'd seemed from a distance, probably much the same age as Mitchell himself.

'Where does she come from?'

'Well, she lives here in Rome, but she's British originally, like yourself. I have an international clientele, so we present international artists.'

'There's a pair at the end,' said Mitchell, 'entitled Aftermath.' His hand strayed again to his pocket. 'How much would she want for one of them?'

The man opened a drawer of his desk and appeared to consult a list. 'I'm so sorry, those are not for sale. I already had someone else ask me the same question.'

He was puzzled. 'Surely you can have any number printed off?'

'Well yes, though there's a deal of work goes into producing the perfect print. So for it to have value to the buyer you want the edition to be limited, you can't have the market flooded. A photographer might agree to sell an image under licence which could make him mega-bucks for sure, but that's not what a collector would be after and I have you figured for a collector. Would that be correct?'

'Well... you know...' Mitchell lifted his shoulders and let a bland expression spread over his face. He'd bought posters of bands and bikes as a teenager but that was about the sum of it. Never an original, never a work of art. There were pictures on the walls at home, he'd even paid for some of them, but they'd all been chosen by Corinne. 'It's a shame,' he said, grateful for a let-out clause. 'It struck me particularly, Aftermath, but if as you say it's not for sale...'

'If you want to leave me your name and number, I could contact Ms Stanhope to see whether she would change her mind.'

'No worries, I'll take another look at some of the rest.'

'She's going to go far. Did you see the review in *Il Messaggero*?'

'No, I didn't.'

'I have an English translation.'

Mitchell's phone vibrated in his pocket. 'So sorry, I really must take this call. But thanks, anyway, for the information.' He backed away across the spotless floor; the tiniest crumb or speck of grit would show up instantly, loom out of proportion. He pressed the phone to his ear. 'Sash? Hello, sweetheart, are you done?'

Reception in the gallery was poor, as if it had been soundproofed to aid visual concentration. He was glad to get out of it, escape from its hushed environment back into noisy street life. 'I can't hear you... Yes, I've already eaten. Shall we meet in half an hour, under the obelisk in Piazza del Popolo? You know where I mean? I'm on foot, but it will be quicker for you to catch a bus. Anything that goes from the Vatican down Via Cola di Rienzo and crosses the river. Should be easy enough.'

Piazza del Popolo wasn't as teeming as Piazza Navona and Piazza di Spagna. It was free from traffic these days, unsullied by exhaust fumes, and its spacious oval allowed for a stately flow of pedestrians. Mitchell knew as he settled beneath the obelisk that he would be in for a wait, but there was plenty to look at. It was like sitting in the world's most rococo theme park: marble arches and statues, copper domes and cupolas, and filigree-fine streets spinning from the central hub like threads from a spider's web.

A living statue was poised below the Pincio, dwarfed by the monumental effigies adorning the fountain beside him. Passers-by didn't take much notice and Mitchell thought it an odd place to stand. As a breed they'd become irritatingly ubiquitous and he usually avoided them, but because he had nothing else to do he kept his sights fixed on the man: a Roman Emperor, he guessed from his robes. He hoped to catch him out and regretted he wouldn't be able to spot any tic or twitch without moving closer. However, he did see a rapid change when two *carabinieri*, all braids, buttons and boots, materialised through the archway leading to the Via Flaminia. In an instant the statue had divested himself of toga and wreath and was sitting on the lip of the fountain, packing them into a box. Afterwards, casually, as if to deflect attention, he began to walk in the opposite direction, towards Via Babuino.

Thereafter Mitchell was taken aback by the speed with which things happened. The *carabinieri* were no longer to be seen, but the statue managed to collide with a woman who wasn't looking where she was going (spiky heels, dark glasses, total absorption in her phone call). There was a slight hiatus, then the woman was screeching and scrabbling for the components of the mobile she had dropped and shattered. Had she also been robbed? Two young girls were running in pursuit of the statue as if they were trying to rescue her purse. When he recognised them as Sasha and Ruby he was confused because they'd emerged from an unexpected direction, but he did what seemed perfectly natural at the time and joined in the chase. He gained on the fellow and brought him down in a rugby tackle.

'Dad!' exclaimed Sasha in horror. 'What are you doing?' She knelt to help the man gather his spilled possessions and return them to his box. '*Stai bene*?' she asked. '*Sicuro*?' Then the two of them rose to their feet and moved a few paces away, deep in conversation.

Mitchell hadn't played rugby for thirty years and was feeling the impact of the cobbles on his elbows. 'What the...?'

Ruby attached herself to him and started to prattle. 'The sightlines from here are amazing, aren't they? So straight. Like the way you can see the Victor Emmanuel monument at the far end of the Corso. I read it used to be a racetrack right up until the nineteenth century. The Romans had so many race courses, didn't they? Or do you call them arenas? There's Piazza Navona and the Colosseum...'

Still winded, Mitchell gasped, 'Does Sash *know* that bloody bloke?'

'...And the Circus Maximus.' Ruby was ticking the list off her fingers. Eventually she added, 'Guess she must.'

'You've not met him before?'

'No. But I think she did last summer. I think he might be a friend of Gina's.'

'Ah.' As if that explained everything. He narrowed his eyes and thought he saw something pass between them, hand to hand, though he couldn't make out what the object was or which direction it had travelled in. Sasha had the strap of her messenger bag across her front, the bag itself bounced on her hip, zipped shut. Probably he was imagining things. 'Sash!' he called and she turned her head guiltily.

'Just coming.' The statue moved off, cradling his box of possessions. Her gaze lingered a moment on his retreating back and then she joined them.

'What was all that about? Who was he?'

'Sami. I met him a few times last year. I was only saying hi. But hey, Dad, you didn't have to be so rough.'

'I thought he'd stolen something. There are pickpockets everywhere. I didn't want to let him get away with it.'

'Well, you picked the wrong guy. He hadn't nicked anything.'

'He was running away. It made him look suspicious. Anyway, let's start again, shall we? Have you had a good day so far?' The girls exchanged looks, shrugged in reply. 'Well then, do you fancy an ice cream in Rosati's?'

'What's Rosati's?'

They had faced each other for almost a century, Canova and Rosati, the two lavish cafés at the entrance to the square, both wildly overpriced but fitted with such opulent elegance and offering such tempting displays of fancy pastries, the girls were sure to be impressed. Of the two he preferred Rosati's. The walnut panelling, parquet flooring and linen napery spoke of a different, more glamorous era.

They chose a central table beneath a dazzling chandelier so they could ogle the *pasticceria*: the glossy fruit tarts, dainty macaroons, confections of chocolate and cream. Mitchell ordered another beer to dull the pain in his elbow and Sasha an apricot *frullata*. Ruby settled for ice cream: scoops of pistachio and strawberry served in a tall-stemmed glass. They couldn't make up their minds about the cakes.

When he asked them again to tell him about their morning they were evasive, possibly they'd overdosed on Renaissance painting. 'My day hasn't been so great either,' he admitted. 'Though I've just remembered where I've seen that living statue of yours before.'

'He's usually in Piazza Navona,' said Sasha. 'Perhaps he thought there'd be less competition here. But he's not really a mate. I only came across him a couple of times.'

'Through Gina?'

'Yes.'

'She took his photo, didn't she?'

'Um... Maybe.'

'I saw it,' he said. 'She's got an exhibition on, did you know?'

Ruby said, 'What? You went to see her exhibition?'

'Yes,' he said, mildly annoyed by the implication. Did they think him such a philistine? 'And he's in it, all dressed up in his toga. A bit freaky if you ask me.'

Sasha was sucking up her milkshake through a straw; she began to choke as if she'd inhaled some by accident and Ruby thumped her on the back.

'Did you... did you like her stuff?'

'Yeah. Some of it was a bit contrived, but on the whole I was impressed.'

A long silence followed, though it may have seemed drawn out because most of the other tables were occupied by vivacious gesticulating Italians. Sasha blew her nose. Ruby carefully scraped every morsel of ice cream from her glass and licked the spoon clean. These feisty young women, he thought fondly, were little girls at heart. Sugar and spice and all things nice. Sasha had braided her hair, exposing the childish curves of her face, the clear soft complexion with its scattering of freckles.

'I was at a loose end,' he said. 'I should have gone along with you two. I didn't get much joy from the agency.'

'They didn't have anything else, you mean? Nothing to swap?'

'That's what they claimed.' He couldn't tell whether Sasha was relieved or disappointed. He pulled the money from his pocket. 'This was the pay-off.'

'Does that mean you're going to stay with us then?'

'D'you want me to move out?'

''Course not.'

'I might look at some hotel rooms... But this...' He flapped the notes. 'This is pathetic. I'm going to blow it.'

'Can we help you?' said Sasha with a sudden urgency.

'Sure you can. What d'you reckon? We hire scooters for the day, pig-out at a top restaurant, buy an audience with the Pope?'

Ruby giggled, seemed about to break in with a novel idea of her own, but Sasha said, 'Um, we could go shopping.'

This was the suggestion he least favoured. For Mitchell shopping was a functional activity, like showering; he couldn't see the attraction of it as a leisure pursuit. Particularly in little boutiques like the ones along the Corso, where impossibly svelte assistants hovered and preyed. Sasha and Ruby would take a hundred and one garments into the inadequate fitting rooms and change their minds a hundred and one times while he waited like a lemon.

'Be my guest,' he said, laying the money on the cloth between them. 'But if you don't mind, I won't come with you. Not really my bag.'

She stared at the notes as if they were on fire and then snatched them up hastily in case he changed his mind. She mumbled something under her breath to Ruby but wouldn't meet his eye. Given that she'd just been presented with 200 euros, he thought his daughter could have looked more grateful.

26

Gina stooped for the little brass pot, threw out the desiccating pieces of foliage and took it to the tap to fill with water. She carried it back to the grave and unwrapped her bunch of tulips and freesias, their golden petals streaked with an apricot blush. Tulips, because Felix had always loved them, admired their form; freesias for their fresh intense fragrance, like bottled sunshine – although today she didn't seem to be able to smell it, any more than she could smell the sharp resin of pine or the honeyed drift of jasmine.

So, she couldn't smell; she couldn't hear, because the lush vegetation absorbed all intrusive sounds; and she couldn't really see because her eyes kept welling up. She'd been before in this familiar place, otherwise known as rock bottom. But this time was different because the shock had come out of the blue, with no warning at all. At least, with Thomas and Felix, she'd been given the chance to prepare. She'd known she wasn't going to be able to keep Thomas, that he could only give her the briefest moment of joy; she would have been a lousy mother. As for losing Felix – she'd had plenty of notice of that.

Felix had gone to great lengths to wangle his plot in the Protestant Cemetery. Just think of the company! he'd said. It was a private enclave: a confusion of angels and cherubs, of

Eastern Orthodox crosses, of graves framed by stubby box hedges, of paths bordered with narrow columns of cypress, a sprawl of roses around the memorial urns, innocent daisies in the grass. At first she'd thought it ghoulish, his choice to moulder underground, but now she was glad to be able to visit him. She plucked a couple of weeds and pieces of blown litter from the earth and addressed his headstone.

'You see how crap I am at coping without you? I'm a total disaster. Okay, so I've never been much good with money, but let's face it, *anything* precious slips through my fingers. I was such an idiot to think my luck might have changed. An exhibition – wow! A commission – bring it on! Two pluses, no? But somebody up there, darling – maybe you've even met the bastard – wants to chuck in a minus before Gina Stanhope gets too big for her boots. The picture wasn't really mine, I know that, the way Thomas was never really going to be mine either. But I should have looked after it better for you. Shit, I am *so* sorry. I should have let David take care of it when I couldn't afford the insurance. I should had trusted him more. I'm not good at that, am I? You were the only person I ever really trusted.'

She'd thought of going to the crypt and unburdening herself to Leone. On the phone he'd been sympathetic, but in the flesh she suspected she'd read disapproval. She knew she was to blame. It was the sale of the photos that had made Joe impatient to try his luck and move on, follow a fantasy instead of biding his time. All he'd managed to achieve to speed up the process was to put himself at risk of deportation. And she couldn't do anything to help because she had been robbed of a single piece of paper. Funny: a piece of paper was what Joe needed too.

Usually her visits calmed her, although today, as she squatted on the ground adjusting the freesias in the pot, she wasn't so certain she'd come away with any sense of reassurance. Even with the best will in the world, Felix would be annoyed. You are the keeper of my flame, darling, he'd said. Keep it burning.

'You thought I wouldn't be able to fuck it up, didn't you?'
She continued, 'With the Lion King checking I didn't fritter
your inheritance, hanging in there at every turn. We wouldn't
have had anything to do with each other if it hadn't been for
you. But I reckon I've been a pretty good supporter of the lost
boys, even if I have been a bit unorthodox sometimes. And
Leone hasn't complained up to now. Boy, he can make you feel
small though. Grubby. How does he manage it? I've never done
anything half as dreadful as he has and yet those black eyes
of his just floor me.' Her head drooped in despair. 'I used to
accuse you of being defeatist, didn't I? Well, now it's my turn.
I so need advice, darling. Where the fuck do I go from here?'

A phone began to ring in the bag at her feet. The caller could
be any one of a number of people: friend, client, colleague. It
might be David with more information about Franco Casale.
Or Bertie himself – not that she was in the mood to handle
Bertie. But it was neither of those.

'*Ciao*, Gina!' said Vicki.

'*Ciao*,' said Gina flatly, wandering away from the graveside
to sit on a low stone wall.

'I promised to call you after the opening and I've been so
busy it's taken me days to get around to it. I'm really sorry
about that.'

'You're ringing to say you're sorry you didn't ring?'

'No! I'm explaining, that's all. Anyway, I had a fabulous time
that night. I thought your show was marvellous and I hope it
got lots of interest.'

'Yeah, there was a review in the culture section of *Il Messaggero*.'

'Anyway, how's it going?'

'The exhibition?' There was a smudge of dirt on the knee of
her trousers. As she rubbed it, it spread. 'Okay, I guess.'

'Gina?'

'What?'

'You sound weird.'

'Do I?'

'Is everything all right?'

'Depends what you mean by everything.'

'Well, not the show then. How are *you*?'

In the distance, beyond the avenue of cypress, she could see a sliver of white pyramid and a shuffling tour group. 'Actually…' She was going to say, I'm feeling shit, but what was the point? What could Vicki do? Instead she said, 'I saw Mitch yesterday.'

'Oh my God!' Vicki's voice soared. 'You mean *the* Mitch, the one who…'

'Whose daughter I met in the summer, thanks to you. Yes. She's back, plus her friend and he's come with them.'

'And you've met up?'

'Yes.'

'Did you?'

'Did I what?'

'Did you tell him anything.'

'We went through all this before. What's to tell?'

Now she was exasperated. 'Don't be utterly ridiculous, Gina. I agree it's a bit late at this stage, but all the same… If only you'd contacted him at the time like I kept begging you.'

'I was kind of low, if you remember. I think they call it post-natal depression.'

'Which is why I finally stepped in and made the effort on your behalf. But up until then you were just bloody-minded. He never got back to us because you wouldn't even let me give him an inkling of what it was about. And then you raged at me for interfering. So we don't dig it all up, I understand. But since he's, what can I say… reappeared – and actually I'm glad about that and whatever part I might have played – surely you have a chance to…'

'To what?'

'Put the record straight. Come clean.'

Gina licked her finger and rubbed again at the smear on her trousers; pale linen showed every goddam mark. 'I mightn't see him again. The girl happened to show up yesterday with him in tow and I had to enlist his help because... Oh Christ, darling, you do *not* want to know the mess I'm in.'

'Try me,' said Vicki. 'We could meet for a drink after work. The twins will be at Nonna's. Sometimes it feels like I only had them for her benefit. I hardly see them. The freedom's nice, but, *Dio mio,* does she spoil them. They're becoming right little emperors.'

'No thanks. I need to go home and lie down. I can feel a migraine starting and I shouldn't be in a public place.'

'Where are you?'

'With Felix.'

'Oh Gina!'

A young brindled cat was weaving between her legs and she leaned forward to scratch between its ears. The cat wriggled in appreciation but its fur was harsh and gritty; her hand felt dirty.

'Do you want me to come over? It sounds as though you need someone.'

'Yes,' said Gina. 'I do need someone. I need a hitman, that's who, to get Bertie off my back. Bury him head-first in concrete. That would be my dream.'

'What's he done this time?'

'Where do I start? You know he sent some joker round to sabotage my show?'

'Really? It is still running, isn't it?'

'Barely. He threatened to close me down so I had to substitute a couple of shots. They were the ones I shouldn't have taken of Sasha and Yusef.'

'Of who?'

'Never mind, that's another story. But Bertie's put this *cazzo,* Casale, up to buying them. I think he wants to prove the apartment's a knocking shop.'

'But Gina – '

'That's not the worst of it! He despatched another of his light-fingered *ladro* mates to steal the Twombly.'

She could sense Vicki's confusion, sitting at her computer, scrolling through the online celebrity magazines, hoping to be grabbed by something of interest. Vicki often referred to the devilry/revelry of their flat-sharing days in San Lorenzo with rose-tinted nostalgia, but she also gave the impression that she considered she'd moved on. She had acquired the standard accoutrements of an upwardly mobile modern woman: a professional husband (possibly faithful, possibly not), two children, home ownership, a job with a pension. These were the goals on which people set their sights. But how could you be deemed a failure if you hadn't striven for such goals in the first place?

'What's a twombly?' she said.

'Cy Twombly,' said Gina impatiently. 'You know, the illustrious American artist. Didn't you come to his opening show at the Gagosian with me? Quite old and more than quite valuable. Felix left me an early drawing. He probably guessed that one day I'd have to cash it in.'

'Valuable? Like, how much?'

'I don't know. I'd have to ask David. Only I can't because it's been stolen.'

'Oh my God! Have you told the police?'

'Darling, whenever have you got a result from reporting anything to the police? There was no evidence of a break-in. I can't prove I had the bloody picture in the first place and I can't go around denouncing Bertie as the perpetrator. They'll lock me up for defamation.'

'I don't know why you get yourself mixed up with these types.'

'You sound like my mother.'

'And I don't think you should be at home on your own.'

'I'll be fine,' said Gina, not moving from the wall; the cat sprawled beside her scratching its fleas. 'I've got to the bus stop now and I can see it trundling towards me. Such a welcome sight, don't you think, the bus home?'

'What you need – ' began Vicki again.

'Apart from the hitman? Yes, I know and I've got David on the look-out. What I need massively is a bloody good lawyer. Any ideas?'

'What about Mitch?'

'He's not a lawyer. He flies aeroplanes.'

'What I meant was, what are you going to do about seeing him?'

'I'm getting on the bus,' said Gina, squinting along the line of box hedging towards Felix's burnished granite slab. She imagined him chortling quietly; he'd enjoyed watching her wind people up. 'My plan is to pick up a bottle of cheap brandy from Signora Bedini, climb into an empty bath with a box of matches, pour it over my head and self-immolate.'

'Gina, that's not funny. You say one more piece of nonsense like that and I'll bring the twins round and bang your door down.'

'You strike fear into my heart.'

Vicki said, 'Will you promise me something?'

'What?'

'You really won't do anything silly? You'll ring me if...'

'If what?'

'If, you know... I'm only trying to be a good friend, Gina, that's all.'

'Right. Thanks.'

She ended the call, tossed the phone into her bag and stood up from the bench. The cat had its hind leg behind its ear and was nuzzling its haunch. She said goodbye to Felix, left the cemetery and caught the bus to Trastevere. In the *alimentari* she changed her mind and bought grappa instead of Vecchia Romana. She poured herself a large slug, took two painkillers, changed into pyjamas and lay down on her unmade bed, willing the headache to go away. When the banging intensified, accompanied by an irritating buzz, she realised someone was at the door. She assumed Vicki was carrying out her threat and resisted opening it. A male voice called her name. She stiffened, listened again.

No, not Bertie.

Mitch.

27

They had been by a lake. He'd forgotten whether it was Italian or Swiss, whether near Milan or Geneva, but he remembered picking their way along its edge until they reached a deserted strip of fine shingle. Gina spread out the towels and Mitchell unloaded the picnic he was carrying – although picnic was too grand a term for a bottle of wine, two ham-stuffed panini and a bag of black grapes. A large flat rock jutted over the water and he buried the bottle in its shade. It was early autumn but the sun was strong and most of the trees screening the lake were conifers; they could have been anywhere, anytime.

Gina removed her clothes and stretched out to sunbathe. He challenged her to a swim.

'The water will freeze your bollocks off,' she said.

'I will if you will.'

'Nah, can't be bothered.' She was long-limbed, athletic – she'd out-run him once or twice – but generally lazy.

'Too soft, you are. We could race to keep warm.'

'You're not tempting me.'

'Fine. I'm going in anyway.' He undressed and waded into the rim of the lake where the waters were shallow and balmy, but the ground sloped sharply and he was soon out of his depth. He felt the hairs rise on his arms as the temperature fell to an indescribable chill. He struck out in a swift crawl to keep the blood flowing. When he turned to look back Gina was on her feet watching him. 'You should come in,' he called, suppressing a gasp. 'It's lovely.'

'Really?'

'See for yourself.'

He didn't think she'd be persuaded, but she climbed up onto the rock and stood poised to dive. Silhouetted against the light, she could have been a bronze statuette on a plinth, a dancer: her arms raised above her head, her breasts small but shapely with their upward tilt, the muscles tautening in her calves as she rose on tiptoe. She was teasing him.

'Bet you daren't jump,' he yelled and then regretted it.

'You lose,' she shouted back, springing off the rock headfirst into the lake. Ripples spread at the spot where her feet had disappeared. He thrashed towards them, his teeth chattering. Diving into unknown waters was a crazy thing to do. They might be too shallow, there might be submerged rocks or the treacherous tug of reeds, the swallow of silt. Why couldn't he see her?

She surfaced twenty yards away, her sleek head breaking through the placid sheen of the water, her legs pummelling fiercely beneath. 'It's fucking perishing,' she said. 'Mind you, I knew it would be.'

'You shouldn't have dived. You could have bust your head open or broken your neck.'

'You know I'm a risk-taker.'

'Is that another name for an idiot?'

She kicked out at him and they tussled for a while. She jumped onto his head, he grabbed her ankles; flailing and spluttering, they cast crystal rainbows, kissed with hot tongues. Then they floated on their backs, sculling with their hands; Gina's red toenails poked into view like poppy petals.

'It's not so bad like this,' he said. 'Gives the sun a chance to warm your skin.'

'Hey, I've done photo shoots in far worse conditions. I mean, *arctic*. I'm not all self-indulgence.' She rolled onto her front. 'Mind you, I'm not a sado-masochist either.'

She began to swim to the shore, but Mitchell was determined to outlast her. Various parts of him were protesting, squeaking with pain, and he tried backstroke, followed by butterfly, in an effort to boost his circulation. Then he saw her clamber onto the bank and rub herself down with the towel in a way that might have been deliberately languid and erotic. It seemed absurd to punish himself by continuing this endurance test. As he headed towards the rock and the small beach he felt the stirrings of his extremities returning to life.

She sat hugging her knees as he dried himself. 'Don't you think,' she said, contemplating the sky's reflection, a deep tranquil blue patterned with silver, 'that there can be nothing in the world more idyllic than a lake with no one about?'

He shook the towel he'd been using, unfurled it and lay down. 'An idyllic lake,' he said, 'with us beside it.'

Gina came over then to straddle him, her long thighs either side of his hips, her long hair, tawny as a lion's mane in those days, streaking damply past her shoulders. She pinned his arms to the ground, allowing him just enough movement to be able to raise his head. He fastened his mouth around her nipple as she lowered her body onto the shaft of his penis, miraculously restored to its full beating energy.

He remembered that day by the lake – he couldn't help it – when, twenty years later, Gina opened the door of her apartment and allowed him to enter it. Allowed, rather than invited. She didn't say 'Come in'. She weighed him up without speaking; her hand fell from the doorknob, she turned and disappeared.

He supposed he should follow her. He shut the door behind him and went into the sitting room. On yesterday's brief visit, when she'd feared a break-in, it had all looked relatively orderly. Today the place was in a state of upheaval: drawers pulled out and upturned, chests and cupboards spilling contents, cushions scattered from sofa to floor.

'What the – ?' he began, but he couldn't see her. 'Gina? Are you all right?'

She had stalked through the chaos and disappeared. He tracked her down in her bedroom. She was lying on the bed with the shutters closed; the light was dim. She was wearing a flimsy vest and matching baggy bottoms. Either she'd been in her pyjamas all day or she was having a very early night. Her complexion was unusually pale, almost grey compared to the day before, though that might have been the effect of the gloom.

'No, of course I'm not all right,' she said. 'I have a stinking bastard of a migraine.'

'And the flat? Have you really been burgled this time?'

'I was really burgled last time. Only I didn't cotton on.'

'Have you reported it?'

'Don't make me go over it all again. Please.'

'Sure. Okay. Fine. Can I do anything?'

'Why did you come here?'

'Why?' He raised the plastic bag he was carrying and its contents clinked. 'I've brought you a nice bottle of wine and a jar of mixed antipasti. Hoped I could persuade you to come out to dinner afterwards. I did try to phone.'

'I'm not taking any calls.'

'No. You're probably not in the mood for dinner either.' He sighed. His offerings of wine and pickles seemed forlorn and inappropriate. 'The girls have gone shopping, didn't want me to cramp their style. You might as well let me be useful. That mess next door – it wasn't made by your burglars? No need for fingerprinting?'

'It was made by me,' muttered Gina with her eyes shut.

'Right. So why don't I tidy up a bit for you? Restore some order?'

'Why? Does it bother you?'

'You can't leave it like that. Someone could have an accident.'

'Is this your health and safety training? Everything has to be shipshape.'

'Well?'

'I don't care,' she said. 'I don't give a shit unless you find my Twombly.'

He didn't know what she was talking about, but on the way to his self-appointed task he stopped to tell her, 'I went to see your show. I liked it.'

Her eyes flew open. 'You did?'

'Yeah. Very strong, I thought.'

'No sales though.'

'That's not what I heard. I'd've bought one myself, only...'

'Only what? No. Don't go on.' She rolled her head on the pillow. 'I wouldn't want you to buy something out of sheer sentiment. And don't kid yourself: that's what it would have been.'

'There's no convincing you, is there?' And no point in trying to combat her present mood. He shouldn't have come. He should have left yesterday's encounter as a one-off. What was he trying to prove? That a little jaunt into the past could be salutary? That he was on the same kind of voyage of discovery as his wife? Would Corinne see it that way? Unlikely. But he couldn't walk out on a sick unhappy woman whose home looked as though a hurricane had blown through. He'd put it to rights, see if she needed anything from the chemist and then catch up with Sasha.

In fact, the mayhem looked worse than it was. He did the easy things first: replacing the sofa cushions, righting the chairs, stacking the magazines on the coffee table, straightening the rugs. Then he sorted the clothes that appeared to have been flung around in a frenzy and folded them into two piles, male and female. He guessed they came from the blanket boxes beside the French windows. Once he'd returned them and shut the box lids, the room looked much more civilised. Now there were merely scraps of paper, letters and documents to collect up; he piled them on top of the sideboard for Gina to sort out later.

He noticed a cup and a plate had been smashed and rooted in cupboards for a dustpan and brush. When he'd disposed of the broken china and wiped up a spillage of something sticky, he glanced around in satisfaction. Perhaps not everything was in its right place yet, but at least it was manageable again.

There was no reason for him to linger. It was impossible to say why he decided to shuffle the papers on the sideboard, whether he'd been subconsciously seeking it, or whether the birth certificate of Thomas Stanhope would have caught his eye in any event. This must be what Ruby'd been referring to. He was shocked that she and Sasha had been going through Gina's papers; he was shocked a great deal more when he saw the date of the boy's birth.

Holding the certificate in both hands, he went out onto the terrace. Large terracotta pots were lined up along one edge, filled with evergreen bay, rosemary and lemon trees. A passion flower twining through a trellis protected a corner seat from sun and wind alike, but Mitchell couldn't sit down. Above him a Boeing 737 glided across the sky, as stately as a cruise liner. What wouldn't he give to be at the controls, to be concentrating on something other than the document before him.

He had left Gina for Corinne in April 1993. The baby had been born in October the same year. This boy could be his. A son. He would have liked a son. His beloved Sasha had been a tomboy of the first order and he'd encouraged her fearlessness. But inevitably she'd become a young woman, with feminine preoccupations (like clothes shopping). She'd never shown any interest in engines; flying; cricket.

The paper trembled in his hands. There was another explanation: Gina could have been two-timing him. She'd had no shortage of opportunity and it might explain why she'd been so ready to let him go, told him nothing. But then why was the space for the father's details blank? Had that relationship finished too? Perhaps, if she'd planned to have the boy adopted, she didn't want the other guy to know in case he staked a claim.

He could imagine that. The circumstances of Gina's own origins would have made her shy from abortion, but she'd often said she didn't know why Phoebe had kept her when she rarely showed her any love.

Somewhere out there roamed the boy who'd been born as Thomas Stanhope. Gina's son (and maybe his own) would be eighteen and entitled to search for his birth parents. He'd heard tales of such reunions: of confusion, denial, then grudging acceptance; sometimes (more rarely) delight. He couldn't believe she had kept such information from him. All that nostalgia for happier times, fornicating by foreign lakes, was replaced with bitterness.

He didn't care how bad her headache was. He couldn't let this lie. He was no longer aware of the dry rustle of the bay leaves, the strong fragrance of rosemary, the imprecations floating up from the street. Gripping the certificate between finger and thumb he returned indoors and marched into Gina's room without knocking.

She was either asleep or pretending to be so, her lips slightly parted. Her brow was pale but smoother than before, as if she'd finally found relaxation. Half an hour earlier he might have tiptoed out again, but in the space of thirty minutes his world had fractured into a kaleidoscope of possibilities, nearly all of them traumatic. He couldn't wait for an answer. He leaned forward to touch her and she stirred.

'Feeling better?' he said, more gruffly than he intended.

She moaned, wriggled, scoured her eyes with the heels of her palms until they opened, bloodshot. 'Are you still here?'

'I've been clearing up for you.'

'You couldn't get me another couple of Nurofen, could you? To be on the safe side? In the cabinet in the bathroom, left-hand shelf.'

He laid the document on the bedside table, but she paid it no attention. He fetched her the painkillers and a glass of water and sat on the edge of the bed while she took them.

He planned to be tactful. Dealing with Gina was unpredictable; she might deny everything. He would never know which were the lies and which the truth. But impatience overcame him.

'Were you ever going to tell me?' he said.

'About what?'

'Him,' He jabbed at the name. 'Thomas.'

'What do you know about Thomas?'

'Only his date of birth. Why don't you tell me the rest?'

'Oh God, Mitch…' She struggled into a more upright position. Her vest was made of some gauzy fabric ripped at the seam; he could see straight through it. 'You've caught me at a low ebb; my bloody head…'

His eyes moved to her face, on the lookout for any hint of deceit. 'Well?'

'Here's the thing,' she said. 'I didn't intentionally keep you in the dark. But there didn't seem to be any point in explaining…'

It was as he'd expected: she'd been seeing someone else. He said, a little awkwardly, 'So I shouldn't have jumped to conclusions? That was a mistake, obviously.'

'*Obviously*!' He'd set her off. Would she start throwing things again or had she grown out of the habit? He doubted it, given the state of the room he'd just cleared up. 'What's that supposed to mean?'

'Well, I'm surmising…' Sweat ran around the collar of his shirt, trickled down his back. 'The boy wasn't mine, that's all.'

'Why?' she glowered.

'How about because I'm not named on the birth certificate? Isn't that a good enough reason?'

'I'd like to know how you got hold of it.'

'Gina, it was floating around the room with all sorts of other debris. I picked it up and saw the date. Look, this is all a long time ago and I'm not going to start recriminating. God, if you had another bloke back then I'm hardly going to make a big deal of it now, am I? I have no claim over you. On the other hand…'

'You're right,' she said. 'It was a long time ago. Still hurts though.'

He cleared his throat, toyed with the links of his wristwatch. 'When we split,' he said, 'we weren't exactly on the best of terms, and I thought you'd be glad to be rid of me. A clean break. No ties. In the past half hour I've learned it wasn't so simple. You must have been pregnant, but you didn't tell me. Didn't you know?'

'You believe what you want,' said Gina. 'What suits you. Clean break? No ties? How mighty convenient.'

'I'm not a mind reader! How was I to know any different?'

'You're right.' He was startled by her change of tone, doleful and contrite. 'It wasn't fair of me. I should have told you.'

'You mean that he really *was* my son?'

'Yes.'

It was like being dealt a ferocious punch. His ears rang with silence. 'Why didn't you let me know?'

'To start with, because I hadn't made up my mind what to do.'

'If only you'd consulted me, we could have talked it over…'

She ignored him. 'And then I had this terrible threatened miscarriage.' She flinched at the recollection. 'I was in Ostia. Felix and I had gone to the beach for the afternoon. The pain, well, it was so… alarming. I'd never felt anything like it. He had to take me to a private clinic.' Her voice dropped to a whisper. 'It might have been better if I'd lost him then, but the nuns, you know, they were determined to save him even though I must have scandalised them. As a person, I mean. They flapped around like swans and put me on a drip. And I did try, really. I stopped drinking; I ate bland food like rice and mozzarella and bananas. I had a crap pregnancy – I was laid up for weeks. Felix looked after me. I was in that apartment, you remember, near the University and he used to come over at lunchtime and after classes and give me the gossip and make me laugh. He was fantastic actually. I wouldn't have predicted it. In the end we both surprised each other.'

'And then?' he prompted, already jealous of Felix, a dead man he'd never met, which was patently ridiculous.

'Have you ever heard the saying: The best thing a father can do for his children is love their mother?'

Mitchell shook his head.

'I think there's a lot of truth in it,' said Gina. 'Don't you?'

This was uncomfortably guilt-inducing. Nonetheless, he nodded.

'I'm not blaming you, Mitch, but you didn't love me, you didn't want to be saddled with me and I sure as hell didn't want to be anybody's millstone.'

He wondered whether she herself had ever truly loved anyone, whether she was capable of it. Independence was one thing, but Gina was positively intransigent. Bloody impossible. He tried to keep his temper, stay rational. 'All the same, you shouldn't have deprived the boy of a father. Everyone has a right to know where they come from. Chances are, however successful the adoption process, he's going to want to know the truth one day.'

'Who told you he was adopted?'

'Well...' He swallowed, massaged the back of his neck, which was sticking to his collar. Her face, devoid of make-up, was bland, inscrutable. He thought, not for the first time, how much easier it was to read a computer screen. All the information you needed in front of you on the primary flight display: airspeed, altitude, barometric pressure. Figures that followed the rules of logic, told you what you needed to know, enabled you to make the necessary adjustments. Intuitive deduction not required. 'Nobody. I didn't think you'd brought him up here by yourself because...' Mitchell knew what a house looked like when it had a teenager living in it.

'Well, you're wrong. I didn't give him away. He was taken.'

He was puzzled. 'By the nuns?'

'Thomas was born prematurely,' she said. 'His lungs weren't developed and he had a hole in the heart. Three actually. So tiny, his heart. I used to picture it like a *fragolina de bosco*, a wild strawberry. Dark crimson and slightly misshapen, but oh so sweet.'

Mitchell's limbs stiffened as if caught in a sudden icy blast.

Gina clamped her hands briefly over her mouth, then knotted them in her lap. She spoke in a low monotone, a story she must have told before.

'He was in an incubator at first, while they decided what they could do. He would have needed an operation, a whole new heart and lungs. Someone else would have had to die, another baby somewhere... But then they let me take him home, wrapped in a blanket like a little doll. I didn't play much with dolls as a girl, though I used to make plasticine effigies of people I didn't like – my stepfather mostly – and stick pins into them. I was a horrid child.

'We were allowed home because there was nothing they could do for him – and those private clinics don't come cheap. We had three days together and I didn't leave him for a moment. Me and Tom, we were inseparable. The bed was our whole world. Most of the time he slept and I watched over him. He was hardly feeding and my milk was leaking as if my breasts were crying too.

'He didn't open his eyes often, but when he did they were this intense violet blue like a night sky. I didn't know that all babies are born with blue eyes, did you? I was so damn ignorant, I didn't know a thing. Babies were totally foreign to me. I couldn't get over how something so perfectly formed on the outside, down to the teeniest whisker of an eyelash or a toenail, could be such a mess on the inside. Stupid of me really. I've worked all my life with superficial images. I should know how deceptive they are.'

'Gina, you should have...'

'What, contacted you? No, you were last person I would have told. I didn't want to share him. I hardly ever put him down. He died in his sleep, in the crook of my arm.'

His reactions were slow, but the poignancy of her situation finally pierced him. 'Why?' he said. 'I don't understand what went wrong.'

'It was just something that happened. You think everybody can be saved, everybody can have what they want in our brave new world, but it doesn't work like that. A granny of sixty-five can have a healthy baby. I was twenty-seven and I couldn't.'

Twenty-seven, he thought, how young; he didn't like to ask if she'd tried again.

'It was for the best,' she said after a pause. 'Some people aren't cut out for motherhood and I'd never had much of a role model.'

'So what did you do, afterwards...?'

'Do? I went back to work. I needed the money. I'd lost quite a bit of weight so no one complained. Friends rallied round; Felix, and my flatmate Vicki.'

'Vicki? Christ, I think she was the woman who rang me... it must have been, I don't know, about the time that...'

'I was in a blue funk for a bit. She was always going on at me for not contacting you.'

'She left messages but they were very cryptic, so I'm afraid I ignored them.' He was ashamed to admit this, but she had spoken to Corinne and in those days Corinne was his new beginning.

'Interfering harpy,' said Gina. 'Kind, I'll grant you, but never happy except when she's meddling. Some people are like that. Usually because they don't have enough to do.'

'She was probably very worried about you.'

Gina grimaced. 'She still is. She called me this afternoon and I made the mistake of telling her I'd run into you. She insisted I came clean.'

'You wouldn't have done though, would you, if I hadn't found the birth certificate?' He didn't ask why she had kept it: the only evidence of a life so briefly lived.

'No, I guess not. It's actually very painful, you know, raking this up. If you bury things deep enough and don't disturb them it's easier to carry on. Isn't that the catchphrase of the moment: going forward. Well, that's what I try to do.'

He seized her hand in an attempt at consolation. She didn't resist but she said, 'Don't look so grim, Mitch. You have the lovely Sasha.'

'True.' Where were the girls, he wondered. Glad to have shaken him off no doubt, toasting themselves with colourful cocktails, carrier bags slung over their arms. 'She thinks Rome is paradise.'

'Any particular reason why you're not making a family holiday of it? You are still married to Sasha's mother?'

'Yes.'

'And you've been with her ever since…?'

'Since you and I split up, yes.' He kept a snapshot of a laughing Corinne in his wallet but he decided against producing it. 'I suppose I met her at a point where I was feeling a need to put down roots. Because of all the travelling. But obviously, if I had known about… the pregnancy… I would have acted differently. I would have – '

'Done what exactly? You'd already fallen for her, hadn't you?'

'I wouldn't have let you down. I'm not that much of a bastard.'

'Here's the thing, I don't want to be anybody's second best. Not then. Not now. Not ever.'

'We had some terrific times together, Gina, but ultimately… I mean, all relationships require a bit of compromise…' He really wasn't handling this very well. He added wryly, 'Corinne's very different from you.' A backhanded compliment if ever there was one.

'So anyway, what's happened to her? Where is she?'

'She's hiking.'

'Hiking! Striding out on her own? I'm picturing some kind of Brunhilde.'

He shouldn't be surprised that she sounded snide; she was unlikely to feel well-disposed towards the woman who'd crashed into her life at just the wrong moment. 'She's with a friend. In Scotland. I would have gone too but we both felt Sash could do with a chaperone and my Italian's better.'

'Ever the linguist.'

'You should hear my Farsi.'

Her hand was still lying between his. He wanted to ask whether she was lonely, but there comes a time when any language, native or foreign, turns into meaningless babble. After a while, he managed, 'Would you like me to stay for a bit?'

'Yes please,' she said.

28

He couldn't sleep. He'd checked on the girls and told them he'd be in touch again in the morning. Under Gina's directions he had pulled out the sofa bed in the spare room and found a duvet. They'd eaten toast and drunk a bottle of wine. Then Gina had taken a Valium and offered one to Mitchell, which he declined. He knew sleep wouldn't come easily when she lay the other side of the wall, when his brain was processing new information, but he had trained himself to manage long periods of wakefulness, to cope without loss of function.

On his back, elbows behind his head, he stared up at the ceiling with its wood-panelled squares, the bevelled edges diminishing inside each section in much the same way his thoughts chased their tails, revolving around this unexpected story: a pregnancy, a baby, a death. What should he have done? If he'd kept in touch with her, what difference would it have made to the outcome? Did he hate her for not telling him? No, probably not. Forgive her? Well, that was another question. And what was he to do with such knowledge that was now out of date; redundant. Where could he go from here?

He was up early, long before Gina. He took a cold shower, wanting to clear his head, scourge his body; every part of him was numb. His mood skittered irrationally from disbelief to resentment, guilt to remorse. He had to do something. No way could he let her off the hook, let himself out of her flat and leave as if the information had never come to light. He would take charge, steer this extraordinary out-of-control situation to its logical conclusion. He would pay his respects to his son.

He took a coffee into her room and put it down on the bed-side table. She was lying with her arm flung out and her cheek flushed, but the aroma aroused her. She stretched and yawned and as soon as she'd opened her eyes, he said, 'I want you to take me there.'

'Where?'

Fresh coffee couldn't mask the sour smell of last night's wine. Gina shifted herself against the pillows in the half dark. In the past twelve hours she had scarcely changed her position, still wore the same grungy pyjamas.

'Wherever he is.'

'I already told you.'

This was true. She had explained through sobs that, unlike Felix, no memorial had been erected to Thomas Stanhope. No grieving group of friends clubbed together for the best quality marble on the best site in the city. No poetry lovers trooped past in search of great names. His ashes had been taken into the countryside on a drab November day and scattered on the surface of Lake Albano.

'I know. I want to go there.'

'Today?'

'Yes.' He opened the shutters and she cringed as the light flooded in. 'You should get up. Have a shower. Get dressed.'

He thought she might protest, but she swung her legs over the side of the bed and stood shakily. He resisted the urge to reach out and steady her. She picked up the small espresso cup and downed the contents. Mitchell took his own coffee outside onto the terrace.

The world should have looked different, but it didn't. The pantiled roofs layered around him in their autumn colours had scarcely changed in centuries. Workmen came along with their bags of plaster and lengths of copper piping and rendered and repainted and re-plumbed, but their alterations were superficial. The threads of the old street patterns remained the same. A bunch of cells had divided and grown, matured into life and withered again within the flash of an eye. A child had breathed on his own for less than a week. Eventually, in the scheme of things, seventy years might have no more consequence than seven days.

He gripped the railings, sensed a movement behind him. Gina was barefoot, in tight jeans, damp hair pulled back from her newly scrubbed face.

'How are you feeling?' he asked. 'Better?'

'Like I'm recovering from the worst ever hangover.'

'Have you thought about what I said?'

'About wanting to go to Albano?'

'Yes.'

'It's okay, I'll show you. You don't need to worry. I can handle it. I'm not going to make a scene. Only...'

'Only what?'

'Please don't make me go on the train. It's so slow and noisy and it won't get us anywhere near the bit you need to see. You'll have to hire a car.'

Mitchell hadn't thought about how they would actually travel there, merely the moment of catharsis he hoped would arrive. Below, at street level, a Vespa curved elegantly around the corner. He straightened up. 'I'd rather hire a bike.'

She frowned. 'What sort of bike?'

'One with a decent engine. I'm not going to putter up and down the hills on 50cc.'

'A motorbike!' exclaimed Gina. 'Like a bloody teenager. Oh my God, this is mid-life crisis behaviour, isn't it?'

Possibly she was trying to goad him, but he refused to be riled. 'I think this qualifies as a mid-life crisis, Gina, for both of us. Don't you want to feel the wind on your skin again?'

*

It cost far more to hire a bike than a car – especially since he went for a Ducati Monster – but wasn't wild extravagance part of the whole deal anyhow? The sensation of owning the road, negotiating the traffic and inhaling its fumes as they left the city; of cresting a hill at full throttle or swooping into a bend as the air rushed past; the simple elemental power of the engine, the growl and the heat it threw out – all these were pure pleasure. Gina leaned against his back with her arms around his waist. It was possible she was scared but he wasn't going to let her inhibit him. Transporting people from A to B was the one thing (maybe the only thing) he could do well.

The lake was a perfect mirror of the sky. In other circumstances, he would have liked to race around it a couple of times, feeling the pull of gravity and the leap of Ducati performance, knowing this was something he could control.

'Left here,' said Gina, indicating. 'Then down that track.'

He followed her instructions and after a few hundred metres the track widened into a asphalted area where inverted rowing boats were humped on top of each other. When he killed the engine he wasn't prepared for the sudden silence – but it was soon filled with birdsong and the far-off whistle of a train trundling along its single track. Gina clambered off the pillion seat.

'Are you okay?' he asked.

She removed her helmet and shook out her hair, bent to massage her calves. 'Feel as though I've been at sea and just got back onto dry land.'

'You weren't frightened? I mean, I hope you trusted me.'

'Funny you should say that. I knew someone who killed his friend on the very stretch of road we've come down.'

He said defensively, 'What are you getting at?'

'Not getting at you, Mitch. I'm in one piece, aren't I? You reminded me, that's all.' She shivered and hugged herself as if she were cold. 'One little mistake, one lapse in concentration. That's all it takes. Self-reproach must be such an awful burden.

I don't know how a person can learn to live with it. They must always be going over that moment, you know, when they'd taken their foot off the brake or pumped the accelerator too hard. Or whatever. How would I know? I've never sat behind a steering wheel. But I do know that sometimes there's a point when things could go either way and you have to keep your nerve or live with the consequences...

'Anyway, it wasn't like that with Tom. You must believe me. I had no influence one way or the other. It was a totally random condition he was born with. We couldn't have made any difference.'

'Right,' he said, trying to smile. No man wants to think he's behaved like a shit, even if he has. 'I would have supported you through it all if you'd given me the chance.'

She shrugged. 'I shouldn't have got pregnant in the first place, but accidents happen, don't they? I'm not blaming *you*. It's easier to think of it really as an Act of God. Bloody God. I've never had much time for Catholicism – all that confession and repentance seems such a cop-out. Felix got pretty close to converting, but he couldn't deal with the whole transubstantiation issue. He and Leone used to argue for hours.'

She was off on a tangent again and Mitchell was worried about her state of mind and whether he'd been wise to suggest the excursion. But then she recomposed herself and marched towards the dense woodland that quilted the sides of the once volcanic crater. He followed.

They passed a mangy dog rooting in the shallows, a family of newly fledged ducklings, a trio of fishermen setting up camp for the day with their canvas stools and their cool-box, fitting their rods together, unspooling their lines. The path wound through thickets of trees and, nearer the shore, palisades of rustling reeds. Mitchell trod pungent wild garlic underfoot, nearly tripped on brambles and whips of twining honeysuckle. He became confused by the direction they were taking. 'Are you sure you know the way?'

'Oh yes, David and Sergio have a place not far from here.'

'Who are they?'

'David's my dealer. And Sergio's family have lived in the area for generations. They have a boathouse and a jetty a little further on. So you see, I do come here from time to time and Sergio's very helpful. He'll give me a lift if I want one, whenever…'

Because he was trying to catch what she was saying he lost concentration, caught his toe in a tree root and went sprawling. Pain stabbed his ribs, struck his knee; he could taste dirt on his tongue. Gina turned. When she saw him spread-eagled, she laughed. It was a laugh with an edge of hysteria, a release of tension. 'Oh my goodness, you look so –'

'What?'

She was trying, not very successfully, to control herself. 'So… helpless.'

'I tripped, that's all. No big deal.' He rose stiffly and dusted his jeans.

'I'm sorry. Are you all right?'

'I'm fine.'

'We're nearly there, anyhow.'

She came towards him, as if she were going to guide him like a blind man or an invalid for the last few yards. Instead she rubbed a smudge of dust from his cheekbone. He'd forgotten, this close, how tall she was, their eyes almost level. She only had to tilt her chin and their lips would meet too. Her hands were resting on his shoulders; his reached around her back to pull her to him. Their mouths joined in so natural and familiar a fit the years spent apart contracted in an instant.

A kiss. A real kiss. A deep, ardent, devouring kiss. A kiss of promises and apologies, of commiseration and forgiveness. A kiss that could be the end or the beginning, that could lead nowhere at all. Only a kiss.

Gina broke away first, tugged him through a gap in the trees. 'Here,' she said.

They were standing on a patch of coarse sand. The water at its edge was utterly transparent, but as it stretched into the distance it took on an intense blue. Although they were now side by side, their moment of intimacy dissolved, her hand slipped into his as Sasha's used to when she was a little girl.

'Here,' she said again. Then, 'Can you feel the breeze?'

He could – a light breath of wind with a nip of spring.

'It's not as easy to scatter ashes as you might think. You don't want them blowing back in your face and it was a blustery autumn day. Felix was with me. He was very consoling but he wasn't like you. He didn't like to get his feet wet. I'd already taken off my boots and waded in. Tom was in a pretty white casket and I threw it as far as I could. It bobbed about for a little while – I had expected it would float for longer, it was such a light frail thing.' Her voice was low. He squeezed her knuckles, rubbed his thumb into her palm. She continued, 'Then it sank, very gracefully, but very quickly and there was nothing left to see. You can't really visit ashes like you can a grave. Or tend them. I should have thought of that, but I wasn't thinking straight at all. And I was so young then. There was still the prospect of tomorrow. Anyway...' She gave a brilliant brittle smile. 'You're here now. Do your thing. I'll wait for you.'

She withdrew, to sit some yards away on a tree stump. He moved closer to the water, till it lapped at the leather of his trainers. The ebb and flow, although slight, had a pacifying effect. He couldn't envisage the features of a child he'd never met – no, not a child, a premature infant, a small pink scrap – but of all the sensations of loss that had been troubling him, shouldn't this be the most acute? He needed more time to adapt to the extraordinary cruel truth of it, but the image of this spot was captured in his head. Later he would reconcile it with everything else he'd been told; meanwhile he would store it, as precisely defined as one of Gina's photographs, for safekeeping.

He walked back up the beach towards her. She was sitting with her legs tucked at an angle like a mermaid. He half-expected to see a flat rock projecting like a diving platform and a thought struck him. 'This isn't the place where we went swimming, is it?'

When she laughed he thought it might have been in mockery – that he should have revived the memory of the pair of them grappling naked on the shore like the couple in *From Here to Eternity* or any of its imitators – but no.

'That was Lake Bracciano,' she said. 'I can't believe you've forgotten.'

'Why?'

'Because you made such an almighty fuss at the time. You wanted to visit the aeronautical museum, but we'd dallied so long it was closed. You were so pissed off. You hardly spoke to me on the way back into Rome.'

He remembered now. The sound of the museum had intrigued him – a twentieth-century history of Italian aviation – and he did, hazily, recall the disappointment of finding it shut. But, if pressed, he would have attributed it to a separate trip, a different compartment of experience. He wouldn't have connected it to their swimming or love-making. 'Christ! I'm sorry.'

'What, sorry that you sulked and spoiled what had been a brilliant day?'

'I don't sulk.'

'Yes you do. I mean, you did. We've both had to grow up since then.'

A duck rose from the rushes with a squawk and skimmed the surface of the lake. The scent of mimosa wafted towards them. The spot was both tranquil and painful. Better, he thought, if they didn't linger. 'Thank you for bringing me here. Let me know when you're ready to leave.'

She uncoiled herself. 'Whenever you are.'

He doubted he would ever come this way again, nevertheless the trail they followed had an aspect he seemed to recognise, as if it were ground he'd covered many times before, every lake he'd ever visited rolled into one. He wasn't likely to forget it.

He smelt charcoal burning. The three fishermen had got a campfire going to griddle their catch.

'Are you hungry, Mitch?'

'Starving.' His stomach was grumbling. Gina was whip thin, too thin really. When he'd embraced her he'd felt her hip bones grind sharply against his own. 'You must know some restaurants around here. You wouldn't let me take you out last night, so what about lunch?'

She could hardly refuse; they were forty minutes from Rome and he was in charge of the bike.

'There's a *trattoria* I've heard recommended,' she said. 'Halfway up the road to Rocca di Papa. It shouldn't be crowded today. It's not high season yet.'

The restaurant appeared to balance on an overhanging spur. The view through the wide glass windows of the dining room was astonishing, like flying low in a glider. But the view didn't interest him. Sitting at the table with its linen napery, condiment set and dainty vase of anemones, put them once more on a formal footing: two old friends who'd happened to bump into each other but didn't have enough in common to meet again. He wanted to recapture the way he'd felt when they touched.

Gina was ordering mineral water and wine. 'Actually, you shouldn't drink, Mitch. Not when you're in charge of the Monster.'

'I wasn't planning to.'

'I'll get a half carafe for myself then, to relax me on the way back.'

'Fine. Go ahead.'

The waiter scribbled on his pad and handed them two menus with a flourish. The body of the text was in Italian, but underneath were some erratic English translations that made Mitchell smile. 'Have you seen this, Gina? *Contorni della terra?*'

'Root vegetables?'

'No, darling.' The endearment slipped out; he couldn't take it back. 'According to this they're contours of the heart. Shall we order some?'

Her feet shuffled beneath the table and the look she flicked at him – quizzical, amused, a little flirtatious – told him she was remembering the kiss.

As the waiter returned with the drinks, Gina's phone rang. She glanced at the screen and took a long draught of Frascati.

'Don't you need to answer?'

'It was an unknown number. They can wait.'

Later, when their starters had arrived the phone trilled again. 'I'd better take it. It might be business. Sorry.'

'Sure, go ahead.'

'Who is this?' said Gina, and he was surprised to hear her speaking English. 'Ruby?' He laid down his fork. 'Hang on a minute.' She covered the mouthpiece and hissed, 'Is your phone working, Mitch?'

He'd thought it was, though he'd been glad enough not to receive messages for the past few hours. He pulled it from his pocket, depressed the switch a couple of times but couldn't connect. 'Shit, it's out of charge.'

'Has Sasha been trying to get hold of him?' Gina asked Ruby. 'Oh, I see. Okay, well, as it happens, yes, he is here with me, but we're not in Rome. We've been on an… excursion. Do you want to put her on the line?'

'Let me talk to her,' said Mitchell, mentally deploying his excuses.

Gina shook her head. 'Apparently it's me she wants to speak to.'

'Really, what about?'

'How on earth should I know?'

29

As instructed, Sasha and Ruby were waiting in Piazza San Cosimato. The market was closed. The wheels of cheese, crimson cross sections of tuna, ruddy slabs of meat were locked into their refrigerated units. The stalls heaped with golden zucchini and purple artichokes, clusters of tomatoes and pyramids of fruit, had been packed away. Children had taken over the piazza. They were drawing hopscotch squares, riding tricycles, chasing pigeons, blithely ignoring their purpose-built play equipment. Around the edges were benches to sit on so you didn't have to buy a drink in a pavement café. This was just as well because the girls had no money left.

Yesterday afternoon Sasha had bought some cheap tat from a street vendor in the hope that her father might be convinced it had cost a lot more. That morning they had returned to the Madonna of all Mercy. As they entered, the American woman, Annie, had raised her head and given them a dirty look, as if she'd discovered they were imposters – though she could hardly complain about imposters who'd joined in the work effort. 'She should be well grateful,' said Ruby. 'Ignore her.'

Sasha, however, was consumed by a need for urgency. 'We've come back,' she said to Annie, 'because we've raised some funds. We'd like to give them to Father Leone personally.'

When Annie smiled, her face crumpled into folds that squeezed her eyes into raisins. 'Well, honey, the organisation has a treasurer who deals with receipts, you know. Father has enough on his plate... That's to say, you don't need to bother him with extra coinage.'

'It's quite a lot,' said Sasha, feeling the roll of notes in her pocket, '180 euros.'

Annie gave her a doubtful look and then made a show of hunting for the whereabouts of the priest. As if I'd nicked it, thought Sasha in indignation.

Aloud, Ruby observed, 'She's trying to protect him, right? Mother him or something. See off the troublemakers. Or maybe she fancies him, but she's wasting her time.'

'Why, because he wears a frock?'

'Yeah, partly. Anyhow I have a nose for these things. I should be a truffle hound, me, sniffing out the best matches. You and Liam were never going to work. Even if you had made the effort.'

'You'll have to wait a while, I'm afraid,' said Annie, returning.

'We don't mind.'

They went to sit on two unforgiving chairs pushed up against the wall. A nervous young man sat nearby chewing at his thumb. He looked as though he'd been waiting a long time. His feet were bare and blistered; he had no toenails.

Sasha spotted Father Leone before Annie could intervene. He must have come down an internal staircase, one that led directly into the church. He came towards them, pausing first to speak to the youth.

Then he said, 'The good friends of Yusef? Good morning.'

'We want to help,' said Sasha anxious to get to the point, 'with his legal fees. We've brought you some money.' She held it out. Foreign currency never seemed real anyhow. It might as well have come from a Monopoly set.

His glasses glinted in the artificial light. 'You are certain?'

'Yes, please take it.'

301

'As a donation?'

'Yes.'

'To our cause?'

'Can you use it to help Joe with his expenses? You said that if he could hire a lawyer he might get a better result. Quicker anyway.'

'There is a difficulty,' said Father Leone. He indicated the shadowy figures hunched in pockets of the crypt, leading their half-lives, waiting for some minor improvement in their lot. A new jacket. A mattress. A few hours' work. 'We believe in spreading our resources as equally as possible. For the basic essentials. It could be a problem to divert funds to a legal case that may bring no result.'

'But Joe shouldn't have been picked up in the first place. He wasn't doing anything wrong. The money he had on him was his. And you said that Gina – '

'*Esattamente*. It is Gina who is trying to raise the fee. Perhaps you should give it to her.'

Sasha let her fist close over the euros and drop to her side. He had a way of making you feel a jerk, this man – something to do with his faith, she supposed. She herself no more believed in God than the tooth fairy, but the Lion King was sincere and unshakable.

She didn't see how she could give the money to Gina. She might ask where it came from and then her father might find out and remember the photographs and put everything together. 'I already gave Sami my bracelet,' she said. 'Was that a stupid thing to do, too? I thought if he could somehow get it to Joe, either as a keepsake or to sell... I don't think it's worth much, but it *is* silver and... I don't know... I hoped it might help...'

Ruby had told her at the time it was mental, that she was acting like some medieval knight and next thing she knew she'd be camping outside all the detention centres in Europe like that page of Richard the Lionheart who went singing in search of his master. 'I believe Sami will try to help his friend and yours,' said the priest. 'Loyalty can be a difficult concept for many refugees because they feel so threatened. But when you have close ties as those boys do, it is different, I think.'

Ruby broke in. 'You're saying we should give this dosh to Gina, not you?'

'I'm sure she would be grateful.'

'I don't know about that. She's not too keen on us. She thinks it's our fault someone broke into her apartment. Because we didn't lock the door properly.'

Leone said, 'The thief would have known what he was looking for. Twombly's work is very distinctive. You have seen it perhaps?'

'Don't think so. What does it look like?'

Sasha couldn't understand why Ruby was getting off the point until the priest answered her. 'He is famous for what some people call his scribbles or graffiti. My preferences are more old-fashioned, but Felix, who originally owned the work and was a great friend of mine, was an admirer, and I understand that –'

Ruby gripped Sasha's elbow and hung onto it tightly. 'When you say scribbles, you mean if you didn't know any different, you could think it was a kid's drawing?'

He laughed as if at an excellent joke.

Sasha gaped. Then she found herself raising her arm again and pressing the notes into Leone's hand. 'It doesn't matter if you can't use it for Joe,' she said. 'We'd like to make a donation to the hostel anyway.'

'You are sure?'

'Absolutely.'

They'd left before he could ask them any penetrating questions and before they could change their minds and wish they'd kept it to blow on something exciting. Sasha didn't know how long the warm glow of generosity would last and, anyway, there was no mobile phone signal in the crypt.

Ruby had made the call and now the pair of them were sitting on the bench in San Cosimato sharing a cigarette. They'd bought a packet of Marlboro to steady their nerves. Her father wouldn't approve but she didn't care. He'd gone off with Gina Stanhope so he had plenty of explaining to do himself.

'You've got nothing to worry about,' said Ruby, inhaling deeply. 'What you've done isn't half as bad as what she did to you. You gave her a fright, that's all. She deserved it. You thought it was just some random scrawl when you picked it up. Put it in your bag accidentally.'

'She's with my dad,' said Sasha who'd been mulling over this ever since the phone call. 'What if he takes her side?'

'He's not going to be a party to this. It's none of his friggin' business. It's between you and her. You'll have to get rid of him.'

'How can I do that? What are they doing together anyhow? Like she's got some sort of hold over him.'

'Oh Sash, you don't even see what's under your nose!'

'Like what?'

'They've got history, haven't they? And old people, that's what they're after.'

'What?'

'Wanting to recapture when they were young and carefree. Trying to turn back the clock.'

'Bollocks,' snapped Sasha. 'Anyway, they're not old.'

'Middle-aged. Whatever.'

Ruby stamped on the cigarette stub and they sat in a grudging truce until a child playing with a ball bounced it in their direction and the mother hastened forward to apologise. The girls, glad to be distracted, tried to practise their Italian on her. The child ran off with the ball into the path of a motorbike which stopped abruptly. The mother screamed and whisked the boy to safety. Instead of continuing on his way, the driver parked the bike a few feet from the bench; its gleaming exhaust cocked in their direction like a double-barrelled gun. Then he and his passenger dismounted and took off their helmets and Sasha identified them with a jolt.

'Jeez!' said Ruby. 'What the fuck!'

'It was his idea,' said Gina, strolling towards them with her helmet under her arm.

Mitchell followed. There was something odd about him, Sasha thought, a vague unfocussed air, like he couldn't tell you what day of the week it was. Nevertheless, she was aggrieved. She and Ruby had been abandoned without explanation while he and Gina had disappeared into the wide blue yonder – on a motorbike, for God's sake.

'Where have you been, Dad?'

'I thought you two would be glad to be rid of me,' he said. 'You'd made the apartment so cosy and you knew I was going to find somewhere else. When I rang you last night you couldn't wait to get me off the phone.'

'But why didn't you tell us anything? Like where you were staying, or planning to have your breakfast or lunch. What were we supposed to do?'

'I'd given you plenty of money, Sash. You weren't going to starve.'

'Like, not even a text!'

'That's not true, you weren't answering this morning. I'd left the charger in the apartment, which was stupid, I agree, and I didn't realise I'd run out of battery. But you're okay, aren't you?' He tried to clasp her but she shook him off. 'When you were little you used to get so worried when I was flying. Especially after the attack on the Twin Towers. Mum kept having to reassure you that planes generally got back in one piece. In the end you learned that I did too.'

Sasha wanted to tell him to shut up, that wasn't the point. She and Ruby hadn't minded getting shot of him, diverting themselves. But she did mind, gravely, that he had spent those missing hours with Gina Stanhope. 'Where did that bike come from?' she demanded.

'I think it's awesome,' said Ruby. 'Can I sit on it?'

'Sure, if you want…'

She'd already hopped astride the warm leather seat and was leaning forward over the handlebars. 'Go on, Sash,' she called. 'Take my picture on your phone.'

Sasha obeyed, but as she clicked on the button she noticed a silver Alfa dawdling past. Kerb-crawler, she thought, what a wanker. Then, with a shock, she recognised the car. Had Signor Boletti recognised them? Perhaps, after all, he wasn't ogling Ruby's bare legs, the grip of her thighs. She lowered the phone. He was wearing sunglasses so she couldn't be certain, but he seemed to be looking past her. She turned. Gina had looped her arm through her father's, in a display of affection that to Sasha was totally unnecessary, and was brushing a lock of hair from his forehead in an intimate gesture. They made a striking couple, she had to admit. She glared.

Mitchell disentangled himself, clearly unaware of the context. 'I suppose you girls want a ride too,' he said with forced jollity. The Alfa slipped away.

'Yes please!' crowed Ruby.

'I can't take you both at once but I've hired it for twenty-four hours so there's plenty of time left, and…'

'Go on,' said Gina. 'Give the girl a whirl. Head up the Gianicolo. You can hammer those hairpin bends and show her the view.' She followed up this suggestion by giving Ruby her helmet to put on.

Ruby fastened the strap around her chin and made faces through the visor, indicating that Sasha should take some more shots on her phone.

Mitchell was reluctant. 'I didn't mean right away. We've only just got back.'

'So? You can see she's itching to go for a spin.'

'What about Sasha?'

'Don't worry, I'll look after her, take her to the flat.'

'Please, Paul,' came Ruby's muffled voice.

'Okay, Sash? I'm not deserting you, sweetheart. You'll get your turn.'

Why was he looking so anxious, as if he didn't want to leave her alone with Gina? Of course, she'd rather have Ruby by her side, but since they had to get him out of the way that wasn't possible. Ruby was doing her bit and Sasha had to man up to this confrontation by herself.

'What are you waiting for?' said Gina. 'Get a move on. Go!'

As Mitchell kick-started the engine back into life and Ruby gave a regal wave, Gina grabbed Sasha's elbow as if she wouldn't let her go and steered her down the street. 'We have some talking to do, you and I.'

'Yes.'

'You've got it with you, haven't you?'

'Yes.'

Gina seemed to unbend a little then. She released Sasha, bounded ahead of her up the staircase, breezed into the apartment and flung open the shutters to let in the daylight.

The sitting room had an even more dishevelled air than usual, the chairs disarranged, a sheaf of loose papers tottering on the sideboard, but to Sasha it was still a significant location. She'd been holed up here with Joe and it wasn't a period she was likely to forget. She sat down on the sofa where she had tried to sleep, where she had lain listening to the chimes of the clock on Santa Maria, and clutched a cushion to her chest like a shield.

'D'you want a drink?' said Gina. 'Tea, coffee, wine, Martini, beer, water, vodka? No Coke, I'm afraid.'

'No thanks.'

Gina poured herself a slug of red wine. 'God, I've had a harrowing few days! I so need this. Mostly,' she scowled over the rim of the glass, 'on account of you.'

'Me!'

'Things were going well. I had an exhibition, something I'd been angling after for years. Some good publicity too. A book commission in the offing. I was flying high. You turn up and

there's that stupid business with the glue and then the picture...
And as for your father – '

This was unfair. 'He used to be your boyfriend, didn't he?
But how could I know that? It's not like you told me anything.'

'What difference would it have made?'

'A lot, if you'd been seeing him recently...'

Gina flapped her hand dismissively. 'Well, I hadn't. We split
up ages ago, when he met your mother.'

'Oh.' She was relieved to hear this, though it sparked another
train of thought. 'Do you mean if she hadn't come along you
two might have stayed together? And then *you* might have been
my mother instead? Wow.'

'Sorry to disappoint, but no. Because you wouldn't have
been born.'

Sasha hadn't meant the observation seriously, but Gina's tone
puzzled her. It was fraught with bitterness. 'Hey, what did my
dad do to you?'

'Nothing. That's the nub of it, Sasha. It's the sins of omission
that matter. He neglected me, you could say. You may have
noticed: I'm an attention seeker. I don't care to be overlooked.'

Every time Sasha decided Gina's attitude was insufferable,
she would make some unexpected remark that showed she was
sensitive after all. Now she'd kicked off her pumps and curled
up in the chair opposite, nursing her glass and looking pensive,
even a little bit tragic. And Sasha couldn't help hauling her
up in her estimation again. If you had a stepmother manqué,
wouldn't you want her to be like this fascinating, enviable,
mysterious woman?

'There's nothing for you to worry about,' Gina said. 'We've
been going over a bit of old ground but I'm not stealing him
back. Too much water under the bridge. So now that's out of
the way, will you give it to me, please?'

'What?'

'You know perfectly well what I'm talking about.'

'No.'

'What d'you mean, no?'

'I mean I won't give it to you.' Sasha's bag was on her lap and the cushion lay on top of the bag. She didn't think Gina would try to wrestle it away from her, she wouldn't want to risk any damage to the drawing. 'Until you tell me why you did it.'

'Did what? Darling, you're the one who owes me an explanation. You hustle your way into my apartment, rummage around until you find a key...'

'We found it by accident.'

'...Unlock what is obviously a private storage box, help yourself to the most valuable item in it and smuggle it out of the building. Theft on a pretty major scale, wouldn't you say?'

'I didn't know it was valuable.'

'Then why steal it? What the fuck did you think it was?'

Sasha couldn't tell her, but she intended to stand her ground. 'I guessed it might be important because it was hidden away. I didn't want to keep it. Actually I wanted to exchange it.'

'For?'

'You must know what for. Those pictures of me!'

Gina rocked back in her chair. 'So you've been to the exhibition. I wondered if you had.'

'Why did you even have to take them?'

'Because that's what I *do*. I'm a photographer. And it was a gift – the perfect shot, no need to retouch or recompose. You've no idea how rare that is. My work can take for ever to get right. The finished product might look artless but there's been a lot going on behind the scenes. Half the time you don't even know what's in the frame till afterwards, when you're uploading. But in the case of you and Joe lying there, I could see it all right. It was so powerful, I couldn't ignore it.'

'Even if it was an invasion of my privacy?' said Sasha.

'You squat, uninvited, in my house. You shag my protégé. I think I'm the one who's privacy's been invaded.'

'Protégé?'

'I'm trying to distinguish between a lad who's lost everything and needs a helping hand and a privileged little daddy's girl like you.'

The insult was deliberate, though Sasha would have shared anything and everything with Joe if she'd had the chance. And she could produce plenty of arguments to show she wasn't half as spoilt or privileged as a whole load of other kids she knew, but that would take her in the wrong direction, which was no doubt what Gina wanted.

'You didn't have any right to stick me up on a wall, though, not without getting my permission. I bet you asked all the others in the show, Sami and such.'

Gina responded more calmly. 'Yes, that's true. In fact, I hadn't intended you to be included in the first place. There were a couple of shots of Antonio I'd taken that I mixed in with the rest. Bertie had originally agreed to let me use them, but then the bastard changed his mind and I had to find a substitute. David picked out the Aftermath pictures. He thought they were terrific, that they made such a good story. It was all very last minute and I never thought you'd see them. I didn't even know how to get in touch with you.'

'Yes you did. You could have used Facebook.'

'Well, anyway,' Gina drained her drink and set down the glass, 'I don't know what you're making such a fuss about. Your own father didn't recognise you.'

'Because he hasn't seen me without clothes on since I was eight.'

'And dozens of other people have?'

'Well, they have now.'

'Darling, nobody could possibly know who you are. Even your hair's different.'

This was true; it was longer, sleeker, but that wasn't the point. 'It's not just about the exposure. That was a special moment in my life and you've totally ruined it.' A single tear slid down the side of her nose.

Gina didn't notice. She was drumming her fingers on the arm of her chair, appearing to reconsider. 'As it happened, I turned down a potential buyer.'

Sasha flushed. 'Someone wanted to *buy* them? Oh my God! He must have been a massive weirdo.'

'Not necessarily. Anyway I said no.'

'If you hadn't, I could have sued you.'

'In the Italian courts? Be my guest. Your father would have to file the suit on your behalf and I'd've had a counterclaim against you for trespass, theft and distress. We'd be batted back and forth to infinity. But don't worry. You can keep your knickers on. I'm not selling.'

'You won't exhibit it anywhere else or publish it or whatever?'

'Not without your permission.'

'Like I'm going to give it!'

'One day,' said Gina, 'you might see things differently. You might even be proud of the image. It's very strong, very beautiful. I appreciate the whole episode was a bit of a watershed for you, but you know what, you'll have other romances, more grounded, more lasting. It was, after all, a particular set of circumstances that brought you together and for such a short time.'

'What makes you think it's over?'

'Do you really need me to spell it out? For one thing, it's hard to make a relationship work if you live in different countries, as I should know... and for another, you're both very young. Joe isn't in a situation where he could commit to anybody. He's fighting for survival – '

Sasha was angry and defensive. 'He was trying to come to England, he wanted to see me again. If he'd made it, he could have been legit...'

'It really isn't that simple. He should have waited, not jumped the gun.'

'He did it because you'd sold those other photos of him. The gay porn.'

'I do *not* take pornographic photographs!'

'Whatever. But he wouldn't have had the money on him otherwise. So that kind of makes it your fault.'

'How do you know this?' asked Gina suspiciously.

'*He* told me.'

'Who? Sami?'

'No, your Lion King.'

'Leone! Ah…' She bit her lip. 'Did I see you with a fag earlier?'

'What's that got to do with anything?'

'I could do with a smoke if you have a spare. Leone always gets my goat.'

'Oh.'

They went out onto the terrace. Sasha struck a match and Gina cupped her hand around the flame. Sasha lit her own cigarette from the tip of Gina's. She didn't smoke much as a rule – mainly rollies late at night when she'd drunk enough not to notice the taste – but there was no doubt the nicotine had a sedative effect. It united them in a temporary truce.

Sasha said, 'Why does he get your goat?'

'It was kind of an odd situation.' Gina plucked a leaf from a lemon scented geranium and crushed it between her fingers, releasing a fragrance more pervasive than the wafting smoke. 'Me, the Lion King and the Raven Queen. It must have been the most peculiar triangle you were ever likely to find. Theirs was a meeting of the minds, Felix used to say, even though they always argued. I'd let them get on with it because I knew they were both cleverer than I was. Jealousy doesn't have to be sexual, you know. Leone thought I was after what I could get, which, when you've had to fend for yourself since the age of sixteen, is likely to be true. That's what you are, isn't it, sixteen? You don't know you're born, darling.'

Sasha said nothing, although she felt very old, positively ancient compared to a year ago, when she'd still been walking the dog and none of this had happened.

'We rubbed along,' said Gina, 'because Felix was dying and the sainted Leone was reassuring him about heaven. I was trying to keep everything together. I was going out with a graphic designer at the time who was helping me set up a new web page. But he flipped out when Felix and I got married, so that was the end of that. Leone wasn't happy either. All I'd wanted was to secure possession of the apartment, but I ended up inheriting the pictures too. And I have bent over backwards ever since to prove that I'm not a gold-digger. I've done my bit for the lost boys.' Her hand was shaking and a column of ash cascaded onto the ground.

'I feel like he can see straight through me,' said Sasha. 'That he knows whether I'm telling the truth or not.'

'Yeah, he keeps people on their toes. Maybe that's his USP. One look from Leone and you have to start examining your motives. Mind you...' She paused to bury her stub in a plant pot. '...You'll find he's not judgemental. Hypocrisy isn't one of his failings. We are all sinners.'

Sasha supposed she was included in this, that Gina was getting at her again for stealing the drawing. Well, she could have it back now; she was through with being lectured at. 'I took care of it for you,' she said. 'It isn't creased or anything. I've kept it clean and flat in the plastic envelope and – '

'So the real irony,' continued Gina as if she hadn't been interrupted, 'is that here are you and I'm feeling guilty about our peccadilloes and misdemeanours while he's committed the greatest crime of all.'

'Who?'

'The Lion King.'

'What did he do?'

'He killed a man.'

Sasha's jaw dropped.

'A close friend, I believe.' Gina seemed pleased with the reaction she had elicited. 'But it was an accident; manslaughter. Years ago, when he was a seminarian at Villa Palazzola – it's in the Castelli region and we went there today, which reminded me. He was driving down the hill, too fast, and swerved to avoid an oncoming car; crashed into a tree. His passenger died of internal injuries. No seat belt – Italians like to live dangerously – so it wasn't entirely his fault. It isn't common knowledge, by the way. It was pretty much hushed up because they shouldn't have been out together that afternoon. Skiving in the woods, letting their passions run away with them. Indulging in a bit of illicit frolicking. Hence the hurry, you see – they were going to be late for the Angelus.

'I heard the story from Felix, and if you're wondering why I'm telling you, it's because I'm trying to get across the fact that you shouldn't take anything – or anyone – at face value. He's a fine man, Leone, a very fine man, who once took a few chances and made an awful error. I'm sure it still haunts him and that's why he can be difficult to deal with. But don't let it get to you. We all have skeletons of one kind or another. We do bad, stupid things from time to time. But we can do the good stuff too.'

Sasha was trying to digest this information, trying to work out whether it made any difference to the way she thought about the priest and his project. She was imagining the consequences of such a dreadful accident when she caught her friend's voice floating through the air and was momentarily disorientated.

'They're back,' said Gina peering over the railings. 'You'd better give me the drawing.'

'You will keep your promise about the photos? I can trust you?' Recalling, as she spoke, that this was a woman whose motto was 'Trust no one'.

'A bargain is a bargain,' said Gina holding out her hand.

'Can I ask you one more thing?' The words came out in a rush. 'What happened to Thomas Stanhope, your little boy?'

Down below Ruby was swinging her helmet. Mitchell rang the doorbell.

'You'll have to ask your father.'

30

Mario drove Gina to David's; she wanted to arrive in immaculate condition. Besides, she couldn't have walked because she was wearing her new, shockingly extravagant, staggeringly high heels from Dolce & Gabbana. Red was her lucky colour. The gallery was closed so she had to ring the bell.

'What have we here?' mocked David as he let her in. 'The Wicked Witch of the East? Or Dorothy trying to get home to Kansas?'

'Sod off, darling. I decided to treat myself.'

He led her through the echoing exhibition space into his office and opened the chilled drinks cabinet set into a faux marble column. 'Ready for a drink?'

'Go on then. White wine. I need it. Is he here yet?'

He shook his head. 'He may be delayed.'

'I don't see why you're being so mysterious about him. Anyway, while we're waiting, I have something to get out of the way.'

She threw herself on the sofa and kicked her shoes onto the limestone floor, where they gleamed like freshly spilt blood. She pulled the drawing out of its folder and handed it to David. 'I thought maybe you could sell this for me.'

When he grinned his teeth were aggressively white. 'Jeez, Gina, you've still got it.'

'Why did you think I hadn't?'

'Well, Felix always had the Cy Twombly in pride of place, right? So when I didn't see it any more I figured you'd already got rid of it. Guess I thought somebody had made you an offer you couldn't refuse.'

'You never said anything.'

'Maybe I was kinda hurt you hadn't consulted me.'

'I never could make up my mind whether I liked it. After it fell off the wall and the glass smashed, I decided to put it somewhere safe. And it's caused me so much hassle lately I don't want to hang onto it any more. I can't take the responsibility. Do you think it's a good time to sell?'

'Sweetheart, none better. The price I could get for this, you could *buy* yourself a goddam apartment. Well, a down payment at least.'

'For real?' This was the news she had hoped to hear, but it still made her gulp.

David opened a drawer and wrapped the picture in a protective parcel of tissue, card and bubble wrap. He unhooked the large canvas from the wall and twisted the combination dial on his hidden safe. He locked the parcel inside. 'You did well out of that guy,' he said.

'I'd rather have him alive, any day.'

'So would we all.' He replaced the canvas and turned to her, shaking his head. 'But he's had you stuck in a rut for years, kid. Time you grew up.'

Fake-youthful, bleached-blond David, indulged by the tolerant, older Sergio as he ran around with adolescents, chasing new blood – how dare he? '*You're* telling *me* to grow up!'

'Somebody has to. Cut yourself some slack.'

'What do you mean?'

'Look, I know this maybe sounds a little harsh, but how long is it since Felix died?'

'Nearly five years.'

'And have you moved on?'

'Well, of course I have.'

'So how come that apartment's such a shrine to him? Why are you hanging onto every single piece of his furniture? Hey, I know it's classy but you've said a million times it's not what *you'd* choose.'

'I bought a new sofa bed. I haven't got around to the rest, that's all.'

'Gina, hon, you will *never* get around to it. I'm telling you, the best thing you could do is start fresh. Right now you could give the head-shrinkers a field day. Sell off Felix's furniture – it should be worth quite a bit – and get some stuff of your own that you really like.'

'I just need to get things sorted…'

'With Boletti?'

'Well, yes, partly. What are you getting at? Is there something I should know?'

David didn't say anything. He'd gone back to the drinks cabinet and was fiddling with the cork of the wine bottle.

Gina glanced into the dim deserted gallery, the shadowy portraits on the walls. 'He is coming, isn't he?'

'I already told you, he's stuck in traffic.'

'He'd better be worth waiting for.'

'I think you'll find he is.'

'I mean, legal processes in this country are such a nightmare. It would make all the difference to have a really good lawyer, someone you can rely on…' Something in his expression alerted her. 'David! Why are you pulling a face? What's going on?'

'Nothing. Cool it. No call to get uptight.'

'Look, the last thing I need is you going back on your word. It was your idea we met for a casual drink, right? You made out I was in for a wonderful surprise, that your mate was the answer to a maiden's prayer, and he could probably walk on water at the same time.'

'Back off, Gina.'

'But he's not the hotshot lawyer you promised when you called me, is he?'

In truth, David had been as cagey as usual, but she'd detected a suppressed note of excitement which had raised her hopes.

'Hon, I said no such thing.' He leaned back, threading his fingers together and cracking his knuckles. The overhead spotlight exaggerated the artificial straw of his hair and the coarse, much darker stubble on his chin; it illuminated the pale creases at the corners of his eyes and the tiny reminders of cosmetic surgery behind his ears. 'How about we start over?'

'Start over?'

'You come into the gallery and take a seat. I offer you a drink. We're civil to one another.' As he took her empty glass, the bell rang. 'There!' he said in triumph. 'You see, I have not let you down.'

Gina stayed in the office, restoring her shoes to her feet, listening to the exchange of greetings, the click of the double doors as they closed against the night. David was a ghostly figure in white. His guest, in a sober dark suit, was harder to discern. She could tell only that he was tall. Even when he appeared in the doorway and she saw his face, with its trimming of beard, it took her a moment to recognise him.

'May I introduce Franco Casale,' said David. 'Gina Stanhope.'

'*Piacere.*' Casale extended his hand.

'We already met,' said Gina, shaking it briefly and returning to her seat. 'At the opening.'

'You did?' David was perplexed. 'You never said.'

'You never told me who was coming here this evening.'

'I have given you my card,' said Casale. He reached into his pocket as if about to produce another.

She said quickly, 'Sorry, I lost it. But I don't remember it describing you as an *avvocato.*'

'He isn't,' said David, waving the wine bottle. He refilled Gina's glass and handed a fresh one to Casale.

Start over, he had said. What on earth did he mean, if this was the kind of nonsense he was going to come up with? 'Then you've got me here under false pretences. I thought I'd made it absolutely clear I was looking for a good lawyer.'

'So is Boletti,' giggled David. 'Franco here has had him under investigation.'

Gina set down her wine, not wanting to spill it. 'You're a cop!' she said in disbelief.

'He's a tax man, hon.'

'A what?' Wasn't this worse? 'You are kidding me!' Nobody ever declared their full earnings but David's dealings with art and artifacts, with objects whose price related to the amount clients were prepared to pay as opposed to any intrinsic value, surely he was the last person to want a tax official sniffing around. Unless he was bribable… She assessed Casale again; he looked dead straight to her – he had a fastidious manner that reminded her of Felix – but you never could tell.

Seeing her expression David said, 'No worries. We're small fry to Franco. He's in the tax fraud section; he's only interested in the big guys. I know you figured a bar would be a neutral meeting ground, but there are confidentiality issues. You understand? But Franco was happy to come over here and share the good news with you.'

'What good news?' said Gina. She was finding it difficult to accept that the man hadn't switched sides. Up until now she'd seen him as her nemesis: Bertie's fixer. The one giving directions and chortling as he brushed flecks of dust from his lapels; encouraging Bertie to sabotage her show, spy on her visitors, bugger up her mortise lock. But according to David he'd done none of those things. He was on the side of law and order, incorruptible, whiter than white.

'We have been pursuing Boletti for some time,' said Casale. 'He has failed to pay not only his income tax, but his property taxes too.'

'Like half the rest of the country, you mean?'

He was unperturbed. 'In his case, there are considerable sums at stake.'

'He'll slither away from you. You'll never catch him.'

'Regrettably he has made too many enemies. And this has helped us acquire the evidence we need.'

Gina recalled Bertie's frequent meetings with 'the bank' – whoever they were. He'd never given her details of names or functionaries, he'd kept everything vague. She wondered if blackmail were involved or if he'd simply become too greedy. Clearly she wouldn't have been the only person he'd pissed off. He had it coming, she thought, with a delicious shiver of vengeance. 'I hope you're going to bankrupt him.'

'Not personally,' said Casale. 'Men like Boletti know how to protect their individual wealth, but the company is in trouble. The assets have been frozen.'

'What does that mean?' He had an attractive smile, she decided, open, *simpatico*. Why had she once thought it sinister? Good posture too, confident without being arrogant, though she could see he was brimming with satisfaction at the outcome of his investigations. And with reason. A warm flush of joy began to seep through her veins.

David cut in. 'It means he can't throw you out, because he won't be owning the building much longer.'

'It's up for sale?'

'It's possible the apartments may be sold off separately.'

'So it's possible,' said Gina carefully, with a covert nod at the hidden safe, 'that I might be able to afford to buy the one I live in? Christ knows, it needs an awful lot of work. David, you bastard, why are we drinking white wine? Why not champagne?'

'I must warn you the process will be slow,' said Casale.

'At least you won't have that hound dog sniffing around, denouncing you, sending you notices to quit,' David said. 'You can sleep easy.'

'Do I still have to pay the rent?'

'We don't perform miracles. But the income will not go to Boletti.'

Gina savoured this. Part of her, the subversive, contrary part had enjoyed confronting each little skirmish – she recalled with pleasure the tightening of his hand on the Alfa's steering wheel and the grim set of his mouth when he saw her nestling against Mitch – but ultimately she'd known Bertie held the cards that mattered. She was grateful to all those unseen creditors, construction companies, bank officials, whatever, whose grievances had toppled him. She couldn't have won by herself.

'And you can guarantee, can you, there'll be no leap in the shares of glue manufacturers?'

'I'm sorry, I don't understand.'

'Roberto Boletti is a devious man with a warped sense of humour. And I'll bet he's got some tricks up his sleeve that you haven't thought of.'

'For this reason,' said Casale, 'I hoped to speak to you when we met here before, but I had chosen the wrong moment...'

'Timing,' agreed Gina, who could now be magnanimous, 'is everything.'

A text message chimed on David's phone. 'Sergio's going to fix a booking for dinner. You'll join us?'

'Sure.' Then she realised he was speaking to both of them as, after a brief hesitation, Casale nodded.

'I'll call him back,' said David, wandering out of the room.

She wanted to chase after him. She wanted to protest that this was going too far, she didn't need any well-meaning friends to set her up on a date with a tax man. Though she could imagine David's response: This guy's saved your ass, hon. Why not be grateful to be onside with the angels for once?

Casale made some throat-clearing sounds and she waited. She couldn't help being wary; she didn't want to be caught out, leaping to any more false assumptions.

'Photography fascinates me,' he said. 'With its ability to convey more than the eye can see. I have been very taken with your work.'

'Really? I'm surprised you should say that. I know I didn't give you much of a hearing at the opening; all the same, I had the impression you were trying to undermine me.'

'Why?' He raised his glass and she noticed expensive cuff links.

'Because you refused to believe my story.'

'Ah, the Trevi Fountain… *Comunque*, it wasn't true, was it?'

'Not exactly,' she admitted. 'Though some elements were. And I had been considered for the campaign. In the end it couldn't happen in the Trevi because there were too many problems with security and road closures and so forth. But you should never call a person a liar in public. And in Italy too!'

'I think we had a misunderstanding.'

'We had a misunderstanding all right. And it was my fault, I know. I had you confused with someone else.'

'I was referring to your reason for becoming a photographer.' He glanced down at her ruby red shoes and smiled his slow warm smile. 'Wet feet?'

Gina arched her instep, admiring the slender shaft of her heel, the neat curve of her toe. Then she stood, rising to his level. It seemed important to explain herself. 'I used to get so fed up with people thinking that I changed career because I was getting too old to model. All that rot. I'm not saying it didn't play a part, but I was actually much more concerned with what I could do, what I could create, with a camera. Only I hate coming across as pretentious. Put it down to being a Brit: if you go on about your artistic vision you're deemed to be some kind of pseud. So instead I embroider a silly tale, which backfires. The wet feet, well, that was just a bit of fun really…' She was floundering but she thought he'd followed her; he'd shown he had a sense of humour.

'I liked listening to you,' he said. 'I enjoyed your account. I could see you in your black dress in the fountain. And the necklace breaking... You created a remarkable image. You do, in fact, create wonderful images. I tried to buy one of your prints but David told me it wasn't for sale.'

Scarcely a week ago had come the thrill and then the disappointment of his offer. And in the meantime Mitch, Sasha and Ruby had blown into her life and blown out again. A week, was that all? 'Now that *was* a true story,' she said, 'which got me lots of hassle. Up to my neck in hot water rather than cold. It was one of those reckless moments...' She shrugged and continued. 'My hands are tied so I can't really say any more about Aftermath, I'm sorry.'

David returned, slipping his smartphone into his back pocket, twirling his key fob. 'You guys done?' he said. '*Andiamo*.'

Gina scooped her bag off the sofa and shouldered it, ready to follow him. She took a step, then halted. She wasn't hungry yet and there were other priorities to consider. 'Could you give us ten minutes?' she said. 'I don't think we're quite finished. There's wine left in the bottle. And could you turn on the lights next door?'

'In the gallery?'

'Yes, darling. It's a bit gloomy and we need to be able to see properly. Franco would like to get a closer acquaintance with my work.'

David snapped on the master switch and in the sudden illumination the walls came to life: the boys with their ball games, the ramshackle campsites, the men's scarred torsos and damaged limbs – all bathed in deep velvety shadows.

This time she would handle her prospective purchaser more carefully, treat him with respect. Everybody deserved a second chance.

AFTERMATH

2013

A wedding. Tonight.

It's a thousand miles away and Sasha would love to be there. Instead she's rushing out of the house, hoping she won't be late for her lecture. The strange conversation she's just had is buzzing in her head. Less than an hour ago, flicking onto Gina Stanhope's Facebook page she'd seen that Gina was preparing for a second exhibition, a solo one this time. Sasha made a sudden bold decision to Skype her and Gina responded with more warmth than she'd hoped for. Sasha needn't have worried; she's kept her word about the Aftermath photos.

She also has to credit Gina with bringing her parents back together. Corinne was rocked by the tragic story of baby Thomas, that was clear, but then she rallied. She turned down the job offer from Dundee and accepted a local promotion instead. Sasha's dad brought home a silky-haired puppy the day after, to celebrate. She's going home this weekend to see him – luckily her boyfriend Adam has a car.

She'll get a stitch if she doesn't slow down. What a piece of news – Sami getting married to a Polish juggler! They'll be like strolling players, she thinks, entertaining tourists and school parties. Father Leone is officiating and Gina will take the pictures. Sasha is delighted for him, of course, but she had to ask – how could she not? – whether Joe would be a wedding guest too.

But it seems that Sami's contact with Joe is erratic. Nothing's been heard of him since the break-out from the centre for identification and expulsion in Turin. Lots of detainees escaped, Gina has told her; he may still be trying to get to the UK.

After her lecture, she'll head straight over to her volunteering project. Every Thursday she helps to prepare and dish up lunch to the asylum seekers who drop into the Centre for advice on legal issues, housing, English lessons. Most of the other volunteers are immigrants who've been through the mill themselves; she's the only student.

The Centre is housed in what was once a large Victorian priory, red sandstone with high ceilings and tall windows, tiled floors that echo. When Sasha gets there she will hang up her coat on the row of pegs – which makes her feel like she's back at school – and go through to the large busy kitchen. She will mash tinned tuna and sweetcorn together and spread the mixture onto baguettes. Then she'll wrap the filled rolls in paper napkins and carry them through on a tray to the serving counter.

Many of those who drop in are regulars, but sometimes there are newcomers too: men who've been journeying for years and finally arrived. Today, after what Gina has told her, if she spots a slim young man in the queue who hasn't been before – perhaps he'll have a beanie hat pulled down to his thick dark eyebrows – she won't be able to help herself. Although it's completely irrational, her glance will stray to his hand as it reaches out for a roll. And she will look for a flash of silver circling his wrist.